About the Author

Tony Sharp studied at the universities of Aberystwyth, Sussex and Berlin. After working briefly in the Foreign Office, he taught Politics and European Studies at the University of Dundee. He is the author of three important historical works. This is his first novel. Dr Sharp lives in Godalming, Surrey.

Dedication

For

Charlotte & Alan

Eileen & Colin

Kay & Keith

and

James

Tony Sharp

C OMMAND PERFORMANCES

Copyright © Tony Sharp (2015)

The right of Tony Sharp to be identified as author of this work has been asserted by him in accordance with section 77 and 78 of the Copyright, Designs and Patents Act 1988.

All rights reserved. No part of this publication may be reproduced, stored in a retrieval system, or transmitted in any form or by any means, electronic, mechanical, photocopying, recording, or otherwise, without the prior permission of the publishers.

Any person who commits any unauthorized act in relation to this publication may be liable to criminal prosecution and civil claims for damages.

A CIP catalogue record for this title is available from the British Library.

ISBN 9781785540677 (Paperback)
ISBN 9781785540691 (Hardback)

www.austinmacauley.com

First Published (2015)
Austin Macauley Publishers Ltd.
25 Canada Square
Canary Wharf
London
E14 5LQ

Printed and bound in Great Britain

PART ONE

OCCUPATIONAL HAZARDS

SEPTEMBER TO DECEMBER 1948

1

MONDAY 6 SEPTEMBER 1948

She weaved through a crowd of commuters, evoking blatant looks and furtive glances from both sexes. Aware that her height and hair prompted such attention, Eve Loxton smiled wryly; recalling how she'd once kept her red mane shorn and dyed black. But that had been in another life.

Life before the secret police invested her with real powers. Life before her cheating husband met with his fatal accident. And life before Claudio's tailoring skills stood at her disposal. Thinking about the new outfit in her rucksack, a contented expression drifted over her face.

It changed into a scowl when 'the Doss-house' loomed into view. For few would dispute that the Waterloo headquarters of DOSS, the Department of Special Security, fully merited its nickname.

The war had done no favours to an already drab building. The lower levels of its brickwork were now blackened, courtesy of a German incendiary bomb. A quirky crenellation topped off this sooty scar, indicating where the fiercest tongues of flame had licked away. Only the windowsills, smeared with pigeon droppings, added patches of lightness to its bleak façade.

The interior of 'the Doss-house' was nothing special either, as was confirmed by Eve's ill-lit climb past mildewed walls to her office. With difficulty she closed its warped door. Struck by the room's warmth, she touched a radiator and wondered why the heating was on in September. Shrugging, she assumed someone must be testing a system which had failed so abysmally the previous winter.

Lowering the rucksack onto her desk, she eased a parcel from its confines. From this, she withdrew the costume and blouse she'd collected on her way to work. After draping each item over hangers, Eve commenced a pernickety examination of both tailoring and materials, before pouting in approval.

She glanced at her watch to check how much time remained before her appointment. Then she peeled off the clothes she was wearing and drew on the latest outfit Claudio Bonomi had made for her. Mirrored appraisal from multiple angles confirmed its perfect fit.

This was hardly surprising, since Claudio had dubbed her his 'maid to measure'. This was his first and only pun in the English language, and he would repeat it *ad nauseam* while trailing his tape around Eve's slender dimensions. The recollection prompted a lewd smile, since the 'new' Eve was not averse to mutually beneficial arrangements, and her splendid bespoke clothes had cost but a pittance.

Peering into the wall mirror, she grimaced at her dark-ringed eyes. Perhaps she should have passed on the weekend's temptations, since she knew her boss would allude to the aftermath. Frown intensifying, she visualised the gross, slovenly figure of Arthur Barber. Then she mimicked aloud the most likely catchphrase that 'Uncle Arthur' would inflict upon her:

'Still working you too hard, am I, lass?'

As if on cue, a heavy thump resounded above her as Barber performed some deed in his room. Eve looked up when the crashing sounds resumed. They were now interspersed with audible grunts. What the hell was he up to?

Being the owner of outsize feet which swelled in warmth, Arthur Barber had found himself short of options. Whereas in high summer he could simply wear size thirteen shoes instead of his normal twelves, that day's sudden increase in room temperature had forced his hand.

Balancing his pipe on the edge of the desk, the 'Dossboss' groped awkwardly beneath it with his left paw. In such a posture his bulk proved a hindrance, and induced the fierce grunts he emitted before finally dislodging both feet from scuffed shoes. Flexing his liberated toes, Barber sprawled back in his chair to catch breath.

At length the heaving belly stilled. Now chewing upon a straggly moustache, he resumed his study of what was to prove a fateful file.

The punctual rap sounded upon his door and Barber bellowed permission to enter. Immaculate in blue silk blouse and navy costume, Eve strode into the room. Fabricating his most avuncular air, Arthur waved her into a chair by his desk. First checking its surface for pipe-ash, she sat, crossed her long bare legs, and primly jerked down her hem.

Barber focused upon the telltale shadows edging Eve's striking green eyes. 'Still working you too hard, am I, lass?'

A bland smile fronted her gritted teeth. 'No, sir,' she lied.

Beaming broadly, he picked at gravy stains mottling his frayed tie. 'Eve, I can't help the long hours. Keeping the lid on this can of worms we call democracy is a full-time job.'

Homilies over, with a grunt of exertion he stretched out for his pipe, and then stabbed its stem at the file before him. 'Herbert Pilling, lass, commercial traveller, killed in a car-crash couple of weeks back.'

'"Minimised"?' queried Eve, employing the DOSS euphemism for murder.

'Nay, lass, he wasn't.' Drooping lids half hooded his eyes. 'But, I can promise you our Herbert would've been, if we'd known about him.' He struck a match. Holding the flame above the cherrywood's bowl, he sucked hoggishly as he spoke. 'After young Pilling was scraped from his wreck, the police went through it and stumbled on some microfilmed Foreign Office documents among his samples.'

'Sounds like a bit of luck at last.'

'Happen,' he countered gruffly. 'Trouble is, Eve, the trail's pretty cold. The only address we've got for young Herbert is his brother's, and he knows nowt about Herbert's movements. And nor do we. With his job, it was all hotels both here and over the Channel.'

'Did Pilling travel abroad a lot?'

'Aye, lass, he was often on the Continent. I reckon that's where he handed over his films. And he could have any number of suppliers back here, who we know sod all about, not to mention a place to do his photography.'

She concurred with a gloomy nod. 'Do we have any idea who supplied him with the microfilmed FO documents?'

'It seems MI5 have their eye on some junior official they reckon fits the bill.'

'Oh,' said Eve in a disappointed tone. 'So this case has been given to the opposition, has it?'

A vigorous headshake set his jowls wobbling like jolted jelly. 'It's what's laughingly called a joint operation, lass.'

She cocked a suspicious brow, when he passed her a lengthy list of women's names and addresses.

'It seems young Herbert was a real ladies' man, Eve. So someone's got to check up on all the names in his address-book, in case there's more than just hanky panky involved. Yon lasses could all be shop-girls or barmaids, but you never know. And Five don't have much of a women's section.'

'Nor do we,' she retorted sourly, 'although we could have.'

A nod of the pipe was all the sympathy she got.

Eve skimmed the list and frowned in frustration. 'Sir, there are some fifty names here. I just haven't got the womanpower for this sort of job.' She punctuated her complaint with a pronounced pout, which augured a major sulk unless remedial action was taken. 'I'm overstretched, underfunded, and unappreciated.'

'Nay, lass, you're very much appreciated,' he soothed hastily. 'But, there's nowt I can do about extra funds.' Lolling back in his chair, paws petting his paunch, he shammed stupefaction. 'Eve, you've always had a fair whack from my budget. What on earth do you do with it all, lass?'

She imagined him using the same slightly indignant, somewhat flabbergasted tone with his wife, when it came to housekeeping bills. Puffing her lips less blatantly, Eve perused the list more attentively. Halfway through the names a spontaneous glint came to her eyes, when they lighted upon one which indelibly scarred her memory.

Switching her expression to docility, Eve feigned a sigh. 'Well, if it's really important, sir, I suppose I'll just have to take it on.'

Sticky, patterned socks tautened over the balls of his feet as Arthur twiddled his toes in triumph. Then he pounced upon his matchbox. 'Any road, how's your investigation of Horner's finances coming along? Is our Stephen fiddling the books?'

Eve noted the familiar way he spoke of Stephen Horner. Many uttered that name with an undertone of awe, but Barber viewed him realistically for what he was. Horner headed a modest department which had outlived its wartime usefulness, and was constantly threatened with absorption into a major ministry, if not outright liquidation. It was the same fragile status that Barber and DOSS enjoyed.

When Arthur finally torched his pipe productively, Eve replied to his question. 'Well, I reckon Horner *has* been on the take, but I'll be more certain about things in a few weeks' time.'

Belching smoke, Barber beamed at her brazenly. 'You're worth every penny I pay you, lass. So keep at it. A bit of success in this matter wouldn't come amiss. It would please our current patrons in the Foreign Office, and help keep the other big boys off our back. I need hardly tell you that fresh moves are afoot to close us down. So bring me some trophy, Eve, which I can shove in Five's face.'

She responded with a cosmetic smile. Behind it her mind was racing, but not with thoughts of Horner or Barber's bureaucratic battles. She was recalling instead the woman who'd finally caused her old world to collapse; and now Eve had *carte blanche* to investigate her.

With the scent of revenge tingling in her nostrils, she left Barber's office and hastened downstairs to her own. Yet by the time she sat at her desk, instinct had given way to calculation. Revenge would certainly be sweet; but, as the Italian saying went, it was also a dish best eaten cold.

In any case, this personal vendetta was all part of the much larger job that Barber had dumped into her lap. It had to be organised, financed, and fitted in alongside all the other tasks she had on. Dismissing Fay Galbraith from her thoughts for now, Eve dialled her deputy's number.

2

TUESDAY 7 SEPTEMBER 1948

Halting on the kerb of a Westminster side street, Jack Randall tipped back his trilby. He stared across the road at his place of work, where the Department of Research and Analysis − or DORA as it was less reverently known − was housed in two adjoining buildings.

His gaze drifted to the top storey, where DORA's director had his office. Whether it was occupied by Stephen Horner that day was a moot point. Horner's absences were becoming ever more marked, and his general behaviour increasingly erratic.

Not that Randall's own was a model of consistency. Ever since selling some landscapes that spring, he'd imagined himself tendering his notice and striking out as a professional artist. But, a stream of bills, product of a less than austere lifestyle, ensured that such ambition remained quixotic. Unable to escape thraldom to a regular salary, he'd settled instead for bouts of job dissatisfaction.

A few days' leave had only made matters worse. Reluctant to face his job, and beset again by problems with women, Randall had to force himself to cross the road. Mission accomplished, he cast a routine glance over the nameplates outside DORA's entrance. This merely confirmed that, as a matter of policy, they hadn't been cleaned.

Since neither body courted publicity, it took a practised eye to discern that these grimy plaques advertised both DORA and a dental practice. The latter's staff were also employees of Stephen Horner. Tending but a few select patients, they fronted for him by occupying most of the ground floor of the two buildings.

Doffing his hat, Randall proceeded along a sepulchral corridor towards the reception desk. He registered the incumbent's changed hairdo and complimented her upon it. Favouring him with more than her standard smile, she pressed one of three buzzers to alert the personnel inside the security foyer.

The responsibility of these men was to react appropriately to 'friendly' green light, 'ambiguous' amber, or 'hostile' red. For green, by far the most common signal, they operated a control which released the foyer's sealed door.

When Randall entered, the tang of stale tobacco smoke made his eyes smart. He picked up too on the antagonistic atmosphere, since Donald McCloy was on duty alone, his demeanour exuding the dislike he'd always shown towards him. Staring back coldly, Randall tossed his ID onto the counter in the centre of the foyer.

Drawing himself erect, McCloy ensured that he towered above Randall, who was himself over six feet tall. Baleful eyes scrutinised the photo on the pass as if viewing its bearer for the first time. When he finally returned it, after painstakingly logging its details, McCloy's manner suggested it was a favour.

Randall stepped inside the nearby lift and pressed the 'up' button. The cage ascended sluggishly towards its sole destination, the third floor of the building. From here internal stairs, passages, and through-doors led to offices honeycombing other storeys.

When the lift juddered to a halt, Randall emerged from it reticently, and then scaled the staircase leading to his own room on the fourth floor. Dumping hat and briefcase on the desk, he peeled off his suit jacket, and loosened both tie and collar. Then he left his office for that of his secretary.

Lucy Temple's room was larger than his, but reduced in space by the filing cabinets lining two walls. Perched behind her typewriter, Lucy beckoned him with a blood-red talon.

Then she extracted a sheet from some handwritten pages, and spread it accusingly upon her desk. The talon guided his eyes to the relevant spot.

'Decipher.'

He squinted at the offending sample of his scrawl. 'It says "AVH" or "Hungarian Secret Police", Lucy.'

'It says nothing of the sort.'

'Well, I've....'

'Print.'

Obediently, the head of DORA's European Communism Section penned the requisite words in block capitals. Lucy checked his efforts and grudgingly nodded approval.

He gathered up the backlog of paper cramming his in-tray, and frowned at the reports of Zhdanov's death headlining the Soviet press. Horner would want to discuss this topic; but Randall's agenda was dominated by other concerns. Fingers raking through dark, wavy hair, he stared at her brimming in-tray.

'Fay won't be in until Thursday,' confided Lucy in mind-reading tones, 'and only until eleven, before she goes on holiday with her husband.'

As usual, he ignored the subtle emphasis she'd placed upon the final word.

From a secluded nook in the Waterloo pub, Eve surveyed the lunchtime scene. 'Snow White and the Seven Dwarves,' she mused, except there were only four men, and they weren't dwarves. They all just happened to be shorter than Sandra Jansen, and, in this respect, they were hardly unique.

Standing six feet without her heels, Sandra was two inches taller than Eve, and, at thirty-three, some four years older. Lithe and leggy, she had short and silky blonde hair, azure eyes, and pouty lips that seemed to be demanding a kiss.

As the male quartet danced attendance, Sandra collected four gin and tonics from the bar. And, although she accepted that the banter and flirtation would do Sandra good, Eve's rule was that business preceded pleasure. To indicate that playtime was over, she beckoned her deputy with a flick of her head. Smiling her leave-taking, Sandra glided through the throng with laden tray.

Eve grabbed a drink and lowered its level drastically. 'Ooh, I needed this! So what's the womanpower situation like?'

Content with but a sip from her own glass, Sandra flipped open her notebook. Then she fiddled with the rings on her left hand, which were now as token as those Eve wore. 'Well, I can get enough girls, Eve, as long as you can rustle up more funds. What you last came up with covers solely our present strength, and only until mid-October.'

'Oh, I'll get you the dosh,' Eve declared confidently. 'I've got a date with a sad little banker, who's in desperate need of an authority figure.'

'"Authority figure",' echoed Sandra. 'The things you come out with, Eve. It'll never catch on. Anyway, what's this banker been up to?'

She produced a taunting smile. 'Sandra, it's most unlike you to show interest in the sordid side of our business. It's always been me who's done the dirty work.'

Sandra pinked slightly. 'I know. But you seem to enjoy it, Eve. And I'm only showing interest, because we've never had a banker before. Just think of tapping into a bank's resources whenever we need to.'

'That thought had occurred to me,' Eve remarked drily. 'But there's more. This bloke's not just any old banker, he's Horner's banker. Anyway, let's return to matters at hand.' She tapped the list of names from Pilling's address book. 'I want a really professional job done. Run checks on all these women.' Her finger stabbed viciously at the name she'd circled in red. 'But, pay special attention to this bitch, Fay Galbraith. I want to know every move that cow makes.'

'Any special reason?'

'Yes, Sandra,' she hissed, 'it's personal.'

'Sorry I asked,' muttered Sandra huffily.

Eve gave a consoling squeeze to the other's arm. 'I'll tell you about it later.'

Sandra managed an abrupt nod of forgiveness. 'Does this Fay Galbraith have a job?'

'Well, when I knew her, about three years ago, Fay was working in DORA. So that's somewhere for you to start. And her home address is there on Pilling's list.'

Having penned some notes, Sandra looked up.

'Are you still annoyed?' asked Eve.

Toying with her pen, Sandra shook her head. 'I'm just a bit touchy, Eve. Unlike you, I've got a husband who's still alive and causing me grief. Derek met me from work the other day. Said he wants to come back, now the bitch he ran off with has thrown him out.'

'You wouldn't have him back, would you?'

'Not a chance! But I'm thinking of moving to another part of London.'

'So do it,' Eve exhorted. 'Now, tell me more about these new girls you've just taken on. Twins, you said.'

'That's right. Delilah and Delphine Delaney.'

'You're kidding!' Eve chuckled into her glass, before polishing off its contents. 'So tell me more.'

'Well, they're both language students, which means one's available to work if the other's at lectures.'

'What else can they do, besides babbling in strange tongues?'

'They're amazing dancers. We first met down the Palais in….'

'That's a hobby,' said Eve sharply. 'What talents do they bring to the women's section of DOSS?'

'Well, they're bright, willing, and quick learners. They can drive, and they're both handy photographers who can work a darkroom.'

'Now, that's more like it,' said Eve, reaching out for her second gin.

Work finished for the day, Randall nipped into a nearby pub. He was seated with newspaper and brandy, when a woman's voice asked if she might join him. Looking up, he smiled at Wendy Page from DORA's Finance Section and waved her into a vacant chair.

For two years now, she'd dealt with his expenses, which Randall, as a member of the human race, naturally padded. She had easily caught him out. But, instead of shopping him, she'd encouraged him to continue; arguing that such financial chaos reigned in her section that no one else would notice. Jack suspected that she had a dip herself, since she was always well-dressed on what was likely to be a modest salary.

He was unsure why she favoured him so. She was engaged, and although she flirted with him, she never suggested that more was on offer. Nor was he sure that he'd accept if she offered, since she both passed and failed certain of his exacting standards.

She had exceptionally attractive eyes, topped by long, natural lashes. Wavy, shoulder-length black hair was another plus, as was her height. On the other hand, although her buxom figure curved in all the right places, there was far too much of it. She was overweight by at least a stone. Then there was her excessive make-up, which he found particularly unbecoming on a woman who was only in her early twenties.

Between sips of port, Wendy told him she was waiting for a girlfriend. They were off to the cinema. She named the film, but it meant nothing to him. Then, setting down her glass, she gazed at him unblinkingly, and inquired how he was getting on with Fay. She saw his eyes harden, but she still pursued the matter.

'Jack, it's not exactly a secret that you two are having an affair. After all, women talk.'

'Too damned much,' he observed caustically.

She tasted her drink again. 'Would you marry Fay if she was free?'

Randall held her probing stare. 'You won't get an answer to that question.'

'I didn't think I would.' Wry smile fading, her expression grew sombre. 'Would you marry someone you didn't love?'

'No, I wouldn't, as I'd only be postponing an inevitable break-up.'

She put down her glass, and stared at her engagement ring. 'That's what I've been thinking too. I can't see it working between Andy and me. I really can't see us happily married.'

'Then don't do it. As they say, there are plenty of fish in the sea, and you're attractive enough to hook them.'

Her eyes lit up at the compliment. Then she sank the remains of her drink, and produced a perplexing smile. 'I heard that you paint in your spare time, Jack. Do you paint women?'

'I have done on occasion.'

'Have you painted Fay?'

He nodded cautiously.

She was about to pose another question, when a woman's voice called her name. Wendy waved back at her friend, who was standing by the entry door to the bar. She collected her handbag and stood.

'We must talk again, Jack.'

Setting down her glass, Eve eyed the package resting on the sofa in her flat. Sent by her mother in Hastings, it was the latest in a stream of parcels, stuffed with bizarre woollen garments, most of which ended up with the Salvation Army.

Her mother knitted constantly and expertly from any wool that she had to hand, and without the slightest reference to her youngest daughter's tastes. Besides knitting, her mother collected husbands. She was on her fourth, as was her favourite film star. Eve was open-minded as to whether this was coincidence.

Eve opened the parcel at one end and reached into it tentatively, like a novice drawing entrails from a chicken. As the red and white hooped socks extended in length, she stared aghast. Apart from their association with her late husband's football team, Eve had no intention of looking as if she was prancing around atop a pair of barber's poles. Shaking her head despairingly, she muttered to herself.

'Ever since I told her I couldn't be bothered wearing fiddle-arsing suspenders and stockings, she's worried my legs will get cold in winter.'

Eve freshened her drink. Then she switched on the wireless, to be greeted by the sound of 'We'll meet again', her stepfather Alf's favourite tune. She stood as if petrified, while memories swirled around her mind. The orchestra was half-way through a medley from 'Oklahoma' before she shook her head clear.

Eve grabbed her glass and gulped down most of its contents. Then she hoisted the residue in mocking toast to the late Alf, one of those husbands no woman should ever have. But, at least her mother had acted when she'd found out, while Eve had acted later.

3

THURSDAY 9 SEPTEMBER 1948

An insipid sun brightened few rooms in DORA, affecting solely those in the upper storeys overlooking the street. Sited at the rear of the building, Stephen Horner's spacious fifth floor office compensated for its gloomy location with an entirely white interior. It was also ablaze with light. The illumination ranged from that afforded by a crystal chandelier to the focused beams of reading lamps atop a massive mahogany desk.

A map of the Soviet Union dominated one wall. Horner confronted it, his forefinger navigating the Black Sea. Having brushed the coastline, it wormed its way through the narrow Kerch straits, skimmed across the Sea of Azov, and docked in the port of Mariupol. When he spoke, his clipped tenor tones seemingly addressed the Ural Mountains.

'Andrei Alexandrovich Zhdanov, born in Mariupol in 1896, died on 31st August in a sanatorium near Novgorod.' Horner spun on his heel. 'Tell me, Randall, what impact will Zhdanov's demise have upon Soviet policy?'

'None whatsoever,' replied Jack tersely from his seat. He reached out for the small glass ashtray that Horner provided for addicts. 'There's only one death which will have any impact upon Soviet policy, that of Stalin.'

Horner took a pace forward, and the brilliant lighting caught his spectacles at such an angle that his eyes disappeared from view. 'So, Randall, you believe that a patently decrepit Stalin remains in total control of the entire red realm, do you?'

The younger man frowned before replying. 'Being sick and old doesn't prevent him from instilling terror, and he's a past master of the tactics of divide and rule.'

'So who will succeed Zhdanov as heir apparent?'

'I doubt that it matters.' He jammed a cigarette between his lips. 'Any so-called heir apparent is simply a temporary top dog, who could disappear the moment Stalin wills it.'

The forefinger came into play again, testily tapping Horner's thigh. 'Randall, could you at least venture to name the likely contenders?'

Jack blew smoke towards his knee, and then looked up. 'Zhdanov's Leningrad faction will continue to fight for the succession to Stalin, and they have two major players. One is Nikolai Voznesensky, the chairman of the State Planning Commission, and the other is Central Committee Secretary Alexei Kuznetsov.'

'Who else will reach for the crown?'

'The faction of Beria and Malenkov.'

Horner adjusted his glasses, pressing them higher on the bridge of a beaky nose. The stern grey eyes reappeared. 'And who will win?'

Randall's mouth tightened into a cynical smile. 'Place your money on Beria and Malenkov. They've both had considerable experience of murdering their way to the top, and their ruthlessness is far better honed than that of the "Leningraders".'

'Whose victory would you favour, Randall?'

He shrugged his indifference. 'I don't make policy. I simply provide information to those who do.'

'Well, speaking as one of the latter, I would favour the triumph of Beria and Malenkov over the disruptive "Leningraders". Despite their sins, I view this duo as businesslike men who seek an orderly, well-policed world; a world divided into stable spheres of influence.'

'Why use the word "seek"?' Jack queried combatively. 'In my opinion, your ideal world is already in existence.'

It was self-serving act, designed to demonstrate — if only to himself — that he still retained critical standards, despite his current attitude to his job. Yet a nagging inner voice wondered why he was embroiling himself with Horner. He wanted to see Fay before she left on holiday, and, according to Lucy, she'd be in her office only until eleven. He glanced at the wall clock, but still ploughed on.

'Europe's political, economic and military division is well advanced. Germany will soon be formally split into two states. The communists are losing the Greek Civil War. There are no longer any communist ministers in the governments of Western Europe, while in the east Stalinist parties rule unchallenged. So what more is required?'

Horner's hand swatted away these contentions as though dealing with a wasp at a picnic. 'That litany does not characterise a concrete division of Europe, Randall; it merely delineates the present imprecise fissures. So I shall tell you what more is required to produce stable spheres of influence.'

Horner marched over to his desk and sat. Removing the stopper from a decanter, he poured a generous measure of malt whisky. Jack consulted the wall clock again, which gave the time as 10:27.

That Horner gambled recklessly remained but the stuff of rumour for his employees. That he'd begun boozing at unearthly hours had passed from rumour into reality. It was generally assumed that both vices were a consequence of the recent death of his wife.

Stubbing his cigarette, he watched Horner's hands come together as if in prayer. His own supplication was that any lecture would be short.

'First of all, Randall, you neglected to mention the fact that the United States alone possesses the atomic bomb.'

Horner's hands parted. One grasped the glass and poured its contents down his throat. Then he placed the glass decorously upon the desk. It was as if he'd simply lubricated his verbosity with a sip of water

'For real stability to pertain in Europe, Randall, this American ascendancy must be offset by Soviet possession of these awesome weapons. Only this can deter certain hotheads in Washington, who advocate using their monopoly against the USSR, from consigning much of our planet to Armageddon.'

The younger man frowned before speaking. 'Surely, it's a mere matter of time before Moscow produces its own atomic bomb.'

Horner planted his elbows upon the desk and layered one hand atop the other. 'Randall, were I to possess information to accelerate that process, and were I to be offered sufficient inducement to part with such knowledge, what do you imagine that I would do?'

Unsure that he'd heard correctly, Jack stared at the carpet. Was Horner drunk? Was he baiting a trap? Had he, in fact, done anything more than speculate? Lifting his head, he eyed his boss, and was rewarded with Horner's enigmatic smile; a gash of pink in the chalky complexion.

Randall settled for another shrug. 'I'll assume that your question was purely rhetorical.'

The tiered hands disengaged, and then renewed their close association in Horner's lap. 'Moreover, there is a second factor militating against stable spheres of influence in Europe, which you have also neglected to consider, Randall. This is the spectre of "national communism", exemplified by Tito's apostasy, and the consequent expulsion of the Communist Party of Yugoslavia from the Soviet fold last June.'

Shaking his head contrarily, Randall lounged back in his chair. 'But, I've never shared your concern that this so-called "Titoist" contagion will infect other communist parties in Eastern Europe. While there are members of these parties, who'd be only too pleased to lessen or loosen Soviet control of their states, I see no chance of them succeeding. The factors which permitted Tito's Yugoslavia to assert its independence do not pertain in the satellites. Tito got away with it because Yugoslavia wasn't occupied by the Red Army, and he, not the Russians, controlled the levers of power; the Party, police and army.'

Horner raised a hand to halt further debate. 'Randall, in my department there is only one party line on the Soviet-Yugoslav rift, and that is the one advocated by my good self. Naturally, you will bear that very much in mind.'

Noting the time, Jack withheld any response.

Horner poured more malt, and on this occasion took only a sip before setting down his glass. 'As should be clear, Randall, I favour waging a real Cold War, not a cool one; with glacial division between east and west, and icy indifference to matters we cannot influence. Let Stalin take whatever action he chooses to quiet his unruly realm. It is no concern of ours.'

Randall peered inquiringly at the older man. 'Well, if current policy is simply to erect "Keep Out" signs on both sides of the Iron Curtain, what exactly do you want my section to do in future?'

'I have outlined an aspiration not an extant situation,' retorted Horner archly. 'As to current tasks, you can produce for me an up-to-date study of conflicts within the Soviet hierarchy. After that, you can perform the same task with reference to the satellite parties.'

Nodding acquiescently, Jack glanced again at the clock. When Horner reached for a file, he took it as a sign of dismissal. Slipping from the room, he hurried down the stairs to Fay's office. It was locked. Cursing, he hastened to his secretary's room, where Fay often chatted with Lucy. There was no sign of either woman.

However, a note from Lucy topped his in-tray. From this, he learned that Fay had telephoned. She had been too busy to come in to see him. She'd be in touch after her vacation. It was at times like this that Randall wondered why he bothered.

Pink towel clutched to wet body, Eve sprinted from the bathroom in her flat. Not for the first time, she wondered why someone couldn't invent a phone you could carry with you anywhere. Grabbing hold of the receiver, she puffed her presence into the mouthpiece.

'Didn't get you out of the bath, did I?' The woman at the other end of the line cackled, and then coughed throatily on her fag. 'Anyhow, Eve, we're all set up for tomorrow with your banker. There's another one in the pipeline too, a judge this time.'

After noting the details, Eve replaced the receiver. Smiling cockily, towel draped champ-style around her neck, she swaggered back to the bathroom. Closing its door, she raised her brows.

'So how about making some room for me?'

The bath's occupant, who was rinsing her hair with an old saucepan, grudgingly complied.

4

FRIDAY 10 SEPTEMBER 1948

To indicate her readiness, Gwen Chambers patted her *Leica* camera. Eve nodded in response. Directing her gaze at the closed bedroom door, she narrowed her eyes by stages, as though adjusting them to X-ray vision. Not that she was in need of such talents, for Eve knew precisely what she'd encounter when she burst through that door.

Coming to her full height in the flat's dingy hallway, she teased a strand of red hair behind an ear, and fussily straightened her black jacket. Then she turned the doorhandle and barged into the bedroom.

On glimpsing the socks, Eve clapped a hand across her mouth to stifle her laughter. Quickly recovering her poise, she reviewed the scene. All was exactly as planned, save for the incongruous socks. Not that they enhanced the man's dignity; for, apart from handcuffs, the socks were all he wore.

Bowed across the back of a chair, wrists fettered to its legs, the tubby, little banker forced up his balding head. Eyes bulging in disbelief at the sight of the smirking intruders, Rupert Eaton's resonant voice launched into a stream of invective.

Ignoring his ranting, Eve sat on the unused bed and layered one leg across the other. Slicking her skirt over upraised knee, she pocketed the key ring lying on the bed, and then peered inquiringly at Gwen. When the photographer nodded, Eve issued her commands.

Already stationed behind the man, two masked women raised their canes and took turns to land them tamely on target. Throughout this simulated scourging, Gwen rattled off shots from all angles, while Eaton mouthed obscenities nonstop.

Once Gwen announced that she'd taken enough photos, Eve rose to her feet, and jerked her head in the direction of the open doorway. Obediently, both 'flagellators' tripped towards the exit.

'Let's have that stick, Gloria.'

Exposed by the mask's aperture, gleaming lips served up a lopsided smile, as Gloria poked the cane into the redhead's hand. 'High-quality import, Eve, so don't bloody well break it.'

Eve grinned back. The women clattered into the hall. Gwen toyed with her camera. Eaton's deep voice thundered more expletives.

Pacing up to the manacled man, Eve grasped his fleshy nose and tweaked it. 'Shut up, Rupert. We need to talk.'

Eyes watering, his voice stilled. But, the moment Eve relaxed her hold, the coarse tirade recommenced. Crouching before him, she clamped his nose anew with one hand and waved the cane in threatening manner with the other.

'One more peep out of you, Rupert, and you'll regret it.'

She released his glowing nozzle and stood. A telling nod greeted Eaton's silence. Tossing the cane onto the bed, Eve perched on its edge, and tugged her hem primly over crossed knees.

'Do you need me any more, Eve?'

'No, Gwen.' Hauling a packet of *Kensitas* from her pocket, Eve extracted a cigarette and lit it. 'I think Rupert's ready to discuss matters sensibly now. So go and join the others.'

She heard the door close behind Gwen. The next sounds were grunts of fury and metallic jingles, as Eaton rattled his chained wrists. Gazing at his apoplectic face, Eve feigned and fanned a yawn.

'For God's sake release me,' he whined.

'Not just yet, Rupert.'

'Then cover me up.'

'First, let's have a little chat.'

'Who the hell are you?'

'My name's Eve Loxton and I work for DOSS, the Department of Special Security.'

'DOSS? I thought they'd closed down you maniacs years ago.'

Eve exhaled smoke through pursed lips, which she then reworked into a sinister smile. 'Lots of people believe that, Rupert, often with dire consequences. But, I can assure you that we're still very much in business.'

His cherubic face screwed up in concern. 'But why pick on me? What have I done?'

'Well, besides being a sexual deviant, Rupert, you run a bank. And, a bank has clients and a bank has money.'

Meagre lips contorting into a sneer, he forced his head up higher to take on her steady gaze. 'So DOSS is robbing banks now, is it?'

'No, Rupert. Although I will be charging you a fee for my services, my primary interest is in one of your clientele. I want to examine your records of Stephen Horner's financial dealings.'

'Horner? But why do you want to…?'

'Why?' she snapped. 'Because I damn well said so, Rupert, and you're in no position to argue the toss.'

Stubbing her butt, Eve stood and ran skirt-smoothing palms down her thighs. Eaton blinked apprehensively. Moments later, his expression switched to indignation, when she began rifling through his neatly hung suit.

'What the hell do you think you're up to?'

Eve delayed her response until she'd finished examining his wallet. 'I'm going through your pockets, like any sensible woman would.'

When another string of obscenities spewed from his lips, Eve grabbed the cane from the bed and glared at him menacingly. The stick swished twice to land a sharp blow upon each fettered hand. His gasp was more surprised than pained.

'I trust there will be no further offensive remarks, Rupert.'

Grimacing impotently, Eaton wisely held his tongue.

Laying the cane aside, Eve reseated herself on the bed and opened his briefcase. It contained solely a sizeable envelope. She withdrew the item within it, and found herself staring at a calendar for the coming year. Resting it upon her thigh, she leafed through the black and white photos accompanying each month. They ranged from erotic to downright pornographic.

Years before joining DOSS, porn had ceased to be a novelty to Eve. It had entered her life along with her late husband. She'd accepted it then, in the same way that she'd accepted anything which ostensibly helped their marriage. In the end, nothing had helped. The fleeting moment of recall prompted her hand to clench into a fist; knuckles whitening as the nails dug into her palm.

Dismissing her savage thoughts, Eve examined the photographs more attentively. She was impressed by the quality of the shots and the subtle use of light. All stood in marked contrast to the crude back-street stuff, seemingly lit by arc lights, and with every detail on show to pander to barren imaginations.

'Pretty porn? Posh porn?' Eve played with oxymorons in her mind. Then she asked Eaton how much he'd paid for the calendar. When he told her, she added 'pricey porn' to her assessment.

'So where did you get this calendar?'

'From a chap at my club,' he muttered sourly.

'And where did he get it?'

'I've no idea.'

'Then find out for me,' she ordered curtly.

Sliding the calendar back into the envelope, Eve announced that she was confiscating it. Eaton said nothing, merely making the sort of face that a thwarted schoolboy might produce.

Laying the envelope aside, Eve came to her feet and eyed the banker coldly. 'Paying for your perverse ways must get rather expensive, Rupert.'

'What's it to you?' he snarled, mustering irritation to veil his vulnerability.

From her pocket, Eve withdrew the key ring and a slip of paper. The latter she placed upon the seat of the chair, allowing Eaton to study the figures inscribed upon it.

'What the hell is this?'

'I'm invoicing you my fee, Rupert. Small denomination used notes, of course. And don't forget to hunt out Horner's file. I'll phone you when the photos are ready, and arrange another meeting.'

She freed one of his wrists, placed the keys atop her 'invoice', and left him to do the rest. Sweeping the envelope from the bed, Eve fired off her parting shot.

'I'm sorry your fun got curtailed, Rupert.' She compensated him with a sardonic smile. 'Still, it means you can get home early and tell the wife all about your day.'

5

MONDAY 27 SEPTEMBER 1948

A man of stocky build, with greased hair cresting a chubbily handsome face, Sid Yates worked the control in the security foyer. When the incomer presented his ID, Yates flicked a glance at it, scribbled the man's details in his logbook, and then returned to the sports pages of his paper.

When the next arrival entered his domain, Sid pigeon puffed his chest and bounced upon his toes. Silently, he intoned words to the effect that he could 'really manage that!' And, although there was little chance of a man managed by Hilda Yates managing any such thing, it was nice to dream.

Despite the onset of autumn, Fay Galbraith wore a sleeveless cream dress with a white cardigan draped over her shoulders. All flesh on display was deeply tanned, and she moved with the sensual grace of a woman entirely at ease with her body. Curvy hips swinging slightly, Fay sauntered towards the counter. A hand swept back long, chestnut hair, and then poked around her handbag for her pass.

Converting his leer into a smile of greeting, Yates took her ID, and entered its details at the staid pace he reserved for detaining attractive women. Throughout, Fay lounged upon forearms squashed against the counter. This allowed Sid to glimpse the iceberg tip of cleavage, before looking up to inquire chirpily where she'd been on holiday.

'The south of France,' Fay responded in the alto voice which she could play like an instrument. Sid always felt a tingle in his spine when she let it go really husky. Hilda had only one tone – hectoring, and one volume – strident.

He was staring into her eyes now, those umber eyes which could really look at you, and were daring him to peek down her dress again.

'Mr Galbraith enjoy it too?' he inquired nosily.

Her mouth staged the jaded smile that said it all, but she tagged on a verbal response. 'He was called away on business on our third day there.'

That would be when Fay really enjoyed herself, Sid wagered. Throwing a fleeting glance cleavagewards, he bet himself that her tits were brown all over. But, you could do that in the south of France, couldn't you? Hilda liked Southend.

Fay ambled towards the lift, trailing his gaze in her wake, until a green light flashing on the counter obliged Sid to return to his duties. His face lit up when a buxom clerk entered the foyer. Bouncing on his toes, he conceded that his wasn't a bad job sometimes.

Randall had almost finished his study of internal tensions within the Soviet party leadership. Before completing it, he needed to access a file, which another researcher was using. While waiting, he'd turned his attention to the Hungarian party.

Fiddling with an unlit cigarette, he tried to concentrate upon a thick dossier, which detailed the careers of the Hungarian Communist Party leadership. He'd obtained it from Fay, after learning that she had popped into the office a day before the formal end of her leave.

She'd handed it to him without acknowledging his existence, let alone breaking off the animated conversation she was conducting on the phone. Obviously, Fay was extremely 'busy'. And, although she'd often treated him in like fashion, he could divine only one reason for such behaviour. She was reminding him of who called the shots in their relationship. Something that was hardly necessary in his case.

For Randall had long ago shed the delusion that a man ever seduced a woman. Despite virtuoso performances by sundry sirens, which aimed at creating such a mirage, he knew this was only ever an introductory act, reserved for hard cases like himself. In the real world of relationships, women commanded and men performed. Therefore, the easiest and most pleasurable solution for the male was simply to abide by this immutable rule.

And, if he was ever asked why a man should then leave one woman for another, Randall's ready answer was that this was no independent decision by that male. He was merely obeying the commands of some fresh enchantress, who'd convinced him that she could raise his performance to some peak he had never yet attained. And, for some men, so it went on, and on.

Jack emerged from his musing just as Wendy Page appeared in his room's open doorway. Closing his file, he beckoned her enter. Hands linked behind her back, she approached his desk, smiling cryptically.

'Jack, would you like to see a part of me that's naked?'

Having no ready response, he just grinned. Wendy's next move was to thrust her left hand across the desk. The engagement ring was gone.

'The deed is done,' she announced with a dismissive flick of her long lashes. Then she peered at the title of his closed file. 'You were in Hungary in late 1945, weren't you?'

He frowned. 'How do you know that? You weren't here then.'

'True, but I did review your entire record on expenses.'

Her salient remark prompted a guarded nod from Randall.

'What were you up to in Hungary?'

'Horner sent me there to report upon their first post-war election.'

'I see. Anyway, thanks for encouraging me to call things off.'

'I simply offered my opinion, Wendy.'

'Well, I might seek your advice again sometime, Jack.'

Switching off another enigmatic smile, she waggled a wave and left. It was with a marked lessening of interest that he returned to the file.

He ploughed through brief biographies of Rákosi, Gerő, Farkas, and Révai; the quartet of nonreligious Jews who constituted the Hungarian party's real leadership. Turning to another page, he found himself staring at press photographs of László Rajk.

Some five years older than himself, one of eleven children, Rajk was born in Transylvania of Protestant parents. Jack recalled the off-colour joke he'd heard in Budapest, that Rajk was only in the Party's Politburo so that someone could sign decrees on Saturdays.

The photos depicted a good-looking man, very tall and slim. His shy smile belied Rajk's role as a ruthless Stalinist, who'd headed the vital Interior Ministry during the years when the communists rose to power. Yet Rajk had lost that post in August, when he was appointed Foreign Minister.

Some people contended that this was promotion for Rajk. However, that wasn't Randall's view, given that Moscow determined Hungarian foreign policy. Jack half-smiled, recalling Horner's complementary opinion that the USA ran British foreign policy. But Horner had no time for the Foreign Office, always referring to the FO as 'the Foe'.

Dark green eyes surveyed the décor of Rupert Eaton's office, digesting the dull dependability of its furniture and wallpaper. Focusing upon one wall, Eve studied the portraits of bewhiskered ancestors, who glared at her prudently from gilt frames. A restrained smile to her lips, she confronted the present incumbent, peeping at her from behind his desk.

'So how many of that lot were perverts like you, Rupert?'

When his chubby pink face deepened in hue, Eve's smile broadened to expose her splendid teeth. Extracting an envelope from her tan shoulder bag, she tossed it onto the desk.

'The photos have come out really well.'

Blushing again, Eaton stared transfixed at her offering. Then he unsealed the envelope and withdrew its contents. Chewing his lip, he flipped through the photos, before shoving them back under wraps.

'Good, aren't they, Rupert?'

He slipped the package into a drawer. 'What happens now?'

Eve treated him to a mercenary smirk. 'Well, once we've concluded today's business, I won't bother you until I pick up my next fee sometime in November.'

He snorted contemptuously. 'So, just like any blackmailer, you'll keep coming back for more.'

Sitting on the chair opposite his oak desk, Eve eyed him stonily. 'Rupert, you really must view things from my perspective. I head the women's section of DOSS, and I operate upon a shoestring budget. I employ several talented ladies who help safeguard this nation's security. But, unlike your female staff, my girls receive the same remuneration as male employees of DOSS. So to fund things properly, I'm obliged to collect fees from those who deserve to pay them. All clear now?'

He screwed up his round face, and then stared inquisitively at the rings on her left hand. 'Are you married?'

'I'm a widow.'

'I'm sorry,' said Eaton mechanically.

'But I'm not,' Eve retorted, nostrils flared in disdain. 'Anyway, let's talk about your predicament.'

'You mean about setting me up.'

'I rather think you set yourself up, Rupert. If you'd been home with the wife that fateful evening, tuned into the Light Programme's joys, none of this would have happened.'

Lowering his gaze, Eaton fiddled with his waistcoat's bottom button, which he left unfastened to ape the 'fashion' set by an obese monarch. Then his eyes flicked up, when Eve, hand outstretched in demand, ordered him to pass over Horner's file.

'Eve, this is quite unethical. Can't we deal with these matters in some other way?'

'Of course we can, Rupert. I can tell Gwen to post those photos to your major clients. But, these might include some stuffy people, who'd look askance at those pics of you....'

'That's enough!' he barked, whipping open a drawer to grab a fat folder. Glowering helplessly, he shoved it across the desk. 'Stephen Horner's fucking file, fully up to date.'

'Thank you, Rupert,' she said sweetly.

As Eve scrutinised the relevant pages, only the sound of his desk-drumming fingers disturbed the silence. When she looked up, her eyes locked onto his.

'When does the next poker session of the "Spats" take place?'

His fingers ceased their tattoo, in order to massage sweat-beads into his balding pate.

'Rupert, I know all about it. At regular intervals, Horner and other wealthy men assemble to play poker for serious money. As a condition of membership of this elite group, they are obliged both to wear spats and to bank with you. At the start of each session, you specify each individual's so-called "worth", based upon your knowledge of their total assets. Any "Spat" can then obtain chips up to his "worth".'

Grimacing, he studied his paunch. 'You're remarkably well-informed about these matters.'

'For God's sake, Rupert, do you think I just strolled into your session with Gloria and Zoë on the off-chance? I've spoken to girls working in your bank, and I've also interviewed barmaids working at earlier poker sessions.'

He looked up warily. 'What about Gloria?'

'Well, she and some of her co-workers are deeply indebted to me. But, it's not just your head they've served up to me on a platter, Rupert. A fair sprinkling of the usual suspects have found themselves on the wrong side of Gwen's camera, and now deem it beneficial to assist me with finance and information.'

'I see,' he muttered miserably.

Eve jabbed a finger at a page in the open file. 'Horner seems to have lost rather consistently of late. So what's he got left, just the Richmond house and a few paintings?'

He huddled lower in his seat. 'Horner retains significant assets.'

'Rupert, stop sodding about! Horner's already sold off the properties his father left him. He's also broken up the art collection he inherited.'

Eaton stared at her in astonishment.

'I *can* read a will, which is a public document,' she lectured, 'and I've got girls working in the Land Registry as well as the major auction houses.'

Gripping both arms of his chair, the banker drew himself ponderously to his feet. 'Do you want a drink?'

'I'll pass, Rupert. For me, it's always business before pleasure.'

An abrupt smile flashed across her face, as she watched him haul a bottle of scotch from the array in a cabinet and pour generously with shaking hand.

'At the end of a session of the "Spats", how do the losers settle their debts, Rupert?'

Eaton swigged from his glass before replying. 'A debtor has up to three months to settle his losses. He may do so either by the transfer of cash between accounts, or, if his creditor agrees, by the transfer of physical assets of the appropriate value.'

She eyed him shrewdly. 'What if the creditor insists upon cash and the debtor has insufficient liquid assets?'

'Then the debtor must liquidate physical assets to raise cash.'

'But, since it can easily take well over three months to sell off a property, for example, what does a debtor do to raise the cash within the time limit? Does he borrow from your bank, Rupert?'

He drained his drink. 'It's not unknown.'

'I presume you charge an interesting rate of interest.'

'What the hell do you expect?'

Eve glanced again at the file. Then she looked up with an artless expression to her face. 'Has Horner ever borrowed a large sum from your bank?'

Shaking his head, he recharged his glass.

'Yet last March, his account is credited with the sum of fifty thousand pounds. Where did that come from?'

Eaton stared at his feet. 'Horner made a cash deposit.'

'A cash deposit of fifty thousand quid?'

'It happens,' he mumbled.

'It doesn't in my world,' she snorted. 'Then in June, he deposits fifty-five thousand pounds and withdraws fifty thousand. Would you care to explain these transactions?'

Clutching his whisky, he plodded back to his chair and sat. 'The deposit comprised various cheques for the sale of assets, while the withdrawal was in cash.'

'So fifty thousand pounds in cash goes into his account, while Horner was waiting for the cheques to cover his gambling debts. Then, once these arrive, the same fifty thousand gets withdrawn. Where did this handy little sum come from, Rupert?'

'I've no idea,' he mumbled into his glass.

Standing, Eve smoothed her skirt, and then paced around the desk. Eaton shrank in his seat as she towered over him, and yelped when she grasped his nose.

'You've no idea?' scolded Eve as she tweaked. 'You know damned well that it was misuse of public funds, Rupert, taxpayers' money. Horner helped himself to his department's budget, and then put the money back again to cover his thieving tracks.'

Following a last spiteful twist, she released him. 'Now everything's fine, isn't it? His department's ledgers would pass external scrutiny. Horner's current account with you is in credit. Most of all, he still has a house and a few pictures to fund his next visit to the poker table. Have I missed anything out?'

Rubbing his nose, he peered up at her. 'Eve, I'm just a banker. Money is simply a commodity. I don't ask about its origins and destinations.'

'When's the next session of the "Spats", Rupert?'

Shying away when her face thrust into his, he stammered a reply.

'So it begins on the night of Wednesday 6th October. This means, Rupert, that following Horner's next performance on the green baize, you will report to me in detail about his then "worth". Understood?'

When he meekly assented, Eve stepped away from the desk. 'Rupert, what do you know about Horner's so-called "Treasure Trove"?'

Eaton tasted his scotch before responding. 'It's the name Horner gave to his collection of sleazy reports, which supposedly could ruin the reputations of many notable figures. It's a clever stratagem. Horner deters attempts to liquidate his department, by threatening unseemly disclosures should anyone take him on. His threat may well be a bluff, but it's one that nobody dares to call.'

'You may well be right. But, should this hoard of Horner's prove to be a reality, and should it ever find its way into your vaults, Rupert, then I expect to be informed. I trust that's perfectly understood.'

'Yes, Eve.'

'Now I'll take my fee.'

Grimacing, he reached into a drawer and pulled out a bulging envelope. Eve plucked it from his hand and stuffed it into her bag.

'Aren't you going to count it?'

Shouldering the bag, she glared at him balefully. 'I'll count it later. And, if you've had the temerity to defraud me, it will cost you in every way. Now, show me out.'

Standing at once, he licked his lip nervously. 'You really are a very demanding woman, Eve.'

'But you like that, Rupert.' Her voice, like her eyes, was mesmeric. 'Constant domination, a bit of punishment, plus payment for your sins, what more could any man ask?'

6

THURSDAY 7 OCTOBER 1948

'Bloody spats!' spluttered Barber from the car's back seat. 'Who does Horner think he is, Fred Astaire?'

As brisk, measured strides brought Horner ever nearer to the watchers' vehicle, Christopher Pratt rubbed at the moist haze inside the windscreen to improve his view. His thin lips tautened smugly. 'Horner is obliged to wear spats, sir, in order to attend his card school. After all, it *is* rather exclusive.'

'I know that, lad,' snarled Barber. Burrowing beneath a shabby mac, he grappled with a blazer pocket's torn lining and disentangled his pipe. The exertion deepened in shade his florid face and accentuated his heavy breathing. Fumbling for matches, he addressed the ginger-haired man in the driver's seat. 'See owt unusual, Eric?'

'No, guv.'

Arthur stoked the cherrywood. The pungent smoke prompted Pratt into a mannered cough. Barber's response was to disgorge another cloud, while his alert pale eyes watched Horner trot up the steps leading to his kingdom, and disappear inside the building.

'Looked right cocky, didn't he? Happen Horner hit a winning streak last night.' He gnawed at a fickle hair straying from his untrimmed moustache, and then lapsed into the murkiest delivery his northern origins afforded. 'But with whose funds, eh, private or public?'

'Sir, these are only rumours,' protested Pratt mildly, as he wound down the passenger seat window. 'To my mind, the suggestion that Horner is pilfering from the public purse is utterly farfetched. After all, his department's accounts have never been challenged.'

'And who's going to challenge him, eh? Think what our Stephen's got tucked away in his so-called "Treasure Trove", Christopher. Files full of indiscretions by people in public life, they say. He might even have a file on you, lad.'

Eyes glued to the rearview mirror, Eric Moon caught Arthur's wink and gurgled a laugh. Disdaining further comment, Pratt fiddled prissily with his bow-tie.

In an office in DORA, the head of its European Communism Section was in close consultation with his deputy; unavoidably so, since she'd just eased herself onto his lap.

'I want a kiss,' announced Fay, adjusting the spread of her bottom, and extending the heat Randall felt far beyond his thighs. Her wish granted without demur, Fay pulled back her head and stared into his eyes. 'You seem somewhat aloof, Jack.'

'Perhaps it's something to do with the fact that until now, you've barely spoken a word to me since you got back from France.'

She shrugged her brows. 'I've been exceptionally busy.'

'So what's changed?'

'Well, Oliver's away from tomorrow until Tuesday evening.' Squashing her bust against his chest, Fay traced a finger over his lips. 'So I wondered if you might possibly be interested in seeing me for a few days.'

'I suppose I could make time in my hectic schedule.'

'You don't have to, Jack.'

'I know I don't. But, most conveniently, I'm on leave all next week. What about you?'

'I've already arranged to have Monday and Tuesday off.'

He made a sour face. 'You knew I'd agree, didn't you?'

'I knew someone would.' Her eyes rounded teasingly above a winning smile. 'I just thought I'd give you first refusal.'

'Only you knew I wouldn't refuse.'

'Then there's no problem, is there, my sweet?'

Fay brushed her mouth against his, slid sensually from his lap, and then pointed at an item in the open newspaper on his desk. 'Have you read about that dreadful earthquake in the Soviet Union?'

Fuzzy though audible, Eaton's secretly recorded tape of their last meeting had just ended; after which the banker had listed his demands.

Hands knuckled on hips, legs planted resolutely apart, Eve stared at an ancestor while she carefully rearranged her features. Surprise, tinged with anxiety, gave way to a ruminative pout, as she contemplated the wiles needed to reassert control.

She unbuttoned her black jacket. Glancing from the corner of her eye, Eve confirmed that his were glued to her profile. Slipping her hands into jacket pockets, she turned to face him. 'Rupert, you must realise that you don't exactly sound like the Angel Gabriel on that tape either.'

He hunched in his chair, a sly smile dimpling his cherubic face. 'I'm aware that I said some very indiscreet things, Eve. Unlike you, however, none of my words constituted a criminal offence.'

'So what exactly are you going to do with that tape, if I don't give you Gwen's films and all the prints she's made?'

'I'll hand it over to the police.'

'But I *am* the police, Rupert.'

'I meant the real police.'

'In my view, the only real police are the secret police,' contended Eve in a silky voice. 'But, be that as it may, what do you think the regular police will do with your offering?'

'I'm not sure,' he muttered hesitantly.

'You haven't really thought this through, have you?' She smiled indulgently. 'Can't you see how irrationally you're behaving, Rupert? This silly state of mutual blackmail won't get either of us what we want.'

'I'm not sure what you mean, Eve.'

'Rupert, I really do need some money.'

Long fingers pushed the white blouse deeper into the waistband of her skirt, causing the prominent nipples of free-range breasts to indent the silk with their presence. Dragging his eyes from her bust, Eaton bit on his lip and grasped his lapels.

'Eve, there's no reason that you can't be guaranteed a regular income. But you don't have to blackmail me to get it.'

'Sorry about that. Force of habit, I suppose.' Miming an apologetic smile, she paced to his side and laid a hand upon his shoulder. 'Now, what exactly do you want for your money?'

His eyes dropped to his paunch. 'I want to be me, Eve, and I'll pay to be me.'

'I understand,' she murmured. 'So what do you want me to do?'

He twiddled the unfastened button of his waistcoat, as though involved in a major scientific experiment. 'There are rather a lot of things, Eve.'

'Well, why not write them down, and I'll see what I can manage.'

Immediately abandoning his contribution to science, he looked up at her with an expression both childlike and artful. 'I've written them down already, just in case.'

'Have you really?' said Eve, forcing neutrality into her tone. She gave his neck a cautionary squeeze, and then reluctantly slackened her fingers. 'Well, you'd better show me what you've written.'

His hand dived into a desk drawer and emerged with a sheet of foolscap covered in spidery writing. A late injection of sweetness tempered her citric smile, as she took the paper from his hand and laid it on the desk to read.

'Do you mind, Eve?'

'Why should I? Just as long as you don't mind paying my fees.'

He leant forward enthusiastically. 'I presume you can get Zoë to help you out. I gained the impression she worked for you, rather than Gloria.'

'Most observant of you, Rupert. I like to have someone I can rely on to be present at such events. But I'm afraid Zoë's not available just now.'

'Well, I can wait.'

'But I can't. I'd like something on account.'

The piggy eyes bulged, and a small and very pink tongue swept along his lower lip. 'In that case, so would I.'

Arched brows queried his intentions.

'Well, Eve, there are certain items in that list which you could perform without Zoë's assistance. In fact, we could begin now. This late in the evening we have the building to ourselves. So choose from my list.'

She scanned his requirements again. 'Rupert, there are a couple of items here that I'm not quite sure about. Now, what exactly is this number fifteen, the "Greek Wedding"?'

His eyes glazed in ecstasy as he explained in detail. Having heard him out, Eve gave a perfunctory nod. Then she located a pencil and printed a price upon his unsullied blotter.

'Ridiculous!' he spluttered. 'No man in his right mind would pay such an exorbitant sum for....'

'But, Rupert, you're not in your right mind. You're a pervert, a fantasist, a fetishist.'

'That's a bit harsh,' he retorted sullenly. 'And you must admit that it's an awful lot of money.'

She paced around the desk and sat in the chair opposite him. Crossing her long legs elaborately, Eve let her skirt ride up her thigh. 'Now, stop haggling, Rupert. You know you're ready to pay.'

When his financially-induced frown was followed by a submissive nod, she sucked in her cheeks. For this she needed a drink. Yet what did the occasion demand?

As usual in such situations, Eve silently recited the mantra she'd composed from experience: 'Gin caused no sin. Wine too was fine. Whisky makes you frisky. And brandy downright randy.' Since Eaton's fantasy was pure theatre and nothing but a bit of acting was involved, she settled for her staple tipple.

'It is, of course, cash on the nail, Rupert. So off to your safe you go. Then you can stoke up the fire, and pour me a stiff gin and tonic.'

He stood at once, hands clasped ingratiatingly before him. 'Is there anything else?'

'Yes, there is. Have you found out any more about that calendar?'

'Well, the chap I got it from is asking the chap he got it from, where it came from.'

'So how are these chaps communicating, by carrier pigeon?'

A flaccid smile crept onto his lips, when the light of understanding finally dawned. 'Shall I tell them to get a move on?'

'Something like that,' said Eve, wasting her sarcasm.

She watched him leave. Then she sprang to her feet to fix a drink herself. Carrying the gin back to the desk, she examined his list again. Moneymaking ideas came to her in embryo, as she emptied her glass in generous gulps.

7

MONDAY 11 OCTOBER 1948

A file open before him, Barber sprawled behind his dilapidated desk. Fiddling with sparse wisps of sandy hair, he pondered matters of life and death. Not for the first time, he'd been left to settle the fate of an individual, whom 'higher authorities' were reluctant to deal with by constricting legal means.

It had begun during the war, when DOSS was set up to counteract Nazi sympathisers by means other than internment under the Defence of the Realm Act. And, while the post-war period had seen DOSS scaled down in size, it was still in business, with its executive functions now directed against adherents of the new enemy to the east.

Arthur's fingers pirouetted around his balding crown. Beneath it, his mind sat in judgement upon the fate of a junior FO official, whose life and guilty deeds were the subject of his file. Was Barber to let him be or not? To 'maximise' or to 'minimise', that was the question.

'Maximising' — or more correctly 'maksimising' — stemmed from the injuctive phrase 'make silent', and utilised such arts as intimidation, blackmail, and bribery to neutralise those who chose to serve Stalin. Confusingly, 'minimising' was a more extreme sanction. This euphemism derived from the acronym 'M.I.N.I.', which stood for 'Murder in the National Interest'. Needless to say, Barber's authority to stage 'suicides' and 'accidents' was not abused through overuse, for, as in all matters, he strove for moderation.

He flipped back a page. It would hardly be outrageous fortune for the treasonable bastard to come to a sticky end. Perhaps it was time to convey an exemplary message to those tempted to betray British secrets to Moscow.

Of course, the fellow did have a wife and kids. Not that this red traitor had shown much regard for their interests. Still, as a family man himself, it could hardly be expected that Barber would be left unmoved by such considerations. Rubbing a finger across his puggish nose, he reflected upon the depths of his merciful nature.

His mind made up, he nodded vigorously, setting off tremors in the wads of ill-shaven flesh beneath his chin. He inserted a blank sheet of paper at the end of the file and, writing without pause, rendered judgement in his surprisingly elegant hand.

Horner confronted the Soviet Union, grim eyes riveted upon Ashkhabad, capital of the Turkmen Soviet Socialist Republic. Jabbing his forefinger down the line of his gaze, he pinpointed the stricken city. It had been devastated six days earlier, ostensibly by an earthquake. Trailing a nail over the linen of the map, he brought it to a halt just north of Ashkhabad, and then allowed it to meander about the wastes of the Karakum Desert.

Striding over to the desk, he unscrewed the cap from his pen, and employed it to compose a memorandum. This conjectured that on 5th October 1948 the first Soviet test of an atomic bomb had aborted.

When Eric Moon stoop-walked into his dingy office, Barber reached for the cherrywood idling in an ashtray. Invoking memories of pre-war quality between expletives, he dispensed with two dud matches. A third fizzed alight, and he inhaled raucously.

'So how was the martial bearing today, Eric?'

'Different, guv. Mr H. never looked dashin' at all.'

A paw engulfed the pipe's bowl, as discoloured dentures released its stem. 'Happen our Stephen's hit a losing streak,' remarked Barber, modulating his certainty as suggestion.

'Want me to keep on watchin' then?'

'Nay, lad, wind it up,' he muttered, blowing out some unimpressive rings of smoke. 'We can't spare the resources just now. Still, our Stephen will come a cropper some day, just mark my words.'

'So what do I do now, guv?'

'What you're good at, lad.'

Moon's red nose glowed happily in his doughy face.

Barber tapped the envelope on his desk with the pipe. 'Foreign Office lad who supplied young Herbert Pilling, it's all in there, Eric.'

Moon produced a jagged smile when Arthur held out the package. Clenching it in a terrier-like grip, he awaited the verbal command.

The lids drooped over Barber's eyes. '"Minimise",' he ordered.

Steel-rimmed spectacles dangled from one hand. The other concealed part of Horner's face; index finger pressing above the cheekbone, thumb indenting the sparse flesh around his jaw. It took a timorous knock upon the connecting door to displace gambling debts from his thoughts.

'Come!' Horner barked.

Correspondence clamped to an amorphous bosom, his personal assistant stole in diffidently from the adjacent office. Selecting various papers from the pile, Ursula Conrad paraded them before him. Hooking his glasses over almost lobeless ears, Horner leafed through items requiring his attention, before inquiring if Randall's report was to hand. Withdrawing it from her pile, she laid it reverently before him.

'That will be all,' announced Horner, without looking up.

As she stole from the room, he transferred his attention to Randall's analysis of the Soviet leadership in the wake of Zhdanov's death. Passages pertinent to his interests Horner marked with his pen. Then he sat back in contemplation.

Spine braced against his chair, he endeavoured to suppress an involuntary shudder. For late the previous night, 'Lady Luck' had finally forsaken him. When his prial of sevens had succumbed to Toby Meredith's flush, Horner had forfeited virtually his entire remaining 'worth'. Of course, he could cover his debts with another 'loan' from DORA's contingency fund, but this would require him to recoup his losses when the 'Spats' reassembled in December. If he lost again, it would mean utter ruin.

He unlocked a desk drawer, slid it open, and fingered an ornate brass key with the label 'TT' attached. Then his hand leapfrogged the pills prescribed for his heart condition, and lighted upon a revolver. Horner extracted it, inserted a single cartridge into the chamber, and caressed its barrel. Some minutes later, he unloaded the firearm and cached it in the drawer.

Pouring drinks in the lounge of her compact flat in Shepherds Bush, Eve watched Sandra Jansen lean over the arm of her chair. The blonde poked her hand into an opened parcel on the floor, shuddered, and pushed the orange balaclava back under wraps. Wearing the expression of one who'd just trodden in something unpleasant, she glanced at Eve.

'Mother?'

Eve nodded. 'I suppose it might make a good Halloween mask.'

'But we don't celebrate it, Eve.'

'We will. This coca-colonisation by the Yanks is unstoppable.'

'Coca-colonisation, did you make that up?'

Eve nodded again. 'It's a bit of a mouthful, but that sort of thing might catch on with French reds, given their current anti-American line.'

Sandra stared again at the parcel, and then faced her friend. 'Your mother's just eccentric, Eve, but mine's a full-time cow. I've never been able to please her. I was always too skinny, too tall, too blonde, too clever, too difficult. I never knew what she wanted.'

'A boy perhaps?' suggested Eve drolly, as she passed Sandra a large gin. 'Anyway, what have you got on Fay Galbraith?'

Sandra flipped open her notebook. 'Do you want all the detail?'

Now lolling upon her settee, Eve's truncated nod was like the peck of a bird.

'Well, Eve, until last Friday, the surveillance was all very humdrum. Following her holiday, Fay just toddled off to work at DORA, and afterwards went straight back home to Chiswick and hubby Oliver.'

'But on Friday,' prompted Eve.

'On Friday evening, we followed Fay from DORA. She had a valise with her, and she went into a nearby pub. There she met up with a bloke we'd often seen coming out of DORA. We'd noticed him, because both Delaney twins had remarked that they fancied him.'

'And you?'

'Well, I could see their point.' Sandra doused a pert smile with a sip of gin. 'Anyway, we followed them to Westminster, from where they travelled by tube to Ealing Broadway. There they nipped into another pub for a quick drink. Then they went to the bloke's place.'

'Do we know who this bloke is?'

'I checked the electoral register. For that address the sole resident is one John Gareth Randall.'

Eve pouted. 'So Fay's having an affair with Jack Randall.'

'You know him?'

'I know of him.' She glanced at her deputy's frustrated face. 'I'll fill you in later.'

'Thanks a lot!' said Sandra caustically.

'I promise.'

Sandra reached into her handbag. Extracting a wrinkled tissue-bag, she offered its contents. 'Fancy one, Eve? They're off-ration this month, and when I see them I just can't resist the urge.'

Eve declined a sweet. 'So how long has Fay been married?'

Sandra's teeth amputated the legs of a red jelly baby. Chewing and sucking in turn, she checked her notes. 'She married Oliver in June 1933. He's about twenty years older than her.'

'What does he do?'

'He's a senior rep for an agricultural machinery firm. So he's often travelling, both home and abroad, and he's away right now.'

'What about Jack and Fay?'

'They must be on leave. They were still at Jack's flat this afternoon.'

Eve winched up her brows inquiringly.

'Well, Eve, there's a flat across the road from Jack's place that's up for rent. It has a little tower, which apparently was intended as a dovecot, and this is well above the tree-line, which otherwise shields Jack's flat from view.' Smiling to herself, Sandra took another pull on her drink. 'I looked it over with the twins this morning.'

'See anything interesting from the dovecot?'

Sandra prefaced her response with a smutty laugh. 'Well, you can see into Jack's attic. Its roof is studded with skylights and dormer windows. Moreover, his bedroom on the floor below has clear glass doors leading onto a balcony, and from the lounge of this other flat you can see into it through the trees. So with the proper camera....'

'Is there room enough for the twins in this flat?'

'Ample room, Eve, it's got two bedrooms. There's also a scullery, which could be made into a darkroom, so the twins inform me.'

'Have they got the right camera?'

'They know where to get one, Eve.'

'How pricey is the flat?'

'Beyond my budget, I'm afraid.'

'Take it,' said Eve magnanimously.

'Money no object?'

'Don't see why it should be. After all, my banker will be paying, and paying through his squashy nose.'

'Have you seen him again then?'

'We've been to a "Greek Wedding".' Pulling several wads of banknotes from beneath a sofa cushion, Eve passed them over.

'You've been where?' asked Sandra, wide-eyed, as she stuffed the cash into her bag.

'I'll tell you sometime.'

'Why not now?'

'Sorry, Sandra, I'll have to turf you out. I've got to drive Eric to a job tomorrow, so I'll need my beauty sleep.'

Sandra drained her glass, and gathered up her things. 'Thanks, Eve. About the flat, I mean. It will be good to get away from my present place. Derek was mooching around at the weekend.'

'Well, get Eric to have a word with him, like he did with my Jimmy. Eric's good at straightening people out.'

Eve glanced at the parcel on the floor. Of course her mother was weird, but at least she'd rid the house of husband number two; someone else who'd needed straightening out.

8

TUESDAY 12 OCTOBER 1948

'Who the hell was that on the phone, Jack?'

Randall settled moodily on the side of his bed. 'I'll give you three guesses.'

Scowling, Fay propped herself on an elbow. 'Horner wants you up there this very minute?'

'Only nine out of ten,' he replied peevishly. 'I've got to see him at one-thirty p.m., precisely.'

'But you're on leave,' she protested, hand straying to stroke his bare thigh.

'Not any longer.'

'But Oliver comes back this evening, and I wanted to spend the rest of the day....'

'Well, you'll have to make do with a couple of hours, my lady.'

'Damn that bloody man!'

'Which damned and bloodied man are we talking about, Fay?'

'Horner, of course. You know I discuss my husband as rarely as I sleep with him.'

'I keep forgetting the merits of marital bliss.'

'Oh, Oliver has his uses, as have you, my sweet.'

Tanned body emerging from beneath the covers, Fay stretched out to clutch his hair. Having flattened him onto his back, she knelt to each side of his hips, and pressed his revitalised erection against her clitoris.

'You did say two hours, didn't you?'

Nodding, his hands reached up to fondle her breasts.

'Well, make sure that's nonstop, Jack.'

Tensing his legs, Eric Moon gripped the passenger seat. He relaxed palpably when Eve screeched their car to a halt behind a ramshackle lorry, which had braked sharply. When Moon's lips ceased expleting, they twitched combatively as he reached for the door handle.

'Don't you dare!' snapped Eve, clipping the words of her command. 'Your job requires total concentration, Eric. This is no time for a bout of road rage.'

When he glanced at her mutinously, she cowed him with an authoritative glare. Then she reversed their vehicle, indicated with her arm, and accelerated into the outside lane.

Docile again, Eric gurgled a laugh. 'Them fings you come out wiv, Eve. Bleedin' "road rage"! Won't never catch on in a million years.'

Belatedly, he entered the fifth-floor sanctum. Toasting his rump by a coal fire, Horner glanced in unspoken rebuke at the wall clock. Ignoring him, Randall peered at the packet on the desk. So he'd been called in to play 'noughts and crosses' again.

The standard routine was for Randall to leave a plain bar of soap in his wash bag in some foreign hotel room. The soap contained microfilm, and its skin was scored with a 'nought'. Only when he noted its replacement by an identical bar gouged with a 'cross', was his mission over. He then returned to base with the proxy. He never knew what this might contain, nor did he want to know. He simply ensured that it came into Horner's hands.

With the post-war contraction of DORA, both he and Fay had moon-lighted as couriers. It was hardly onerous work. Nor did he view it as dangerous, for Horner hadn't sent him anywhere in the Soviet sphere since a visit to Prague in 1946. He didn't count trips to Berlin and Vienna, both of which were under quadripartite control. In any case, once the Berlin Blockade had fully commenced the previous June, Horner hadn't sent him there either. In fact, most of his jaunts were to Paris, with the odd trip to other cities of Western Europe thrown in.

'Amsterdam. Tomorrow,' he heard Horner say, as he collected the packet. So that was the rest of his leave taken care of. Still, it would give him the opportunity to look at paintings in the *Rijksmuseum*. He turned to go, but Horner's disciplined nod assigned him to a chair on the unheated side of the desk.

'Informative,' acknowledged Horner. 'Your paper upon conflicts within the Soviet leadership. You can take it with you. Now the file beneath. Contents might be of interest.'

Stifling a yawn, he nudged Horner's purple-coloured file across the desk. Its sole entry, a memorandum in Horner's barely legible hand, was untitled, undated, and unsigned. In an attempt to occlude the room's extravagant light, he studied it through half-closed eyes:

'The world's leading seismographs recorded the occurrence of an earthquake of "unusual intensity" in the general area east of the Caspian Sea at 20:00 hours GMT on Tuesday 5th October 1948.

This region contains a desolate expanse of more than 100,000 square miles known as the Karakum Desert. There have also been reports of a large explosion in this general area causing thousands of deaths and extensive property damage.

I am of the opinion that this phenomenon was a Soviet atomic test which ran amok because their nuclear device was "overloaded".

Moscow must now be very much in the market for "short cuts".'

Randall looked up from his reading. 'What does "overloaded" mean?'

'You must ask Miss Temple,' said Horner, his expression as opaque as his reply.

'And what does the last sentence mean?'

'Precisely what it says. Now the buff envelope between the lamps, Randall. Put names to some faces.'

Obeying these crisp instructions, Jack extracted another purple binder, opened it, and stared in astonishment at snapshots of senior Soviet leaders. Their casual poses suggested that the photographer too was a member of the inner circle.

The photos were numbered, and upon a separate sheet of paper Horner had printed the names of those characters he recognised in each. The senior Politburo members featured here. Molotov, Mikoyan, Malenkov, Voroshilov, Kaganovich and Beria grinned back from the photos. Even the late Zhdanov put in an appearance. There were no shots of Stalin.

As Jack waded through them diligently, Horner quit hearth for throne. Seated behind the mammoth desk, he deployed his resources against a crossword.

'I've never seen any of these before. Who took them?'

Wrestling with an anagram, Horner refrained from looking up. 'They came into my possession, Randall. That is all that you require to know.'

He had hardly expected more of an answer. Horner acquired many things from many sources.

'Tell me, Randall, who are the two unknowns standing behind Molotov in photograph number seven?'

Jack glanced at this print. 'The fellow with the round Slavic face and pouty lips is Voznesensky. The man with a long, quite handsome face is Kuznetsov.'

'Zhdanov's acolytes,' muttered Horner darkly. 'Does Abakumov, the head of the MGB, feature in any of those photographs?'

'I've no idea. I've never seen any photos of the Minister of State Security. It's possible that none have been published.'

Horner eliminated two more of the clues arrayed against him, and then seemingly invited testimony from an inkwell. 'The uniformed chap attending Beria in numbers nine to thirteen, what of him?'

'He's an MGB officer.'

'That I discerned for myself, Randall.'

'From his insignia he would appear to be a colonel.'

'Randall, I did not drag you out of bed and off the bottle for you to relate his rank. From you, I foolhardily expected more.'

'Well, you may be in luck.'

Horner looked up from a tussle with ten down.

Randall sat back. 'The most obvious fact about this colonel is that he's a real tich. Even Beria is taller than him, and Beria's no giant. And his small size makes me certain I've seen another photo of him.'

'Where?' demanded Horner, laying his crossword aside.

'Well, we obtained a massive batch of photos in 1946, which should be in Records Section. They were a collection of unpublished shots taken by the press at the so-called Paris Peace Conference. Anyway, this little man was there, ostensibly as part of the Soviet delegation. If I recall correctly, there were two other people with him in the photograph.'

With grudging conviction, Horner penned an instruction for Records Section, and inserted both this and a photo of the officer into an oft-used envelope. Battening this down with staples, he ordered Randall to deliver it. Then Horner sat back in his chair, elbows installed upon its arms, fingers tented beneath his chin.

'Randall, what is your opinion of Beria?'

'It's the same as my opinion of any mass murderer and serial rapist.'

'Other than that,' said Horner dispassionately.

Jack smiled cynically at this response. 'Well, Beria is plainly a ruthless and energetic survivor. He must also be a very talented manager. Otherwise, Stalin wouldn't have placed him in charge of the Soviet atomic bomb project.'

'Are you certain that this is Beria's current role?'

'Well, there's hardly been any public announcement about it. However, we learned in early 1946 that Beria was superintending those ministries deemed essential to the Soviet nuclear programme. That same year, he was also deprived of direct control of his old fiefdom. Neither the MGB nor the Ministry of Internal Affairs are currently headed by Beria's placemen.'

Horner's hands disengaged and gathered up a pencil. He spun it meditatively, his eyes anchored to a corner of the room. At length they rediscovered the man seated by his desk.

'That will be all, Randall.'

Eve had dropped off Eric in the Essex countryside. There he'd take stock of the lie of the land, prior to a later and lethal rendezvous with the condemned FO official. Leaving him to catch a train home, she'd popped into 'the Doss-house', and then driven back to her flat mid-afternoon.

She squatted before the gas fire in her lounge. Thoughtfully flipping through the confiscated calendar, she reflected that this was certainly one way to produce a nice steady income. But, she had nothing with which to found a comparable empire, in order to finance expansion of the female section of DOSS. Naturally, she discounted Gwen's shots of sad, middle-aged men caught in compromising situations.

'Just one more,' she promised herself, as she stood and topped up her glass to the brim. Carrying it over to the fire, Eve sat on the floor, and reached out for the calendar again. Then she pushed it away. Photos were all very well, but she was in the mood for more; but who with?

Zoë was treading the boards on the south coast, while Abigail was pursuing some civil service course out of town. Eve was about to ring Alice, when she recalled that the daft cow, bought off with some exquisite jewellery, had agreed to 'try again' with her wealthy, philandering husband.

Eve pouted. So it would have to be a bloke. It was several weeks since she'd last bothered to pull one, even though for her they didn't pose the usual problem. While marriage had demonstrated that she couldn't have children, the converse was that she could now enjoy carefree sex.

Pushing to her feet, Eve hunted out a notebook. Turning its pages, she reviewed the names she'd penned in it, as well as the scores she'd awarded for each man's performance.

Following the requisite visit to Records Section, Randall wandered into his secretary's room. 'Horner said I was to ask you what "overloaded" means, Lucy.'

Since she was busy recoating designated nails, his request evoked an intemperate glare. Relenting momentarily, she pointed a drying talon in the direction of a filing cabinet. Then she instructed him where to delve and what to withdraw.

Ending up with a skimpy booklet, Randall glanced at the title page. It was a classified publication of the United States Atomic Energy Commission. Pocketing his catch, he retreated to his room to learn how to 'overload' an atomic bomb.

9

FRIDAY 29 OCTOBER 1948

'About "Red Freddie's" little helpers,' announced Barber, the moment Eve had swept punctually into his office.

A perplexed frown lightly creased her brow. 'Sorry, sir, you've lost me.'

He tapped a file upon his cluttered desk. 'I've just got round to this load of bumph, lass. It's about a joint parliamentary committee to investigate British trade with Eastern Europe. It's been set up under the chairmanship of Lord Whatsit, Frederick the third summat of some place.'

'Let's settle for "Red Freddie",' suggested Eve, redundantly straightening the green jacket clinging to her slender body.

'I never can remember all these tossing titles, Eve. Any road, I reckon the House of Lords in its hereditary form should be abolished.' Blubbery cheeks expanding with his grin, Arthur reached for his pipe. 'Not to worry, lass. Your boss isn't turning red. I just happen to think I should have the right to elect them what runs this country.'

'I trust you'd draw the line at elected secret policemen, sir.'

Chortling at her cynical rejoinder, he poked the pipe between his fleshy lips, put it to the torch, and gulped down smoke. 'Do you know why his lordship's called "Red Freddie"?'

'Bit left-wing?' she guessed.

'Nay, lass, Freddie's as steady as they come. But, though his hair's now white as snow, when he was in his prime, it was your colour. That's how he got his nickname.'

'So how are we involved with steady Freddie?'

'It's because of his lordship's committee, Eve. While I doubt the government will take the blindest bit of notice of its findings, it's what this body sees on its way to producing its report that could cause some problems.'

'I'm still not clear, sir.'

'Well, lass, the MPs are on it, because they've got even less to do than usual, given the size of Attlee's majority. So the parliamentarians will avail themselves of the junkets. But the spadework will be done by civil servants seconded from various ministries. And, since they'll be seeing loads of secret stuff, the chosen ones must be whiter than white.'

'I'm with you now.'

Lids sliding to half-mast over his eyes, he proffered her a list of names. 'These are the candidates, lass. So get your pretty mitts on their personal files, and get hold of some solid references too. I doubt yon bureaucrats were properly vetted when they joined.'

Nodding, she threaded a strand of hair behind an ear. 'How long have I got to check them out?'

'Give us summat by the end of the year, lass. Reckon you can manage that?'

'Yes, sir,' she said, stifling a yawn.

His chins quaked in a sympathetic nod. 'Eve, I know you're tired and overworked. We all are in this underfunded department. But we just have to soldier on.' His message to the troops concluded, both paws patted blazer pockets in search of the elusive matchbox. 'Any road, how's your investigation of Pilling's harem coming along?'

Eve permitted herself a satisfied smile. 'Well, I've discovered that one of the women on that list works for Horner.'

He relit the pipe clamped between his tarnished teeth. It steamed limply and then expired. 'So has she done owt to raise your suspicions?'

'No, sir,' said Eve glumly.

'But you're still not happy, are you?' he asserted shrewdly.

'No, I'm not.'

Barber and his pipe pondered together. 'Feel it in your water, do you?'

'I'll let you rely on that, sir. I'll stick to feminine intuition.'

His pudgy jowls shuddered at the concept. 'Any road, lass, keep me informed, as usual.'

'But of course, sir,' Eve lied in honeyed tones.

They left the *Forum* cinema in Ealing, nipped between two buses to cross the Uxbridge Road, and then strolled hand in hand past shops leading up to the tall steeple of Christ Church. When he asked her if she'd enjoyed the film, Fay replied that she'd enjoyed Clark Gable, and added that Oliver had looked quite like the film star when he was younger. Randall stayed silent until they reached the crest of Spring Bridge Road.

'I thought you rarely talked about your husband.'

'It's a woman's right to change her mind.'

Jack had mouthed the last four words into the night in refrain.

'Do you ever feel jealous of him?' probed Fay, as they veered to the right to cross Haven Green.

'Why should I be jealous of a bloke whose wife is always off with other men?'

'Man,' she corrected him. 'You know full well that the others have been mere caprices, and that I always return to you.'

Smiling cynically, he halted on the path and released her hand. 'I find the concept of the faithful adulteress rather hard to grasp, Fay.'

'You bastard!' she hissed, swiping his arm. 'So would you be jealous if there was some real competition, as there was with my cousin Caroline?'

'That was ten years ago. In any case, it was no more than a brief affair.'

'Then why keep that photo on the wall in your flat?'

'Fay, I keep that photo because of the boy. Do you want me to cut Caroline out of it? She is his mother, after all.'

Her eyes narrowed. 'But you're not the father, Jack.'

'How the hell do you know?' he replied testily. 'It could only have been Imre or me.'

Fay shook her head in mock despair. 'I know you're not Zoltán's dad, Jack, because I saw both Caroline and her boy in May 1947, when Horner shipped me off to Budapest.'

'You told me that. I do have a memory, you know.'

'But, what I didn't tell you then was that Zoltán looked just like Imre. And I'm talking about a boy of eight, as he then was, with developed features; not the baby you've got hanging on the wall.'

'It's the only picture I've got,' he muttered ruefully.

'Well, I think I've still got one of the photos I took in Budapest. I'll dig it out sometime, Jack. Then you can see for yourself.'

'Hell, I'm not likely to see him whoever his father is.' Randall reached out a hand. 'So there's no point in us arguing.'

'I'm not arguing,' said Fay crossly, hands remaining pocketed.

'Good. So shall we walk on?'

Eve stared at dusty photos arrayed on a lounge wall. Her gaze strayed from those of her father and sisters, to snaps of her mother with her third and fourth husbands. Naturally, there were none of the second. But Eve didn't need any; pictures of him were indelibly imprinted in her mind.

Alf was several years younger than her mother when they wed, and Eve had to admit that he was an extremely handsome man. He knew it too. The touches and gropes had begun when Eve was fifteen, shortly after she'd left school to work in an insurance office. But it was only when her mother went into hospital that the next stage began.

He started it, but Eve never told him to stop, and she hated herself for it. Even when her mother came home he carried on, creeping into her room in the early hours. Then one day he wasn't there on her return from work, and nor were his things. Eve's thick red hair disappeared too, when her mother hacked it short and dyed it black.

'It's this red hair you get from your father that's to blame,' she contended irrationally, tears spurting from her eyes.

Eve withdrew into herself thereafter, free time spent reading. At eighteen, when husband number three hove into view, her mother evicted her. Eve found a bedsit, and kept on reading. She kept on cutting and dying her hair too, and hated herself for it.

She turned to drink, ballooned in size, and hated herself for it. However, she stayed sober one night a week and learned German at night school. It was there that she met Jimmy in autumn 1938, shortly after the Munich crisis.

War came, and the government directed Eve from her office to the Board of Trade. She married Jimmy in 1942, shortly before his battalion left for North Africa. After Jimmy deserted her, she eventually turned her life around. It was only then that her thoughts returned to Alf.

'We'll meet again,' he'd sung, and so they did. Only Eve had company, and he'd never known what hit him, when the men bundled him into a car, cuffed him, and drove him to a secluded wood.

Now, instead of Eve kneeling naked in her bedroom, complicitously serving his needs, Alf was grovelling before her on a carpet of mouldering leaves. Begging for his life, he protested that he'd committed no crime, since she'd never told him to stop.

'I never told you to start either, Alf, and you made me hate myself. That was your crime. You made me feel guilty and I suffered for that. You see, I don't like feeling guilty.'

At her signal, Eric Moon and Phil Dove had emerged from the trees and hauled the terrified man to his feet. His body, with the restraining cuffs removed, was found four days later by a dog-walker. The cause of death was adjudged to be suicide by hanging.

Fay came hurtling up the stairs to the attic and slammed the door. Grabbing her scotch, she crouched before an electric fire, shivering extravagantly.

'Jack, is there no heating on the floor below? Your bathroom's like ice!'

'I'll light a fire later, if you want, but I'm a bit short of coal.' He pushed up onto one elbow on the thick Spanish rug where he was lying. 'Anyway, you usually prefer it up here in the attic.'

She glared at him. 'That's because it's the only civilised part of your flat. When are you going to fix the décor downstairs?'

'When I can afford some decent paint,' he replied equably.

'There's plenty of paint around, Jack.'

He thought of those colours, which were only too readily available in vast quantities in post-war Britain; fetching battleship grey, and the sludgy shades of green, brown and yellow so essential to camouflage.

'For colours I can live with, Fay, it means paying black market prices.'

She drained her glass and reached out for the nearby bottle to replenish it. 'You can make up a bed here tonight. I'm damned if I'm going to freeze to death down there.'

Recalling their last spat, which had flared up on entering his flat, he lofted his brows inquiringly. 'So you've decided to stay?'

'Yes, but I'll be leaving Sunday morning.'

Masking his irritation at her latest change of plan, he reached out for his drink. 'I thought Oliver was away until Tuesday.'

'He is, but I've got things to do.'

"Things to do", "I'll be busy", "Something's come up": Such phrases all conveyed the same message. Sometimes Fay's mini-affairs away from him were dictated by a man's wealth, sometimes by looks, sometimes by youth. On occasion, political leanings played a role, or intellect was the attraction.

Randall never inquired about the competition, since she treated him as father-confessor afterwards. In any case, given his own behaviour, he had no intention of sitting in hypocritical judgement.

As he made up a bed in the attic, Fay inspected the canvases stacked against the wall. She remained silent until he finished his task, and then turned towards him. 'Jack, you could at least hang that picture of me when I'm here.'

'Like the royal standard is displayed when the king's in his palace?' he teased. 'Well, if you like looking at that nude portrait of yourself so much, Fay, you could always take it back home with you.'

'Oliver would love that,' she retorted drily. Then she narrowed her eyes, when some barely-associated thought struck her. 'Have you heard what happened to that busty trollop in Finance, who doles out your expenses?'

'I presume that bitchy remark refers to Wendy Page.'

'It's not bitchy at all,' she sneered, unappeased. 'It's common knowledge that she fancies you.'

'That's news to me, Fay. Anyway, what's happened to Wendy?'

'Well, she's in hospital. Evidently, her enraged former fiancé shoved her down some stairs last night. Her leg's badly broken.'

'Poor girl,' said Randall softly, his tone tinged with a feeling of guilt.

10

SUNDAY 31 OCTOBER 1948

'Bit of a climb,' puffed Eve, once she was admitted into the flat in Ealing. 'So show me around your new place.'

Thrusting her hands into the pockets of a blue cardigan, Sandra led Eve into a sunny room, whose appalling floral curtains clashed sublimely with the covers of a lumpish suite.

'This is the lounge,' she announced superfluously. She glided over to the window. 'From here you can see through those hideous conifers into Jack's lounge and bedroom.'

Eve stared across the street to confirm this. 'So how do you get into his flat?'

'You go through that door in the wall, then down some steps to his garden. There's an entrance and staircase to the first floor at the back of the house. The twins checked it out when Jack was at work.'

'Who's on the ground floor?'

'An elderly couple. They have a separate garden and their own front door. But they're away a lot.'

She ushered Eve into her own bedroom next to the lounge.

'Nice and bright,' remarked the visitor, now gazing at the sofa bed strewn with cushions. 'That's a bit narrow. Not expecting any company?'

Sandra pulled a face. 'I'm expecting to be busy.'

Pacing past Eve, she opened a door on the other side of the corridor, to reveal the room shared by Delilah and Delphine Delaney. Poking her head around the jamb, Eve was confronted by two single beds with identical bedspreads, upon which lolled identical teddies. From two bedside tables, identical pictures of identical twins smiled back at her in identical fashion.

'Hell, Sandra, which one's which?'

'No idea, Eve. I just say "Del... er" and let them fill in the rest of the name.'

Sandra led the way past bathroom, kitchen and 'darkroom'. At the end of the hallway was a door, which opened onto a steep and narrow staircase. Ascending this, they emerged into a boarded attic, faintly illuminated by grimy skylights. Sandra edged her away along a narrow strip of flooring towards another door. This she opened to reveal the interior of a brick tower topped by a wooden 'dovecot'. A secured ladder led to a platform halfway up the structure.

Standing at the bottom of the ladder, an anxious frown filtering onto her face, Eve scoured the dovecot's interior. 'I bet it's full of bloody spiders.'

'Oh, Eve, a big girl like you!'

'I happen to be very traditional in certain matters,' asserted Eve, before clambering up the ladder to the platform, followed by Sandra.

In this compact space, there were two chairs, the seat of one occupied by binoculars. The wooden walls were punctured by numerous small apertures, now filled with glass. In addition, there were two sizeable windows, with one overlooking Randall's attic.

Eve settled on the vacant chair, grabbed the binoculars, and peered through the window. 'Just as you said, Sandra, you don't miss much from here.'

'We certainly didn't miss much that happened yesterday. The twins were using a camera with one of these long-range lenses, and there was lots of sunshine.'

'So what's Jack like?'

'Let's go downstairs, and you can see for yourself.'

Back in the lounge, Sandra made up drinks. Then she extracted a large envelope from a sideboard drawer and planted this in Eve's lap. 'The twins produced those prints last night.'

Eve flipped through the wad of snaps, her smile broadening. 'Now you know why most of us have got net curtains.'

Sandra joined her on the settee. 'Bit intrusive, isn't it?'

Eve shook her head. 'Blokes have been spying on women since time immemorial, Sandra. It's nice to turn the tables.'

'So what do you think of Jack?'

She peered at a photo. 'Tall, slim, good-looking, nice hair. A definite bit of alright. And I've certainly seen worse tackle.'

'Me too. I was married to it.'

'Well, right now, Sandra, you'll just have to make do with a photo, if you can bear looking at that fat, round bitch with him.'

'Eve,' she protested, 'Fay's not fat, she's curvy. Loads of blokes would go for her.'

'They'd get her too,' Eve riposted caustically. She flicked through more snaps. 'That toffee-nosed tart certainly has a wide repertoire.'

'Eve, are you going to tell me what there is between you and Fay?'

The green eyes held Sandra's forthright stare. 'Tell you what. Come over to my place Saturday week. We'll have a real heart-to-heart and a good drink.'

'Okay, let's do that.'

Eve thrust most of the photos back into the envelope. 'Where are Jack and Fay right now?'

'Fay left this morning. Jack's probably down the pub.'

Eve laid the bulging envelope to one side. Gathering up the photos she'd retained, she slipped them into her bag. 'I'm holding on to certain snaps of Jack,' she explained. 'There's something I've noticed that I want to check more closely.'

Sandra's eyes widened, but she made no comment. 'What are you going to do with those photos, Eve?'

'I'm not sure yet. Blackmailing Fay is an option. Or I could just post them to Oliver, should he need evidence for a divorce.'

'I reckon he must have a pretty good idea of what goes on when he's away, Eve. Their marriage is either very open or very ended.'

Eve lit a cigarette and inhaled thoughtfully. 'Select the best pics of Jack and Fay with their clothes on, Sandra. Then show them to Beatrice, that former official in the CPGB who helped you out before. Find out if Fay and Jack were ever in the Communist Party.'

'Is this just guesswork, or do you know something else you're not telling me?'

Eve peered back through wisps of smoke. 'I'll fill you in later. Now, do you know where to find Beatrice?'

'I'm not even sure if she's still alive. Last I heard she was in hospital. You know she was a boozer.'

'All good things in moderation,' pronounced Eve, emptying her glass and holding it out for a refill. 'So, what about the rest of Herbert Pilling's harem? Have your girls come up with anything?'

'We've found a couple of militant shop workers,' Sandra related half-heartedly, as she trickled tonic into Eve's glass.

'Well, I'd be militant too, if I worked in a shop, especially if I had to serve me.' Frowning, Eve took the proffered glass. 'Is that all?'

Sandra reseated herself on the sofa. 'There's also a woman called Rita Prior.'

'What about her?'

'Well, she has an address in Putney, but she's never there.'

'So where is she?'

'I don't know.'

'Then bloody well find her!' snapped the redhead. 'Sandra, you were in the Ministry of Home Security in the war. You've got contacts in the Passport Office, and we still carry identity cards. We don't lose people in this country. Not yet, anyway.'

Sandra's cheeks pinked. 'You told me to concentrate on Fay.'

'Your girls are tailing Fay when Oliver's home.' Eve gesticulated towards the window. 'In any case, she's likely to be right under your nose when hubby's away. So, since the eagle-eyed twins will follow her every twist and turn when she's at Jack's, that leaves you free to get on with some detailed research.' She screwed out her cigarette in the ashtray. 'If Rita Prior was in Pilling's address book, then I want to know why. Understood?'

Sandra glared back.

'You're thinking that I'm being hard on you,' said Eve gently. 'Especially, since you've had such a rough time of it of late. But I'm also hard on myself, Sandra. After all, someone has to be.'

Chiselled flawlessly in the mode of saviour of oppressed mankind, a bust of Stalin dominated his desk. The short, balding man cast a nervous glance towards it. Behind pince-nez perched on an aquiline nose, Lavrenti Beria's eyes flashed uneasily, as if fearful that this effigy would report his words to the master.

'Georgi Maximilianovich, his silence is ominous. The Boss is plotting a major purge. I saw the same signs in the thirties. Once he's finally identified his enemies, he'll act against them with his usual ruthlessness and liquidate them.'

Gazing gluttonously at the platters on a nearby table, Malenkov speared a chunk of herring with his fork. His chubby, feminine features changed little as he chewed, and he swallowed before venturing a reply. 'Then we must make damned sure he doesn't act against ourselves. That's why I've detailed some sins of the "Leningrad gang" in that report.'

Drawing damp palms down his lapels, Beria perused the document which Malenkov had placed upon his desk. Guardedly, he raised his eyes. 'It's a start, but we'll need more.'

'We'll get more. Abakumov will help.' Malenkov scooped onto his plate a portion of chicken breasts swimming in cherry sauce. 'In the meantime, we must distract the Boss with some new external enemies. This will give us time to prepare the ground against the enemies within, and ensure that we keep our heads.'

Standing, Beria plodded over to a bulletproof window, and grimaced at the threatening Moscow skies. 'So what do you have in mind?'

Malenkov poked around his piled plate, as if reading entrails. His dark eyes narrowed slyly. 'There are "Titoite" sympathisers among the leading cadres of every party in power in Eastern Europe. We should focus Comrade Stalin's attention upon their existence.'

Beria's thick lips contorted into a sneer. 'We'd be spoiled for choice. In public, they were all admirers of Tito before his fall.'

'That was then.' Malenkov jabbed his fork into a prime morsel. 'But now Tito is an outcast, these comrades are outbidding each other in their denunciations of him, since none of them wants to be identified as a surrogate Tito.'

'No surprises there,' muttered Beria mordantly.

Lifting another titbit, Malenkov wavered between mastication and speech. 'In my opinion, Lavrenti Pavlovich, we should offer some fraternal advice about which candidates might be selected as blood-sacrifices to the Boss.'

'Are you suggesting we should prepare the way for show trials in Eastern Europe?'

'Yes, I am, comrade.'

Mopping his glistening dome, Beria trudged away from the window, and huddled his stout shape conspiratorially in the chair next to Malenkov. 'Now, I do know something about show trials, Georgi Maximilianovich. To stage them successfully requires time and patience, and more than a little artistry.'

Malenkov swept a hand through lank, dark hair. 'I grant you that.'

'Well, time is just what I don't have. Running our atomic programme consumes my every waking moment. I have to scrounge materials for our pampered scientists, and pray that our agents in America have produced some more information we can use. Added to that, I'm constantly facing the suspicions and accusations of the Boss. Would you want my fucking job?'

'I've enough worries of my own. So, since Abakumov and I will be fully involved in preparing the case against the "Leningrad gang", what do you propose that we do regarding the selection of "Titoites" in Eastern Europe?'

Restraining himself no longer, Beria stood and grabbed the opened bottle of *Tsinandali* standing on his desk. Pouring two glasses of the Georgian wine, he passed one to his ally.

'Well, since I've no time and you've no time, it means that Volkov must handle the initial preparations.'

11

SATURDAY 13 NOVEMBER 1948

Trying hard to keep a straight face, Eve conducted a hobbling Sandra Jansen into her lounge. Briskly skirting the coffee table, she resumed her position on the sofa, and reached for the bottle.

'Oh, my poor feet!' moaned Sandra, pulling off her high-heels.

'Well, if you refuse to wear sensible shoes,' lectured Eve without sympathy.

Scowling, Sandra collapsed into an armchair. 'Pins like mine are not shown to their best advantage in lace-ups, Eve.'

Holding out a glass, her hostess smirked. 'Well, do you want to drink this gin, or shall I rub it into your tootsies?'

'Internal application only,' confirmed Sandra, catching hold of the proffered drink. Following a generous swig, she massaged the sole of a stockinged foot. 'This comes from following Fay for most of the day. We've been wandering round the shops in the West End.'

'I thought you were meant to be researching, not watching.'

'The research is in hand,' clarified Sandra hastily. 'But I had to do a stint of watching, because we were so short-staffed.'

'Have you found Beatrice?'

Sandra nodded. 'She's been in intensive care, but the doctor said I could try talking to her in a couple of weeks.'

'What about Rita Prior?'

'She's abroad, Eve, but due back soon, according to what her milkman told Janice when she was feeding his horse.'

Eve's brows arched above a growing grin, as she pictured her most flamboyant employee in action. Then she refocused her attention and leant forward inquiringly. 'So who was Fay out with, Jack Randall?'

'No, Oliver's home, so today she trailed hubby around in her wake.'

'Any aberrant behaviour from Fay, besides her trysts with Jack?'

'Well, last Monday she popped into a bloke's flat for a couple of hours, following a meeting of her constituency Labour Party.'

'So what do you reckon? Was it a discourse about nationalisation or a quickie?'

'I've no idea, Eve.'

'And the bloke?' inquired Eve, lighting a cigarette.

'He was younger than Fay, quite nice-looking, a teacher. Nothing on him though.' She puckered her lips. 'Eve, you said it was personal between you and Fay, and that you'd tell me about it tonight.'

Eve nodded. Sitting up straight on the sofa, she grabbed the gin bottle on the low table before her and topped up her glass. 'Well, Sandra, our paths first crossed when I worked in DORA's European Communism Section in 1945. Jack Randall had just been promoted to head it, but I never got to meet him. Both he and his deputy were abroad while I was there. So Fay was acting chief.'

'You worked in DORA?' Sandra set her glass upon the table. 'I thought you were in the Board of Trade before joining DOSS.'

'And so I was. But the transition wasn't exactly seamless.'

'So when did you join the Board of Trade?'

'Late 1941, just after my twenty-second birthday.'

'You weren't married to Jimmy then, were you?'

'No, I married him in 1942, just before he was posted to Egypt.'

'"Desert Rat", was he?'

'Just a rat, Sandra.' She drew deeply on her cigarette. 'Later, Jimmy fought in Italy, and after he took a bad leg wound there in 1944, they returned him to my loving arms.'

Sandra tucked her legs behind her in the armchair. 'What was he like then?'

'Like the proverbial total stranger. But I pretended nothing had changed, that we just needed time to get used to each other again. Every day after work, I went home, tarted myself up, cooked Jimmy's meal, and waited for him to return some time.'

Eve stared at her gin as though it was lethal, before imbibing generously. 'Well, one night in early 1945, he didn't come home at all. After that he stayed out frequently. You know how it is. Even when he did come home, he wouldn't talk about things, and he started sleeping in the spare room. It was like having a lodger, not a husband, in the flat.'

Nodding grimly, Sandra reached out for her drink. 'But you must have known he was having an affair.'

'Of course I did, but I didn't want to admit it was all over.' Her eyes shone with a naivety borrowed short-term from her past. 'Jimmy was my man, Sandra. Even with all the opportunities offered by the war, I never looked at another bloke.'

Dangling her empty glass, Sandra smiled. 'Been making up for it since, haven't you?'

'You bet I have!' retorted Eve fiercely. 'But back then I just went to pieces. My work at the Board of Trade suffered and I was absent a lot. So they recommended that I got myself a new job.'

'They sacked you?'

Eve passed over the other's gin, and then reclaimed her cigarette from the ashtray. 'No, they didn't sack me. They were really good to me. They suggested I made a new start, and fixed me up with the post in DORA. So in late summer 1945, I transferred to Horner's mob, and began working in the unit dealing with the Soviet Occupation Zone of Germany.'

'So what went wrong?'

Eyes vindictive, Eve ground out the butt. 'Well, I came back one evening to find Jimmy moving out half the furniture from the flat. Finally, he was open about things. He was setting up home with his new woman and he wanted a divorce. Having relayed his glad tidings, he jumped into his van and drove off.'

'What about you?' asked Sandra solicitously.

'Well, Jimmy's news tipped me right over the edge. As a result, my attendance and work at DORA went completely to pot, and soon I was summoned to an interview with Mrs Fay Galbraith, my acting boss. Fay told me she'd give me a week for things to improve; otherwise, she'd recommend to Horner that I be fired.'

'Didn't you tell her about Jimmy pushing off?'

'Of course I did. Between floods of tears I poured out my story into her sympathetic ear. And Fay's response was to tell me, and I quote: "Oh, stop snivelling, woman. Pull yourself together."'

Sinking the last of her drink, Eve reached again for the bottle. 'Well, I couldn't pull myself together,' she confessed in a hushed, hurt voice. 'Instead, I missed more days. And, when I finally made it back to work, I found this note telling me to report to Fay. God, I was utterly terrified.'

Lips curling bitterly, Eve swilled the contents of her glass. 'Anyway, when I finally found the courage to see Fay, she just sat there, sneering. Then she announced my dismissal in this remote, clinical voice. It was all so unfair. It was as if I'd been condemned for being innocent. I was in this absolutely desperate state, but I had no one to turn to. I simply burst into tears.'

Pausing, Eve brushed a knuckle against first one eye and then the other. She made a sniffy sound, and then took a long pull at her drink. 'Fay just stared at me as though I'd escaped from a freak show. There she was, this confident and successful woman, with a look of utter contempt stamped on her face, for I must have epitomised all the opposite traits.'

Eve pulled another cigarette from her pack and lit it. Her eyes, though glistening, now hardened markedly. 'But she wasn't quite done. With her scornful look augmenting, she spoke again. "Let me give you some advice," said Fay sweetly. "If you're wondering why you lost your husband, try looking in a mirror".'

'The utter cow!' snapped Sandra. 'What a way for a woman to treat another woman.'

'Sandra, be realistic. Forget the sisterly solidarity. Women treat other women in all sorts of ways and always have done. I do so myself.'

'So what happened after that?'

'I just went down and down, Sandra. I didn't have a job and I'd lost all my self-esteem. I never went out, but a really kind neighbour did my shopping and collected my prescriptions. Luckily, I had some savings to pay the rent, although I was spending loads on booze too, and I was so full of pills I must have rattled. In short, I went so far down that the only way left was up.'

Fastidiously, Eve flicked a speck of ash from her black slacks. 'Well, that's more or less what happened. One day in January 1946, I woke up totally devoid of any feeling. It was like a raging fire had burned itself out, leaving just the ashes of my old self.'

'Then a new Eve emerged from the cinders, like some Phoenix,' suggested Sandra supportively.

'Something like that,' said Eve, a weird smile dusting her lips. 'That same day, I took a really long, hard look in the mirror, just as Fay had advised, and I saw there a woman I didn't know. I'd lost loads of weight, Sandra. I used to be fat and round. And, in those days, I used to feel conspicuous as a redhead, so I kept my hair short and dyed it black. Now, it was long and red with frizzy black ends, which I hacked off there and then.'

Glancing at Sandra, whose expression mixed amusement and amazement, Eve emitted a hollow laugh. Then her face grew solemn. 'Far more important than my changed looks, though, were the changes I felt in my heart and my head. I just knew that this woman, gazing back at me from the mirror, felt and believed in different things from the old Mary Wilcox. So, soon afterwards, I changed my surname back to Loxton, my maiden name, by deed poll.'

Sandra's brows zoomed up inquiringly. 'I knew your married name was Wilcox, but where did the Mary come from?'

'It's my middle name. Dad, who was a man of few syllables, called me Eve, and Mum called me Mary. These were the names they'd personally chosen. It was as if they were fighting for my soul. But they quarrelled about everything. My older sisters told me later that their rows had got worse after Dad came back from the trenches. So, once he'd pushed off when I was ten, Mum had free rein, and I was always called Mary by everyone. In fact, I never again thought of myself as Eve, until this time in January 1946.'

'So when did this new Eve Loxton start working for Barber?'

'The following May.'

Her listener frowned. 'You just walked into the job?'

'No, first I got off the pills and the booze. Then I needed some clothes. Nothing I owned fitted me anymore. In any case, dumpy Mary was a pretty frumpy dresser. So I blew the last of my savings on some black-market material, and took it to a bespoke tailor to have it made up. I'd never owned a fitted costume before.'

'Can I pour myself another?' asked Sandra, waving an empty glass.

'Oh, give it here!' Stubbing her cigarette, Eve mixed their drinks as she spoke. 'Well, this tailor was an Italian widower, called Claudio Bonomi. He'd been briefly interned when Mussolini declared war on us in 1940.'

Nodding her thanks, Sandra reached out to accept the refill.

'Claudio and I got on from the moment we met, Sandra. I saw this tall, wiry man, with a magic smile. Pushing sixty, it's true, but still very handsome. Moreover, I couldn't help noticing that he was utterly fascinated by my thick red hair.'

A hand shot up to Sandra's gaping mouth. 'Eve, you didn't.'

'Of course I did.' Lighting another cigarette, she blew smoke from the side of her mouth. 'I knew how I wanted to look, and Claudio knew just how to make me look like that.'

'But sixty, Eve.'

'Older men are more grateful, Sandra, and usually more tolerant. So, to cut a long story short, it was that randy old Italian who made me feel like a woman again.'

'So how many outfits and blouses has Claudio made for you?'

'He's made them all. Every item meticulously made to measure. And he loves measuring me, Sandra. It takes him hours.' Phasing out a salacious smile, Eve drained her latest glass and set it on the table. 'Anyway, once I'd got my first outfit from Claudio, I presented my new self to my old friends at the Board of Trade, and asked about jobs. Amongst those on offer was this post as a clerk in DOSS. It was pretty low-grade, but there was something about it I found appealing. So I applied and got the job.'

'Did Barber interview you?'

'Yes, he did, and in an odd way we hit it off at once. Within months he'd made me his personal assistant. Then he directed me to build up the female side of DOSS. Well, I jumped at the opportunity. The trouble was that "Uncle Arthur" neglected to provide me with adequate funds to fulfil my ambitions. But, overall, I have to be grateful to that fat old closet feminist. He just gave me my head from the outset.'

'You mean he let you follow your instincts?'

'That's right, although I picked up loads of things from working with him and Eric too. Blokes are unsentimental in the main. So I just learned to look at the world and exploit situations like they do, but without ever compromising those talents that only a woman can possess.'

'So what talents have you been using to bring in all this much-needed loot, or shouldn't I ask?'

Eve stared back coolly at her friend's rather prim expression. 'Well, as I mentioned before, I picked up the last load of dosh at a so-called "Greek Wedding". You know, Sandra, where the guests pin banknotes to the bride and groom. Only this time there was just my little banker pasting them all over my goose pimples.'

Sandra's stifled laughter escaped as a splutter. 'What was it like?'

'It was just theatre, but I got well paid for performing my role.'

'And he didn't want anything else?'

Her brows rose in disdain. 'Sandra, he couldn't manage anything else. But he got what he wanted and so did I. Rupert has some memories to help him wank in the dark, while we have fresh funds to help us strengthen woman's place in DOSS.'

'Then we take over the world, do we?'

'No, Sandra, we proceed step by step from one small victory to another, just like women do all the time. Emancipation is a process, not an event.'

12

MONDAY 22 NOVEMBER 1948

He smiled optimistically when Fay paid his office a surprise visit. 'Is Oliver going away?'

'Yes, he is, Jack, and I'm going with him.'

'That's twice this year,' he observed, a tinge of sarcasm overlaying disappointment.

'We're going to Paris.'

'Lucky you!'

'For six months, Jack. We leave on Thursday.'

His brows arched in surprise. 'That's a bit of a turn-up for the books.'

Easing her bottom onto an amazingly uncluttered desk, Fay planted her palm upon its surface and leant towards him. It was all very deliberate upon her part, causing maximum frustration upon his. Every desirable aspect of her body was on view, and he could scent the musk from her hair dangling but inches from his face.

'Oliver's taken a post in Paris. It's to do with implementing Marshall Plan aid. I'm sure I've told you that there's very little he doesn't know about agricultural machinery.'

'I must have been sleeping when you imparted that information.'

He reached for his cigarettes and offered her one, never knowing whether Fay was or wasn't smoking. She was, and the odours of lighter-petrol mixing with sour smoke expelled the intensity of her presence from his senses. It helped too that she sat up straight to talk.

'Originally, I was going to resign, Jack. But when I spoke to Horner, he expressed great interest in having "one of my own", as he inevitably phrased it, hanging around the various organisations operating there. He's even fixed me up with a position. Then from 1st June I resume work here.'

He lolled back in his seat. 'So what do I do for a deputy in the meantime?'

'Is that all I am to you?'

'You know damned well what you are to me.'

'Do I? I know what I do with you, Jack, but I don't know what I am to you.'

Randall chose to pass the onus, rather than respond in any depth. 'It's not me who's married, Fay, and I'm not disappearing for six months.'

She produced her jaded smile. 'How did I know I'd get that sort of answer?'

He shrugged. 'So what am I supposed to do while you're in Paris?'

'What you usually do between our trysts. You'll find somebody else.'

Stubbing her cigarette, Fay slid from the desk, and left without another word.

A film of sweat gleaming on his brow, Eaton indicated the coat which was to feature in number twenty-four on his list. 'It's mink, I think.'

'Musquash,' said Eve dismissively. 'Still, it will have to do.'

'So we've got all we need.'

'Not quite,' she retorted sternly. 'There's the small matter of my fee.'

Stammering an apology, he reached into a desk drawer for an envelope and passed it to her. Eve checked its contents in cursory fashion, and then stared at her empty glass. Apologising again, he turned to his cabinet and provided her with a refill.

'What have you found out about that calendar, Rupert?'

'Well, I've finally discovered the name of the chap, who sold several copies to the other chap. The chap who sold one to me, that is.'

'I only require the name of the first chap.'

'Well, he's a peer. I've not met him, but I've heard lots about him. He goes by the name of "Red Freddie", he's the third….'

She smiled to herself as Eaton maundered about 'Red Freddie's' deeds. She'd already received a handwritten invitation to dine with his lordship. He wanted to meet in person, the woman who'd be assigning officials to service his committee.

Slumped in his lounge, Randall effaced his melancholy smile, but only to take a sip of brandy. He put down his glass when the telephone rang. Hoping it might be Fay calling, he leapt to his feet. However, it was Louise, an even older flame, who was on the line, and when she implied that she was free that weekend, he invited her round at once.

Fay was right. During her absence he'd find somebody else, no matter how short-term. So, temporarily at least, he was cushioned against the dark moods which beset him, when there was no woman in his life to offset the tedium of work.

'Good of you to come by,' said Horner, as he closed the door of the Richmond house behind his guest.

'Well, I was in London anyhow, Stephen. But then you knew that.'

Stripping off his gloves, Thomas Quaid placed them and his hat on the hallstand. His host assisted removal of the overcoat. Lastly, Quaid shed his scarf.

'You know, it's colder here than in Paris.'

'Then come through into the study. I am disbursing a portion of my coal ration.'

Following Horner into a room, which was book-lined on three sides, Quaid took stock of the remaining wall. Where paintings had hung during his last visit, brighter blocks now chequered the faded wallpaper. He wondered whether gaming losses had also compelled Horner to sell the Millet, which had dominated the dining-room.

Settling into a durable leather armchair beside the fire, Quaid nodded when Horner suggested a nip. Passing a generous measure of malt to the American, Horner perched upon the arm of a chair, facing his guest.

'Great whisky,' lauded Quaid. 'How come you can get your hands on it?'

'Clan connections, Tom. My late wife, who as you know was Scottish, came from a family of distillers. I continue to receive an adequate quota of annual output.'

Quaid took another sip and then set his glass in the hearth. Reaching into a pocket of his double-breasted suit, he produced a pack of *Lucky Strikes* and lit one. 'So what can I do for you, Stephen?'

Horner gazed at the almost boyish face. Only the lined forehead, plus flecks of grey in the chestnut hair, even hinted that Quaid was well into his forties.

'Who is your current employer, Tom?'

The brown eyes narrowed cagily. 'Washington, Stephen.'

'Tom, you were in the Office of Strategic Services during the war. Are you now perchance a member of this new Central Intelligence Agency?'

'Me in the CIA?' A spurious note of surprise was injected into the mellow New England voice. 'Stephen, I work as an advisor for our Economic Cooperation Administration in Paris, handing out Marshall Aid to you Europeans.'

Standing, Horner lifted from the mantelpiece the photo alluded to by Randall, and subsequently supplied to him by DORA's Records Section. This he presented to Quaid like an indictment. 'Tell me, what advice were you tendering to the two gentleman pictured with you in that photograph?'

'Oh, this and that,' muttered the seated man.

'Tom, shall we cease fencing? Despite his civilian attire, the very small fellow in that photograph is a colonel in the MGB.' He wafted another photo into Quaid's hand. 'This one shows him in the entourage of Marshal Beria.'

Hurling his cigarette into the fire, Quaid grabbed his glass and emptied it. Horner refilled it, and then placed the decanter upon a table set between the armchairs. On this occasion, he lowered himself fully into the comforts of his own.

Face set in taut mask, Quaid deposited both photos upon the table. He took his time lighting another *Lucky*, and exhaled fiercely. 'What do you want to know, Stephen?'

'Firstly, the name of the Soviet colonel.'

'Yuri Pavlovich Volkov,' replied the American, without hesitation.

Horner selected the picture from Records, and wrote the Russian's name upon the reverse side, taking the spelling from his guest.

'Are you going to write my name there too, Stephen?'

'Hardly, Tom. I know who you are. In fact, I shall literally be cutting you out of the picture.' He sipped his malt frugally. 'So who is the third wise man?'

'Max Stern.'

'Precisely when was this photograph taken?'

'May of '46, Stephen. I recall the date because that was the only time I met Volkov.'

After jotting further details upon the back of the photo, Horner hitched his trousers at the knee, and then sipped again from his glass. 'Is Stern a fellow American?'

'He's a naturalised American.'

'So where did this Stern fellow originate, before he dived into the melting pot?'

'I'll tell you what I know, but I can't vouch for its accuracy.'

'There is so much deceit in this world of ours, Tom.'

Quaid managed a specious grin, and then lolled back in his chair. 'Max Stern claims to have been born "somewhere in the Habsburg Empire", to use his own line. The smart money says he's from Budapest, with an each-way bet on Vienna. Others reckon he's from Prague, Zagreb, Bratislava....' He broke off with a shrug. 'Hell, who knows? Some reckon he's a peasant's son, others say his pa was a baron. Max could pass for each and any.'

'When did Stern arrive in your country?'

'Max arrived stateside in the fall of '29, almost to the day Wall Street climbed on the helter-skelter.'

'Hardly the most auspicious time to search for the American dream,' observed Horner caustically.

'Like you say. So, just as he steps off the boat, the Wall Street Crash hits Max along with the rest of us. In the early Depression years, Max was sifting through garbage on New York's East Side, and picking up his new lingo waitering in dog-and-pony joints. And he still talks that way some. He can sound crude and abrasive, but believe you me, Max Stern is a real smooth operator.'

'How did he rise from the ranks, Tom?'

Quaid tossed his butt into the glowing coals. 'In 1938, Max started up small-time as an art dealer on Long Island. Then came World War Two, and Max, with his language skills, got taken on by the OSS. After the war, he stayed on in Europe, basing himself in Paris.'

'So what is Stern's current profession?'

'When he's not dealing big in paintings, Max calls himself a "political broker".'

Horner tasted his malt. 'Tom, I am familiar with stockbrokers and insurance brokers, but what service, pray, does a "political broker" purport to perform?'

'He brings together those wanting to trade political objectives, and helps set up their deals.'

'For a commission, I presume.'

'You got it. Max is pricey, but he's goddam effective.'

'Is he entirely venal?'

'That's a hard one to call.'

'And what sort of deals has he been setting up with Volkov?'

'Stephen, you know I can't tell you that.'

The grey eyes stared levelly at the American. 'Has he perchance dealt with Moscow on behalf of certain circles in the United States, but outside of official channels?'

Quaid's expression remained masked by the glass tilted to his lips. When he lowered it to speak, his tone was cold. 'Why the hell do you want to know, Stephen?'

'Tom, I am not concerned about the details of Stern's activities upon your behalf. However, I would like to meet him.'

'Why so?'

'Tom, you know I cannot tell you that.' Horner tented his fingers beneath his chin. 'Is it such an outlandish request? Can you not mention to Stern my interest in talking with him?'

Quaid's lips pursed reflectively. 'Okay, Stephen, I'll mention it. But, if you hear nothing back from Max, you can take that for an answer. That's the best I can do.'

Horner offered a taut smile of thanks. 'Shall we eat? Cook has left us to serve ourselves.'

Quaid followed his host through to the dining-room. There he gazed enviously at the Millet, which still hung in pride of place.

13

SUNDAY 5 DECEMBER 1948

'Where are the eagle-eyed twins?'

Sandra closed her front door. 'Up in their eyrie, Eve.'

'Doing what?'

'Watching Jack.'

'Is he with somebody?'

'No, he's painting.'

In the lounge Eve lowered herself onto the settee. She straightened her beige skirt, lit a cigarette, and sat silently until her hostess passed over the requisite glass. 'Has Jack had any other women in his flat besides Fay?'

'Just one. She stayed with Jack last weekend.'

'Do we know anything about her?'

'Blonde, attractive, good figure,' detailed Sandra. Extracting a battered folder from the sideboard, she passed over a wad of photos. 'She arrived by car. We're still checking her out.'

Eve flipped through the snaps, and then laid them aside. 'Keeps her pearls on when she's at it,' she observed. 'So when did Fay depart?'

Sandra coiled up in an armchair, feet drawn behind her. 'She and Oliver left eleven days ago. She's not due back until 1st June, according to what her milkman told Janice.'

'Then we'll pick up her trail when she returns to London.' Eve glanced around the lounge. 'I suppose you'd like to keep this place on.'

'Of course I would.'

'So what do we do about Jack Randall?'

'I know what I'd like to do.'

'Seriously, Sandra.'

Straightening her face, she eyed Eve inquiringly. 'Is Barber still interested in Pilling's contacts?'

'Well, since the source who leaked the FO documents has been dealt with, I rather think his interest in the Pilling affair has waned. In any case, Sandra, the existence of DOSS is again under threat, so I fancy his attention is focused elsewhere just now.'

'What about you, Eve? Are you still interested, now Fay's abroad?'

'Why?'

'I've finally had a word with Beatrice.'

'So what did she have to say for herself?'

'Well, Beatrice recognised both Jack and Fay from the photos I showed her. She even gave me their Party names, "Comrade Luke" and "Comrade Natasha". She said they'd both been in the same CPGB branch in West London from 1936 to 1938, when they were both expelled on exactly the same day.'

'Fancy that,' said Eve softly. 'So why were they expelled?'

'Beatrice couldn't remember the details, but she said there were rumours that these were phoney expulsions. Meaning that they were designed to let Jack and Fay distance themselves from their previous political backgrounds.'

Eve inhaled thoughtfully. 'Thereby permitting them to worm their way into positions of responsibility, where they could be activated later by Soviet intelligence.'

A sceptical expression drifted over Sandra's face. 'That's how the "sleeper" concept was supposed to work in theory, Eve. But, it was only rumoured that the expulsions of Fay and Jack were staged.'

'Go on.'

'Well, they might have been chucked out of the Party for perfectly sound political reasons, Eve. Lots of people passed through the ranks of the CPGB in the late 1930s, during the Popular Front period. Many of them were just idealistic, middle-class antifascists, who ultimately rebelled against the twists and turns of the Party line.'

Nodding in noncommittal fashion, Eve stubbed her cigarette. '"Comrade Natasha" and "Comrade Luke", you said. Is there any significance to those names in their pasts?'

'None that I've found so far.'

'So, keep looking into both their lives, Sandra. Now, have you learned anything more about Rita Prior?'

'Yes, I have. Since Rita returned from Europe, she's rarely been at her home address. Most of the time she stays in Belgravia with her friend.'

'Belgravia, indeed! So who's this wealthy friend?'

'Jessica Deacon.'

Eve's brows arched with interest. 'You mean the photographer and travel writer?'

'That's the one.'

'How long have they been together?'

'No idea, Eve.'

'How old is Jessica now?'

'She's forty. I've put a recent picture of her in the file. I must admit that I was really surprised how attractive and feminine she is.'

Eve's brows ascended heavenwards. 'Did you expect suit, tie, and cropped hair?' she queried acerbically.

'I suppose I did,' Sandra confessed in a subdued voice.

'Well, given her profession, I suppose Jessica could have helped Pilling with his microfilms.'

'It's possible, Eve. On the other hand, Jessica has always been a fellow-traveller, just a progressive name on the headed paper of a Party front. She's never been a member of the Party itself, according to Beatrice. She was always deemed to be too much of a loose cannon.'

'So what do we know about Rita?'

'She's thirty-eight, and was a model before she married one Charles Prior, a member of the fast set. Rita lived the life too and got heavily into drugs. She may still be on them. She looks somewhat fey in her photos. She's divorced now, Eve, and doesn't seem to have a job.'

'Presumably, she lives off Jessica's immoral earnings.'

'You mean those sublimely illustrated apologies for Stalinism that masqueraded as her travel books.'

Eve nodded. 'Anyway, what did Beatrice say about Rita?'

'She'd never seen her face before.'

'Did she recognise Herbert Pilling from his photo?'

Sandra shook her head.

'What was Rita's maiden name?'

'Fairfax.'

'Where was she born?'

'Canterbury.'

'Well, so was Pilling, Sandra, and my recollection from his file is that his mother's first husband was a bloke called Fairfax.'

'So Rita was Pilling's older step-sister, and that was why he had her address?'

'It may be as simple as that, but keep digging.'

'I will, but I'd better warn you that we're short of funds again.'

'No, we're not,' said Eve smugly, extracting an envelope from her shoulder bag. 'I saw my banker a few days ago.'

'Another "Greek Wedding"?'

'No, this time I had to perform number twenty-four, the fur coat fantasy. It wasn't very imaginative. In future we're going to have lots of props, hired from theatrical costumiers.

And to stage his next productions, Rupert has taken a place down in Sussex.'

'As a matter of interest, Eve, how much information is Barber getting from you?'

'About as much as I get from him. In any case, he's distracted by bureaucratic politics.'

'In what way?'

'Well, as you know, Sandra, MI5 wants to gobble up DOSS, and, of course, the Home Office is backing them. But, the SIS also wants to swallow us whole, and they're responsible to the Foreign Office. So for now the FO acts to keep us out of MI5's clutches, and a condition for this support is that Barber helps remove DORA from the scene.'

'Why?'

'Because some stuff produced by Horner's outfit has left the FO with egg on its face.'

Sandra shook her head dazedly. 'It all seems terribly complex. We're just little cogs in the wheels of power, aren't we?'

'Well, I leave the big time politics to "Uncle Arthur", and the more bureaucratic infighting he's involved in, the better for us. It gives us more freedom of movement.'

'So if Barber nails Horner, we might survive?'

'We'd certainly be in a stronger position.'

'How vulnerable is Horner?'

'As vulnerable as any gambler is, Sandra. His fate depends in large part upon the fickle ways of "Lady Luck". So, with Rupert as my snout, I've kept Barber broadly informed about Horner's financial problems. I've even given him the date of the next game at "Spats" in December. Of course, he knows nothing about my own financial arrangements with Eaton.'

'So what is Horner's current situation?'

'Dire,' retorted Eve vindictively. 'His house and some paintings are mortgaged to one of his creditors, and his residual "worth" is about five thousand pounds. Yet recently, he made a cash deposit of twenty thousand pounds into his account.'

'Where did he get the money?'

'I think you can guess, Sandra.'

'What happens if Horner loses this twenty-five grand?'

'Well, he'll be homeless and penniless, and entirely ruined if the Treasury auditors should then swoop.'

'But if he wins?'

'In that case, everything reverts to seeming normality for a while. Yet there may be another way to destroy Horner. What if we could expose DORA as being riddled with communist spies? That would certainly redound to the credit of the women's section of DOSS.'

'So that's what you're up to.'

'That's my maximum aim, Sandra. But, as a minimum, I just want to take belated revenge upon Fay Galbraith.'

Sandra sipped her drink reflectively. 'There's something you've never explained to me. Why did you ask me to check with Beatrice, whether Fay and Jack had been members of the Communist Party? Was that just your famed intuition at work?'

Eve shook her head. 'I wish it was that easy. In any case, I only included Jack in the inquiry because he was involved with Fay. It was her about whom I had a niggling suspicion.'

Sandra's expression grew more puzzled.

'Well, do you remember that load of material we inherited from some defunct anti-communist outfit?'

'Do I?' retorted Sandra with a wry smile. 'It took me ages to sift through those mounds of magazines and newspapers, and most of the material was of no use to us, anyway.'

'True enough. However, some of the foreign language stuff was interesting. I was particularly intrigued by a glossy French periodical, put out by one of the anti-Stalinist groups operating in Paris. Only seven numbers appeared, all published in 1937, but each one was full of quite classy photos and barbed cartoons.'

'So what's this got to do with Fay?'

'I'm getting to that,' said Eve, following a swig of gin. 'One edition had an illustrated article, entitled "Solidarity with the Women of Spain", featuring demonstrations in Paris, New York, Prague and London. In it, there were some photographs of the British event, which I've frequently studied with a magnifying glass.'

Sandra leant forward attentively. 'So what had you found?'

'Well, in the very front of the London demonstration was a woman in her early twenties. Fist clenched, shouting some slogan, she looked like a younger Fay. The figure and long hair were certainly like hers.'

Eyes narrowing, Eve paused to ingest more gin.

'Most of all, though, it was the look of sheer enjoyment on this woman's face that convinced me it was Fay. It was exactly like Fay's expression, when she advised me to take a look in a mirror. And I've carried a clear memory of that look for years.'

Sandra smiled sympathetically. 'So it seems you were right all along. But, all that proves is that Fay was once a communist. We've no idea about her current politics, Eve; nor Jack's, if it comes to that.'

14

FRIDAY 10 DECEMBER 1948

DORA's finance officer waylaid Horner outside his room. 'Sir, have you examined my estimates?' he inquired in a nasal monotone.

'I have indeed,' proclaimed Horner, 'and I fear that you have erred upon the side of parsimony, Ikin. So go away, and conjure up sufficient fresh items to justify my claim for a further fifty thousand pounds.'

'Only fifty thousand, sir?' responded Leo Ikin, the register of his voice too inflexible to convey the sarcasm.

Horner eyed him coldly. 'In this unique instance, Ikin, you are correct to chide me. Make that sum seventy thousand.'

'I got a card from Fay,' reported Lucy Temple.' She seems to be having fun in Paris.'

Flexing her claws, she examined the paintwork, and asked her boss if he'd also heard from her. When Randall shook his head, Lucy whisked a file from her desk, and inquired if he spoke Albanian.

'*Jo,*' he replied.

Her eyes widened over a pert smile. 'Is that "no" in Albanian?'

'*Po.*'

'And that's "yes" in Albanian"?'

'*Po.*'

'Do you know any other words of the language, Jack?'

'*Jo.*'

She poked a purple binder towards him. 'Horner wants an immediate analysis of this.'

Randall flipped open the file, whose sole content was a recent cutting from *The Times*. This reported the arrest of Koçi Xoxe, Albania's former Minister of the Interior, and several of his supporters, following a campaign against them as 'Tito's friends'. Closing the file, he laid it next to others he'd extracted from his secretary's cabinets.

She eyed him quizzically. 'So how come you knew the Albanian words for "yes" and "no"?'

'I know those two words in several languages, Lucy. I like to respond appropriately to all offers.'

'I'd have thought a nod or shake of the head would be enough.'

'Now, that could be confusing, even fatal, in Bulgaria. There a nod means "no" and a shaken head means "yes".' He gathered up his files and grinned. 'Isn't this a wonderful place to work, Lucy? You learn something new every day, don't you?'

'*Po,*' she replied, shaking her head.

Seated at a rickety table in DORA's canteen, the head of Records Section dissected a corned beef rissole. Deftly, Vic Welles directed a lump of gristle to the side of his plate. Opposite him, Leo Ikin poured scotch from a hip-flask into a cracked Utility mug, whose bottom was still frosted with sugar from his earlier tea.

'The man's mad,' complained Ikin. 'How the hell can I squeeze seventy thousand pounds out of the Treasury in today's financial climate?'

'Tell them to stop compensating the impoverished former owners of our mines and railways,' suggested Welles sourly.

'Do you think you should express such views so publicly, Welles?'

Vic rummaged amongst a mound of tepid greens. 'I remember the time, Ikin, when you used to castigate me for my moderation. You were a real firebrand then.'

'Shut up! That's all in the past.'

Ikin glanced over his shoulder, to check whether his surprisingly loud tone had drawn attention to their table. But the canteen was deserted, save for Sid Yates and a companion. The security guard sat with his back to them, chair positioned close to that of a young clerk, his hand resting lightly against her back. Its gradual descent to grope her bottom evoked an unconvincing squeal of protest.

'Must be from Italian Section,' observed Welles drily, stroking a knuckle along his clipped moustache.

'She's in Finance,' said Ikin, glaring pruriently. 'It's high time I saw to her transfer.'

Pushing his plate to one side, Welles focused his watery eyes upon the smaller man. 'While you're about it, Ikin, perhaps you can finally see to the transfer of some outstanding expenses as well. I'm still owed them from my trip to Warsaw, and I put in my claim months ago.'

Turning to face him, Ikin swigged more whisky, exacerbating the pong of his malodorous breath. 'You'll just have to wait, Welles. The money isn't there.'

Vic inserted his spoon into a bowl of coagulated rice pudding. 'So where is the money?' he demanded in a hostile undertone.

'Three guesses.'

'Horner?'

'His creditors, more likely.'

Having gummed up his mouth with tepid pudding, he swallowed a way clear for his words. 'You mean my expenses have helped finance the old bugger's gambling debts?'

'That's exactly what I mean, Welles. And until our lord and master hits a winning streak, and repays what he's pleased to call his "loans", the cupboard's bare. So don't ask me to find money that isn't there. When it is, you'll get your expenses.'

'Why do you go along with it, Ikin?'

'It keeps him quiet.'

'There's nothing to keep quiet about,' snarled Welles. 'You ought to shop him, Ikin. You're the numbers man. You could do it.'

Again Ikin glanced over his shoulder. Yates and his companion were just exiting from the canteen. The doors swung closed upon a stifled female shriek, which crescendoed into a complicitous giggle. Ikin turned to face his colleague.

'Welles, I can't shop him. Horner's got a record of every employee who was formerly a member of the Party.'

'How the hell do you know that?'

Ikin hunched in his chair, compact shoulders swallowing a scrawny neck. 'Some weeks ago, Horner ordered me to transfer all unallocated reserves from DORA's contingency fund into several new accounts, to which he alone had access. When I refused, he recited to me a summary of my political past, retracing my years in the Party?'

'Christ! Did he mention having a file on me?'

'No, Welles. He simply said that he could produce a record of the activities of every ex-communist in his employ, should it be required.'

'So how many former Party members are there in DORA?'

'How in God's name should I know, Welles? I only know about you because we were in the same branch.'

Vic's fist thudded onto the stained laminate surface. 'Damn it all! It wasn't a crime to have been in the Party. There were many reasons why....'

'Try explaining that to your next employer, Welles.' Even acerbity floundered in Leo's adenoidal delivery. 'Right now we're living in a world of goodies and baddies. Our pasts are the political equivalent of indecent exposure, and Horner could strip us of our fig-leaves of respectability, should we ever step out of line.'

Amongst the fresh acquisitions adorning the spacious Paris apartment, the Monet took centre stage. Grimacing, Quaid mounted an intense and covetous inspection of the painting.

Max Stern swamped the ice in two glasses with bourbon. 'Tom, why in hell's name did you hand the low-down on me and Volkov to this Horner guy?'

Quaid spun on his heel to take the drink proffered by his host. 'Max, I reckoned I had to give up the names of you and that Russkie runt. For all I knew, Horner had them already from some other source.'

Stern rustled a Havana adeptly between his chunky fingers before lighting it. 'What's Stevie Horner after, Tom?'

'Dough, I guess.'

'And you say Stevie's got some classy pictures?'

'He sure as hell does.'

'So maybe sometime I'll take a gander at his "for sale" sign.'

Late that night, Horner strode away from the baize table at 'Spats'. Playing upon his lips was a species of smile once common at public executions. Behind him, he could hear Toby Meredith's protesting voice hover on the verge of tears.

With two queens and sublime gall he'd bluffed and raised until Meredith, his principal creditor, had folded a full house. On that one hand alone, Horner had scooped a pot which effectively restored both home and paintings to his good self, with a few grand in loose change thrown in.

'What do you reckon, Eric?' demanded Barber, as Horner swaggered past their parked car in the lamp-lit Knightsbridge street.

'Like a bleedin' march-past, guv.'

Barber stabbed the stem of his pipe in Horner's direction. 'That cocky bastard was on his uppers yesterday. I know that for a fact, Eric. All the whispers said the same. And now he's gone and bloody won, hasn't he? Horner's got all his resources back. Now all the books will balance, and he'll be right back at the helm.'

'If it works that good, guv, maybe you oughta go gamblin'.'

Arthur's fat lips slimmed slightly with his smile. 'I fear my cosy low-church conscience would trouble me, lad. But, one day I'll get into DORA. And when I do, God help anyone with their hand in the till, or balled in a clenched fist.'

PART TWO

WHOSE DEAL?

FEBRUARY TO MAY 1949

15

THURSDAY 3 FEBRUARY 1949

Randall slipped through the open door of his secretary's office and came to a halt; stopped in his tracks by the woman doubled over a filing cabinet drawer. As he stared at the skirted posterior, the woman straightened to her full height. Turning towards the desk, she complained to Lucy Temple that she couldn't find a particular file. Jack smiled in surprise. It was Wendy Page, and a slimmer version of her old self.

A half-smile playing upon her lips, Lucy asked, 'Is there a green slip in there, Wendy, where the file should be?'

'Yes, there is. So what does that mean?'

'It means he's got it,' pronounced Lucy, an accusing talon fingering Randall like a suspect in an identity parade.

Turning, Wendy smiled warmly. 'Hello, Jack. It's lovely to see you again.'

'Likewise, Wendy. Are you okay now?'

'Yes, thanks.'

'Anyway, I see you've met the boss.'

First treating him to her special glare, Lucy scowled at a chip in her nail varnish, and then spread her claws before her like an eagle about to pounce.

'I've been put on light duties,' explained Wendy. 'Mr Horner wants me to collect material to present to a parliamentary committee. It's all to do with British commerce with Eastern Europe. However, it's been arranged that I'll be seeing mainly statistics and reports. So I won't be poking my nose into your secrets.'

'Secrets?' he echoed derisively. 'Wendy, there aren't any secrets in this section. Lucy sees to that.'

His last words were drowned by a clatter of typewriter keys. When the carriage return pinged more frequently, as Lucy moved into top gear, he beckoned Wendy into the corridor.

'So have you finished with that file, Jack?'

'Yes, it's in my office. You can have it now.'

She followed him to his room, and grinned at the mounds of files and newspapers fringing his desk. Seating himself behind these paper parapets, Randall tugged the required file from one heap and laid it aside.

'So, Wendy, does this new task mean that you now officially have brains, as well as slimmed down beauty?'

Given the coating of face powder she still wore, he couldn't tell whether she had blushed at his compliment.

'I lost over a stone in weight while I was in hospital, Jack. No alcohol, of course, and I couldn't stomach the food. Moreover, I had to do loads of exercises to strengthen my leg, after it came out of plaster.' She smiled teasingly. 'And recently, I was invited out by a man who's even older than you.'

'So I'll have a chance, if you ever become free again.'

The smile grew hesitant. 'I never know how serious you are.'

'Nor do I, Wendy. But, in your absence, I've been careful not to pad my expenses. Unfortunately, it seems I'll have to remain wary.'

'Oh, don't worry, Jack. I'll still be working part-time in Finance, and that's a subject I want to discuss with you. In return, can I ask you for help with this Eastern Europe job?'

'Of course you can. So what did you want to discuss about expenses?'

Hands planted to each side of a stack of papers, she leant across the desk. 'Jack, you must know that we have major problems in Finance.'

This oblique reference to Horner's rumoured behaviour prompted him into a guarded nod. Shifting his gaze, he tried unsuccessfully to ignore her jutting breasts. They were hovering perilously close to the summit of his piled copies of *Pravda*, the Soviet Party daily. Beneath them, he could just about make out an upside-down photo of Stalin.

'Our records are in such chaos, Jack, that I could provide you with several times the pathetic amounts you've fiddled so far, and nobody would notice a thing.'

He realised that he found her startling proposition tempting. He'd never reconciled himself to that genteel poverty, which had been the lot of most Britons for a decade of war and so-called recovery. And he could certainly do with extra cash, to fund some sorely-needed improvements to his flat.

Despite such errant notions, caution just about prevailed. 'We'd still be stealing public money,' he observed, 'only more of it.'

She leant closer. When Stalin vanished beneath her substantial bust, it was with difficulty that Randall overcame some surreal musings.

'Jack, what control does the public have over how its money is spent? In any case, I'd be drawing upon accounts which no external auditors would ever find, even if they knew of their existence. In any case, I'm not proposing some massive one-off fraud. I'm talking about getting hold of reasonable amounts at regular intervals.'

As she sought to lead him yet further astray, he found himself peering at the plump vermilion lips. That particular shade of lipstick was too bright to suit her, and she still used too much powder. But, it was impossible to fault those eyes or the slimmed down body.

Notwithstanding these distractions, he'd still absorbed her every word. 'So tell me more,' he invited in a casual voice.

'You're abroad a lot, Jack, and you make regular claims for expenses. I'm simply proposing that you increase the amounts, submit the forms directly to me, and let me handle matters from there.'

By now, Randall was acutely aware that he'd slid over enough moral objections to find himself well down the slippery slope. This easy journey led to a mercenary afterthought.

'What's your cut going to be, Wendy?'

'We'll go fifty-fifty, Jack, on all that I produce in excess of your legitimate expenses. And, should we become partners in crime, I'll suggest other things to help cover our tracks.'

'I've only one more question, Wendy. How will you obtain Horner's signature to release the money?'

'That's no problem, Jack. There's a set of blank papers pre-signed by him in Finance. He provides these to facilitate day-to-day administration.' The dark eyes constricted. 'So what do you think?'

Fingering his lean jaw, he felt it nodding gently, in a motion of consideration rather than consent. She'd obviously given the matter much thought and he had no objection to her terms.

'I'd like to think things through for a bit, Wendy.'

Her lips tightened into a satisfied smile.

16

MONDAY 7 FEBRUARY 1949

The door was on the latch. Once inside, Randall dropped the snib and turned the mortise-key in a second lock. Announcing his arrival, he mounted the stairs to the landing, where subdued light shone through the half-opened doorways of bedroom and bathroom.

'Go on through, Jack,' her voice called out from the latter. 'I'll be with you in a trice.'

Depositing his things in the hall, he entered the bedroom. He lowered himself onto the springy bed, and then lolled back on the feather-filled *Dauerndecke* covered by a gaudy quilt. She'd bought the duvet while visiting him in pre-war Vienna; a concession to his view that lovemaking beneath tucked in English bedclothes was like sex in a straitjacket.

And this was why they were together now, with neither questioning the motives for their behaviour. Both accepted that it derived from their common pasts, and that being who they were, they just did what they did. Yet, with nothing for them to share beyond the intense sexuality of their relationship, they parted without regret once this had run its brief course. Thereafter, all contact between them remained sundered, until the next time that she commanded and Jack colluded, and they repeated the whole self-serving performance.

He looked up when he sensed her presence. Motioning him to stay put, Pamela Armitage bent forward to impress her lips briefly but firmly against his. She smelt of high-class perfume, but tasted of toothpaste and scotch. Drawing herself to her full height, she produced a perplexing smile, before rounding the bed to pose before the wall mirror.

'And who's the fairest of them all?' she chanted softly in a refined alto, as she revelled in her reflected glory. Full-lipped, blue-eyed, and fair-skinned, her face held all the hauteur of icy beauty.

'Forty today,' she announced, dabbing at her wavy, blonde hair. 'I can hardly believe it, Jack. Yet I still seem to turn men's heads.'

'Only if they aren't screwed on tightly, Pam.'

She smiled crookedly into the glass, and then spun around to face him. Blue dress hugging her fine figure, she held her pose like a statue. 'So just how tightly is your head screwed on tonight, darling?'

He grinned. 'I'm always prepared to lose it for a while.'

'Good,' she said, accompanying her response with a satisfied nod. 'I'm drinking scotch. You can take whatever you want.'

'I saw the twins at the bus stop as I was driving by,' griped Eve, when Sandra let her into the flat. 'Why aren't they up in their eyrie watching Jack?'

'I don't think he'll be home tonight, Eve. He was carrying his rucksack when he left this morning. Anyway, Janice and Norma followed him this evening, as usual. They rang in some minutes ago and reported that Jack had slipped into a mews house in Kensington.'

'Does that mean we've got another lovely to investigate?'

'Looks like it,' said Sandra, pouring drinks.

Taking the proffered glass, Eve seated herself on the sofa. 'So let me have details about her as soon as possible.'

'I'll do my best, Eve, but I'd best warn you that we're running out of cash again.'

'Problem solved,' announced Eve, hauling wads of notes from her shoulder bag.

Sandra fetched some rubber bands, and began sorting the readies. Her lips pursed primly. 'So what have you been up to this time?'

'Number six. I've been on a rocking horse at Rupert's place in Sussex.'

'Doing what?'

'Riding, Sandra. Gorgeous horse. I've never seen one that big before. I had to ride it wearing various scanty outfits, and nothing at all when I was Lady Godiva. All the while Rupert just kept on saying, "Gee up!" in a babyish voice.' She pointed at the cash that Sandra was meticulously counting. 'Not bad for three hours of saddle-sores, is it?'

Sandra bound the last banknotes. 'You're certainly an outstanding fundraiser.'

Eve reached out for a bundle and tossed it into the other's lap. 'Expenses, Sandra, for the head of my new research department.'

'Thanks a lot, Eve. That will really come in handy.' She smiled bemusedly. 'I like this grand title you've awarded me. But, as far as I'm aware, I'm the only member of this research department I'm now heading.'

'Nothing like being your own boss, Sandra.'

The buffet she served up was excellent, primarily because it was the creation of a master chef. Randall doubted that Pam had ever cooked a thing in her life. Carrying their drinks, they quit her small dining-room for the lounge, which was at best a way station for the bedroom.

Seated upon the sofa, Pam hunched forward excitedly and peeled the wrappings from his gifts. The scotch, which she preferred to malt whisky, provoked a curt nod of approval.

However, the perfume purchased in Paris induced her to sniff and assess, before mouthing him a kiss.

'Yes, I can wear this. Thank you, darling.'

Opening the final package, she extracted from it the silk scarf he'd bought in Bologna. Her face lit up. 'It's utterly gorgeous, Jack, but I've absolutely nothing to wear with it.'

'I'm sure you'll find something appropriate, Pam.'

'Yes, I'm sure I will,' she concurred, smiling to herself. Then she laid the scarf aside and stared at him inquisitively. 'So how are you making out without Fay?'

'I'm managing.'

She plucked a *Du Maurier* from an onyx box, screwed it into her holder and lit it. 'Has she left her woebegone husband yet?'

'I've no idea.'

'Fay uses you, darling.'

'I suspect we use each other, Pam, just like you and I do.'

'At least you make a better job of it than your father did.' A flash of hatred in her eyes accompanied this brusque retort.

Surprised by this rare disinterment of her past, he smiled forbearingly. 'Should I take that remark as a backhanded compliment?'

She shrugged. 'Take it in any way you want.' Carefully flicking ash, to allow her face to fully recompose, she probed again. 'Do you think Fay's being faithful to you?'

'I don't think it's any of my business. Fay's either available or she's not, and I refuse to concern myself with her life otherwise.' He lounged back in the armchair. 'Anyway, what's new with you?'

'Well, I think I might marry "Smarmy",' she replied matter-of-factly. 'Naturally, it won't interfere with our arrangements, Jack, or his, come to that. So what do you think?'

'That you're old enough to know your own mind, and young enough to keep on making mistakes.'

She blew smoke from amused lips, and then anchored her eyes on his. 'Do you know what I'd like from you as a wedding present? I'd really love you to paint me again.'

He gazed back coldly. 'Only I won't do it, Pam.'

She produced what would have passed for a wounded expression, had she been someone whose emotions were less armoured. 'Why on earth not?'

'You know perfectly well.'

'But that was all so long ago.'

'It shouldn't have happened at all, Pam.'

She puffed once more on her cigarette and then ground it out. 'Jack, you can be terribly stubborn at times.'

But not often enough, he reflected, particularly where women were concerned. His abrupt smile queried whether this was in fact a fault.

She rose to her feet. 'I'm going next door. I want to try on this gorgeous scarf you bought me.'

'I thought you said you had absolutely nothing to wear with it.'

'Yes, I did. So absolutely nothing is what I'll be wearing when I try it on. Anyway, come through soon, darling, and tell me what you think.'

17

FRIDAY 25 FEBRUARY 1949

'Nice smell,' said Eve, sniffing keenly, as she passed from hallway to lounge in the Ealing flat.

'We're having stew, salad, and gin,' announced Sandra.

'I think you've got the order of dishes back to front, my girl.' Lowering herself onto the settee, Eve swished the hem of a charcoal skirt over her knees. 'Where are the twins, down the pub?'

'They'll be off soon,' said Sandra, opening a bottle of tonic. 'But, just now Delphine, at least I think it's Delphine, is in the darkroom.'

'Developing more photos of Jack?'

'Hardly, Eve. The twins haven't snapped a thing since the blonde with a car visited in November. Other than his excursion to Kensington earlier this month, and the times he's been abroad, Jack's done nothing but work, paint, and drink. So they're producing some enlargements.'

'What of?'

Sandra reined in a ribald smile. 'I haven't dared ask.'

'And Delilah, if it's Delilah, where's she?'

'In their room, writing an essay, or maybe two.'

Eve rested her drink on the coffee table. 'Now, they're both pretty little things, Sandra. Aren't there any men in their lives?'

'Well, there's one bloke down at the Palais whom they *both* fancy, of course. So far it's gone no further. But I know they're a bit bored. They've even started on the gin.'

'So tell them to play with their enlargements until Jack goes into action again, as I'm sure he will. No men in this flat, Sandra. I don't want the operation jeopardised.'

'I'll make sure of that,' said Sandra compliantly, 'although, until recently, I've often wondered if there was anything to jeopardise.'

'And now?'

'There have been certain developments,' she replied teasingly.

The green eyes glittered above Eve's expectant smile. 'Well, I'm all ears.'

Sandra extracted a file from the sideboard, and from it withdrew some photos which she passed to Eve. Then she curled up in an armchair, the file nestling in her lap. 'The lady in Kensington goes by the name of Pamela Armitage. The twins took those photos while she was strolling in the park.'

'She looks predatory,' observed Eve, after leafing through the snaps. 'There's something familiar about her too.'

'That's just what I thought, Eve. And, although there was nothing on Pam Armitage in our files, I was certain I'd seen her face before. So I showed our snaps to a trustworthy journalist. She recognised Pam at once, and provided me with some items from her paper's archive.'

Stretching out, she passed two press photographs to Eve. The first, dated September 1936, depicted Pam in profile in almost philosophical pose; elbow propped upon crossed knees, chin resting lightly on her knuckles, an intricate bracelet surrounding her right wrist.

The second cutting, dated July 1934, featured another striking photo of Pam. This time she was bare-shouldered and exhibiting a full face. This shot was but one in a set of six women. They were presented under the headline, 'ANOTHER SELECTION OF BRITAIN'S BEAUTIES'. At the bottom of the page, there followed a list of their names. Eve's gaze halted at that of Pamela Randall.

Face tense, she demanded the full low-down. Making little effort to suppress her cocky expression, Sandra flipped open her file and narrated.

'Well, Eve, she was born Pamela Elaine Napier in February 1909. In March 1930 she married a well-off widower called Luke Randall. Luke already had a young son, John Gareth Randall, who was born in October 1914. Pamela and Luke formally separated in early 1931, and later divorced. In 1940 Pamela Randall married one Gilbert Armitage. Reportedly, it was a fraught marriage. It was also short, since Pamela Armitage was widowed when Gilbert was killed in North Africa in 1942. All clear now?'

Eve's smile exposed her flawless teeth. 'So Pam Armitage is Jack Randall's stepmother, and "Comrade Luke" used his dad's name for his Party moniker.' Her eyes lit up in anticipation. 'So what else have you discovered?'

Smiling smugly, Sandra tasted her drink. 'Luke Randall had an older sister Daisy. She married a man called Geoffrey Deacon, and bore him three daughters. Their names were Jessica, Nancy, and Amanda.'

'Wow!' exclaimed Eve in delight. 'So Jessica Deacon is Jack's cousin, and there must be a fair chance she knows Pam Armitage too.' She squeezed out a satisfied smile. 'Sandra, I'm really impressed. Now, dare I ask if there's anything else?'

Sandra nodded. 'The blonde from November is called Louise Grainger. She's Pam's cousin. We're still investigating her.'

Eve coddled her glass thoughtfully. 'Do we know anything about Jack's other two cousins?'

'Only that they're both older than him. Why the interest?'

'I was wondering if Jessica was the only red in her family.'

'So you want me to continue researching?'

'I most certainly do.'

'Good,' said Sandra, rising to her feet. 'Anyway, let's eat, Eve, and no shop talk at the dining table, please.'

It had taken only two days for him to agree to Wendy's proposals. A week later, Horner sent Randall to Copenhagen. On his return he'd submitted his first expenses claim under the new regime. They had since arranged to meet in his room late that evening, when the other staff had departed.

He looked up to see Wendy in the open doorway. Stepping across the threshold, she eased the door to and leant back against it.

'I've got your expenses here, Jack.'

He lolled back in his chair. Pacing over to his side, she unclipped her handbag and withdrew from it various items. Intent on arraying them on his desk, Wendy stretched across it. This last act prompted him to maintain his position, in order to enjoy the contest between outthrust bottom and tightened skirt. When she glanced over her shoulder, a conniving smile formed upon her lips.

'Seen enough, Jack?'

'I've seen enough to know I'd like to see more.'

'Perhaps you will,' she replied lightly. 'But, right now, I'd like you to pay attention to something else.'

Sitting forward, he studied her paperwork. As arranged, the cheques were made out to different accounts for smallish sums, with no eye-catching round figures.

Having verified that he'd opened two fresh bank accounts, she pointed at the cheques 'Put those in your accounts in stages, Jack. Once they've been cleared, you can start paying me my cut. Use the payee names, account numbers, and amounts exactly as I've indicated on that sheet of paper.'

'I'm really surprised at Jack not seeing any women,' said Eve, hanging up a damp tea towel. 'I wonder what he's up to every night at the office. I suppose he could be merrily microfilming documents.'

Sandra untied her apron. 'Eve, we've got Jack permanently tailed, and he's never broken his routine to suggest he's making a delivery.'

'Well, he could have stuffed a load of documents into his rucksack when he visited Pam in February. Then Pam could have handed them over to Jessica for filming.'

'Talk about scraping the barrel,' countered Sandra waspishly. 'Eve, have you got the slightest evidence that Pam is anything other than a pampered society beauty?'

Spinning on her heel, she led the way from kitchen to lounge, and coiled herself in an armchair. Lolling on the sofa, Eve slipped off her shoes and pensively rubbed the sole of her bare foot. Then she looked up.

'What do you reckon Pam's doing these days, besides screwing her stepson now and then?'

'I haven't the faintest idea, Eve.'

'Perhaps we'd better find out.'

'Does that mean you want me to put a tail on Pam as well?'

'Yes, Sandra, let's do that. In fact, let's get hold of a place near Pam's, like you did with Jack.'

'Whatever you say, Eve, but Kensington's pricier than Ealing.'

'I know. But, you should have plenty of dosh left from what I earned by riding Rupert's rocker, and there'll be more to come.' She pushed to her feet. 'Anyway, there's something I want to show you.'

From the rucksack she'd dumped by the sofa, Eve withdrew a large envelope, and then assumed a side-saddle posture on the arm of Sandra's chair. 'I want you to look at some erotic pics, but try to see things from a purely investigative angle.' She placed Eaton's calendar in her deputy's lap. 'Start with January.'

Sandra opened the calendar and her fair brows steepled. 'Wow! I wonder what that's like.'

'Me too,' said Eve, leering over her shoulder. 'Anyway, do you recognise the woman performing the handstand?'

Sandra turned the page upside-down. 'No, Eve. Her arm's obscuring her face, and the lighting's all arty.'

'What about the bloke?'

Sandra spluttered. 'How can I? His head's....'

'Turn to February and March, and tell me what you see?'

Sandra pinked slightly as she perused these shots. 'Well, all three photos were taken at the same session. The rug pattern is the same in all three pics, and there's a wine bottle lying on its side in each one too.'

'Good. So what else do you see?'

'Not a lot. Although the bloke and both women are really uninhibited, you can't identify them, because of their positions and the lighting.'

'For goodness sake,' said Eve in frustration, 'look at the bloke's left forearm. There's a long snake-shaped scar on it.'

'I know. What of it?'

From the envelope Eve plucked out the photos she'd commandeered in October. She held one of Jack with Fay in front of Sandra's face. 'Can you work it out now?'

Sandra clapped a palm over her gaping mouth.

'The scar on his arm is identical. I've examined it from all angles.' Eve slipped the snaps back into the envelope, and then directed Sandra back to 'February'. 'Now, what about the two women with Jack?'

'What about them?'

'Well, look at the right wrist of the woman on the left.'

'She's wearing a bracelet with an unusual clasp.'

'And?'

'You tell me,' Sandra retorted testily.

Standing, Eve retrieved one of the press photos and handed it to Sandra. The seated woman stared at the picture of Pamela Armitage in reflective pose. The bracelet on her right wrist exhibited the same conspicuous clasp as the calendar photograph.

'I'm really unobservant,' conceded Sandra, making an apologetic face. 'So the wicked stepmother is one of the women with Jack.'

'And who's the other one, wearing a pearl necklace?'

'Keeps her pearls on? Is it Pam's cousin, Louise?' She turned back to "January". 'It must be Pam doing the handstand. I can just about see the bracelet in this shot.'

Reseating herself on the arm, Eve told her to turn to "April".

Sandra scrutinised the photo attentively. 'This shows a third woman with Jack, and this time you can see some of their faces,' she related. 'Jack looks like he's in his late teens, and both of them seem to be drugged up to the eyeballs.'

She flipped through the other months, but none featured Jack, Pam or Louise. Lips pursed, Sandra rose to replenish her glass. When she turned with drink in hand, a frown scored her brow.

'So who compiled that calendar, Eve?'

'Jessica Deacon, I imagine. Not only is she a professional snapper, but she must know Jack, Pam, and Louise. Moreover, the chap who marketed the calendar was "Red Freddie". And when his lordship's in London, he lives in the flat above Jessica.'

'How do you know his address?'

'He sent me a letter on headed notepaper, inviting me out to dinner. He wanted to discuss certain matters relating to the work of his committee.'

'I didn't realise you'd been slumming it of late, Eve. So what was Freddie like?'

'He's very attractive for his age, but somewhat seigneurial, and distinctly frisky. And I fancy he'd have been a damn sight friskier, if his wife hadn't been there.'

'Well, I'm sure you could have handled that, Eve. But let's get back to the calendar. Although it's been produced recently, those photos of Jack, Pam, and Louise were all taken well before the war, weren't they?'

'Yes, they were. So it seems Jessica's been making and flogging porn for years.'

'But why would she need to rake in money in such a way just now? She'd be risking at least public exposure and political humiliation, if caught.'

'True. But she's probably in dire need of lucre. There's a Cold War on, Sandra, so it's unlikely that her pro-Soviet books would hit a mass-market, like they did pre-war. So that's one source of income gone. Moreover, you suggested that her lover Rita was probably still on drugs, which would mean she's costing Jessica plenty too.'

'Well, Eve, if she really does need money that badly, then perhaps Jessica *did* microfilm those FO documents for Rita's stepbrother, Herbert Pilling. And, another thing, do you think Jack, Pam, and Louise know they're on display in this calendar?'

'That's a good question, Sandra. However, except for that photo of young Jack in "April", it would be impossible to identify any of the three from those pics. Even in that photo, given his youth and the lighting, Jack's only recognisable to those who know him, like we do.'

'So what are you going to do with all this new stuff?'

'Right now we're going to do nothing, Sandra, other than to observe and add to our files. In any case, Jessica and Rita are in Morocco until early June, according to what Rita's milkman told Janice.'

Lolling in his lounge, Randall sank another brandy. It did little to blur his maudlin mood. He recalled Wendy's words regarding the prospect of seeing more of her: 'Perhaps you will, Jack.' Then again, perhaps he wouldn't.

Other than the torrid weekend with Louise, and the bout of sexual abandon with which Pam had abandoned her thirties, his life had been shorn of women. Work, travel, drink and painting had been his lot.

Although Louise had invited herself round again, she'd cancelled this arrangement the next day. Trapped in a loveless second marriage, she continually balked at freeing herself from it entirely, and resuming her career as a scientist. However, he was as used to her erratic ways as he was to those of Pam and Fay.

Like Randall himself, they all wanted to have their cake and to eat it too; an outlook on life which could lead to spells of acute hunger, such as he was experiencing now.

18

MONDAY 11 APRIL 1949

Bearing a bottle, whose contents he rated as mouthwash, Max Stern gazed at his bar. Then he switched his stare to the tiny, blond Russian, who stood inspecting the Monet.

'You really gonna drink this, Yuri?'

Yuri Volkov turned from his long perusal of the painting. 'Max, you should know by now that I only ever ask for what I want.'

Although markedly accented, Volkov's English was still more elegant than Stern's. They always spoke in the language of commerce when they traded, since Russian, not being a major tongue of the Habsburg Empire, had eluded Max in his colourful youth. Conversely, none of the Slavic languages that he did know were sufficiently intelligible to Volkov.

Stern loaded ice into pristine glasses. Over his own he swished bourbon lavishly. He made a sour face as he filled Volkov's. 'Jeez, Yuri! What kinda Russkie are you? You don't smoke, you don't drink liquor, but you're happy wit' this piss.'

Accepting the proffered drink, Volkov settled himself into an armchair. Big blue eyes widening above his smile, he raised his glass. 'Cheers, Max!'

'*Na zdraví!*' muttered Stern in Czech; the toast being near enough to the Russian. 'So why you here, Yuri, and why'd you say not to tell Tom Quaid you was coming over?'

'Business reasons, Max, and business solely between we two. "Under four eyes", as the diplomats say. But don't worry. Nothing detrimental to American interests is involved.'

'Okay, if nothing bad's gonna happen to Uncle Sam by way of this, then I'm listening. So how about your backers, Yuri? They know what you're at?'

'Let's say, Max, that the proposals I shall put to you are in line with their objectives.'

'Hey! You a diplomat now?'

Volkov laughed aloud. 'No, Max, I'm still a secret policeman.'

'So what's your pitch?'

'I want you to buy me an English agent, Max.'

Smile-creases deepened around Stern's inky eyes. 'You want for me to buy some guy? Like from who?'

'From a man called Stephen Horner.'

Stern's jawline hardened. Frowning, he ambled around the seated Russian towards a low table, where he flipped open an ivory cigar box. He cut and moistened a Havana. 'Now, listen up, Yuri. I'm gonna spill some beans.'

'Why should you do that, Max?'

'So we don't get blown outta the water.' Clamping the cigar in the corner of his mouth, Stern took the seat facing his guest. 'This Stevie Horner guy knows we talk. Is that news to you, Yuri?'

'Yes, that certainly is news to me.' Volkov took a reflective sip from his glass, and then placed it on the table between them. 'Max, has Horner played any role in our affairs?'

Stern shook his large head. 'What you and me's got, Yuri, is the direct line from Washington to Moscow. The train don't stop no place else.'

'And for that very same reason, Max, I can't make a direct approach to Horner. I need a middleman.'

'So, Yuri, you still want for me to buy a guy from Stevie Horner?'

Upping a shoulder to afford his hand room, Stern fished matches from a pocket. As he lit the cigar, he observed his partner's decision-making process. Pouching an olive from a dish on the table, Volkov's small fingers popped it into his mouth, like a bitter pill. Then he sampled his drink again before speaking.

'Max, go ahead and make the purchase.'

'Okay. And you know for sure Stevie's in the market?'

'Horner is certainly in the market for money. According to our sources, his severe gambling losses last month completely negated the gains he made at the end of 1948. Even his Millet is up for sale.'

'Is that a fact? And Stevie's got what you want, for sure?'

'He's got what I want, Max.'

He peered into Volkov's elfin face. 'Moscow's gotta guy in Stevie's joint. That how you know, Yuri?'

'Does it matter how I know?'

'Ain't no skin off my nose,' muttered Stern, twitching his beefy shoulders. 'So tell me what I gotta do.'

Volkov pointed towards the briefcase parked beneath the Monet. 'I'll be leaving that with you, Max. Inside is everything you need.'

Stern drummed his fingers against the table, retracted them into a fist, and cracked his knuckles. 'My dough there too?' he asked seriously.

The little man checked his laughter. 'Your fee is there too, in a mixture of dollars and Swiss francs. The less you pay Horner for your purchases, the bigger your commission.'

'So I got dollars and francs,' said Stern, following a deliberate, cigar-chomping pause. 'Stevie's gonna want Sterling. And Sterling ain't easy to come by, Yuri, by reason of London's exchange controls.'

'But you can manage?'

'Sure thing. So Stevie's wearing a "for sale" sign. And, while he ain't gonna sell his country, he'll trade me one of his guys for the right price. That the play, Yuri?'

'That's correct, Max. However, I want one particular breed of agent from Horner. Your full instructions are in the briefcase.'

Leaning back in his chair, Randall reciprocated Wendy's smile and greeting. She posed in the open doorway, mac draped over one arm, her dark, expressive eyes holding his all-encompassing stare.

'Sorry to disturb you, Jack, but you've got another file I need. This one's concerned with Bulgarian economic policy.'

He waved her into the room, and then fished among the files littering his desk. The hunt ended in singularly rapid success. 'Is this the one you mean?'

She advanced across the room to inspect his offering. 'Yes, that's it.'

Somehow she found room to deposit mac and file upon his cluttered desk, when she accepted an invitation to embellish the room's spare chair; but "just for a bit", because she had "something on".

'Jack, are you really interested in such an arcane subject as Bulgarian economics?'

'I'm interested in the politics underlying it. Horner wants to know about a man called Traicho Kostov, who's been running Bulgaria during the long illnesses of Georgi Dimitrov, the nominal communist boss there.'

'So why is Horner interested in this Kostov man?'

'Well, he's in trouble, and not only with his rivals for the succession to Dimitrov, but more importantly, with the Russians too. Kostov was recently denounced by the Bulgarian Party's Central Committee for his "lack of friendship and sincerity" towards Moscow. More specifically, he's been accused of withholding information from the Soviets concerning the prices at which Bulgarian goods have been sold to Western countries.'

'That could be very dangerous for him, couldn't it?'

'It could prove fatal, Wendy. Such an act can be presented as an economic variant of "Titoism", as another outbreak of so-called "national communism".'

She peered at him through lidded eyes. Then she turned in her chair to inspect a distant nothing, and thrust back her shoulders. The prominent bosom banished Bulgaria from his thoughts, and briefly he was allowed to sit and stare. When Wendy restored her eyes to his face, a smile dimpled her cheeks.

'Anything wrong?'

Letting just a little lewdness into his expression, he shook his head.

'Now, Jack, what about Nikolai Voznesensky, the head of Soviet state planning, who was dropped from the Party's Politburo last month? Is he for the high jump as well?'

'Probably. But he's just disappeared from sight. Naturally, Horner has also expressed an interest in him and the other "Leningraders" who seem to have been purged.' He raked a hand through his wavy hair, and then pointed at a pile of files. 'So that's another chore I'm landed with.'

She cocked her head in query. 'Jack, what exactly do you do on your trips abroad, or shouldn't I ask?'

'I deliver things to Horner's men in the field, and I write reports about the local situation afterwards. I'm not a secret agent, Wendy, I'm just a researcher. I'm a deskman, not an operative.'

'To me the boundaries look somewhat blurred.'

'A fair point,' he conceded. 'I certainly wouldn't like to try and convince a hostile interrogator that I was just a glorified paper-pusher.'

She puffed her lips before posing her next question. 'Have you heard from Fay?'

'Not a word.'

'What a strange woman.'

'What makes you say that?'

She beamed away his question and stood. 'I must go, Jack. I've got to meet Sam, the man who's even older than you.'

19

TUESDAY 3 MAY 1949

Making his way from the turnstile, Stern checked his change. He halted, confused by the coinage of the realm. After a run of failures at converting half-crowns and florins into their dollar equivalents, he poured the silver into a pocket. Then he scanned the letters of the stands. Having located the appropriate block, Max climbed to the top of the staircase, and was met by polite applause.

Dotted about an expanse of grass were some men rigged out in white. Two of them, with heavily bandaged legs and carrying chunks of wood, loped leisurely past each other. Another unhurried individual stooped, straightened, and jerked an arm. Loitering by three sticks knocked into the ground, another bandaged figure caught the reddish ball in his big gloves. He then chucked it to an unbandaged man, who tossed it like a hot potato to another.

Lowering his briefcase, the American watched the ball move down the line. Nobody seemed to want the goddam thing. Stern's eyes screwed up suspiciously, when one guy not only seemed keen to hang onto it, but rubbed it near his crotch as he took a walk.

The ripple of handclapping had come from the few spectators, seated in isolation or huddled in pathetic clusters. One of them was Horner, who stared alertly ahead of himself, as Stern edged along the otherwise vacant row. Taking a seat next to the Briton, Max pulled a face when his rump landed upon hard wooden slats.

Since Horner didn't speak, Stern watched with him as the joker with the ball spun around at the end of his walk. Then he charged at an old guy in a white cattle-coat, who was guarding three more sticks. Narrowly avoiding collision, his body contorted violently, but he fluffed the cartwheel.

'T. E. Bailey. Fast-medium,' remarked Horner. 'However, we require someone far faster, a new Larwood. Do you know of any other way to deal with the Australians, Stern?'

Patience eroding, Max made no reply.

'We had a frightful time last year at the hands of Lindwall and Miller. Fifty-two all out in the final Test at the Oval. What do you say to that, Stern?'

'You all through, Stevie?'

Dependency and curiosity blinding his eye to the other's familiarity, Horner turned his head. 'Stern, some six months ago, I intimated my desire to speak with you. You hardly strike me as bashful, so why such delay in returning my call?'

'My business,' retorted Max curtly. 'But now I'm right by your side, pal, and I got work for you. You wanna talk about it here?'

'Stern, at Lord's my accustomed vantage point is there.' Reverential eyes focused upon the pavilion. 'I suggested that we meet on the popular side, because for the last day of Essex versus the MCC it was likely to be deserted, which is indeed the case.'

'Okay, Stevie, let's deal.' Max set his briefcase between them. 'Take a gander inside.'

Horner moved the case onto his thighs, unfastened it, and peered into its depths. 'How much is in there, Stern?'

'Two grand Sterling. Used bills. It stays when I go.'

'This trivial sum represents my consultancy fee?'

'That's appearance money, pal. You want more, you gotta work for it.'

Horner repatriated the briefcase to Stern's care. 'So what services am I required to render, in order to garner these rewards?'

'I wanna buy from your payroll, Stevie, if you can fit my bill.'

'So what are these specifications?'

'You got any one-time commies on your books?'

Horner's thin lips tightened into the suggestion of a smile. 'In my department, Stern, I employ all sorts. Regarding former members of the Communist Party of Great Britain, I am able to present you with the precise figure of five.'

'So let's run the reel on these five jokers.'

Mulling over the quintet of former communists working in DORA, Horner translated his knowledge into mental sketches.

'Well, Stern, number one is a former comrade who still believes ardently in the cause, despite his expulsion from the Party. Each day, he undergoes the cruel ordeal of reading the *Daily Worker* from cover to cover. Upon occasion, he endeavours to rejoin the diminishing congregation of his former branch.'

Max lit a Havana. 'And this guy sees secrets?'

'No, Stern. Number one has no access to confidences. I use him as a doorman. During the war he served as a paratrooper. Now he ensures that nothing inimical to my interests shall cross the foyer of my department.'

'I read you, Stevie. So how's number two shape out?'

'Number two resigned from the Party of his own volition, as a protest against the Nazi-Soviet Pact of August 1939.'

'And still ain't sure he done right?'

'Precisely. Thus he is stranded in that no man's land inhabited by fellow-travellers. Unable to render full homage to the mercurial writ and fickle icons of the creed, but still attracted by the Party's camaraderie and spurious optimism.'

Horner restored his gaze to the cricket. 'Number two is exceptionally good with figures, Stern. Whenever there are unsavoury exchanges with the Treasury, concerning the funds allotted to my department, my little bookkeeper does wonders with his ledgers.' His hands tapped together to acclaim an event offstage. 'A good catch.'

'You reckon?' Max muttered dubiously to Horner's profile.

'At short-leg.'

Stern too gazed at the circus ring. An unbandaged guy sprawled upon the grass. A bandaged guy stalked off, swinging his club. He turned back to Horner. 'So shine a lamp on number three, Stevie.'

'Number three was a committed and knowledgeable Marxist. At a certain juncture, unpalatable facts ceased to tally with the comforting ideology, and brought on that dreadful business of theoretical doubt. He volunteered his disquiet to the Party, and found himself rewarded not with debate, but with denunciation and expulsion as a "Trotsykite".'

'So what gives with number four?'

'Again expelled from the Communist Party, this person is currently aligned with the left-wing of Labour.'

Max exhaled a ragged ring of smoke. 'What's the scene wit' number five?'

'Yet another expellee, Stern. An intelligent and debauched character, whose major fallibility is an unfailing love of comfort and security.'

'That it?'

'Such is my motley crew. Worth their weight in gold, are they not?'

Stern gazed at a sparrow hopping along the boundary. 'Could be.'

'When?'

'When it's all sewn up.' Drawing upon his cigar, Max let a few seconds dribble by. 'But, you know what, pal? I need more.'

'I need more too, Stern.'

Picking up Horner's scorecard, Stern penned some details upon it and handed it to the Briton. 'Time and place, Stevie. No show, no go. You want more dough, pal, then be there. Make sure you got the real McCoy on your five jokers wit' you. Pretty pictures too.'

'I shall require extra for all such details, Stern, particularly for photographs.'

'You want more, huh?' Max hauled himself to his feet. 'Every mother's son wants more, Stevie. So name your price, but wise up too. You go through the roof, then I go some place else. You got me?'

With the words 'you got me' ringing in his ears, Horner's hands clasped each other with the limp dependency of marathon dancers. 'I understand,' he responded icily.

Stern glanced at the cricket, where the fielders were leisurely changing ends, and a sight screen needed adjustment. 'I'll leave you wit' the action, Stevie. Don't forget your dough.'

On reaching the top of the stand, he looked back. Horner was writing studiously upon his scorecard. Stern grinned.

'See you soon, Stevie,' he muttered assuredly to himself.

Eve handed Sandra her drink, and then lolled along the length of her settee. 'So what's Jack been up to of late? Any more jaunts abroad?'

Curled in an armchair, Sandra stifled a yawn and opened her notepad. 'Well, recently he's made two trips, each time taking the boat train to Paris. Perhaps he went to see Fay.'

Eve propped herself on an elbow. 'Sandra, he could have gone anywhere, once he reached Paris, and we've no idea why he's been travelling or where to. Supposing Jack was a Soviet courier, like Herbert Pilling, then his job would be ideal cover for such activities, wouldn't it?'

'Is that fact, intuition, or guesswork?'

'I'm just trying to keep all possibilities in mind.' Eve reached out for her cigarettes. 'So have you located Jack's cousins?'

'Well, Nancy Deacon now lives in Australia, but we've tracked down cousin Amanda.'

'Did you show Amanda's pic to Beatrice?'

'Yes, I did, and she identified Amanda as another former member of the CPGB. She joined the Party in 1933, and left it in 1939 at the time of the Nazi-Soviet Pact.'

'Fancy that,' said Eve in a satisfied tone. 'So what did Beatrice have to say about Louise and Pam?'

'Well, she didn't recognise Louise from her pics at all, but she knew Pam's face. She recalled seeing Pam and Jack at a party hosted by Jessica Deacon in summer 1939.'

Eve frowned. 'Was this a Party party?'

'It was more of a do for intellectual and artistic left-wingers, Eve. Some of the guests were party members, but these were invited solely as members of Jessica's circle.'

'This was summer 1939,' noted Eve. 'So it seems that Jack was still hanging around party circles, despite being expelled in September 1938.'

'That's one interpretation. On the other hand, Jessica might simply have invited Jack as a relative.'

'Well, keep digging, Sandra.'

'I'll do my best, Eve. However, I'm afraid the financial situation is precarious again.' Her eyes widened above an ambivalent smile. 'Have you any plans to see your banker?'

'I'm seeing him soon to perform number thirty on his list. So come round Monday week, and you can collect the latest instalment of the wages of sin.'

20

WEDNESDAY 11 MAY 1949

There were thirteen booths in the renowned Paris restaurant. The *maître d'hôtel* escorted Horner to number seven, and then left the Englishman to inspect his surroundings.

On three sides privacy was guaranteed by plush velvet drapes, which extended from a ceiling of latticed beams to the carpet's deep pile. A wall panelled in cedar completed the cubicle. Given the absence of any natural light, the recessed lamps were essential.

Horner looked up when Stern drew the curtains apart to enter. He then tugged them back to cloister the two men. Wriggling his broad beam, he settled upon the seat opposite Horner, and pressed the wall-mounted bell.

'Wanna drink?'

'Why not?'

'Wanna eat?'

'Later, Stern. I prefer not to negotiate upon a full stomach.'

'Negotiate, Stevie?'

'Deal?'

Max summoned the waitress, in response to her respectful call of '*Monsieur*' from outside of the drapes. In almost faultless French, he ordered bottles of Horner's nominated malt and his own preferred bourbon. Then, after checking the availability of a particular dish, he explained that they would order dinner later.

Once she'd left, Max loosened his garish silk tie, and reached down to pat a black briefcase. 'Dough's in the bag.'

Horner gestured towards the attaché-case parked next to his seat. 'Some details are contained therein, others I carry in my head.'

Stern unbuttoned the collar of a navy shirt and his neck squirmed in relief. 'Okay, Stevie, let's talk about your guy number one, the janitor.'

'Doorman,' corrected Horner, making it sound like promotion.

'Now, I gotta feeling he ain't too big in the brains department.'

'Distinctly limited, Stern.'

'You use him on foreign jobs?'

'Good grief, no! Given his fragile temperament, which appears to be not untypical of that part of Glasgow from which he hails, I would have courted a diplomatic incident.'

'So scrub number one.'

'Consider him eliminated from the proceedings, Stern.'

The waitress returned, and deposited the contents of her tray upon their table. She produced a charming smile for the approving Stern, and then sidled through the curtains.

Max reached with silver tongs into the ice bucket and loaded his own glass. Horner restrained him from sacrilegiously adding ice to the malt he'd just poured. Both made noticeable inroads into their drinks before Stern spoke again.

'I gotta problem with number two.'

'Further elimination?'

'Yep, he's outta the running, by reason of him quitting the commies off his own bat.' Stern refilled his glass. 'So we lose number two, Stevie, leaving us wit' three guys.'

'Stern, does the word "guy" signify solely the male of the species?'

The craggy face crinkled in a smile. 'Why you asking, Stevie?'

'For this reason.' Replacing his glass upon the starched tablecloth, Horner circled a finger around its rim. 'Number five is a female.'

'A dame? Hell! Dames mean trouble.'

'Is she to be scrubbed?'

Max simulated a frown. 'I ain't sure.' Expression lightening, he swigged from his glass. 'So tell me about numbers three through five. Any of them do duty in Prague? And we're talking just post-war here.'

'Number three has been in Prague in that period.'

'Moscow?'

'None of them.'

'Warsaw?'

'Solely number four.'

'Budapest?'

Horner watched Stern scribble notes on the back of his menu card. 'Three and five have served in Budapest.'

'Belgrade?'

'Again three and five.'

The large head nodded ponderously. 'So, Stevie, numbers three and five've done duty in Budapest and Belgrade post-war, but number four ain't. That right?'

'That is correct.'

'So lose number four.'

'In which case, is the candidate to be number three or number five?'

'I'm thinking about it,' muttered Max in seemingly pensive tone. He hauled a Havana from his inside pocket and lit it ceremoniously 'So how old are these jokers?'

'The man is thirty-five in October, and she is thirty-six, today in fact.'

'Happy birthday, babe!' Stern emptied his glass in toast and then refilled it. 'Are both these guys up and running?'

'Both are in rude health, physically and mentally.'

'Not much to choose, I guess.'

A mirthless smile skirted Horner's lips. 'There is the sexual differentiation, of course.'

Stern shammed on, to reel in Horner further. Volkov had categorically forbidden him to purchase the female candidate, in the unlikely event that the target male did not emerge from the elimination process.

'Yeah, dames mean trouble,' he growled through cigar-filled teeth.

'Well, surely that relieves you of any predicament, Stern.'

'Like you say, Stevie. You hold onto the dame. I'll buy the guy.' He hoisted his glass. 'So here's to number three.'

Horner did not participate in the unseemly toast. He waited for Stern to speak again before raising his glass to his lips.

'How much for number three, Stevie?'

'What precisely is he expected to do?'

'He's gotta go some place.'

'Will he return from this unspecified location?'

'I dunno, Stevie. God's truth.'

'Might a diplomatic incident occur, on account of number three's departure to an unknown destination for an indeterminate period?'

'I ain't no wiser than you, pal. I'm just the middleman.'

'Then, as "appearance money" for number three, Stern, I would suggest the sum of ten thousand.'

'Bucks?'

'Sterling.'

Hamming incredulity, Max delved into his briefcase and slapped wads of used notes upon the table. Lifting them up diffidently, Horner layered them inside his attaché-case.

'Hey! How about that, Stevie? Buying and selling guys.'

'Such is hardly a unique occurrence in the history of our two nations,' rejoindered Horner frostily.

Stern jammed the Havana between his teeth. 'Okay, Stevie, I put up good money for number three. So let's give the guy a name.'

'A name tag comes with a price tag, Stern.'

'Don't it just. How much?'

'A further ten thousand.'

'Okay, I'll see you for that.'

Stern laid more bundles upon the table, and Horner transferred his latest gains to the attaché-case. Then he inspected a thumb, which he held uplifted in the manner of a charitable Caesar. 'Number three's name is Jack Randall, although in his passport it will read John Gareth Randall.'

'You got all Jackie boy's passport dope there?'

'Your assumption is correct. Upon engagement, each member of my staff is obliged to present their passport to my good self, together with some photographs of recent vintage. All such details are logged in their personal files.'

'So how much for this background dope?'

There was little haggling, as the details of Randall's passport changed hands for money. Even his 'distinguishing mark', the serpentine scar on his left forearm, was auctioned off without friction. This brought them to his photo. Max balked at the asking price which the Briton optimistically ventured, while Horner masked his delight at being 'knocked down' as low as the American's counteroffer.

On completion, Stern lolled back in his seat, thumbs hooked into his waistband. 'So tell me one thing, Stevie. How in hell's name have you been keeping all these one-time commies on your books, seeing how things have shaped up post-war? It sure ain't that way stateside. Uncle Sam's taken a stand against reds working in government.'

The grey eyes gazed back unblinkingly. 'I retained the services of my five former communists, by recommending that this questionable quintet be ousted from my department.'

'You lost me.'

Bringing the glass to his lips, Horner rolled the malt around his mouth, as though lubricating his tongue for its next bout of prolixity. 'It was merely a question of timing, Stern. Having anticipated the vehemence of contemporary Cold War sentiment, I advocated the discharge of these five persons as early as August 1944. I intended that my disquiet regarding their unsavoury pasts should be evinced promptly.'

'So how'd it pan out?'

'I was informed that, on account of the fleeting popularity of our gallant Soviet ally, prior membership of the Communist Party could not, of itself, warrant dismissal. However, I was invited to furnish supplementary reports, if I deemed it imperative.'

'Did you get back to them?'

'I have compiled some anodyne memoranda over the years. However, my initial action patently deterred subsequent investigations. None of these five could ever be accused of being "plants" or "moles" or some such.' Horner's lips dabbled with a smirk. 'In point of fact, rather than incurring such infamy, my department is now perceived as one of the most secure bastions of the so-called "Free World".'

'Nice work,' muttered Max. 'But let's get back to Jackie boy.' A penetrating stare ironed out the deepest creases in his rugged face. 'How about the dirt? Randall gotta record, a liquor problem? Does he go wit' dames? You know, Stevie, that sorta dope.'

Horner sipped his malt as though rinsing away a sour taste. Then a finger pointed like a spear at Stern's briefcase. Once Max had doled out more dough, Horner informed on Randall's personal life in stunted and awkward phrases, far removed from his typical grandiloquence. When he'd finished, he stared at his hand as if reading his palm.

'This lucre is literally filthy, Stern.'

'Used bills,' said Max, massaging his nose. 'But we eat soon. So go wash your hands. Bathroom's to the left.'

Having locked his attaché-case, Horner disappeared through the drapes. Stern peered into his briefcase. It was still almost half-full. Smoking placidly, he awaited the other's return. When Horner resumed his seat, Stern laid the Havana aside, and produced a slip of paper.

'One last thing, Stevie, I gotta give you orders for Randall's meet.'

Picking up his own copy of the menu, Horner turned it over like a crucial playing card, and wrote upon it Stern's directive. Then he unlocked his attaché-case and added the menu to its contents.

'So let's eat.' Max pressed the bell. Then, with smile-creases indenting his face, he peered at Horner. 'Stevie, I heard tell you got some paintings for sale.'

21

MONDAY 16 MAY 1949

She stood in the open doorway. 'I see you're working late again.'

Folding shirtsleeved arms across his chest, Randall lounged back in his chair. 'What about you, Wendy?'

'Well, I've got to meet Sam near here later, so there seemed little point in going home. In any case, I had things to do in Finance.' Pacing into the room, she picked up a copy of the Cominform journal from his desk and read aloud its title. '"For a Lasting Peace, for a People's Democracy". What a mouthful! Is it interesting?'

'It's dire, but it contains information relevant to Kostov's fate.'

She returned the journal to its place. 'So when are you next abroad?'

'Horner's sending me to Paris Saturday week, and then I have to hang around there for at least a fortnight.'

'At least a fortnight,' she echoed thoughtfully. 'That means Fay might be back by the time you return. So have you heard from her yet?'

When he shook his head, she stared at a wall, smiling to herself. Then she turned towards him. 'Would you give me your opinion about something, Jack?'

'Of course.'

'So come down to the third floor in ten minutes time.'

Once she'd left, he made a few notes while he waited. Then he locked his door and descended the stairs. Wordlessly, Wendy took his hand and led him through warren-like passageways. She halted outside an opened door and ushered him inside. Palming the door to, she glanced at him before turning its key.

He took stock of her office. It contained much the same furniture as his own, although her desk was devoid of any clutter. Switching his gaze to Wendy, he watched her slink towards a corner of the room. She held up a dress draped over a hanger. Then she hooked it on a shelf, and paced over to where he stood.

'Sam and I are off to a party later and I'm wearing that dress.' Eyes fixed alluringly upon his, she slowly unbuttoned her blouse. 'I'd like your opinion about it when I eventually put it on.'

Randall grinned; he liked the word "eventually".

Eve laid several bundles of banknotes on the table between her and Sandra. Narrowed eyes and smirking lips heightened her louche demeanour. 'That should keep us going. But I'll spare you the shocking details.'

Sandra leant forward, an irked expression to her face. 'Eve, while I've no desire to participate, I'm happy enough to be told the shocking details.'

'Want to see the photos too?' She reached under a sofa cushion for a brown envelope and passed it to Sandra. 'Gwen took these pics at Rupert's place in Sussex.'

Sandra perused the photographs, which showed 'Pharaoh' Rupert ensconced upon his 'throne'. Fanning him were two nude women, one wearing a jackal mask, the other that of a crocodile.

'Crocodile suits you, Eve. I've seen you smile like that.' She flicked through the snaps again. 'So who's the jackal woman?'

'That's Zoë, an actress I know. Works for me sometimes when she's "resting".'

Lips pinched primly, Sandra forced the issue that had bothered her for some time. 'Eve, are you comfortable with naked women?'

'Perfectly comfortable,' Eve responded casually. 'It's quite simple, Sandra. I like options. Sometimes I fancy meat, and sometimes I have a yen for peaches and cream.'

Wrinkling her nose, Sandra shook her head. 'I don't know how you can do that.'

'Sandra, let's be clear about how my world works. I don't want to possess or be possessed by a woman, any more than I want that from a bloke. But certain women find me attractive. Some are drawn to my aura, some are just curious about having sex with a woman, and some are seeking time away from heavy-handed or skirt-chasing blokes. Whatever their motive, if they've got something that appeals to me, I simply go ahead and enjoy them, and that's all there is to it.'

'Do you find these relationships satisfying?'

'Depends what you mean,' said Eve, twitching her shoulders. 'I'm in favour of having relationships that make sense. So I'm quite prepared to spend a night with a man or a woman and then walk away. Or if I feel it's right for me, I'll have another night, then perhaps another, and so on. In short, I'll stick around for as long as things suit me. That sort of pragmatic relationship I can accept.'

She fiddled with her rings, and both her gaze and voice grew colder. 'But to promise some open-ended commitment is ludicrous. I did that once, Sandra, and look where it got me; the depths of degradation and despair, a plunge into madness, and a flirtation with suicide.'

Sandra had stared at her knees throughout Eve's vindication. When she looked up she was frowning. 'Is Zoë one of your peaches?'

'We've had the odd bite out of each other.'

'I'd have thought she was too fat and round for you, Eve.'

'A touch of inconsistency never hurt any woman, Sandra.'

'Eve, what you do in bed is your business. I just happen to think that bisexuals are greedy.' Her expression one of disdain, Sandra shoved the photos back into the envelope. Then she reached out for her drink, and asked about the survey of Pam Armitage's house.

'Well, Pam's had three regular male visitors, all of whom the press preposterously deem to be men of substance.' Eve rummaged under another cushion, and handed over a folder containing three photos. 'Recognise them?'

Peering at the first, Sandra nodded. 'Bald and bucktoothed, I've seen him on the financial pages.'

'What about the second?'

Sandra screwed up her face in disgust. 'Look at that bloated gut. Is he in breweries?'

'No, land, Sandra, lots of land. And do you recognise the third?'

'It's good old "Smarmy", a Shadow Cabinet hopeful.' She closed the folder. 'So what do you reckon Pam's after?'

'A ring from the highest bidder, I imagine.'

His eyes were fixated on the dress she now wore. It hugged every curve of the shape that buttressed it.

'Do I look all right?'

'You look gorgeous.'

She rewarded him with a pleased smile. 'I'd love you to see me to the station, Jack, unless you're desperate to get back to your files.'

'I'll happily escort you.'

'So go and get your jacket,' she said, as she gathered up her strewn clothes. 'I'll meet you by the lift.'

When he joined her there, she stretched out a hand and entwined their fingers. 'Let's leave separately, Jack. I don't want little Sid Yates gossiping about us.' The pressure of her hand augmented. 'What I *do* want, though, is to spend as much time as I can with you before you leave for France. So can I come and stay with you this weekend, and see your etchings?'

His brows soared, and then his eyes narrowed. 'I'd love that, Wendy. But now I'll pose the obvious question. What about Sam?'

'He'll be playing golf in Scotland. So it's his fault for leaving me alone.' Eyeing him fondly, she kneaded his fingers. 'Actually, that's not true. I'll be with you because I want to be.'

'That's very flattering.'

'Isn't it?' Laughing, she stepped into the lift.

When he joined her in the street, she clutched his hand again. 'Will you paint me too this weekend?'

'I'd love to, Wendy, but that means I'll want to paint your face and not a mask. So wear little or no make-up.'

'I knew you'd say that. But, since you're the artist….' Her hands reached behind his neck. 'Can I get one more kiss, *with* lipstick?'

Seated in a car parked near to DORA's entrance, Janice Marlow smiled beatifically at their embrace. Then she issued instructions to her passengers.

22

SATURDAY 21 MAY 1949

A Delaney twin burst into the lounge. 'Wendy Page has just got out of a taxi to visit Jack.'

'Who's Wendy Page, Del... er?'

'Delphine,' said the petite blonde. 'She was with Jack the other night, Eve. So Norma and I followed her home and found out her name.'

'Then we checked it against a list of DORA's employees provided by Barber's snout,' explained Sandra.

Eve rose from her chair. 'Well, let's go and see this latest addition to Jack's harem.'

Randall smiled when he opened his front door. The mask was gone. A touch of mascara enhanced the stunning eyes and there was a light gloss to her lips. Taking her small suitcase, he ushered her up the stairs.

'It's a bit of a tip on this floor, Wendy. I still haven't got round to buying the paints I want. But the attic's presentable.'

He helped her doff her coat, and observed that she was wearing the same dress.

'Well, you seemed to like it,' she said innocently. 'Anyway, let's go up to the attic.'

He followed her up the stairs, and stood aside while she scrutinised the photographs scattered around the walls of the large room. She devoted considerable attention to one of Pam, and then turned towards him.

'Who's that beautiful woman?'

'That's my stepmother Pamela.'

Frowning, she came close to him. 'What about your real mother?'

'She died when I was a baby.'

'Sorry,' said Wendy, squeezing consolingly upon his hand. 'Is your father still alive?'

'Possibly.'

'You don't know?'

'I haven't seen or heard from him for twenty years.' His hands linked around her waist. 'So is my interrogation over?'

'For now.' Rocking back in the cradle of his arms, an enticing smile skipped around her lips. 'But I shall need to pose more questions, after you've kissed me adequately.'

'She's a big girl,' observed Eve, peering through a telescope into Randall's attic from the dovecot. 'So which section of DORA does Wendy work in?'

'She's in the Finance Section,' said Sandra.

'Interesting,' remarked Eve thoughtfully. 'Just the sort of job that could pay for that very tasty dress she's wearing.'

'That will do for now,' she said, easing herself from his hold. 'I have more questions.'

'Such as?'

'Where are your paintings? Why don't you hang them?'

'They're stacked in the corner.'

'I see. Well, I'll interrupt your interrogation temporarily, Jack, by posing a separate question. Do you have any red wine?'

'Plenty, but I'll have to nip downstairs for a bottle and glasses.'

When he left the attic, Wendy paced towards the stack of paintings. Moving the large landscape, which hid the others, she arrayed the canvases along the wall and studied them. Then she walked over to another wall and inspected the photograph of a woman with a baby.

She turned when Randall appeared with the necessities. 'You should hang those three nudes, Jack. They're all fine paintings.'

'Thanks,' he said in surprise. 'I'm impressed that your praise includes my portrait of Fay.'

'Jack, I simply said that it was a fine painting. I can say that, even though I don't like Fay, dressed or naked, any more than she likes me.'

'Point taken.'

'Of course, I shall expect an even higher standard when you paint me tomorrow. Were you planning to paint me nude as well?'

He matched her growing smile with his own. 'That's up to you. I'll happily paint you in whatever mode you choose.'

'We'll see. Anyway, I'll leave until later my questions about the other two naked ladies, one of whom appears to be your stepmother.' She switched off an ambivalent smile. 'Instead, you can tell me about that photo of the dark-haired woman holding a baby. Is the baby yours?'

'It's possible,' he answered awkwardly, 'but I've never seen him in the flesh and I doubt I ever will.'

'What's the baby's name?'

'Zoltán. Only he's nearly eleven now. He was born in Hungary in 1938.'

'In Hungary? So what's his mother's name?'

'In English it's Caroline King. Later, she changed it to its exact Hungarian equivalent, Karola Király. Her father was an austere British businessman, but her mother came from Sopron in western Hungary.'

'And you had an affair.'

'It was hardly an affair, Wendy. She stayed with me briefly in early 1938, after she broke up with her lover, Imre. However, they were soon reconciled, and later that year she followed him back to Hungary. Caroline was several months pregnant by then.'

'So you don't know if the baby is yours or Imre's.'

'No, I don't. But Fay, who is Caroline's cousin on her father's side, claims to have a photo proving that Imre is the father.'

In the hope that he could produce a pause in her questioning, he waved the wine bottle.

'We'll drink when I've got to the bottom of all this,' she responded tartly. 'What happened after Caroline followed Imre back to Hungary?'

'Imre returned to his political activities. He was a member of the miniscule Hungarian Communist Party.'

'Was Caroline a party member too?'

'No, she wasn't, although she might just as well have been. She was just an ardent fellow-traveller when I knew her.'

'So what happened next?'

'Well, the Hungarian Communist Party was illegal then, and Imre was eventually arrested and jailed. So for some time Caroline brought up her son alone. By now she'd changed her name and effectively become Hungarian. She was bilingual, having learned the language from her mother.'

'Can you speak Hungarian, Jack?'

'Little and badly. It's a hellish difficult language, but Caroline taught me some.'

'How did you get to know all these later details about her? Have you seen Caroline since 1938?'

'I only heard from her once after she left Britain. In summer 1939, she sent me that picture of her and the boy. The other details, including the fact that Caroline had a second son in 1942, I learned from Fay. She was posted briefly to Budapest in 1947 and met up with her cousin.'

'So is Caroline a communist now?'

'Yes, she joined the Hungarian Party during the war. Both she and Imre, who'd been released, were also in the Hungarian resistance movement, such as it was. Imre was murdered by the Arrow Cross regime during the last terrible months of the war in Hungary. But Caroline survived. Fay said that she was now working in their Foreign Ministry.'

'Jack, when you knew Caroline and Imre in the thirties, were you a communist too?'

He levelled his eyes at her probing gaze. 'Yes, I was.'

Her face tensed perceptibly. 'And now, Jack?'

'I was expelled from the Party in September 1938, and I've never had anything to do with it since.'

A relieved smile rewarded his answer. 'Why were you expelled?'

'The Party said I was a "Trotskyist".'

'That sounds nasty. So were you one?'

'Who knows?' said Randall, reaching for a corkscrew resting on a shelf. 'At the time, I didn't have a clue what "Trotskyism" was. Nor do I intend explaining what I now understand it to be, while finally opening this damned bottle.'

'Poor man!' she mocked. 'Can't you manage two things at the same time?'

He hauled out the cork, and then stared brazenly at the two things he could unfailingly manage at the same time. Smiling provocatively, Wendy tautened her shoulders. Putting lust on hold for a little longer, Randall finally poured two glasses of wine.

From the foot of the ladder in the dovecot, Eve addressed the nearest voyeuse. 'What are they up to, Delphine?'

'Delilah,' corrected the twin, eyes glued to her binoculars. 'They're being rather creative, Eve.'

'Well, I've brought you some drinks. I'll leave them down here.'

Eve paced back to the lounge, where Sandra lolled in an armchair, seemingly engrossed in a newspaper. Lowering herself onto the settee, Eve licked her lips and then let them stage a scheming smile.

'Fay should be back in a few days, which might be interesting.'

Looking up, Sandra nodded.

Eve reached for her drink. 'Pam Armitage and Jessica Deacon had an affair back in the thirties.'

'How do you know?'

'I asked around at a club I sometimes frequent.'

'A ladies only club?' queried Sandra in a prudish voice.

Nodding, Eve sampled her gin. 'Anyway, who did I see there for the very first time but Pam Armitage. She was obviously well-known on the circuit. So, after she'd left, I did a bit of discreet questioning and learned about the affair between her and Jessica.'

'Did you find yourself a fluffy little peach?'

'No, I was in a carnivorous mood, Sandra. And, talking of blokes, has there been any more nonsense from Derek?'

'Not since Eric had a word with him. Anyway, I'm getting a divorce. I've got the papers.'

'That's good. So have you got anything new to tell me?'

'Well, I've been delving into Fay's background.'

Eve sneered. 'I bet it was privileged.'

'It was to start with, Eve, but later her father went bankrupt.'

Sandra explained that the parental address given on Fay's birth certificate in 1913 was a large house in Hendon, while that noted upon her father's death certificate in 1929 was a dingy flat in Willesden. She then mentioned that Fay's father had worked in Russia for several years.

'But don't get excited,' advised Sandra, dousing any Loxtonian outburst of triumph. 'Fay's father worked there before the 1917 Bolshevik Revolution, and he wasn't political, he was an engineer. That's how he made his money.'

Eve frowned, pondering her question before posing it. 'So what was Fay doing before she married Oliver in 1933?'

Sandra vented a long-suffering sigh. 'Eve, I'm not a bloody private eye. I looked over the addresses in Hendon and Willesden simply to get a feel of things. Do you really want me to go round knocking on neighbours' doors as well?'

'I'm sorry,' said Eve genuinely. 'I always expect so much from you, because you're so efficient. But let me have the addresses, and I'll get Janice to have a nose around.'

23

SATURDAY 28 MAY 1949

The train drew into the *Gare du Nord*. The pretty Englishwoman smiled her thanks, when Randall lifted her cases off the luggage rack. He hailed a porter at her request, and she smiled her goodbyes. Wiggling off in pursuit of her luggage, her alluring hips prompted him into a brief recall of recent events.

Wendy had stayed with him twice more after her initial visit, allowing him to complete two paintings of her. However, neither had broached any arrangements for the future. There was Sam, and there was Fay.

A postcard from Fay, holidaying in La Rochelle, had arrived at his flat the previous day. It made no reference to the fact that she'd not otherwise written to him since leaving for France. It merely anticipated some sort of reunion on her return to DORA on 1st June.

Shouldering his rucksack, Randall strolled along the platform. As he walked, he allowed women and their ways to float from a mind now fixed upon his mission.

At his briefing on Friday the thirteenth of May, Horner had given him instructions for making contact with a person unknown. After this, he was to book into a particular hotel for a fortnight, in case further orders had to be cabled to him. It was all very woolly, but no less opaque in purpose than some other jaunts on which Randall had been sent.

The man in the scruffy, green windcheater was lounging against a wall by a kiosk, apparently engrossed in a copy of

Libération. Short and heavily stubbled, the butt of a *Gitane* jutted from his lips. Pulling out a pack of *Player's*, Jack asked in French for a light, and the man complied. When Randall uttered the words *'Pour un paix durable'*, the other rattled back *'Pour une démocratie populaire'*. In French, the title of the Cominform journal assumed a modicum of style, although Jack still wondered who had dreamed up such a password and response.

He thanked the man for the light, moved away, and set his rucksack on the ground. He'd half-smoked his cigarette, when his contact dumped his newspaper in a bin and scurried off. Randall heeled out his butt, and hauled on his rucksack. Giving the other a start of some fifty yards, he paced purposefully in his wake.

Once they left the main thoroughfares, he closed up to twenty yards, all the while noting street names. By the time they entered a warren of alleyways, he was beginning to sweat in the heat. A rat scuttled across his path, and behind him he sensed a presence. He glanced around. Attired in a beige suit, the man tailing him was strongly built and swarthy. Staring ahead again, he observed contact-man waiting, chewing his fingernails. As Jack approached, he scampered into a drab courtyard and beckoned. Opening the door of the house, he ushered Randall into the vestibule.

He passed into a large room, its primrose walls set off by an ivory ceiling. To his left was the only window, whose prospect comprised mossy cobbles and bricks. Positioned in a corner were two armchairs. A standard lamp glowed above them. Opposite him stood a desk, furnished with telephone, lamp, and brass ashtray. Behind the desk was a chair padded in green leather. Behind the chair was a closed door.

Randall felt a heavy tap upon his shoulder and turned his head. The swarthy man pointed at an armchair. Stepping across the room, Jack dumped his rucksack and sat. From his lowly perch, he gazed at the two contrasting sentinels staring back at him. All three men looked towards the door behind the desk when it opened.

A burly, middle-aged man entered. Seating himself behind the desk, he flipped open a dossier. Randall frowned in recall, unsure whether he recognised the lived-in face, topped by thinning hair.

From a desk drawer, the man withdrew a pistol, and laid it next to the ashtray. Randall was sufficiently startled to pucker his lips. He glanced across the room. The swarthy man was also toting a gun. It was pointed directly at Jack's head.

'Mi a neve?' queried deskman in Hungarian.

Randall shook his head, hoping to clear it. 'I'm sorry, what did you say?'

Again in Magyar, deskman asked his name. For emphasis, he placed a palm over the butt of his pistol.

Trembling fingers wiped at his forehead. Yet he still remembered that, as a foreigner, he didn't have to give his surname first, as would a Hungarian. Dry-throated, he croaked a reply. '*A nevem John Gareth Randall.*'

'*Hány éves?*'

At that particular moment, Jack felt considerably older than thirty-four. He stammered his answer. '*Harmincnégy éves vagyok*'

'*Mi a foglalkozása?*'

His occupation? What the hell was going on? If he'd been addressed in French, he might have believed that this was a bizarre and very heavy-handed ID check. Occupation? What was 'civil servant' in Hungarian? Dredging his memory, he recalled a word he'd both needed and used in Hungary in 1945.

'*Tisztviselő vagyok,*' he managed, pronunciation stumbling over the operative word.

Deskman lit a large cigar before posing his next question.

Well, how tall was he? What was six foot one in metric, and what was that in Hungarian? Jack's brain buzzed as he made the calculation. He hoped his response of one metre eighty-five was about right.

Although he recognised the Hungarian words for 'hand' and 'leg', the next demand in its entirety was too much for Randall's limited knowledge of the language, and hoarsely he said so. *'Nem értem. Sajnos csak egy kicsit tudok magyarul.'*

Deskman laid his cigar in the ashtray. 'On your feet, pal. Hands against the wall. Spread the legs.'

Randall obeyed, staining the primrose plaster with perspiring palms. Contact-man left off nail-chewing to frisk him.

'He's clean, boss.'

Americans? What the hell was going on?

'Az útlevelet, legyen szíves,' ordered deskman with formal courtesy.

'A kabátzsebemben,' Jack informed the wall. The agglutinative suffixes might not be correct, but it was comprehensible.

'The coat for the passport,' translated deskman.

Contact-man slipped it out with a pickpocket's finesse. He carried it over to his superior, who examined its pages attentively before speaking again.

'Okay, Jackie, lose the coat. Step this way. Roll the left sleeve and show me the arm.' When Jack complied, he peered at the scar. 'Okay, we're through. Now go sit.'

Jelly-legged, Randall almost toppled into the armchair. *'Szabad dohányozni?'* he inquired haltingly, unsure whether to use English.

'Yeah, you can smoke.'

After rolling down his sleeve, he tugged his *Player's* from the jacket he'd draped over the chair's back. His shirt was sopping and the trousers clammy beneath his thighs. 'Do you have names?' he ventured.

'Sure. I'm Csillag, little guy's Dee, big guy's Jay.'

'Chill-log,' Hungarian for 'star.' Well, if he said so. Csillag had the gun and the gun was the real star of this puppet show. Jack's role was simply to twitch into action, when others yanked the strings attached to his sticky limbs.

Jay now occupied the other armchair, legs crossed, pistol pointed at Randall's chest. Dee lolled against a wall, either nail-chewing or listlessly scratching at the stubble coating his throat. Csillag puffed serenely upon his Havana, while thumbing through the passport once again. He swatted at a fly. Jack finished his cigarette.

There was a rap at the entry door. Csillag glanced at his watch and nodded. Dee unzipped his windcheater, drew a Derringer from its holster, and cautiously opened the door. A small man in his fifties entered, carrying a battered valise. He glanced at Csillag, who flicked a finger in Jack's direction.

Jay stood and extended his pistol arm, the weapon trained upon Randall's head. Then he circled the seated man, holding him in his sights. Beads of sweat stung Jack's eyes and coursed down his spine. When Jay disappeared behind him, he closed his eyes in terror, and prayed silently to some being. The gun nuzzled against the nape of his neck. The muzzle felt like ice.

'*Monsieur.*'

Randall forced open his eyes to observe the Frenchman parading a syringe. He pointed at Jack's left arm.

'*Retroussez la manche de votre chemise, s'il vous plaît.*'

Jack glanced at Csillag for confirmation and received a stolid nod in return. Finding a dry spot on his shirt, he wiped his palm against it. As he rolled his sleeve towards the elbow, he stared at the serpentine scar.

PART THREE

VANISHING ACT

JUNE TO AUGUST 1949

24

MONDAY 13 JUNE 1949

'The rotten sods, how dare they?'

Lucy Temple's vexed tones sounded from behind a fully-opened copy of *The Times.* Only vivid fingernails, pinching affrontedly at the paper's far-flung edges, suggested her corporeal presence in the chair behind her desk.

'Just listen to this, Wendy.'

The disembodied voice proceeded to recite a report from Tirana, the Albanian capital. This informed the world that, after a month-long trial in camera, Koçi Xoxe had been sentenced to death for 'collaboration with Tito'.

'That sounds like another job Horner will dump on Jack's desk,' remarked Wendy, slamming shut a filing cabinet drawer. 'When and if he deigns to return, that is.'

Lucy's head emerged into view when she relaxed her grasp upon the newspaper. 'You don't understand, Wendy. That was my "X" that just went down the drain. The bloody Albanians are going to bump off Xoxe, and he's my one and only "X".'

'"X"? "Ex"? You've lost me, Lucy. You said something like "Dzodze".'

'That's how you pronounce it, but he's *spelt* with an "X".'

'Good grief! Do you speak Albanian, Lucy?'

'*Jo*,' she replied, laughing. 'No, of course I don't.'

She laid the newspaper aside. Then, with a typically-female gear-change, Lucy smoothly directed their conversation back onto the verbal road they'd seemingly passed but moments before. 'Jack's only a few days overdue, Wendy, and he's been late before.'

'Well, that's some relief. But I'm still worried about him.' She squared her shoulders. 'Anyway, I'm sure he'll find you another "X", Lucy. There's bound to be one lurking around the Balkans somewhere. So what other endangered species are there in your files? "Ys" and "Qs" must be a problem.'

'They are, Wendy. I thought about opening a file on Monsieur Queuille, the French prime minister, but he's not a real red, just a Radical. "Vs" aren't too hot either. I've got a few Van thingmies, but Dutch communists don't do anything of note.'

'What about Mr. Voznesensky?' suggested Wendy helpfully.

Lucy stretched out for a recent cutting from the *New York Times* and passed it over. 'I doubt I'll be adding much to Voznesensky's file, except an obituary notice.'

Wendy skimmed through the report, which detailed the purge of Zhdanov's faction. 'I must agree, Lucy. Mr. V's for the high jump. But at least you have a "Z", this Zhdanov chap.'

Lucy shook her head. 'Dead, drink, last August.' Hunching forward, she lowered her voice into a conspiratorial whisper. 'Actually, I do have another "Z" on file, namely ex-King Zog of Albania.'

'Really? I thought the European Communism Section dealt with active reds, not out-of-work monarchs.'

'Well, it does. But I reckoned it would be nice to introduce a spot of glamour into this grey decade, by keeping a file on European royalty. It's in the CPV.'

'What on earth's the CPV?'

Standing, Lucy beckoned Wendy over, and pointed at the bottom drawer of a filing cabinet. 'What does it say on the label there?'

Hitching her skirt, Wendy lowered her tall body into a crouch. '"Communist Party of the Vatican",' she read out, giggling. 'Well, that should be sufficiently underutilised to cater for your kings and queens.'

'Open it, it's unlocked.'

'Heavens!' said Wendy, after complying. 'Is this all Jack's booze?'

'Jack's only responsible for the brandy. The scotch is Fay's, and the Empire sherry is mine. So could you pass it up, please? I fancy a drink.'

Eve yawned into the mouthpiece of her phone. She let Eaton witter on, until finally he came to the point. 'Yes, Rupert, they're absolutely identical. So in your chosen role of Herod, you'll be seeing double, and, of course, paying double too. After all, it's not every day you can enjoy "the Dance of the Fourteen Veils".'

Ending the call, Eve returned to her lounge, and placed a gin and tonic before her guest. Eyes sparkling, Sandra had a sip, slipped off her shoes, and tucked her long legs behind her in the armchair.

'Is Jack still away?'

'Apparently, Eve.'

Retreating to her sofa, Eve stretched out on it. She picked up the report she'd been reading earlier, and then glanced at its author. 'Interesting,' she pronounced, stringing out the word. 'Have you noticed the date Jack's mother died?'

Sandra nodded.

'This stuff about Louise Grainger's first husband is also noteworthy.' Eve's brows rose above her smile. 'Mind you, when I think of those pics of her in the calendar, I still find it hard to accept that Louise was once a talented scientist.'

Sandra ignored this subject in favour of another. 'Did Janice find out anything from nosing around Fay's youthful haunts?'

'Yes, she did. Janice talked to a bloke, who was still living next door to where Fay and her father resided in the late twenties. Since he was badly disfigured in the Great War, the poor bastard tended to hide himself away. But his room overlooked Fay's bedroom, so he saw her quite a lot.'

'So she'd have been fifteen or sixteen then.'

'That's right, Sandra. Yet, according to this bloke, she looked a good deal older, particularly when she dolled herself up to go out. Apparently, she had loads of different outfits.'

'At fifteen? So who paid for all that?'

'Possibly, it was Daddy, even though he was now ostensibly bankrupt. Or perhaps Fay had another daddy, of the sugary sort.'

'Perhaps she was simply on the fiddle at work, Eve.'

'I doubt embezzlement is Fay's style.'

'So where do you think she got the money for all these clothes at such a young age?'

'Perhaps she was on the game.'

Sandra pulled a face. 'Eve, I appreciate that you've got no time for Fay, but what evidence have you got for an accusation like that? Or are you just going to say "intuition"?'

Eve shrugged. She was sure the crippled former soldier knew much more than he'd told Janice, and she intended visiting him sometime.

'Eve, how much of this have you told Barber?'

'The short answer is nothing. Well, we don't really know anything yet, do we? As I've said before, Sandra, we're just looking for whatever's there.' She reached out for her glass. 'Still, it wouldn't hurt to stir things up a teensy bit, now that Jessica and Rita are back in London.'

25

MONDAY 20 JUNE 1949

The sweating and itching were bound to get worse. Crushing out her latest cigarette, Rita Prior forced spittle into her dry mouth, and then drank greedily from the glass of water. Twice she'd been to the loo. They'd made no objection, except to insist that the Amazonian figure they called Brenda should accompany her. Not that there was anything to witness, other than a genuine call of nature, since her stuff was all in the flat. And Rita had been but yards from her front door and the needed fix, when the kidnappers had swooped.

A woman looking like a charlady approached her in the Putney side street, flashing a card. At the same time, an exotically-dressed redhead twisted her arm behind her back. Then a car had rolled towards them with both nearside doors already open.

Having bundled Rita into the rear seat, next to Sandra, Janice Marlow hopped in to make it a squashed threesome. The 'char' scrambled into the front. Norma Atkins was still hauling the door to, when Delilah Delaney hit the accelerator, and the vehicle hurtled along back streets in response to Sandra's calm directions.

They were into Sussex before Rita spoke, to inquire timidly about their destination. Smiling, Sandra lifted the tissue bag from her lap and proffered its contents. Rita took a jelly baby and sucked in silence. Unlike Norma, who screamed unashamedly and crossed herself according to both rites, when Delilah overtook a bus on a blind bend.

Eventually, they screeched to a halt in the driveway of Eaton's rural retreat.

'What took you so long?' carped the redhead in the immaculate black outfit, when she yanked open the rear door. 'My directions were all right, weren't they?'

'Eve, we'd be in bloody Berkshire by now, if I'd followed those.' Smiling smugly, Sandra scalped a white jelly baby. 'Luckily, I had a map.'

'You read a map?' Eve hoisted her brows in homage.

Alighting from the car, Sandra beckoned Rita to follow. 'Where to?'

'Put our guest in the rocking horse room.'

'*That* rocking horse?'

Eve nodded. 'But today I'm more interested in Trojan Horses.'

Fay Galbraith caught sight of Vic Welles eyeing her table, as he paid at the canteen till. The flaccid wave of a huge hand, and a finger brushing against his military moustache, failed to conjure up the coveted aura of heartiness. Such foundered upon the intense set of his angular frame and the gloom in his watery eyes. When he towered into her presence, Fay manufactured an acceptable, but determinedly unflirtatious smile.

'All right if I join you?' asked Welles, already lowering his tray and newspaper onto the grimy tabletop.

'Of course, Vic, but I'm just off.' Fay took another nibble of her sandwich to hasten this prospect.

'Seen *The Times* today?' he inquired, as he allocated two dishes of overcooked and now tepid nosh to their places.

'Haven't had a chance. I've been writing reports all morning, while this afternoon I'll be ploughing through our allocation of FO incoming telegrams.'

He folded back the paper to the page he required and passed it to her. 'What do you make of that report from Budapest, dead-lined yesterday?'

Fay scanned the appropriate column, and learned that the Hungarian Interior Ministry had announced the detention of László Rajk and others by the state security authorities. The ideological milieu, which had spawned Rajk and his 'accomplices' in an alleged 'espionage gang', was described as 'Trotskyism, Fascism, Zionism and anti-Semitism.'

She handed the paper back to Welles, her lips bunched for sarcasm. 'What do I make of it, Vic? Well, the equation of Trotskyism with Fascism is hardly new. However, this novel juxtaposition of Zionism and anti-Semitism is quite breathtaking. So, with that array of sins already laid against him, and with a large dollop of "Titoism" doubtless to be added to the charge-list, I can only conclude that Stalin must really want Rajk's neck.'

'Hell! You certainly don't give Uncle Joe any quarter, do you?'

'And how much mercy do you think that avuncular assassin will show to Rajk and his co-accused?'

'"Royk",' echoed Welles tentatively. 'Is that how you pronounce it? I thought it would be like "Reich", as in "Third Reich".'

'So it was originally. Rajk's ancestors were Saxons living in Transylvania, when that province was part of Greater Hungary. Then there would have been an acute accent on the "a" of Rajk to produce something like the "Reich" sound. However, plain and unadulterated Rajk sounds more Magyar.'

His fork mashed a questionable carrot into the lukewarm stew, which had already formed a wrinkly skin across its surface. 'Are you working on Rajk for Horner?'

'He's one of several jobs we have on just now. Actually, Jack wrote a good profile of Rajk before he went abroad. But, now Rajk is likely to go on trial, Horner will want an update.

Luckily, the old sod's not in until Thursday, so I won't have to produce it in five minutes flat.'

Welles stared at her as keenly as his morose eyes would permit. 'Any idea where Jack is?'

'I have no idea whatsoever.' Her clipped syllables and snappish tone were sufficiently foreclosing of the matter for even Welles to absorb.

'What about Rajk's arrest? No smoke without fire, do you think?'

'Oh, there'll be plenty of fire, Vic. There always is following trials for witchcraft.'

Welles pursed his protruding lips at this caustic response. Then he opened them in piscine manner to receive a forkful of sludge from his plate. Next he switched subjects. 'Did you get my letter in Paris?'

Nodding, Fay bit into an apple.

'So what do you think?'

Her frown of incomprehension caused the dreaded tread of small crows' feet to stamp their ineluctable presence around her eyes.

'Don't you remember, Fay? I mentioned Horner's file on ex-CPers working here.'

His voice level hadn't dropped one iota. It was as if he assumed that his crude phrase for former Party members was sufficiently esoteric to thwart any eavesdroppers.

Fay glanced around. The nearest occupied table was about thirty feet away, but she still lowered her voice. Her now almost husky timbre masked her irritation too. 'So Horner has a file. So what? So he knows I was once in the Party. Again, so what? It doesn't seem to have worried him overmuch, does it? He hasn't sacked me, or you, or Leo Ikin, has he?'

'Or Jack,' said Welles, as though suggesting an item to be added to a shopping list.

'Did Jack ever tell you he was in the Party?'

'No, Fay, he's never admitted it to me, but….'

'Well, there you are.'

He pared the fat from a chunk of meat and poked the residual sliver of flesh into his mouth. 'Are you saying Jack was never in the Party?'

'Why not ask him when he comes back? Not that you'll get an answer.'

'Do you think he'll be back?'

'Not a doubt in my mind.' Fay bit off the last flesh from her apple, and digested it before speaking again. 'Jack's like the proverbial bad penny, he'll turn up.'

Welles chewed lugubriously upon his latest mouthful. 'Fay, should you feel at a loose end, I'll.... Well, you know.'

She veiled any shudder with a coy twist of her shoulders. 'That's awfully sweet of you, Vic, but Oliver's at home right now.'

'What if he goes away?'

'I daresay Jack will be back by then.' Fay rose to her feet. 'Anyway, enjoy the rest of your lunch, Vic. That bread pudding looks simply divine.'

Her cigarettes were finished, so she nibbled her nails. Her head hurt, her skin was puffy and blotched, and her eyes sore and dark-ringed. Now she was seeing double, but only because both twins were present. Rita focused upon the one astride the huge rocking horse, who was jabbering animatedly in German to her sister. The latter cavorted on the floor beneath a tiger-skin rug, holding the beast's bared fangs inches from her face.

Rita scratched frenziedly at her matted black hair. The itching and the sweating were getting worse. She knew this whole matter somehow concerned her dead stepbrother, and would involve Jessica too. The boss redhead had promised to supply her with a fix, but only after Rita told them about Herbert Pilling.

The twins were now gabbling in Italian, a language that usually soothed her ears. But, today her ears itched and, just as Eve anticipated, the Delaneys were driving her nuts. Unsteadily, Rita rose to her feet.

'*Basta!*' she screamed in a hoarse voice.

The twin under the tiger-skin told her sibling to summon Eve. The rocking twin conveyed this order to Brenda, who simply bawled down the corridor. Soon the boss-woman marched in, accompanied by the leggy blonde. The other women trooped out.

Lips curving in a callous smile, Eve again indicated the 'prize' Rita would earn for cooperation. Having emptied the clogged ashtray, she sat, lit a cigarette, and pushed the pack across the table. With trembling hands, Rita too lit up, and gazed desperately at the 'prize'. Then she confronted Eve's piercing eyes.

'Rita, did Jessica ever microfilm documents for Herbert?'

Confirmation came through an abject nod of her head.

'What do you know about the characters who supplied him with these documents?'

'Nothing,' she whispered.

'So how did it work between Herbert, you, and Jessica?'

Rita brushed at a tear, and then scratched at her shoulder. 'Herbert would simply contact me out of the blue, whenever he had some stuff to be filmed. Then he'd bring his material to Jessica's studio.'

'Did Herbert always bring over a lot of stuff?'

'No. Usually, there was very little.'

'But at other times?'

'Well, on occasion he'd produce piles of documents, which had to be returned to their source next morning. So Jessica would be microfilming virtually all night.'

Eve glanced ostentatiously at the 'prize'. 'And, at the end of these sessions, Herbert would hand over your supplies, wouldn't he, Rita?'

Tears streaming down her cheeks, she nodded limply.

'Rita, didn't you have any pangs of conscience about what you did?'

'A few, I suppose, at first.' She drew smoke deep into her lungs. 'But, Jessica and Herbert said that, by helping the Soviet Union, we were fighting for world peace.'

'Has anybody tried to make fresh contact with you and Jessica since Herbert's death?'

Rita shook her head and Eve accepted her denial. All links to Pilling would have been shut down in the wake of his death, while investigations into its cause and consequences were under way.

'Why did you agree to get involved, Rita?'

'I did it for Herbert. We were very close. As for Jessica, I suppose she did it for me.'

Dropping off Rita near to Jessica's flat, the women in the car watched the slender addict draw her coat tightly around her body and scurry across the road.

'I guess you're wondering what I'm up to.'

Declining the bait, Sandra decapitated a yellow jelly baby and then popped the torso into her mouth.

'As things stand, Sandra, I can do them for drugs, or porn, or espionage. I could even nail Jessica for all three, if I felt vindictive. And, very soon, she'll be receiving that particular message loud and clear from Rita, my Trojan Horsey.'

'What then, Eve?'

'We'll see how they run.'

26

SATURDAY 9 JULY 1949

Their meal finished, Horner sipped some *Saint Emilion.* He stared at his guest, who had said barely a word since arriving, and then placed the wineglass upon his dining table. Reaching for a decanter of malt whisky, he poured two generous measures.

'Is there a reason for your virtual silence, Stern?'

Eyes narrowing, Max cracked his knuckles. 'Stevie, you wrote me about needing to talk over some problem. So, if there's something on your mind, I reckon it's your call.'

Following a perfunctory nod, Horner layered both hands beneath his chin. 'Stern, I wish to resolve certain matters concerning Randall.'

'That being so, Stevie, first off, we gotta talk terms. If you wanna know about Jackie, it's gonna cost you that Rosetti hanging back of your head. Ship it out to my place, like you done wit' the Millet. So you got till I finish my whisky to say yes, or I'm outta here.'

'Very well, Stern, my Rosetti for your wisdom.'

Max hoisted his glass, and then loosened his collar and tie. 'For openers, Stevie, I gotta question to you. You heard the name Noel Field? You gotta file on the guy?'

Horner swilled some malt around his dentures. This brief act of reflection inspired no positive response from his memory. 'I confess that this name is quite unknown to me, Stern. Are you perchance offering to sell me your own file upon this Field character?'

Max countered with a taut smile. 'There ain't no file, Stevie. So, when I talk about Field, write it down. And, if you got some questions, could be I got some answers.'

Quitting the table, Horner opened a drawer and withdrew from it a pad and a selection of sharply-pointed pencils. Resuming his seat, he lowered the level of his drink by half.

'Stern, what happened to Randall in Paris?'

'Jackie met a guy called Csillag.'

'Chill-log,' echoed Horner. 'Is that Hungarian?'

'Yeah, Stevie, it's Hungarian for star.'

'While Stern is the German word for star, as I recall.'

'Is that a fact?'

'What did Csillag do with Randall?'

'He delivered him, Stevie.'

'In an easterly direction?'

'Now you mention it, yeah. Csillag's boys took Jackie to a little airfield east of Paris. Then some other guys took over.'

'Stern, what has this Field fellow to do with Randall?'

'Maybe nothing, maybe plenty.' Producing a Havana, Max let his stubby fingers work the cigar, and then lit it. 'Stevie, you sold me Jackie boy because you needed the dough. But why in hell did I buy him?'

The minutest hint of colour blushed the chalky complexion. 'I presume you had your reasons, Stern.'

'Quit bullshitting, Stevie, and grab yourself some sense!'

The grey eyes stared coldly from Horner's recomposed face. 'Stern, you purchased Randall, because you needed someone who might credibly be portrayed as a British agent.'

'That it? Do I have to draw you a diagram, Stevie?'

'No, Stern, you do not. Randall fitted particular specifications. He is a former member of the British Communist Party, who was expelled for the heinous sin of "Trotskyism". Moreover, during the post-war years he has served in the damning locations of Tito's Yugoslavia and Rajk's Hungary.'

Max rolled the cigar into the corner of his mouth. 'And so?'

'I presume that Randall will be implicated in some manner in the forthcoming trial of Rajk and his co-defendants.'

'So what's your problem, Stevie?'

'That should be obvious. Randall's entanglement in this charade will implicate my department in a diplomatic incident.'

Stern grinned. 'Maybe, just maybe, you're off the hook.'

'You will have to clarify that remark.'

'Now, supposing I tell you Noel Field disappeared in Prague early May. Supposing I tell you how back in wartime Switzerland, Field had dealings wit' the top guy in American intelligence in Basel.'

Horner drained his glass. 'You said that Field disappeared in Prague, so....'

'It ain't a long drive to Budapest, Stevie.'

'Has Field simply disappeared or has he been arrested?'

Max exhaled a cloud of smoke. 'Noel flew *Air France* Paris-Prague on May 5. He took a room in the Palace Hotel. On May 11 Noel goes somewhere in Prague. After that, ain't nobody seen him. Some weeks back, some guy paid off the hotel bill and took away Noel's things.'

'Stern, where on earth do you get all this information?'

'A lotta people owe me, Stevie, and a lotta people talk wit' me. I hear a lotta things.'

'So you deduce from this flood of information that Field is now under arrest in Hungary?'

'That's how I got it figured.'

Horner lifted the decanter and replenished their needs.

'So, Stern, given that Field can boast these superior qualifications, are you implying that the Russians will utilise him, rather than Randall, as the Western imperialist bogeyman in Rajk's trial?'

'Unless I miss my guess, Stevie, that's how it's gonna happen.'

Horner drank deeply from his glass. 'If the Russians now hold Field in their clutches, have they any further need of Randall?'

Smile-creases etched deeply into Stern's rugged face. 'It ain't sale or return, Stevie. Or maybe you wanna buy Jackie back, huh?'

'That was hardly my intention. Randall's reappearance at court would be somewhat embarrassing, to say the very least.'

'So you ain't worried none about Jackie's welfare?'

'Stern, my sole concern is with my department's welfare. I washed my hands of Randall in Paris.'

'Still washing?' asked Max, lips locked around his cigar. The eyes gazing through wisps of smoke were as wintry as Horner's own.

'Is Randall definitely in Hungary?'

'Stevie, the only definites I know is death and taxes. Hell, who knows where Jackie is? I figure Hungary, but I can't say for sure.' He sank the remains of his malt. 'I got things to do, Stevie. I'm back here in a month. We can talk more then. And, case you're wondering, the Rosetti only covers you today.' Standing, Max stabbed a finger towards another painting. '*Az idő pénz*. Time means money, pal. So don't sell the Waterhouse.'

Ignoring the lift, she climbed the stairs. On the penultimate landing, she paused and glanced towards Jessica

Deacon's unlit apartment. Smiling smugly, Eve mounted the final flight.

The door to the top floor flat was held ajar by a tall, wiry man in his fifties, clad in faded cords and blue shirt. The once legendary hair of 'Red Freddie' was now a white peak above a tanned and vital face.

'Greetings, my lord.'

'Oh, Eve, do call me Freddie,' he drawled, as he ushered her inside. 'Lovely to see you and your gorgeous red mane. Makes me quite envious. Moreover, I really must apologise for fixing our appointment for this late hour, and thereby depriving you of your beauty sleep.'

'Freddie, my innate beauty does not depend upon sleep,' retorted Eve haughtily. 'But, regarding the late hour, and speaking as a specialist in compromising situations, I imagine your wife is away tonight.'

Smiling artfully, he shepherded her into the lounge. 'She's in the country.'

Lowering herself onto the settee, Eve smoothed her green skirt. Then she glanced at the peer, who was hovering by a cabinet stocked with bottles.

'Eve, you said on the telephone that this had something to do with Jessica.' The foxy eyes twinkled. 'Has she been a naughty girl?'

'Very naughty, Freddie.'

'Oh, what fun! I do like naughty girls.'

Eve parried with a tight smile. Their meeting was already heading in the direction she'd anticipated. Freddie was feeling frolicsome, just as he'd been when they had met officially for dinner. But she'd have to play along, since she suspected he held the best cards.

'Drink, Eve?'

Needing to be frisky at least, she requested a whisky. Freddie placed their drinks upon a low table near the settee, and then sat next to her. Eve sampled her scotch. When she sat back, she took the opportunity to layer one bare leg over the other. Her raised hem she left unadjusted.

'You really do have superb legs, Eve.'

She inclined her head slightly. After all, there was a genuine compliment there, whatever the ulterior motives. She took another sip from her glass, set it down, and riveted her eyes to his face.

'Jessica and Rita left for France yesterday, Freddie.'

'Yes, I know. A friend has lent them her place in Normandy.' His gaze was shrewd. 'I take it you've had them under surveillance.'

Nodding, she slid cigarettes from a pocket and lit one. 'Of late, Jessica's been terribly busy. She's visited her bank, her lawyer, her publisher, and even an estate agent. She also made three trips to her studio, each time driving home with several boxes of material. And a kind neighbour helped her unload the car upon each occasion, didn't he?'

His latest smile was laboured and fell shy of his eyes. 'Manners maketh man, Eve. I hate to see women struggling.'

Eve blew a stream of smoke from her lips. 'Freddie, I hope those boxes weren't full of official documents that were to be microfilmed.'

'Good God! You're serious, aren't you?'

She widened her eyes for effect. 'Well, if it was simply a matter of drugs and porn, it wouldn't involve DOSS, would it?'

'Is this all official?' he inquired gravely.

'Not yet,' she bluffed. 'Anyway, what was in those boxes Jessica left in your care?'

He stretched out for his drink and sipped it meditatively. 'Eve, there are no official documents in those boxes. The contents are exclusively photographs and personal material.'

Eve's satisfied look reflected the fact that all was still there to play for. She'd doubted that Jessica possessed any documents, while her own interest was in the photos. But, to avoid pressing too hard on this matter, she changed subjects again

'Is Jessica's flat hers to sell?'

'Yes, Eve, it is. It was left by her grandfather to her mother Daisy, and she, in turn, willed it to Jessica and her sisters. Later, Jessica bought out her sisters' shares.' He screwed up his face. 'However, I doubt she'll get the best price. It's at the wrong end of Belgravia.'

It still surpassed the right end of Shepherd's Bush, thought Eve.

'You rent your place as a *pied à terre* from Jessica's uncle, don't you, Freddie? So do you have any idea where Luke Randall is these days?'

He rewarded her evident knowledge of his affairs with a frown. 'I heard he was in Rhodesia, but that was some time ago.'

She crushed out her butt. 'So, with Jessica selling up and moving abroad, will it now be you who's in charge of making a mint from her porn?'

He sank the remains of his drink before replying. 'You're way off target, Eve. I prefer to do rather than to look, although I'm not averse to the latter. As for the financial side, well, Jessica was always too selective regarding her clientele. Certainly, she made money, but she could have made considerably more.'

Eve nodded understandingly, for she intended to make the most of such a business, once it came into her hands. 'Where are the boxes, Freddie?'

'Stowed away in my loft.'

'I'd very much like to see what's up there.'

The wily eyes narrowed. 'Now, have you got a search warrant?'

She shook her head. 'I've only pretended that my visit was official.'

'I was hoping for more than pretence, Eve.'

His amused expression prompted her into a hesitant smile, but when he stood, she followed him into the corridor. He hauled down the loft ladder, told her where to find the light switch, and warned her of the attic's dusty condition. This advice prompted Eve to slip off her jacket. She was hardly surprised when he flagrantly ogled her bust.

She stepped onto the ladder and felt his hand clutch her backside. Eve grimaced. How could she deal with a peer of the realm groping her bum, when she couldn't opt for her standard response? Barred from kneeing him in the balls, because he had something she desperately wanted, she plumped for dulcet tones.

'Freddie, that's naughty.'

'Yes, I know. But I find your contours most fetching.'

Eyes glinting unashamedly, he terminated his accolade with a slap to her rump, which spurred Eve to scale the ladder. Inside the loft she flipped through the contents of the cartons. Even such cursory inspection was enough. Intuition rewarded, and financial gain beckoning, she knew she must have the lot. Stepping back onto the ladder, she addressed Freddie below.

'What did Jessica say was going to happen to these boxes?'

'She said that somebody would collect them in the near future, Eve.'

'Well, perhaps that somebody could be me.'

'It could indeed. The collector's identity was left unspecified.'

'Thanks a lot, Freddie.'

'My pleasure, I'm sure, Eve.'

Catching the emphasis in his voice, she postponed her descent.

'Surely, Eve, you'd agree that one good turn deserves another.'

'So whose turn is it?' she inquired fatalistically.

'Yours, Eve.'

She looked down, and was impressed by the unalloyed loohery monopolising his expression. Fuck! But she'd always known it would come to that. And why not? She'd done plenty of worse things. Fated to succumb to peer pressure, Eve began her descent.

27

THURSDAY 21 JULY 1949

Panting, Eve carted into her flat the final box of items from Jessica's archive. After humping it onto a table, she returned to the front door and slammed it shut.

Thank God, that was fucking over! She'd made six more visits to Freddie since that first occasion, because he'd only allowed her to get her hands on one box at a time. And, for that privilege, she'd been shafted in lordly fashion for nearly a fortnight. Anyway, that was enough meat to last her for.... Well, for a while at least.

Her hand dipped into the box, and emerged with the diary she'd noticed on her first trip to Freddie's loft. She flipped it open and read again its rather flamboyant title: '"Daisy Days": Being the Confidential Diaries of Cheltenham Solicitor Walter Alfred Finch.'

'Fay, did you ask Horner about Jack when you saw him?'

'I did, indeed, Lucy. And, for my pains, I got one of those arctic looks that almost give you frostbite.'

'Horner's covering up something,' asserted Lucy, extracting a file from a drawer. 'Jack's never been this late back. He's been away nearly two months now.'

'So have you heard the latest rumour?'

'The one about Jack defecting to the East?'

'I wonder who launched that canard,' mused Fay. 'I think my money would be on Vic Welles. Or maybe Horner's covering his back, in case something really has gone wrong.'

'I heard it from Sid,' said Lucy, settling behind her typewriter. 'But I still reckon something's happened to Jack.'

'Well, in the meantime, something's happened to Traicho Kostov,' announced Fay busily. Putting on the specs she used for reading, she opened that day's *Times* and read aloud the report from Sofia announcing Kostov's arrest.

Plucking a powder compact from her handbag, Lucy examined her face in its mirror. 'That looks like another one for the high jump. Luckily, I've got plenty of "Ks".'

Radiating optimism, Eve spoke as she paced around her lounge.

'Look, Gwen, Europe will soon boom. Once the German powerhouse starts driving the European economy again, living standards will rise, and people will buy gadgets like Hoovers, fridges and washing machines. Now, although these labour-saving devices will give the masses much more leisure-time, many people just won't know what to do with it. So, such fripperies as pornography will help to fill the vacuum in their lives, while the suppliers can make a mint. All clear now?'

Gwen Chambers swigged from her glass, and then eyed her boss warily. 'So we're going into Europe, are we?'

'Exactly, Gwen.' Settling upon the sofa, Eve crossed her legs and flicked the hem of a cobalt skirt over her knee. 'Now that we've got control of Jessica's stock and outlets, we'll be ready to meet demand. For now we keep going small-scale, but when the time is right, we'll switch to mass production and growth.' An uncompromising expression to her face, Eve stared, in turn, at the other two women. 'But, until I say it's time for expansion, everything stays under lock and key, and I mean *everything*. Understood?'

Effacing her shifty look, Gwen swallowed the last of her drink. 'Eve, you said there was something special for me to do.'

Eve pointed at a cardboard box. 'That contains some old photographic plates, which once belonged to a man called Walter Finch. See if you can get anything from them.'

'I'll do my best.'

Hoisting the carton, Gwen struggled towards the front door. Eve accompanied her, and a few minutes later returned to the lounge.

'So who's Walter Finch?' inquired Sandra.

'He was a solicitor and amateur photographer, who wooed Daisy Deacon after she was widowed. He later left his entire estate to Daisy's daughter, Jessica. I've got his diary too. It mentions a relationship between Luke Randall and a woman called Eleanor Vere.'

'What sort of relationship?'

'That's what we'll need to find out,' said Eve, picking up a package. 'Now, before I forget, Sandra, give the twins these snaps. Gwen took them during their fine performance in number thirty-seven last month.'

Face succumbing to a frown, Sandra shook her head reproachfully. 'Eve, I can't believe you made the twins take their clothes off in front of that pervert.'

'For goodness sake, Sandra, nothing happened to them. Rupert just sat on his throne, watching them dance and unveil. In any case, why shouldn't I encourage the twins to use their talents to advance the cause of women in DOSS? It's high time someone else brought in some dosh.'

Striking a match, Barber bellowed Moon's name. The torrent of breath extinguished the flame. He lit another, coincident with the meek rap on his door.

'Here, Eric!'

Moon shuffled to attention in front of Arthur's desk.

Pipe steaming like a ship's funnel, Barber peered pugnaciously at his underling. 'That last report of yours makes for fascinating reading, Eric. Your spelling's bloody atrocious though, lad.'

'I never got much in the way of schoolin', guv.'

'Not to worry, lad. You weren't hired for your literary prowess.'

Moon's mournful face took on the elation of a patted bloodhound. 'No, sir. Fank you, sir.'

The lids slid down Barber's eyes, half-hooding them. 'I've heard whispers about one of Horner's lot, Eric. The word is that this lad, Jack Randall by name, has been absent from his post for nearly two months.'

'Done a runner, 'as 'e, guv?'

'Well, some say he's defected, while others say he's on a mission.'

'So what do we say, guv?'

'We say we'll find out about lots of things when we get inside DORA. And we will, Eric. I can feel it in my water.'

'Your water's never wrong, guv,' mumbled Moon, contorting his neck to view some upside-down photographs displayed upon the desk.

'Customs impounded yon mucky pictures,' explained Barber. 'That's Rupert Eaton, one of our respectable merchant bankers, Eric. Look at him, sitting on a throne, ogling yon lasses dancing in the altogether.'

Moon craned his neck further. 'Looks like twins, guv.'

'Aye, lad, they are. Now, why would nice little twins do summat like that?'

'Maybe they needs the money, guv.'

'Need the bloody money!' bawled Barber, damson blotches dappling his sanguine complexion.

Sniffing danger, Moon's bulbous nose reddened.

'Eric, they've no bloody business getting up to such tricks. My three lasses would never have dreamed of doing such things.'

That he hadn't the remotest inkling of his daughters' dreams was neither here nor there. High on hypocrisy, as well as family values, Arthur focused pallid eyes upon his shuffling minion, and then struck below the belt.

'What would you think of any lass of yours doing such things?'

Moon's nose beaconed. 'We don't 'ave no kids, guv.'

Barber tutted. 'Eric, why not take Maisie out for a real treat, and then….'

'Take 'er out?' moaned Moon. 'She ain't never bleedin' in, guv!'

28

SATURDAY 6 AUGUST 1949

Eve answered the door to her flat and gawped. Clutching roses and a magnum of champagne, 'Red Freddie' essayed a jaunty smile. It soon foundered upon the strain marking his haggard countenance.

Her face screwed up in irritation. 'How the hell did you find out my address?'

'From certain items in your shoulder bag,' he stammered. 'I noted it that last rapturous night.'

'You nosy old sod!'

'Eve, please, we must talk. For more than two weeks now, since I last saw you, I've hardly slept a wink.'

'Then take a pill.'

'Eve,' he whined desperately, 'I can't help it. I've never met a woman like you.'

The brows lifted slowly to crown her haughty stare. 'No, I don't suppose you have, Freddie. However, I've often met men like you.'

His head shook miserably. 'It's not like that now. Don't you understand? I need you.'

'Well, if I ever need you, Freddie, I'll let you know. But don't hold your breath.'

'Eve, how can you be so cruel?'

'Practice,' she retorted brusquely, slamming the door in his face.

His fists hammered upon it. 'You won't be able to keep me away,' he screamed. 'I'll be back every night.'

Pressing herself against a wall, Eve tended to believe his threat. A man who'd screwed her so seigneurially was quite capable of treating her flat as some peasant hovel, and battering on her door nightly. His shouts diminished in volume as he staggered down the stairwell. Relaxing her body, Eve strode purposefully towards the telephone.

Since Maisie was out, there was no rapid answer in the Moon household. When Eric eventually lifted the receiver, he informed Eve that he'd been cleaning out his tropical fish tanks. Drumming her nails, she tried to sound interested in the feeding habits of guppies. When Moon stopped in mid-sentence, like someone who'd simply run out of vocabulary, Eve took the opportunity to specify her needs. Her voice was set to coo-mode.

'Oh, Eric, could you and Phil do me another really big favour?'

Fastidiously, the diminutive colonel flicked a speck of dust from the sleeve of his uniform. Then he massaged a dab of sweat into his cropped blond hair, and glanced towards the swimming pool. Malenkov sat by its edge, paddling his feet, while Beria thrashed away at an esoteric version of the backstroke. Beyond the pool, Yuri Volkov spotted a pair of Beria's bodyguards. They shared a joke, as they patrolled the outer walls of the Black Sea villa. He'd counted twelve others, all shirt-sleeved arsenals.

Dragging himself from the pool, Beria floundered on its edge, water dripping from his podgy body. Baggy crimson trunks complemented the lobsterish shade of his skin. After patting himself dry, he looped the towel around his neck, and picked up his pistol.

'Where's your report, Volkov?'

'I placed it on what I took to be your desk, Comrade Marshal.'

Scratching at his sunburn, Beria waddled over to the crude but functional table, constructed in local style from planks and barrels. Resting his automatic upon its surface, he clipped on his pince-nez, grabbed an open bottle of *Khvanchkara* from a tub of ice, and filled a crystal goblet to its brim. Seating himself on a bench, he moved weapon and wine into near reach, and adjusted the position of the small, silver-framed portrait of Stalin. Shoving both telephones further back on his "desk", Beria opened the red file.

Malenkov materialised beside Yuri. His outdoor complexion was always incongruous amongst the ghostly masks displayed by courtiers haunting the Kremlin Palace. Now he was bronzed, save for some paler streaks, where excess flab had blocked the sun's rays. Eyes austere, he peered into the colonel's elfin face.

'How's the weather in Budapest, Volkov?'

'August is a very hot month in Hungary, Comrade Secretary.'

'Still, you're inside most of the time, are you not? It must be cool in the cells.'

'But there's still plenty of warm work to be done there, Comrade Secretary, in order to expose the treacherous and degenerate enemies of Comrade Stalin.'

Malenkov blinked at this impeccable response. Studying Yuri's sincere expression, he nodded approvingly.

'Now, hopefully, there'll be a place that's as hot as hell in a few weeks time.' Beria's intervention was followed by a long slurp from his glass. 'You take my meaning, Volkov?'

'I do, Comrade Marshal. And, given your inspirational leadership, I am certain that the test of our atomic bomb will be successful.'

'Well, if it's not, Volkov, it won't be through any lack of effort on my part. As long as there are no further technical hitches, the USSR will finally become a nuclear power on

Monday 29th August. The world will then be a very different place, Volkov.'

'Of that there can be no doubt, Comrade Marshal.'

Beria tilted back his balding head to relish the sun. 'So, after I've delivered the bomb into the grateful hands of our leader, whose star will be on the rise, comrades?'

Ignoring this preening, Malenkov fingered the fruit on a tree splayed against a baking, whitewashed wall. Twisting free a peach, he bit into its succulent flesh, flecks of which smeared his lips.

'That trial in Hungary, we've lost control of it, haven't we? Since that Field fellow appeared on the scene, the Boss and Abakumov have taken charge. Is that not so, Volkov?'

The colonel looked for guidance towards his superior.

Beria waved magnanimously. 'So speak up, Volkov. You're my man on the spot.'

'Well, the situation has certainly changed, Comrade Secretary,' Yuri replied carefully. 'By the time Randall was delivered to us at the end of May, Field had been in the hands of the AVH for more than a fortnight, and their cells in Budapest were overflowing with his Hungarian accomplices. And the AVH were working under the orders of Bielkin, Abakumov's man in south-eastern Europe.'

Malenkov's piggy eyes narrowed. 'Has Bielkin kept you informed of developments?'

'Yes, Comrade Secretary. However, matters have now extended far beyond my plans. You see, Field's contacts were exceptionally wide-ranging. Many men and women he knew are now important officials in the people's democracies. His links were not just with Hungarians, but with Poles, Czechs, and Germans too. Therefore, in the hunt for traitors, the net is being cast ever wider. Now there will be trials of persons I'd not even considered, and in states where I'd made no preparations.'

'It will be just like the 1930s here,' concluded Beria, thoughtfully cradling his wine. 'This political contagion will spread, until the Boss has drunk his fill of blood. So, since matters are now out of our hands, I suggest we stay out of this imbroglio.'

'I agree.' Settling into a wicker chair, Malenkov wiped at peach juice trickling down his chin. 'Let's just attend to matters here. And, if your test is successful, we'll have a divided Europe underpinned by the atomic might of two superpowers, ourselves and the Americans.'

Beria's cold green eyes now stared at Volkov. 'This might mean you're out of a job, colonel. No more jaunts to Paris to see your friend Stern.'

Malenkov buried his teeth in the peach. 'What I'd really like to know is this, Volkov. You suggest that an epidemic of trials will now break out all over Eastern Europe, because of this Field character. But, could we ourselves really have limited the number of trials?'

'If the situation had been left undisturbed, Comrade Secretary, it might have been possible. For example, Koçi Xoxe was a genuine "Titoist". He was literally Tito's man in Albania, while Enver Hoxha was ours. When Comrade Stalin excommunicated Tito, Hoxha used that authority to purge, try, and execute Xoxe. It was simply an old-fashioned Balkan knife-fight, which we could exploit for our own ends.'

'Bulgaria is another such case,' supplemented Beria. 'There was a battle for Dimitrov's crown and Kostov lost. Making him into a "Titoist" at his trial will require rather more artistry than our comrades in Sofia possess. But who cares? The world will lose little sleep over events in Albania and Bulgaria.'

Malenkov dislodged a lump of peach from his nostril. 'What about Hungary, Volkov? Whom did you intend to put on trial there, if this Field character hadn't helped promote Rajk to the post of chief "Titoist" and candidate for the gallows?'

Volkov glanced at Beria, who flicked assent with his eyelids.

'I also intended to bring Rajk to trial, Comrade Secretary, but by a different route.'

'Might I know more?'

Again Beria signalled permission.

'Well, Comrade Secretary, this Englishman Randall once had an affair with a woman called Karola Király, who worked in Rajk's Foreign Ministry. He may even be the father of her first child. It was intended to use their relationship as the foundation of an extensive conspiracy, ultimately embroiling Rajk.'

'That seems a little thin.'

'The Király woman had wide contacts both in Hungary and abroad,' countered Volkov, 'while Randall's background was ideal for our purposes.'

Malenkov managed a grudging nod. 'Were both interrogated?'

'Extensively,' confirmed the colonel. 'The AVH conducted inquiries on behalf of both Bielkin and myself.'

Beria's thick lips curled cynically. 'As a goodwill gesture, I agreed that both Randall and the Király woman could be integrated into the case against Rajk, which Bielkin and Abakumov were preparing. But events aborted this outcome.'

'Meaning what?'

'Tell him, Volkov.'

'The Király woman died during interrogation, Comrade Secretary.'

'I see.' Malenkov tossed away the peach stone. 'What about the Englishman, is he still alive?'

'Yes, Comrade Secretary. However, he will not feature in the trial of Rajk and his accomplices.'

'Why on earth not?'

Beria shook his head in response to Volkov's unspoken request for guidance. 'Sorry, Georgi Maximilianovich, but I have to keep the odd little secret, even from you.'

Scowling, Malenkov wiped his sticky fingers on his swimming trunks. 'So what are you going to do with the Englishman? Surely he's surplus to requirements, now that Field is hogging the limelight.'

'Exactly,' concurred Beria. 'As we've no further need of Mr Randall's services, we're going to dispose of him.' He drained his goblet and held it out to his subordinate. 'See to it, Volkov.'

29

SUNDAY 14 AUGUST 1949

Lugging a laden basket, they left Sandra's building, crossed the road, and pushed open the door set in a high wall. Then they descended the steps leading from the street down to Randall's sizeable garden.

'Are you sure we should be doing this, Eve?'

'Sandra, we're secret policewomen, we're allowed to trespass. Anyway, it's Sunday afternoon. There are no postmen, milkmen or paperboys around, the neighbours are away, and Jack has disappeared. So I doubt we'll be disturbed.' She drew her hand across a moist brow. 'And I don't fancy being caged in your flat on such a glorious day.'

Kicking off her shoes, Eve carefully selected a spot upon the smaller of two tufty lawns. Screened from the steps by shrubbery, it was also near to the shade offered by a tall laburnum, still dangling its spent racemes. Trampling flat the uncut grass, she whisked a blanket from the basket, flailed it like a matador's cape, and then spread it over the ground.

Sitting on the blanket, Eve drew her black skirt high up her thighs. She looked up as Sandra returned from wandering around the unkempt but colourful garden. Her arms folded, fingers tapping against her biceps, there was a noticeable frown to her face.

'So what's up with you? You look a bit twitchy.'

'I am, Eve.' Sandra too sat on the blanket, legs hooked to her side. 'Just after the twins left for Richmond, I got a call from Dad. Mother's not well, and he thinks I should see her. Well, you know we don't get on.'

'So why not pop over for a bit? You can take my car.'

Sandra made a face. 'I'll think about it.'

With deft movements, Eve coiled her thick hair away from her neck and pinned it up.

'By the way, Eve, did you know that some cowardly thugs attacked "Red Freddie" recently and put him in hospital?'

'Oh, the *poor* man!' exclaimed Eve in her sincerest voice.

Sandra's fidgety fingers plucked a copy of 'Nineteen Eighty-Four' from the basket. 'This new novel by George Orwell, that everyone's talking about, is it any good?'

'Let's say it's providing food for thought. Moreover, there are things in it which might catch on, like '"Room 101", "doublethink", and "thoughtcrime",' recited Eve. 'Then there's "Big Brother". Now, that might really catch on.'

Sandra uncorked a bottle of red wine. Filling two glasses, she passed one to Eve, who sipped this neglected elixir and pouted appreciatively.

'Hell, it's hot,' grumbled Sandra, tilting the brim of a straw hat further over her face.

'It's certainly too hot for clothes,' announced Eve. Unbuttoning her white silk blouse, she peeled it from her shoulders.

Sandra eyed her over the rim of her glass, envying the audacity. 'Don't you ever wear a bra, Eve?'

'Not since I rose from the ashes, Sandra. I don't need one, so I don't wear one. The same goes for all the other stuff restricting woman's freedom of movement. Besides that, my policy saves money, washing, and drawer space.'

Standing, Eve draped the blouse over the crown of a choysia. Then she wriggled out of her skirt and hooked it on a laburnum branch.

Sandra shook her head bemusedly. 'Eve, what on earth are you wearing, some stripper's G-string?'

'I call it a thong, Sandra. Claudio has made me a few. More freedom of movement,' she asserted, 'and I foresee a day when millions of women will be wearing them.'

'You're crazy,' said Sandra, downing the remains of her wine. 'Anyway, I've decided to visit mother. So can I have your car keys?'

Eve fished in her bag and passed them over. In return, Sandra handed Eve a key to the flat and her hat. Levering herself gracefully to her feet, she stood twirling the car keys.

'Well, I should be home in a few hours, while the twins are due back from Richmond Park about eight-thirty. Now, you'll be okay without me, won't you?'

'I expect so,' said Eve, adjusting the hat over her coiled hair. 'That is, unless Jack Randall chooses today, of all days, to return.'

Sandra smiled. 'Now, there's a thought.'

When Eve relaxed upon the blanket, Sandra turned towards the steps. Halfway up them, she glanced through a rare gap in the shrubbery and saw two long legs extend in turn, as Eve whipped off her thong and basked in the baking heat.

'Dash it all!' moaned Delphine Delaney in exasperation. She struggled into a sitting position, after sprawling across the pavement. 'I've broken the dratted heel of my shoe. I caught it in a gap in the paving.'

'Well, you can't walk like that,' said her sister, helping Delphine to her feet. 'Take the other one off too. Then we'll get a bus back, and you can change into another pair.'

'Oh, Delilah, I don't want to ruin your day. It will hardly be worth going out again. So I'll go back, and you go on.'

'Don't be so utterly silly, Delphine. What on earth would I do all by myself?'

Eve sank more wine, laid her book aside, and stared in the direction of Randall's front door. Springing to her feet, she doffed the straw hat, and ransacked her shoulder bag for the skeleton key that Eric had given her. Then she padded over to the doorway, and grinned at the antique lock.

Once inside, she checked Jack's post, before bounding up the stairs. Ignoring the kitchen, she stuck her nose into the spare bedroom and wrinkled it reprovingly. Mounting the stairs to the attic, her gaze fixed upon the large trunk wedged in a corner of the brightly-coloured room. She scampered across the floor, opened the chest, and rooted out a battered photo album.

'Cooey! Anyone in?' trilled Delphine. She turned towards her twin. 'I thought Eve was coming round.'

Closing the front door behind them, Delilah pointed at the black jacket hooked over a coat peg. 'That's Eve's. But her car's not here. She and Sandra must have gone for a drive.'

In their bedroom, Delphine pulled on another pair of shoes. Then she looked inquiringly at her sister. 'Shall we go out again?'

'No, it's far too hot.' With an inquiring look at her sister, Delilah suggested that they devote themselves to a pressing translation.

'Yes, let's do that. But we'll need the big dictionary, and it's up in the dovecot.'

'And to keep Sandra happy, Delphine, we'd better take a tray, and collect all the glasses and plates we've left up there.'

Eve leafed through the photographs in the album, most of which dated from Randall's childhood. Then she returned it to the chest. With access to Jack's flat guaranteed, she could examine things more fully later.

Turning, she inspected the paintings hanging on the walls. Fay's portrait incited a malevolent glare. Next to it was one of a younger Pam, which earned an appreciative gaze. She glanced at the portraits of Wendy, and then studied that of Pam again. The painting of Louise stimulated another lengthy review.

Reaching out for an empty gin bottle, Delilah peered habitually through the window and surveyed Randall's flat. Baby-blue eyes bulging, she seized the binoculars

'Gosh! Eve's in Jack's attic, and she hasn't got a stitch on.'

'Golly! What shall we do, Delilah?'

'We shall obey orders, Delphine. And Eve's strict instructions were to photograph everyone who entered Jack's flat.'

Following a final survey of her favoured paintings, Eve trotted down to the lounge to fix herself a drink. Carrying a large brandy into Jack's bedroom, she opened a glass door and strutted onto the balcony. Rapidly quaffing the Cognac, she set down the glass. Her amused eyes gazed over the tree-line at the dovecot. She wondered how the twins would have reacted to her current manifestation, had they been nestling on their perches, instead of rambling around Richmond Park.

Arms raised to the heavens, Eve saluted the blazing orb in the cerulean sky. The sun toasted her body. Her blood felt as hot as her skin, and her head nicely woozy from booze. She felt an almost primal urge to do something outrageous.

Examining her reflection in the glass door, she ran both hands extensively over her body. Then she spun around and swung a leg over the balcony's broad iron railing. Straddling the hot metal, Eve casually directed a hand between her legs.

Delilah lowered her binoculars. 'She seemed to enjoy that.'

'Perhaps she hasn't had her quota of men this week.' As if astounded by her own indelicacy, Delphine abruptly straightened her face. 'Delilah, do you think we're becoming utterly debauched and decadent? Nothing seems to shock us anymore.'

Delilah vacated her chair. 'I think we ought to toddle off somewhere, before Eve returns here.'

'So what shall we do with these films I've taken of Eve?'

Delilah responded with an evil grin. 'Well, what would Eve do?'

Delphine produced a carbon copy of her twin's expression. 'She'd just sit on them, in the belief that they might come in useful some time.'

'Exactly! In any case, we've only done what Eve ordered us to do. It's hardly our fault if we've no conception of her *grand dessin.* We can't see the big picture, can we?'

'"Big picture",' echoed Delphine. 'That's good. It's a much punchier translation than "grand design". It's the sort of neat phrase Eve would like.'

Delilah's gauzy brows rose. 'I expect she's invented it already.'

'And how was mother?'

'Don't ask,' snapped Sandra, unable to suppress a scowl. 'So what have you been up to in my absence?'

Rubbing at hot flesh beneath her blouse, Eve glanced up from the miscellany littering the kitchen table. 'I've been examining Jack's past.'

Sandra leant over Eve's shoulder. 'These photos and letters, where are they from?'

'They're from Jack's attic. I managed to lay my hand on a key, so I'll replace most things later. However, I'll be holding on to a very interesting letter, which he wrote to Pam as a teenager, but seemingly didn't send.' She pouted in frustration. 'You know, I'd really love to get hold of Jack Randall's file in DORA.'

'Why, Eve? What exactly has he done?'

'I don't know, but he's done something.'

'Everybody's done something,' retorted Sandra tartly. 'Look, Eve, we've opened files on Jack and all the ladies in his life, and in the final analysis what the hell have we got?'

'We've got background, connections, and relationships.'

'Eve, if it wasn't for the fact that your intuition has been right before, I'd say we've got sod all.'

'Oh, we've got something,' Eve insisted stubbornly. 'I'm just not sure what. But, I reckon Jack could greatly assist our inquiries, if ever he deigns to return.'

PART FOUR

RETURN TO SENDER

SEPTEMBER 1949

30

MONDAY 5 SEPTEMBER 1949

Donald McCloy scrutinised the photo on the ID, comparing its genial gaze to the hard, bronzed, and unshaven face confronting him in the foyer. When McCloy finally poked his pass towards him, the incomer snatched it from his hand. Then he nodded at Sid Yates.

'Nice holiday, Jack?' probed the other security guard. 'With that tan, it must've been good weather. So where've you been?'

'I've just come from France, Sid.'

Once Randall had entered the lift, both men dived for phones; McCloy to alert Horner, and Yates to brief Lucy Temple.

A gauche smile to her face, Fay was standing by Lucy's desk when he entered.

'Hello, stranger,' she said softly.

He greeted them both, and then lowered his rucksack to the floor.

'Some tan you've got there, Jack.'

'It's dried blood, Fay.'

'Oh, charming! You haven't changed, have you? So where the hell have you been?'

'Hungary.'

'Stop kidding!'

Shrugging, Randall hauled a bottle of VSOP Cognac from his rucksack and inserted it in the CPV. Then he faced the two women again. 'You'll find some phials of perfume in the side-pockets of my rucksack. I bought them on my outward trip. Just take what you fancy.' He rubbed his stubbled chin. 'I'm going to see Horner.'

Fay pursued him into the corridor and grabbed an arm. 'For God's sake, Jack, what's going on? You weren't really in Hungary, were you?'

He jerked his arm free. 'We'll discuss matters later, Fay. Right now, I need to talk with Horner.'

When he glimpsed Wendy approaching along the corridor, he halted by the stairs leading up to Horner's sanctum. Then both he and Fay looked up in response to the scream for help. Ursula Conrad's desperate face was just visible above the balustrade.

'Please, please, help! I think he's had a heart attack.'

Shoving past Jack, Fay pelted up the stairs, as did Wendy.

Barber slammed down the phone like an angler braining a fish. 'I've just had a very interesting call from DORA, Eric. It seems Jack Randall's turned up there, looking very lean and tanned.'

'So 'e ain't defecated then?'

'He may well have done.' Beaming broadly, Arthur picked at a blob of congealed egg yolk on his cardigan. 'Who knows what shit our Jack's in? But there's more, Eric. Poor Stephen Horner's had a heart attack.'

'There a connection, guv?'

'Who knows?' The pulpy lips pouted around his pipe. 'However, my informant said that Horner looked quite ghastly when he arrived at DORA this morning, and he was wearing the mandatory spats.'

'Been gamblin' then.'

'And perhaps losing, Eric, and losing very heavily.'

'So 'ow is 'e now?'

'Dead as the proverbial doornail, lad. And, now he's gone, DORA won't have a cat in hell's chance of surviving in its present form.'

Moon's rubescent nose twitched. 'We goin' in then, guv?'

'Oh, I should think so, lad. Happen I might have to do a bit of wheedling first.'

'Your specialty, guv. Well, one of 'em,' Moon added hastily.

The pipe puffed out forgiveness.

'So why send us in, guv, and not the opposition?'

'Because I'll make it perfectly plain, Eric, that this is a job for the small man, rather than one of the big firms. No fuss, no publicity, no glory-grabbing inefficiency.'

Dressed for departure, Lucy popped her head around his door. 'Jack, are you planning a night shift?'

Randall looked up drowsily from a pile of files and newspapers. 'I need to catch up on certain things.'

'I guessed as much. So I've left the CPV unlocked, in case you need to catch up on your boozing too.'

She sauntered over to his desk and lowered her head. 'Smell,' she ordered.

'Very nice, Lucy. Did I buy that?'

'Yes.' She kissed him lightly. 'Thanks very much.'

His surprised smile was overwhelmed by a firmer kiss. 'That one's to reward you for returning safely, and I hope you're glad to be back.'

The grey eyes narrowed. 'I fancy I'll soon be finding out.'

'You'll be okay,' she said gently, before kissing him again. She opened her eyes to catch sight of a bemused Fay in the doorway.

'Am I disturbing something?'

'No, nothing at all,' said Lucy brightly, sweeping her handbag off the desk. 'All yours, Mrs Galbraith. See you tomorrow, perhaps.'

Fay closed the door behind her. 'And I never knew.'

'Nor did I,' said Jack, a half-smile lingering on his lips.

Slinking over to the desk, Fay squeezed her hips between it and Jack's chair, and landed on his lap. 'Well, I want more than a kiss.'

'Perfume not enough for you?'

She brought her neck against his face. 'Like it?'

'Very much.'

'You've got good taste.'

'Except in women.'

'Don't try and charm me, Jack Randall.'

She nipped his lip with her teeth, and followed up this call for attention with a smother of mouth and tongue.

'Fay,' he said seriously, once they'd uncoupled, 'this really is not a good time.'

'Well, it nearly is, Jack, since Oliver will soon be off again, flogging tractors in foreign parts.'

'Fay, I need....'

'Listen! He's taking me shopping tomorrow, and on Wednesday and Thursday I'll be in and out of DORA. Then on Friday I'll be driving him to the airport.' Her fingers trailed around his throat. 'After that, I'm all yours, Jack, until next Tuesday when Oliver returns.'

'All mine,' he echoed laconically. 'So why did I only get one postcard during the time you were in France?'

'I was busy, Jack. Anyway, I'm sure you managed to fill the hole that my absence left in your life.' She enveloped his mouth again and then pulled back. 'Jack, I'm asking for a couple of nights in bed, not a lifetime commitment. Why behave like a man who's spent time in a monastic cell?'

'I have spent time in a cell, Fay.'

'With that tan? What sort of idiot, do you…?'

'The tan came in the last few weeks, after they let me out.'

Her eyes saucered. 'You were imprisoned in Hungary?'

'That's right.'

The expression in her eyes mellowed from disbelief to compassion. 'You poor lamb! You need a cuddle.'

He thwarted its execution by restraining her arms. 'Not now, Fay. I need to catch up on certain matters.'

She wafted a hand at the material littering his desk. 'Are you really going to plough through all that stuff?'

'Fay, until I bought *Le Monde* in Paris, my reading of late was restricted to the odd copy of *Szabad Nép*. And, as we both know, the Hungarian Communist Party daily is not exactly acclaimed for its full and frank coverage of the news.'

'But this desk-load of capitalist crap is?'

'Spare me, Fay!' he countered testily. 'I'll be using these sources to ferret out facts. I don't read anything for opinion, since I can make up my own mind. Once I've got the facts.'

'Okay, Jack, calm down.' She planted a teasing kiss upon his neck. 'So you want to be left alone, and I want….

'We'll talk on Friday, Fay.' Collapsing his thighs, he caught her before she fell. 'Now, out!'

She turned at the door. 'Nine months, Jack. We've got a lot of catching up to do.'

In the seedy Waterloo office, the phone jangled on his desk. Barber allowed it to ring while he methodically filled his pipe. Beaming at Moon, he prophesied that "Puss" was on the line. Eric gurgled a laugh, when Arthur used his pet name for the PUS or Permanent Undersecretary. This hapless official ostensibly supervised DOSS and its activities.

Arthur lit his cherrywood, bit tightly on its stem, and swivelled the bowl in an arc. Porky fingers gathered up the receiver. He spoke but twice before the other party rang off. Once to mutter confirmation of the blindingly obvious: 'I understand. I'll have full authority.' Later, to snarl a caveat: 'Well, we don't yet know if there's been any breach of security.'

In their secluded nook in the Waterloo pub, Sandra raised her glass. 'So, Jack's back.'

Eve nodded. 'Only Barber didn't tell me about Randall's return, Eric did. And, since Barber didn't put a tail on him, I did. Janice reported that he just went back to his flat. Now you and the twins can watch him again.'

'It will be my pleasure, Eve.' She sipped her gin thoughtfully. 'Do you want me to maintain the tail we've had on Fay, ever since her return from France?'

'I most certainly do, Sandra. And I want you to put one on Wendy Page as well, because we'll need our own entry-points into this case.'

'I'm not with you, Eve.'

'Sandra, right now, it seems that I'm being frozen out. Barber's going into DORA on a recce tomorrow, and he's taking with him just Eric and Christopher Pratt.'

'Pratt by name and prat by nature,' remarked Sandra snidely.

'Exactly. But, after they've done all the he-man stuff, it's possible that "Uncle Arthur" will remember the chief source of brainpower in his organisation. So, while we'll need to be patient, Sandra, we must also be ready to exploit any opportunity that arises.'

'Understood,' she replied, her face brightening. 'Eve, just think of all those lovely files we might find in DORA.'

Eve frowned. 'Let's hope there wasn't some instruction to destroy the juiciest ones, in the event of Horner's death.'

'You mean like Jack Randall's?'

'Just dying to get your hands on it, aren't you? Well, so am I.'

'Of course I'd love to get my hands on it.' Sandra stifled a snigger. 'You can have the file though.'

31

TUESDAY 6 SEPTEMBER 1949

Followed by his henchmen, Barber shambled up to the receptionist's booth in DORA and fumbled for his ID. When he finally produced it, she checked his name, as well as those of Moon and Pratt, against her register. Fabricating a plastic smile, she pressed the green buzzer.

When the entry door opened, the trio passed into the security foyer. Donald McCloy conducted a painstaking scrutiny of their IDs, and then printed their names on purple passes. Barber's head jerked minutely, and Moon and Pratt followed him into the lift.

Horner's deputy awaited its arrival at the third floor. Beckoning Barber to follow, Ifor Evans led the way to his office. Arthur stared unimpressed at the Impressionist prints dotted around lilac walls, doubting that either were official issue.

Evans seated himself behind an elegant walnut desk. Upon its surface lay a folder, from which he extracted a single sheet of paper. Looking up, he stared at the 'Dossboss' through beady eyes.

'I find these instructions from the PUS somewhat confusing, Barber. You have "full authority to initiate an investigation" into this department; while I'm to "afford you that degree of cooperation which is consonant with the security requirements of the Department of Research and Analysis".'

'Seems perfectly clear to me,' pronounced Arthur, slumping unbidden into an armchair, and pulling out his pipe.

'No smoking in this office,' Evans ordered brusquely. 'So, precisely what are you supposed to be investigating?'

'The financial affairs of DORA.'

Evans sneered. 'Since when has finance been your field, Barber?'

'Money matters are at the root of most of my concerns,' he mumbled tritely.

'Then you'd better speak with Leo Ikin, our finance officer.'

'Oh, I'll speak with anyone I want to, Evans.' Eyelids drooping to half-mast, Barber patted the pipe rhythmically against his palm. 'I'll be nosing around gently, lad, to see if things warrant a more robust investigation. If they don't, you'll never know I've been here.'

The pipe-patting ceased, and Arthur shoved his red face forward, lips jutting beneath the straggly moustache. 'But, if I'm impeded in any way, lad, then I'll be back mob-handed, and I'll tear this fucking place apart.'

When the door to Horner's office opened, Ursula Conrad's red-rimmed eyes swept a survey of the two men approaching her. An obese and tousled figure, trudging on elephantine feet, led the way. The other curbed his catlike tread, in order to remain a deferential pace behind his boss.

Greeting her with the mien of a mortician, Barber wrapped both hands consolingly around hers as he introduced himself and Pratt. Then he ushered Ursula into a seat alongside Horner's desk.

She stared in distress at the flower-filled vase she'd set before Horner's vacant throne. Then she turned her glistening eyes upon the duo, both of whom remained respectfully on their feet.

'My dear, I need to ask you a few questions,' said Arthur gently. 'Do you feel up to answering them?'

An apathetic nod followed her slight sniff.

Lumbering up to the desk, Arthur manoeuvred his legs between it and Horner's chair, and eased his bulging behind onto the seat. Having ordered Pratt to find an ashtray, he tugged out his cherrywood, and sent his other hand on a matchbox-hunt.

'Now, I'll do my best not to add to your obvious grief, my dear.'

Twining the soggy lace hanky around her finger like a shroud, Ursula sat immobile for several seconds, teetering upon the verge of fresh tears. Then she hauled herself from the brink. An upward thrust of a cleft chin tilted back her head, and her nose rose nobly.

'I am so sorry, Mr Barber. My emotions are still terribly raw. I worked very closely with Stephen for many years. I thank you sincerely for your consideration, but please feel free to pose your questions.'

'Well said, my dear. Now, part of my job is to investigate financial irregularities relating to this department.'

'That is what I feared.'

He masked any unseemly curiosity by clamping his teeth around the pipe's stem. Then he extracted it, and asked guilelessly what it was she'd feared.

'I had in mind the consequences of Stephen's gambling, Mr Barber. Although I have no doubt that he replaced his borrowings from his winnings, it is my opinion that Stephen should not have behaved as he did.'

Barber held a match above his pipe. Only when the tobacco glowed did he respond. 'I couldn't agree more. Whether or not Horner replaced the cash, his initial act constituted embezzlement of public funds.'

'I know,' she said meekly. 'But then we all knew in a way.'

'Well, once these tangled accounts have been sorted out, we'll have a clearer picture of what occurred. However, I can't guarantee that there won't be consequences.'

Her head shook contritely. 'I just wish I could atone in some way. I should have spoken up. I suppose I'm a prime case of misguided loyalty.'

Arthur puffed reassuringly. 'You probably could atone, my dear.'

She looked up, eyes glimpsing salvation. 'Just tell me how.'

'Well, it would save me a lot of time and effort, if you could point me in the direction of Horner's secrets. How he moved the money back and forth, that sort of thing.'

'For that sort of thing, Mr Barber, I fear that you will have to approach the Finance Section. I have no knowledge whatsoever of any such details. I simply shared in the general suspicion of wrongdoing.'

Barber frowned in frustration. 'So you have no secrets for me?'

'I didn't say that.'

His expression switched from thwarted to neutral, while Ursula stared at the flowers, as though inviting Horner's spectral guidance.

'I'm really not sure what I should do.'

'You should do nowt to impede my investigation,' he lectured. 'Now, I feel you want to tell me summat. Is that not so?'

Ursula met his eyes. 'I should have destroyed them. Stephen left me instructions to destroy everything, in the event of his death.'

'Everything?'

'Everything in his safe.'

Barber's bushy brows lifted, and then fell to fringe his eyes. He scowled at Pratt. Seated behind Ursula, he'd looked up from his notes, and begun fiddling with his bow-tie.

'Where is this safe, Miss Conrad?'

She gestured at the map of the USSR. 'Behind there.'

Obeying Arthur's curt order, Pratt approached the map. He rolled it up ineptly, and then unhooked it at the third attempt to reveal the gunmetal door of a wall safe.

'I presume you have the combination handy, my dear.'

She smiled eerily at the flowers. 'The eight numbers of the combination are derived from Stephen's date of birth, the 28th of November 1890.'

'Got that, lad?'

Perplexity shimmered in Pratt's sombre features. 'What comes after twenty-eight, sir?'

'One-one-one-eight-nine-zero,' he translated for the boy, whose slender body soon tensed over his task.

'I've got it open, sir.'

'So what's in there, lad?'

'A box file,' said Ursula, before Pratt could reply.

'You've looked through it?'

'Of course I have. After all, I was meant to destroy its contents.'

Head and pipe nodded in confirmation of this fact, tipping flakes of ash onto the desk. 'So why didn't you?'

'It just didn't seem the right thing to do.'

When Pratt placed the box file before him, Barber drummed a finger against its lid. 'So how would you adjudge what's in here, Miss Conrad?'

'That is not for me to say. All I can tell you is that there are several references to atomic weapons in there.'

Barber almost bit through his pipe. He relit it hastily, in order to hide his flabbergasted expression behind a mushroom cloud of his own. With the name 'Pandora' flitting through his thoughts, he opened the lid tentatively, and prised out Horner's slim file on Noel Field.

'I added that this morning,' said Ursula unbidden. 'I found it in my in-tray. I cannot imagine how it got there, but Stephen was reading it when he had his…, his….' She began bubbling again. 'Then, as I knelt beside him, he whispered, "I could say sorry, but it is such a little word". Those were his last words to me before….' Her own last words dissolved into a wail.

'Lad!' barked Barber. 'Take Miss Conrad to her room, find some lass to console her, make some tea, tell her….'

His litany faded into cluelessness, as he watched Pratt and Ursula stagger from the room, entwined like drunken lovers.

'What the hell's going on?' Arthur muttered.

To make room for his elbows, he shoved the vase of flowers to one side. Following this act of desecration, he thumped the debris from his pipe into the minute and now overfilled ashtray. Cursing all non-smokers, Barber released a raucous grunt as he levered himself to his feet. Grabbing the ashtray, he tottered over to the waste-bin.

He was about to tip out the crud, when he caught sight of the fivers. Arthur bent down, and was finally reduced to kneeling before Mammon. He pulled out six banknotes that were lying loose, plus four others still held in a wrapper. Numerous empty wrappers littered the bottom of the bin, each bearing the name of an American bank in Paris.

He smoothed out each one, and then deployed them over the carpet. Staring at them fixedly, he munched away at overhanging hairs of his moustache, before gathering them together. Groaning, he creaked by stages to his feet. Having caught his breath, Barber tramped back to the 'Pandora's Box' lying open on the desk.

'It's not often you telephone me at home, Fay.'

'Oliver's down the pub.' Her voice paused. 'Jack, have you heard of a man called Noel Field?'

Randall breathed out heavily. 'My interrogators in Hungary asked me several times if I knew a man of that name.

I didn't, unfortunately. It might have saved me a few beatings if I had. I've been scanning the press and TO telegrams for some sign of him, all to no avail.'

'You should have confided in me, Jack. I've got a file on Mr Field.'

'A file on Field?' His words crescendoed in astonishment. 'Fay, how long have you been keeping it, and more relevantly, why?'

'Oh, it's not my file, Jack. I purloined it from Horner's room yesterday, made a copy, and returned the original to Ursula's in-tray. I've only really had time to study it tonight. You'll find it very interesting.' Fay paused again to adjust the timbre of her voice. 'Naturally, I'll expect a most handsome reward for such assistance when we meet on Friday.'

Seated at his cluttered desk in Waterloo, Barber scowled at the occupant of the spare chair. 'You know Rupert Eaton, don't you, lad?'

'Yes, sir,' said Pratt, effecting a practised flick of the greased lock flopping over his brow. 'He's related to an aunt of mine.'

'Now, besides being Horner's banker, Rupert's a member of this card-school where Horner used to gamble, isn't he?'

'He's a very important member, sir.'

'Correct me if I'm wrong, but my understanding is that no cash changes hands at these poker sessions.'

'That's not quite right, sir,' said Pratt condescendingly. 'You see, all the regular players, the "Spats" as they're called, must bank with Rupert as a condition of membership. At the start of a session he specifies their "worth", based upon his knowledge of their total assets. Any "Spat" can then obtain chips up to their "worth", all guaranteed by Rupert. Later, when they cash in, Rupert notes gains and losses, and simply adjusts their accounts accordingly.'

'So nobody uses cash,' grumbled Barber.

Pratt contrived an indulgent smile. 'I hadn't quite finished my explanation, sir. Cash can indeed be brought in and exchanged for chips, but chips cannot later be redeemed for cash.'

'Interesting,' conceded Arthur. 'Any road, I've got a little job for you, lad.'

Eagerly, Pratt unscrewed his fountain pen.

'Now, Christopher, I want you to get onto Rupert. Tell him I want full, up-to-the-minute details of Horner's "worth", including what's in his current and deposit accounts, and any other accounts he might have held. I also want a full record of Horner's transactions over the last five years. In addition, I want to know of any occasions in this period when Horner purchased chips with cash, and how much these amounts were.'

Pratt peered at what he'd written and nibbled his lip. 'Sir, I really don't think that Rupert would agree to....'

'Oh, he will, lad.' Arthur lifted a sealed brown envelope from his desk and served it like a warrant into Pratt's hand. 'If he makes any difficulty, just say the magic word "twins", and tell him to look inside. Tell him too that it's only the first instalment.'

Pratt's lean face lengthened in perplexity. 'I'm not sure I understand what....'

'Just do what I tell you, lad.'

'Yes, sir.'

'Well, get weaving!' roared Barber.

'Now, sir? It's hardly a civilised hour to....'

'Lad, don't you come the old soldier with me.'

Leaping to his feet, Pratt grabbed his hat and dashed out of the door.

32

WEDNESDAY 7 SEPTEMBER 1949

Moon held open the car door as Barber clumsily alighted. When he stared down the street, his florid face darkened angrily.

'There's no keeping secrets in this bloody trade, is there?' he snarled to his minion. 'Who the hell let on to the opposition about all this?'

Barber stumped towards a stocky man lounging against a car parked near to DORA's entrance. Further up the street straggled the intruder's cohorts, plus a dozen uniformed Bobbies standing by their vehicles.

'You!' Arthur's outstretched finger pointed like a pistol at the interloper's head. 'What the hell are you doing here, Unwin?'

The Special Branch officer waved a hand dismissively in Arthur's direction. 'Clear off, Barber! We're just about to go in.'

'Oh, you are, are you? On whose authority, lad?'

'You know bloody well who,' snapped Terry Unwin, spreading a neatly typed memorandum upon the bonnet of his car.

Groping inside his blazer, Arthur tugged out his warrant, and thumped it down like a trump over the other document. 'So whose sodding signature is that, Unwin, eh? Eh?' He stroked his moustache, with what in a less ungainly man might have passed for panache. 'The powers-that-be know this is a job for the "Dossers", lad.'

Beard-shadow, like smudged charcoal, darkened Unwin's features from pronounced cheekbones to creamy shirt collar. It heightened the redness of his sneering lips. 'Barber, your bleeding mob couldn't crack a peanut, let alone a case like this.'

Bristling, Arthur eyed his rival like a blackbird homing in on a worm. 'How's your daughter, lad? Has she had the abortion yet? And the wife, does she still see the chief-superintendent?'

Fascinated, Moon observed how reserves of knowledge, aimed at vulnerability, could produce an effect every bit as devastating as his own combination punches. Following an involuntary but audible gasp, Unwin's neck shrank into his collar, as his shoulders hunched in humiliation.

'You'd be surprised at the things I can crack,' purred Barber, his vowels broad and menacing. 'Now, bugger off, off my patch!'

As Unwin retreated, Barber's ruddy face signalled victory; the yellow-fanged grin resembling a peach-slice set in red jelly. Then he pointed at the uniformed policemen.

'Eric, go and round up that lot. I could use a few more bodies.'

The receptionist's plastic smile melted into confusion, when she observed a posse of police striding behind the trio who'd entered so meekly the day before. She stared down at her three buzzers, bit her lip, and pressed amber for 'ambiguous'.

'Open up, lass,' commanded Arthur.

'I can't, sir. I've pressed amber, which means the security men must summon Mr Horner to the foyer before they can open the door.'

'Horner's done a Lazarus, has he?'

'Oh, silly me!' Her hands darted to her cheeks. 'I just can't get used to   Well, it's Mr Evans who'll be coming down to see you.'

'I'll be coming down on people too, lass. Mark my words.' Barber whipped out his paperwork, and directed her gaze towards the signature. 'Now, open up!'

'I just knew it would be this sort of day when the cat was sick,' blurted the flustered woman. She prodded the green buzzer timorously, as though it was booby-trapped.

When the foyer door creaked open, Arthur jabbed a fat finger at the senior cop, then at the receptionist, and then at the sole policewoman present. 'Nick her for obstruction and put her on reception. Then close the main door. Station two men there. No one allowed in or out. Rest of you follow me.'

With Eric to heel, Barber clumped into the foyer, where Sid Yates was on the phone. When Donald McCloy's powerful frame blocked progress towards the lift, Moon's nose twitched combatively.

'Out of the way, there's a good lad,' ordered Barber.

McCloy's response was to square his slabs of shoulders.

'Guv?' Moon's inflection of the word sufficed, given their longstanding relationship.

Unleashing Eric with a pugnacious nod, Arthur's lips pursed in approval as Moon swirled into action. A headbutt, right uppercut, and well-directed knee left McCloy prostrate. As three policemen lugged him away, the lift's doors opened, and Ifor Evans stepped primly from its confines.

'You've taken your time,' said Barber sharply, patting his pockets for matches.

'What on earth is going on? We've had an "amber alert".'

'Well, now it's the green light, lad.' He ushered Evans back into the lift, and unfurled his warrant. 'Read that. I'll be back in a tick.'

Bridling in silence, Evans ploughed through the bureaucratic jargon. However, the signature at the end sufficed to quell any protest. When the 'Dossboss' rejoined him in the lift, he returned the document.

'So who's in charge?'

Arthur kindled the cherrywood before replying. 'I am, Evans.'

'And what do I do?'

'First you can work the lift,' said Barber, expelling clouds of smoke into the confined space. 'Now, have you moved into Horner's room yet?'

'No, not yet.'

'Just as well, lad, it saves you having to move out.' He blew an acrid jet into the other's face. 'I'll be commandeering the boss's room, of course.'

When they reached the third floor, he ordered Evans to carry his briefcase. Having plodded up to Horner's room, Barber sprawled in the chair behind the desk, panting heavily.

'Stick my briefcase by the fireplace.'

Evans performed his latest chore. 'Will that be all, sir?'

'Nay, lad.' Baring tarnished teeth in a callous smile, he relit his pipe. 'Next, Evans, you can inform DORA's staff of the following: first, that my men will be in and out of their rooms; second, they may be called for interview; and last, they are not to leave the building until they receive the all clear. Got that?'

'Well, that should do wonders for morale,' responded Ifor in a soft, sardonic tone.

Arthur shrouded himself with a fresh smokescreen. 'They won't need their morale, Evans. The war's over, and time's been called on this relic of our finest hour as well.'

'So you'll be closing down DORA?'

'Well, it's long overdue for demolition, lad. But, my guess is that its assets will simply be divvied up between various ministries.'

'What about its debits?'

'Depends, Evans, upon who's an asset and who's a debit. Or to put it another way, lad, who's in the black column and who's in the red.'

'Those in the red column,' mused Ifor, 'must they still be marching to Moscow's music?'

'Not at all, lad. A man's past always interests me too, since it helps me understand his present.' The lids sagged over his eyes. 'You see, Evans, yesterday I came across a copy of a typed memo, dated August 1944 and signed by Horner. In it he recommended that five ex-communists in his employ should be dismissed.'

'I see.'

'But there weren't any names in the memo.' The hoods drooped further. 'Was your name one of the five, Evans?'

'Hardly,' the other replied disdainfully.

'So where do I find these five names?'

'The names are to be found in the original document. This was returned to Horner, with a notation that he need take no further action. It's in another file. I cleared his desk and cabinets of all compromising material on Monday evening.'

Barber's shaggy brows lifted in threatening fashion.

'Those were Horner's written instructions,' added Evans hastily. 'I have them on file. I can show them to you.'

'Why didn't you clear his safe of compromising material as well?'

'Which safe?'

Smiling knowingly over the virtues of divide and rule, Barber scoured the bowl of his expired pipe with a used matchstick. 'So, have you destroyed this document with the names of the five reds?'

'Of course not.'

'Can I assume, lad, that if they're still working here, you can put your hands on their personal files as well?'

'You can, indeed, assume that.'

The 'Dossboss' cowled his eyes once more. 'So what else have you got that I might want?'

Ifor's lips slipped into a supercilious smirk. 'Would Horner's file on the activities of your own organisation be of interest, Mr Barber?'

Arthur shoved the pipe into his tobacco pouch, 'Do you think I should see it?'

'That's not for me to say. However, I would personally adjudge this file to be decidedly compromising.'

The ballooning cheeks deflated when he audibly blew out air. 'So what do you want for the entire job lot, Ifor?'

'Transfer to a major ministry, promotion, secured pension rights.' Horner's erstwhile deputy paused for effect. 'I also want the guarantee of a knighthood within the next five years.'

First glazing his lips with a reptilian lick, Barber jammed the pipe between them. Peering beyond the flame of the circling match at the other's tense demeanour, he shammed a smile. 'It's a deal, Sir Ifor.'

Evans relaxed, his shoulders dipping and then straightening again, as though readied for the sword.

'I'll put matters into motion later, Ifor. Of course, it won't all happen overnight.'

'I hardly expect that. But as long as I have your word.'

'Oh, you have my word, lad.' Choosing an appropriate expletive, Barber enunciated it to himself. Then he looked up slyly. 'Now, what do you want for Horner's "Treasure Trove", Sir Ifor, a fucking peerage?'

Evans grimaced. 'Don't you think I looked for that too? If the damned thing exists, which I doubt, then I certainly haven't found it.'

Barber eyed Evans steadily for some moments. Then he hauled the cherrywood from his lips, and engaged in a jowl-jolting nod.

'Aye, you're probably right. Truth be told, I always reckoned it was a phantom too, just summat to spook the powers-that-be.'

Fortified by the contents of Horner's safe, plus the files supplied by Evans, Arthur swung briskly into action. Certain of DORA's employees were summoned to the new head's study.

Sid Yates was the first to stand before Horner's desk. Arthur tossed some readies onto its surface, flipped his wallet closed, and shoved it back inside his shiny blazer. 'That's a bonus, Sid, a token of my appreciation for some top-class whispering of late.'

'Thanks, Mr Barber.' Gathering up the notes, Sid's large eyes rounded inquiringly. 'Heard we're getting closed down, sir.'

'Just keep your eyes and ears open as usual, lad. I'll look after you. If I can't get you a transfer to some gossipy ministry, you can come and work for me.'

Jack, Fay, and Vic Welles were ordered to surrender their passports, and sent home under police escort to collect them. All three were given times at which they were to attend 'interviews'. Randall's was to be held first.

Leo Ikin was instructed to assemble all material pertaining to DORA's accounts, and present this to a team of Treasury investigators. His hipflask long emptied, his face ashen, he left DORA ringed by an entourage of towering coppers.

Lucy Temple learned that most of her filing cabinets were to be moved to Records Section, which was to be quarantined. She rescued the CPV, by sharing sentiments with a monarchist policeman. Together they flipped through her photos of European royalty, all the while quaffing toasts of Empire sherry.

33

THURSDAY 8 SEPTEMBER 1949

In a rare act of chivalry, Arthur chaperoned her from door to seat. Having loaded his bulk onto Horner's throne, his fat body squirmed into a semblance of comfort.

'Miss Conrad, you acted both wisely and correctly in not destroying the contents of Horner's safe. But, as you must realise, these matters are exceptionally hush-hush. Not a word to anyone.'

'Mr Barber, I would never dream of....'

'Miss Conrad, I'm reminding you of your responsibilities for one reason only. It's because I seek your assistance in interpreting the material contained in Horner's safe.'

She nodded in a collusive manner. 'I would be only too happy to help in any way that I can.'

'Thank you, my dear.' Florid face radiating satisfaction, he passed her an item from his file. 'Do you recognise the two men in the lacerated photo?'

She studied the faces. 'I'm sorry, but both are quite unknown to me.'

'Kindly turn the photograph over. Is that Horner's writing?'

'Oh, yes.' She gazed devotedly at the few words, as though they formed a sonnet. 'It was extremely individual.'

'I'm having problems reading Horner's handwriting, my dear. But, after all these years with him, I imagine you can transcribe it with ease.'

Ursula raised her eyes coyly at what sounded like a plea. 'That is indeed the case. Do you want a transcription? There is very little here. But if it should help in any way.'

'Would you, my dear?' He switched to a tone marrying gratitude and complicity. 'As a poor form of thanks, I can only say that the help you're affording me is absolutely vital to my investigation.'

Glowing extravagantly in the warmth of praise, she dropped her eyes and caught sight of a pristine sheet of paper, which he'd slid across the desk. Ursula reached into her handbag for a pen, studied the hieroglyphics on the reverse of the photo, and then speedily transcribed them into her own crabbed but legible hand.

Arthur asked her to read aloud what she'd written.

'Max Stern. Colonel Yuri Pavlovich Volkov. Paris, May nineteen forty-something. I'm afraid that the last digit was lost when the photograph was cut.'

'Don't worry about the date, Miss Conrad. But do you recognise the men's names printed there?'

'I have never heard of either one.'

'I see,' said Barber, not altogether surprised.

Ursula slid the photograph back across the desk, and received in return a scorecard of the Essex versus MCC match.

'Turn the scorecard over, Miss Conrad. Ignore the writing there, which isn't Horner's, but if you could interpret the rest.'

Ursula drew a line under her first transcription, and soon composed the second. 'All done,' she announced gaily.

Arthur gouged goo from his cherrywood, and ladled it into the huge ashtray he'd commandeered. 'There is a little more though. Would it be too much trouble to…?'

'Oh, just pass it over, you silly man.'

Again finger-powered, a menu glided across the desk. Hooking it into her possession, Ursula's eyes darted over it. Her lips pinched pruriently at the profligacy of the dishes

'It can only be expected of the French, such ostentatious displays of gluttony,'

'Hardly the fare to be found in our austere land,' he concurred. 'You'll find Horner's squiggles on the other side, my dear.'

Rapidly executing her task, she looked up brightly to ask if there was 'any more'. Nodding, Barber passed over Horner's speculative memorandum about an abortive Soviet nuclear test. The transcription of this completed, again she inquired if she could assist further. When Arthur shook his head, she prodded his offerings and her own handiwork towards him.

He studied her transcriptions, and then looked up. 'Miss Conrad, when Horner had his heart attack, was his safe open?'

Her eyes filmed. 'I believe it was, but everything was so….'

'Who came to your assistance at the time?'

'Fay Galbraith and Wendy Page rushed to my aid. Wendy telephoned for the ambulance, while Fay was dreadfully calm and collected. She loosened Stephen's collar and tie, and took his pulse. Although it was far too late to achieve anything, I was impressed by her attentiveness and efficiency.'

'Did Fay remain in attendance until the ambulance arrived?'

'Yes, she did. Wendy escorted me from the room, because I was so overcome. I was also afflicted by yet another dreadful migraine. So Fay was left alone with Stephen's body.'

Nodding commiseration, Arthur wrote a note to himself about the open safe and the temporary disappearance of the file on Noel Field, to which Ursula had alluded earlier. Then, puffing his cheeks thoughtfully, he switched to other matters.

'Miss Conrad, I'd like to confirm something for the record. The date on that Paris menu was 11th May. So was Horner in the French capital then?'

'Yes, Stephen was in Paris from 9th to 13th May.'

'Tell me, did Horner keep a diary?'

'Yes, he did,' she replied, giving way to a slight blush. 'It was not a real diary, Mr Barber; simply sporadic entries that he made over the years. I took it from his safe when I went through its contents. I wanted to establish whether it contained any personal entries.'

'I understand.'

'Thank you,' she whispered.

'Miss Conrad, is this diary handwritten?'

'No, it was typed by Stephen himself on random sheets of paper, which he then inserted into a binder.'

Relieved, he manipulated his tobacco pouch from a blazer pocket. 'Could you kindly bring Horner's diary to me?'

Rising to her feet, Ursula tested him with a smile. Barber bared some yellowed fangs in response. 'The connecting door to your office is locked, my dear, so you'll have to take the long way round.'

When she slipped through the main door into the corridor, Eric's nose popped round the jamb and sniffed inquiringly; unsure whether it should follow the scent.

'It's all right, lad, she's coming back.'

More Moon came into view, when he stoop-walked into the room, as though a leash attached his collar to Barber's beckoning finger.

'Eric, I want her kept at our country place until we've wrapped this thing up. Get on the blower and tell Eve to set it up. Then get back here.'

When Moon, buoyed by orders, disappeared, Arthur again studied the transcriptions made by Ursula. Then he copied her handiwork onto fresh sheets of paper, and inserted these into his thickening file.

On her return, Ursula placed Horner's diary before him. Barber motioned her to sit. Drawing fruitlessly on his pipe, he scratched his stubbly chin, producing a sound like sandpaper at work.

'On Tuesday, I came across a large number of wrappers from an American bank, Miss Conrad, plus fifty pounds in used fivers. The whole lot was in Horner's waste-bin, and I wondered how these items had got there.'

Her eyes moistened, but her expression verged on the incensed. 'After Stephen's body was removed on Monday afternoon, I went to his safe to deal with his secrets. There I found numerous wrappers that had once held great sums of money, all doubtless squandered at that wretched card table. I flung everything into the bin, because I hated to think of all that talent and service being sabotaged by his addiction.' She blinked away a film of tears. 'Later, I was overcome again, and I forgot that these wretched items were still in the waste-bin.'

'Was it your job to dispose of its contents?'

'Yes, for security reasons Stephen wanted it so. Normally, I would destroy whatever was there each evening.'

Rekindling his cherrywood, Barber nodded consolingly. 'Why did he leave fifty pounds behind, despite squandering the rest?'

'Living expenses!' she retorted acidly. 'He always had to have fifty pounds handy to see him through the day. Of course, that too was probably stolen, or "loaned" as Stephen would have it. That is why I threw the banknotes out as well. They defiled his memory.'

Arthur puffed to ten, allowing a pregnant pause before advancing his conclusions.

'Miss Conrad, since major elements of national security are involved in these matters we've discussed, it would be remiss of me not to be concerned about your own well-being.'

'You really think that I am endangered in...?'

He held up his pipe for silence. 'My dear, if I should err, then I intend to err upon the side of caution. So, until this investigation is concluded, some skilled ladies in my employ will be with you night and day in a secure place.' He dredged his mass from Horner's imposing chair. 'And I may need your help again.'

'If there is anything that....'

Her offer was drowned by the sort of piercing whistle used by dog owners. Immediately, the door snapped open.

'Guv?'

'Eric, fetch the lady's things and see her down to her escort. Then I want you back here.' With a grateful expression wreathing his ruddy face, he shepherded her into Moon's charge.

Lucy's room was unoccupied, since she was on leave that day. Randall opened the CPV and grabbed the Cognac he'd placed there on his return. He filled a glass, sat at her desk, and drank. He was pouring again, when Wendy entered the room. Clad in white blouse and charcoal skirt, she stood facing him, hands laced before her.

'Hello, Jack.'

'Hello, Wendy.'

Smiling warmly, she advanced around the desk, and eased her bottom onto its grainy surface. 'I wanted to talk to you on Monday, when I learned you were back. Then everything went haywire.'

'It still is, Wendy.'

Her expression projected both confusion and concern. 'Were you really in prison? Are you in trouble now? How can I help, Jack?'

He stared up at her questioning face, its attractiveness again marred by excessive make-up. 'Wendy, you can help me best by keeping far away from me. This is no time to flaunt our association.'

'But, Jack, I....'

'Just listen, Wendy. I'm being investigated by this bunch from DOSS. I can't tell you where it will all lead to, because

I'm not sure myself. And, while there's no reason for them to know about our affair, there is the small matter of your role in fiddling my expenses.'

'But those tracks are well-covered.' She beamed assurance towards his troubled expression, and then grasped his hand. 'Jack, can't we be together? There's nothing to hold us back now. I finished with Sam weeks ago.'

'Wendy, I'm flattered by your interest.' He gently squeezed her fingers. 'But, the fact remains that you'll have to do things my way, or else you'll be involved in matters you won't be able to handle.'

Her lips puffed sulkily. 'You'll be with Fay, won't you?'

'Yes, I'll be with Fay, because there are certain things between us that need settling.'

'You're not making much sense, Jack.'

'Good. The less you understand the better.'

More dandruff showered his shiny blazer, when he ploughed a palm through sparse wisps of sandy hair. Barber let his paw rest against the base of his skull, before planting it upon Pratt's report.

'So, lad, Horner's personal account was virtually empty in April. But, Rupert suspected that he'd indulge in his usual ploy of borrowing from DORA's assets to fund his gambling.'

'That's correct, sir,' conceded Pratt sheepishly.

'But, after he got back from Paris, Horner began to use cash.'

'Right again, sir. From May until late August, Horner purchased his chips exclusively with high value used Sterling notes. And when he settled his winnings, Rupert simply transferred the requisite funds from the losing players' accounts to boost the balance in Horner's own. It was from these increased assets that he paid off his so-called "loans".'

'So Horner was winning consistently throughout this period until Monday 29th August, when his luck turned.'

'Indeed, sir. That night, he apparently had no more cash with which to purchase chips. So he was forced to draw upon his "worth", which by then was substantial. However, from that point on, Horner lost very heavily.'

Arthur snaffled the pipe idling in an ashtray. 'Then Horner came back for more on the night of Sunday 4th September, didn't he?'

'He did, indeed, sir, and again he lost on a grand scale.'

'So how much cash did he have left at the end of that last session?'

Pratt glanced at his notes. 'Six pounds and seven shillings.'

'About what I've got in my account,' chortled Arthur. 'Well, no wonder our Stephen was looking green around the gills, when he arrived at DORA next day. He must have been just about ready for a heart attack.'

Pratt looked him in the pipe. 'But, in her written statement, Miss Conrad says the seizure occurred shortly after McCloy telephoned Horner to inform him of Randall's return.'

'True enough, lad,' said Barber, rummaging through his pockets on a matchbox hunt. 'But it was the gambling that brought it on.'

'Not Randall's reappearance?'

'Nay, lad.' He rubbed a bit of sleep from his eye. 'Horner would have wanted Jack back. He needed him to deliver his next load of secrets to the Russians. Conversely, Randall needed Horner to cover up his own treacherous activities. So Horner's death was certainly not in our Jack's interest.'

'I don't quite follow your train of thought, sir.'

The cherrywood nodded understandingly over the defects of a degree in Classics. 'That's because this job requires a very special way of thinking, lad.' He applied a seasoned light to the pipe. 'So did you have any trouble getting this stuff out of Rupert?'

'Not after I handed him that envelope you gave me, sir.'

'Worked like a charm, eh?' Arthur puffed away, a wily smile to his lips. 'Any road, it's time for me to start assembling the jigsaw, so get my file from the safe. I trust you can remember the new combination.'

'It's your date of birth, sir.'

'So the combination is?'

'22111892, sir.'

'Excellent, lad! You'd do well in the services, or prison perhaps, and you've no reason to forget my birthday card now.'

His smile strained, Pratt removed the map of the USSR, fiddled with the safe's combination, and then carted the file over to the desk.

'Now, lad, I've got something else for you to do.'

Pratt stared back keenly.

'Correct me if I'm wrong,' Barber dared, 'but isn't Rupert an MCC member?'

'Naturally, sir.'

Barber extracted the scorecard and a photo from his bulging file.

'Now, Christopher, I'm certain Horner was at Lord's for this match. So find out from Rupert and his chums, if they saw Horner talking to anyone special. If he was, then show them this enlargement of Max Stern's photo, and see if it rings any bells.'

Beaming maliciously, he pressed Stern's photo and a sealed brown envelope upon his reticent aide. 'If Rupert won't play, just hand that over, and say the magic word "pharaoh".'

Sandra Jansen eased herself onto Eve's desk. 'Has Barber got in touch with you yet? After all, you head the feminine side of DOSS.'

'Sandra, I think we're finally getting somewhere. "Uncle Arthur" rang, and invited me to attend Jack Randall's interrogation tomorrow, as an observer. He also wants to meet with me alone on Saturday.'

'Let's hope this means we'll see some files at last.' Sandra frowned thoughtfully. 'So what's Barber after, Eve? There must be a reason for him to question Jack.'

'I asked Eric the same thing. He said Jack was one of five employees in DORA, who used to be in the Communist Party. Something we ladies had discovered already, of course.'

'There must be more to it than that.'

'I reckon so too, Sandra. Perhaps I'll find out on Saturday where his train of thought is heading. Eric also told me that Barber was putting the blokes on Jack's tail. So make sure you and the twins don't bump into them in Ealing.'

'I'll see to it, Eve.'

'Anyway, at least he's got in touch with his feminine side, like you said.' She pouted approvingly. 'Nice little turn of phrase that, Sandra. Could catch on.'

34

FRIDAY 9 SEPTEMBER 1949

Brooding in pride of place, Arthur sprawled behind Horner's desk, a bulky file open before him. Lean face exuding zeal, Pratt sat to his left behind a table. As befitted a right-hand man, Moon covered Barber's other flank.

Randall sat at a low table positioned in front of the desk. Behind him loomed Phil Dove; a massive man, whose handsome face featured kindly brown eyes, and a luxuriant moustache he was wont to twiddle.

From the corner of his eye, Jack caught sight of thick red hair, when Eve slipped into the room and settled upon a chair to his left. She primped the navy jacket which she wore over a white blouse. Then she produced pen and pad from her shoulder bag. Turning towards Randall, she granted him a Delphic smile. Their eyes broke off contact when the 'Dossboss' spoke.

'You've been away, Mr Randall.'

'Yes, I've been away,' Jack confirmed.

'For how long?'

'I left for Paris on 28th May and returned here on 5th September.'

'Where were you in the intervening period?'

'I was in Hungary.'

'I see,' said Arthur equably, poking the pipe between his lips. 'So where did you get that nice tan, cavorting on Lake Balaton?'

'No, I was in Budapest and latterly Pécs.'

Barber flipped nonchalantly through Randall's passport. 'I can't find any recent visas for Hungary in here.'

'There aren't any.'

'Then how did you get there?'

Randall lit a cigarette. 'I think I flew.'

'And how did you get back?'

'I think I must have flown back as well.'

A sardonic smile flitted around the cherrywood's stem. 'Have you sprouted wings, Mr Randall?'

A chorus of laughter ensued from the others present. Randall waited for it to subside before replying.

'I had the impression that I was in an aeroplane. I was drugged.'

'So who drugged you, lad?'

'In Paris it was some Americans, I think, and in Hungary it was probably the Russians.'

'Now, why should they drug you?'

'In order to kidnap and return me with minimum fuss, I imagine.'

'Why should they kidnap you and take you to Hungary?'

'I'm not sure.'

Arthur lit his pipe flamboyantly. 'Have a guess, Jack.'

'Well, I suspect that I was to feature in a political trial.'

'In what capacity?'

'As a member of a British intelligence organisation, who'd served in both post-war Hungary and Tito's Yugoslavia.'

'Why should they want such a person?'

'To add a little credibility to their enterprise, and in this way convince the doubters.'

'So why aren't you on trial, Jack?'

'I think they found somebody more suitable.'

'Somebody more suitable,' Barber echoed derisively. 'Now, in what way was this more suitable person more suitable?'

'Well, this person is American, and he had a tenuous connection to the United States wartime intelligence agency, the OSS.'

'So what's the name of this mystery man?'

'Noel Field.'

'Have you met this Field character?'

'No. But, when I was imprisoned in Budapest, my interrogators asked me the same question, whether I'd met Noel Field.'

Barber blew out a contemptuous cloud of smoke. 'Jack, lad, you don't much look as though you've been in prison.'

'I know. But I got the tan later, along with food to fatten me up and medical attention for my injuries. This was after they decided to return me to the public world.' He stubbed his cigarette. 'Those going on trial in Budapest will look normal too. They can hardly display publicly men who can barely stand, because their feet have been beaten to pulp by frequent "solings". The Hungarians call it that. It's a refinement of the old Turkish torture.'

'So who performed this alleged torture?'

'The Hungarian secret police, the AVH, did the dirty work, but under Soviet supervision. It's Stalin's show though, designed to demonstrate to the satellite parties the consequences of disobedience and nationalism. Those in the dock will just be surrogates. It's Tito and his so-called "national communist" heresy that will really be on trial.'

A finger brushed sternly across Barber's unkempt moustache. 'Let's leave the power politics, lad. I'm only a humble policeman.' He kneaded his ill-shaven chin. 'Now, you claim you were tortured, Jack, but in what way?'

'I took a few "solings", together with the occasional beating from their heavies. Then there was the constant electric light in the cells, plus petty interruptions by the warders every few minutes. This was all intended to continually disrupt your sleep, on the rare occasions you actually got any.'

'I know all about sleep deprivation, lad. I've got three daughters.'

When Arthur extracted the pipe to chortle, Eric gurgled, and Pratt produced a copycat chuckle.

Remaining poker-faced, Jack lit another cigarette, and then added for the record, 'I was also deprived of warmth, soap, clean clothes, liquids, food, fresh air, natural light.'

Barber jammed the pipe between his teeth. 'So what was all this alleged ill-treatment designed to achieve?'

'Well, the ultimate aim of the torturers and interrogators is to remould you, so that you're ready to say anything they demand. They make you write your "autobiography", on which they question you intensively. They later work some of these details into the script of a trial. Some of these facts are true, of course, but, as they're overlaid with so many lies, the end product, the show trial, is also a lie.'

'Communists lying, that's hardly news, lad.'

'It's bad news for the victims though. In the final analysis, you have a bunch of committed communists, many of whom endured torture and imprisonment at the hands of the previous regime, publicly confessing that their entire lives have been a lie. That must be the ultimate torture for them; a total negation of their dedication and sacrifices.'

Barber's ruddy face creased with hostility. 'I'm sure you know far more about what makes a communist tick than any of us, lad. But, why don't these fellows simply renounce their confessions when they come to court?'

'I imagine that the main reason for such behaviour is the question of hostages.'

'Hostages?'

'People react differently to torture. Some crack at once, others after a time, and some not at all. At least, they don't break because of the torture of their own bodies. But, if there's a threat to use these methods on someone's mother, wife, or child, then even the strongest might cave in and collude with their torturers.'

Barber prodded a finger behind his soiled shirt collar to scratch an itch. 'So why did they go from "soling" to sunbathing in your case?'

'I've already told you. I think they decided that this man Noel Field fitted the bill better, and that I was surplus to requirements. After the first three weeks or so, they left me alone in my cell. Then in late June, by my calculations, they moved me to a villa in the Buda hills, where I was allowed to recuperate both in and out of doors. Later, I was transferred to Pécs, in the south of the country, for more restoration work.'

'So how did you get back, lad?'

'Well, on 3rd September, I think it was, I had a meal in Pécs. Soon afterwards I felt woozy. I presume they'd drugged my food. Then someone stuck a needle in me.' Pausing, he ground out his cigarette. 'I woke up in an empty warehouse. My rucksack was by me. My passport and money were in my pockets. Once I'd got out of the warehouse, I saw the Eiffel Tower. I walked for a bit, and then I caught a bus to the *Gare du Nord*. From there I travelled home by train and boat. Once I arrived in London, I came straight here.'

'Just dying to get back to work, eh, Jack?'

'I was looking for some answers.'

'Who from?'

'From Horner.'

'So what did you think when you learned that he was dead?'

The grey eyes iced over. 'My feelings were distinctly mixed.'

Barber turned another page of his file. 'Now, tell us what happened in Paris on 28th May, when you say some Americans drugged you.'

Randall proceeded to relate the events of that day, from alighting at the *Gare du Nord* to undergoing the hypodermic needle. When he'd finished, Barber glanced at his notes.

'If this lad Csillag was an American, why did he speak in Hungarian?'

'I imagine he was checking whether I knew the language.'

'He seemed very interested in your passport details,' asserted Arthur in an insinuating voice. 'It was as though he was expecting someone like you.'

'Meaning what?'

'Does Csillag mean anything in Hungarian?'

'It's the Hungarian word for "star".'

'And you'd never met Csillag before?'

'Never.'

Barber transformed his pouting lips into a mocking smile. 'Well, that'll do for now, lad. But I'll be calling you in again. Just stay away from here till then.' He wagged Jack's passport. 'I'll be keeping this.'

'I can go?'

'Certainly, lad. I've got no reason to detain you, have I?'

Pocketing his cigarettes, Randall headed for the door. Once it closed behind him, Barber lugged his bulk into a standing position, hitched the sagging waistband of his baggy trousers, and rounded on his aide.

'So what did you make of all that, lad?'

'I thought it was a quite fascinating tale, sir.'

The bushy brows shot up in despair. 'Lad, that's the talk of a tosser not a "Dosser",' he rasped.

Dropping his eyes, Pratt glared at the patterned socks exposed by his chief's half-masted trousers.

'Lad, Jack Randall's fascinating tale was a load of codswallop.'

'You mean he hasn't been in Hungary?'

'Oh, he's been east of the Iron Curtain, lad, but not as a prisoner. Moreover, I'm sure the Russians had good reasons to talk with him.'

'I don't quite follow, sir.'

'I'll explain later, lad, when I've fitted more pieces into the jigsaw.'

When Fay arrived that evening, Randall was in the garden. He was staring at the long grass of the smaller lawn, still curious as to why it was beaten down in parts. On reaching the foot of the stone stairs, Fay lowered her small suitcase.

'Thinking of mowing it?'

He responded with a robotic smile.

'Don't I get a kiss?'

'Perhaps later.'

'Jack, what the hell's wrong with you?'

'What the hell do you think?'

Fay bit back any retort. If she was going to extract information from him about Hungary and his 'interview', she would have to handle tactfully his current disposition.

'I'm going to get a scotch, and then I'll try to put you in a better mood.'

She picked up her case, and wandered down the path towards the front door. When she reappeared a few minutes later, Randall was not overly surprised that she was naked.

Her eyes widened appealingly. 'Have you no interest in me anymore?'

'Fay, it's been a long time since….'

'I'll help.'

He stared at her body. 'I've never seen you brown all over before.'

She shrugged, a candid smile to her lips. 'I've friends both in France and here, who own very secluded places.'

'I spent the summer in some very secluded places too, Fay.'

'Jack, I didn't know you were in prison,' she protested.

'No,' he thought bitterly, 'but it was you who put me there.'

Her eyes rounded above a suggestive smile. 'Can we go inside, Jack? I'm getting goose pimples.'

He followed the sensuous swing of tanned buttocks along the path, and then up the stairs. With every step, he felt a volatile mix of lust and anger boiling within him.

When they reached the landing, Fay grabbed his hand, and hauled him up to the attic. He resisted neither her kisses nor the hand pressing between his legs. Squirming from his hold, she stretched out along the made-up bed. Taunting eyes fixed upon his face, Fay fondled her breasts and squeezed the hardened nipples. Then she turned onto her front to flaunt the inviting cushions of her curvaceous bottom, and glared at him over her shoulder

'Think you can manage now?' she demanded.

Blood hot, rage cold, he tore off his shirt.

In the dovecot, Delphine trained her camera and Delilah raised her binoculars.

'Thank goodness they're getting straight down to things, Delilah, since there's only about an hour of decent light left.'

Delilah frowned. 'There's something wrong, Delphine. Jack's never like that with women. He seems angry, almost violent.'

When he rolled off her body, Fay pummelled his chest with her fists.

'That was hideous!' she shrieked. 'You used me like a receptacle, you bastard! I'm a woman, not just some fucking hole!'

Randall slumped onto his back. 'I warned you I'd been brutalised.'

Face warped with fury, she pushed onto one elbow. 'So, because of that, I deserve to be treated like some piece of meat, do I?'

She was right, but it was over now. His rage had left him with his seed. Yet he felt no need to apologise, for she'd betrayed him. Horner had orchestrated his ordeal, but it was Fay, however unwittingly, who'd set him up as the patsy. Pulling her face close to his, he spoke softly in an icy tone.

'Fay, in the last three months, I've had guns at my head and needles in my arm. AVH thugs have battered my feet, when they weren't just indulging in run of the mill brutality. I've been drugged and imprisoned. I've been used and betrayed.' His hold upon her face relaxed. 'Yes, I was rough with you just now, Fay, but if you're implying that I raped you, then phone the police. Right now, it's the least of my worries.'

Her expression had softened while he spoke. 'Okay, Jack, I get the drift.' Tentatively, she touched his shoulder. 'Do you think the fat man believed your tale about Hungary?'

'Probably not. But, all I could do was to provide rational and honest answers to his questions. I couldn't concoct a load of lies and evasions, even if I wanted to. The truth is hard enough to hold in my head.'

'In any case, you don't know what they know or what they're after.' Her fingers skirted around the hair on his chest. 'Perhaps I ought to have a word with Barber.'

'He'll be having a good few words with you at your "interview" next Wednesday. I wouldn't volunteer for an extra shift.'

'But, if I take the initiative, then perhaps....'

'Fay, don't assume that every man is a sucker for your charms.'

Returning his taut smile, she ran a palm over his stomach. 'I think you're in need of the soothing charms of a good woman.'

'And tomorrow my world will look totally different, I suppose,' he retorted acidly.

'The world looks different at every moment in time, Comrade Randall, given the dialectical nature of material reality.'

Not yet ready to confront her, he slowly shook his head. 'I sometimes wonder, Fay, whether you've really escaped from the thrall of that Marxist-Leninist crap.'

Fay made no answer. Instead, she relaxed on her back, eyes fixed upon his gaze. Opening wide her arms, she thrust out her breasts.

'Pillows to rest your weary head, my liege, arms to enfold your scarred body, and petals of hands to caress burdens from your brow. Can you refuse the healing powers of a good woman?'

He shook his head.

'You can cry too. I won't mind.'

Randall smiled sourly. What a luxury! If a man started crying all those saved-up, pent-up tears, he'd never know when they might cease.

35

SATURDAY 10 SEPTEMBER 1949

Seated behind the desk in Horner's room, Eve had perused Barber's file from beginning to end. Although riddled with elements of a latter-day Arthurian legend, his train of thought was obvious. Barber believed that he'd stumbled upon a ring of 'atom spies'.

Eve was not yet convinced of this, although her intuition had always suggested that both Fay and Randall had been 'up to something'. But if 'Uncle Arthur' believed, then she could certainly make-believe.

She conceded that the information he'd assembled had the makings of a case, which her own deeper knowledge of Jack and Fay could make even more tenable. And, given the time and resources she'd devoted to it, she was determined that it would be her case, and not his.

Slouching near the mantelpiece, Barber struck a match. Circling the flame above the pipe tobacco, he gulped in smoke. 'So what do you reckon, lass?'

'I think you're on to something, sir. But I'd like to go through it all once again, just in case I missed some important detail.'

'Go ahead, lass. There's a lot to take in. There's more to come as well, when I can find time to add the stuff from Horner's diary.'

Returning to the first page of the dossier, Eve studied Horner's speculative memo about an abortive A-bomb test in the Karakum Desert. Then she glanced at the photos of Beria and the tiny MGB officer, identified as Colonel Yuri Volkov. Next she inspected the lacerated photo of Volkov and Max Stern. Her brow creased lightly.

'Who's been cut out of this photo of Stern and Volkov, sir?'

'Who do you think, lass?'

'I imagine it was Horner, sir.'

His plausive paw patted the mantelshelf.

Eve turned to Ursula Conrad's rendition of what Horner had penned on the back of the scorecard, when noting the huge sums that he anticipated obtaining for 'photographs' and 'other details'.

'Horner wasn't playing for pennies, was he, sir?'

Arthur removed the cherrywood, allowing the droll words to ooze unhindered from his lips. 'Not a bad price for selling atomic secrets to our foes. The money he got must have funded a good few hands of poker at "Spats" exclusive gaming club.'

'So have you any idea, sir, how much was contained in those wrappers from the Yank bank in Paris, which you discovered in Horner's waste-bin?'

He shook his head.

Eve stared at the reverse side of the menu, where on 11th May Horner had written the instructions he was to give to Randall for making his later contact in Paris.

'This is rather damning, isn't it, sir? What Horner wrote here was confirmed word for word by Jack yesterday, when he described making contact with Csillag in Paris on 28th May. And, I presume we agree that the name Csillag is just an alias of Max Stern's.'

Barber nodded, the downturn of his mouth exaggerated like a clown's.

Next Eve pored over a report about an American WB-29 weather reconnaissance plane, which was patrolling in the Pacific on 3rd September. When east of the Kamchatka peninsula, the crew routinely exposed filter-papers sensitive to radioactivity. These showed levels twenty times above normal. They were now under study in laboratories, where they expected to discover fission isotopes. This would confirm that, very recently, the Soviets had detonated their first atomic bomb.

Eyes fixed upon the file, Eve attuned her thoughts to Barber's wavelength. Then she looked up to display a solemn mask. 'So helped by the likes of Horner and Randall, it seems the Russian cavemen have discovered fire.'

'Exactly, lass.' Clawing at an itchy armpit, he gazed at Eve shrewdly. 'And, sometime in the near future, HMG will need to produce an "atom spy" to assuage the wrath of Washington.'

'Presumably, sir, HMG would shower its gratitude upon any of its security agencies, which just happened to have an "atom spy" to hand.'

Grinning, he blew her a smoke-ring as reward. 'So tell me why you weren't convinced by Randall's tale.'

'Well, sir, although I thought Jack put on a brilliant display, there was one major problem with his account. Let's concede that this Field bloke was a more suitable Western agent to use in Rajk's trial. But why on earth should the Russians then release Randall? Why not just send him to a labour camp or bump him off? Why return him?'

'So what do you reckon about Fay Galbraith?'

A matter-of-fact tone cloaked her malice. 'I haven't the slightest doubt that Fay was also part of this ring transferring atomic secrets to the Russians.'

'I agree, lass. But I don't intend to arrest either Fay or Jack just yet. We're dealing with clever folk, Eve, who've served Moscow's cause both as Party members and Soviet agents. They won't just blurt out the truth. So we'll play cat and mouse a bit longer, slowly knocking them off balance, and letting them entrap themselves in their lies. In the final analysis though, we'll need their confessions.'

Head awhirl with machinations, Eve nodded. If there were confessions, then any gaps in the overall evidence would matter little, if at all. Moreover, she was convinced that she had a far better chance of getting a confession from a man like Randall than Barber ever had; while extracting one from Fay would be sheer pleasure. And, if she could pull the whole thing off, the credit would go to her section, and it would enhance her own status too.

Standing, Eve smoothed her black skirt. 'I can get confessions from them both, sir. But I'll need more resources.'

'And where do I find the money, lass?'

'Oh, that's easy, sir. You borrow Leo Ikin back from the Treasury investigators, and get him to turn Horner's contingency fund over to us. And, if there are any problems, you get Eric and Phil to have a little chat with Leo.'

'You've certainly been working your brains of late, lass.'

'Well, I was left with a lot of time to think.'

'All right, Eve, I take your point. I've neglected the feminine side of DOSS of late.' He dredged the pipe from his mouth. 'But, there's a problem with your plan, lass, because Ikin topped himself yesterday.'

'Oh, sod it! But what about the contingency fund, sir?'

'According to the Treasury, there was only a few hundred pounds in it, and they've grabbed that, of course.'

She gazed at him disbelievingly. 'Just a few hundred quid?'

'There's no way of disproving it, Eve. Evidently, DORA's accounts were a total mess. So they're abdicating all interest and sending them back to us. And if your lasses want to look them over, they'll be here soon. As for Horner's so-called "Treasure Trove", there's no sign of it anywhere. But his files are all next door, if you want to go through them.'

Eve covered her frustration with a moody pout. 'Is that all I get, after coming up with some ideas? You want me and my girls to act like a bunch of glorified clerks, do you, sir?'

He stared at her sulky expression. He'd never been able to handle the temperamental turns of his wife and daughters either.

'As I said, Eve, I've been neglecting your talents. So I'll make it up to you, and let you and your lasses run on a long leash in your investigations.'

Her voice withheld any trace of triumph when she thanked him.

'A long leash, lass, but just that.' His eyes peered coldly from beneath half-shuttering lids. 'You don't get *carte blanche*, Eve. I never give anyone a totally free hand.'

No, he wouldn't willingly grant her free rein. But did it matter? For as soon as the next attack on the independence of DOSS took place, Barber would need to man the barricades against the external bureaucratic enemy. This would leave him no time to peek over his shoulder at Eve's activities.

'I'm fully aware that I won't have a free hand, sir,' she said gravely, reinforcing her lie with a face frozen into a mask of obedience.

Seemingly reassured, he switched subjects. 'Incidentally, Eve, we've now got a pretty full picture of Horner's embezzlements from public funds.'

She tensed slightly. 'How did you manage that, sir?'

'Well, do you know the name Rupert Eaton?'

Holding his stare, Eve simulated a frown of recall. 'I think I've heard the name, sir. Banker, isn't he?'

'He was Horner's banker, lass.'

'Was he really?'

'Aye, lass, he was.' A broad grin compressing his pudgy face, he fiddled with the dormant pipe. 'But Rupert's managed to lay himself open to pressure.'

'What sort of pressure, sir?'

'Well, our Rupert's been showing himself off in mucky pictures. There was a big batch sent abroad, which Customs confiscated. An old colleague of mine sent them on to me, like he always does. You never know when they might come in handy, lass. All sorts of folk turn up in mucky pictures.'

Eve forced her posture to appear relaxed. 'Like who, sir?'

'Oh, we've had politicians, aristocrats, West End actresses.'

'Goodness me! So who's in these pictures with Eaton?'

Barber grimaced. 'They're not the sort of thing I'd show my wife, lass, but there's a selection in the envelope at the back of yon file. Take them for your records, Eve, I've got tons more.'

She found and opened the envelope. Flipping through the photos of herself in a crocodile mask, she was unable to suppress a sharp intake of breath.

'Eve, what makes a woman do things like that?'

'I really couldn't say, sir.'

Heaving his mass off the mantelpiece, he scooped up his file. 'Any road, lass, you've plenty to do. Just keep me informed of everything.'

'Of course, sir,' said Eve, lying through the teeth that her demure smile had exposed.

36

SUNDAY 11 SEPTEMBER 1949

As they passed the library in Ealing's Walpole Park, Fay glanced over her shoulder again. Striding through the main entrance, Phil Dove made no effort to remain unobserved.

'That huge fellow following us, Jack, is he one of Barber's creatures?'

'Yes, Fay, and so was the red-nosed man who trailed us to the *Odeon* cinema yesterday.'

'What the hell do they want?'

'Shall we turn around and ask?'

Shaking her head, she leant over railings surrounding a small pool and peered at the goldfish. 'Do they think we're planning to run away?'

His eyes narrowed. 'I've nowhere to run to, Fay. What about you?'

'You keep making these little digs, Jack.'

'Well, I hope you're getting the message.'

'What message?'

He produced a taut smile. 'Let's talk.'

Taking her hand, Randall led the way to a bench overlooking a pond. Screwing up his eyes against a watery sun, he undid his windcheater, and sat forward, hands clasped. Tugging off her beret, Fay shook out her hair.

'Fay, when they made me write my "autobiography" in Budapest, amongst other things I wrote about knowing you.'

Tearing some bread she'd brought with her, she tossed morsels to the clamouring ducks. 'Why did you do that?'

'Simply to avoid a beating. But, the point is that they already knew more about us than what I'd told them.'

Her attention switched from the birds to his face. 'But how?'

'That's a very good question, Fay.'

'So what are the very good answers, Jack?'

'Well, perhaps Horner told them. After all, Horner quite deliberately sent me on a mission which resulted in me getting locked up in Hungary. I wasn't just plucked at random from the streets of Paris. I was set up.' He lit two cigarettes and passed her one. 'However, there's a problem with that interpretation.'

She questioned solely with arched brows.

'Well, I don't think Horner knew about my relationship with your cousin Caroline. It was over and done with two years before I joined DORA.'

'They asked you about her too?'

'Yes, they did. So possibly Caroline told them about us. I know she was arrested during this purge that's going on in Hungary.'

Her eyes widened with shock. 'How do you know that?'

He stared at her unblinkingly. 'For now, Fay, you'll just have to accept that I know what I'm talking about.'

Turning away from his gaze, she drew deeply on her cigarette.

'Fay, did you talk to Caroline about us, when you saw her in Budapest in 1947?'

'Oh, I expect so. We had a lot to catch up on.'

'Have you had any contact with her since then?'

Flinging her cigarette away, she tore up more bread to serve the needs of a persistent duck. 'Jack, are you interrogating me?'

'I'm trying to answer some questions, Fay.' His gaze followed the smoke he exhaled, and then locked onto her profile. 'So, if you've had no contact with Caroline since May 1947, can you explain something?'

She dusted crumbs from her hands. 'Like what?'

'How did they know how I got this scar on my forearm?'

'They asked you about that too?'

'Yes, they did, to demonstrate that I wasn't being full and frank about my life story. I got a "soling" for that.'

'Good God!' Mortified, she looked away again, and ripped more bread into pieces. 'Well, Horner must have told them about the scar.'

'Horner would have known it existed from my passport details. But, I can't imagine he'd have ordered his minions to discover how it happened.'

She hurled bread towards some sparrows, which were being muscled out by the bigger birds. 'Then Caroline must have told them.'

He ground out the cigarette butt with his foot. 'Fay, I never told Caroline the story.'

'Well, perhaps I told Caroline.'

'When?'

'When we met in Budapest in May 1947.'

'And when did I tell you about the scar?'

She fashioned a tentative smile. 'When you were painting me.'

'Which was when?'

'Shortly before I went to Budapest.'

'Fay, if you'd posed naked in my attic, just before you went to Budapest, I'd have painted you as a mass of goose pimples, given how cold the winter of 1946–47 was.'

'So when did you paint me?'

'So unforgettable was it?'

'No,' she replied, a fond expression lighting her face.

'I painted your picture, when the model could make herself available, in July 1947.'

'But you told me the story before that, Jack. It was shortly after we resumed our relationship on 12th March 1947.' She gazed at him wide-eyed. 'I remember that date clearly, because it was the day President Truman announced his so-called doctrine.'

'There your chronology is perfect, Fay. But I told you about the scar in July 1947, which means you couldn't have mentioned it to Caroline in May.'

Her shoulders set obstinately. 'Well, I maintain that you told me the tale in March. Anyway, does it matter?'

'It certainly matters to me that this episode was known to the AVH and their Russian masters, Fay. It matters too that the *only* person to whom I've ever told the story is sitting right next to me.'

Her fixed smile faded before his ominous look.

'Fay, it was you who passed on that story about the scar, and much else about me as well. However, it no longer matters to me what you've been up to with the Russians. I'm not going to shop you, Fay, but nor am I going to protect you. I'll be too busy watching my own back.'

When she goggled at him open-mouthed, he rewarded her with a sardonic smile.

'Fay, for me your acting is all part of your allure. But, just because I'm charmed by it, don't assume that I'm also fooled by it.'

'Shall I just go home, Jack?'

'No. I'd like to enjoy you and your antics for the little time I've got left. What about you?'

Her arms circled his neck. 'Well, if we've got such little time left, Jack, why are we out here?'

The hospital room was curtained and dimly lit. Eve placed her flowers upon the bedside table. Pulling up a chair, she sat next to the bed, and took the patient's clammy hand in hers. The woman's head stirred in its cocoon of pillows. Eve's tentative smile provoked a surprisingly mettlesome grin from Ursula Conrad.

Only two days after arriving at the safe house in Surrey, Ursula had collapsed while enthusiastically playing Canasta with Janice and Norma. Later, it emerged that she'd suffered both 'migraines' and blackouts over the preceding weeks. The diagnosis was an inoperable brain tumour.

'How are you, Ursula?'

'Decidedly on the way out, my dear.'

'Well, I've been told not to plague you with questions.'

'Oh, stuff and nonsense! I shall soon be dealing with the biggest question of them all. So, if I still hold any information that would be of assistance to you, Eve, then I shall be only too pleased for you to prise it from me, to help atone for my sins.'

Eve swallowed the small lump that had risen to her throat. Gently, she compressed the hand she held before releasing it. 'Ursula, please take me through all the events surrounding Horner's death. I'd also like you to tell me about his so-called "Treasure Trove".'

As if to aid her powers of recall, Ursula squeezed her eyes shut before speaking again. 'Regarding the "Treasure Trove", Eve, I heard rumours of its existence. However, I saw no material in Stephen's possession which was worthy of this rather grandiose title.'

She reopened her eyes in time to catch a scowl of frustration, which Eve hastily converted into a banal grin.

'However, I now recollect certain things that might be of interest to you, Eve. So let us go back to that tragic and bewildering day when Stephen died. Now, not only can I confirm that his safe was definitely open, but I have since recalled that there was something missing from its contents. A few days previously, I had seen a red leather case in the safe; a case that I had never seen in his possession before.'

'Do you think it contained the "Treasure Trove"?'

'That is a possibility, Eve, but only that.' Her mouth puckered to underscore her point. 'Now let us turn to the events surrounding his death. As I have already related, when I entered his room Stephen was consulting his file on Noel Field. He looked distinctly poorly. Naturally, I was aware of his heart condition. Then his telephone rang. The call was from McCloy in the foyer, and it ended with Stephen muttering the words, "I see".'

'Referring to the fact that Jack Randall had just returned?'

'I imagine so. Then, shortly after putting down the receiver, Stephen clutched at his chest, pointed at his key ring, and then at a drawer of his desk. So I unlocked this drawer, and in it were a revolver, some bullets, and a bottle of pills. There was also a very ornate brass key there with a tag attached to it.'

Eve noted these details in a pad she'd slipped out of her shoulder bag. In Barber's report, there was no mention of a key.

'Presumably, he wanted you to get his pills.'

The pale lips smiled. 'Eve, in retrospect, I am unable to exclude the possibility that he simply wanted to put a bullet through his head.'

When Eve's eyes widened momentarily, Ursula grinned.

'But, let us return to the scene. Stephen now stood, gasping, and then he toppled to the floor. I leant over him, and he mumbled what proved to be his last words. Following that, I screamed over the balustrade for help. Fortunately, Fay and Wendy heard me and came running up. Then, while Wendy used the telephone on his desk to call an ambulance, Fay did her best to resuscitate Stephen. Of course, it was all in vain.'

'Was the desk drawer still open when Wendy telephoned?'

'It must have been. I certainly did not close it.'

Having already drawn her conclusions, Eve did not pause to ponder. Putting away her pad, she reached again for the other's hand and pressed it gently. 'Thanks very much, Ursula. That was really helpful.'

'That pleases me greatly.' She squashed Eve's fingers in turn. 'Now, let me see if I can be of further use. Tell me about the budget for the female section of your department?'

'It varies from minuscule to nonexistent,' remarked Eve drily.

'Just as I thought.' She nodded towards the bedside table. 'In that envelope, Eve, you will find a cheque made out to yourself. I hope that you will use it to help pay the salaries of the ladies in your employ. And, please, give a bonus to Janice and Norma, who were so kind and entertaining during my brief stay at your retreat.'

Spontaneously, Eve squeezed the hand she still held.

'Furthermore, I have instructed my lawyer to redraft my will. I was originally going to leave my entire estate to a cat's home. However, the bulk of it will now go to you, to help you and your ladies put the world to rights.'

'Poor pussies!' thought Eve, blinking away tears.

Randall sat on the side of his bed, and passed a scotch to Fay. She frowned as she took it. 'Jack, why do people torture other people?'

'Primarily to get information and confessions.'

'But why use torture?'

'For various reasons, I suppose. It can be very effective, as even the threat alone can work. It produces speedy results in most cases. Moreover, it's a versatile technique, Fay, since the torturer can normally find some variant of pain and fear to fit his victim's personality. Of course, there's no guarantee that the information given under torture is true. Many victims just say something to end the agony they are suffering.'

Her face screwed up in distaste. 'Do you think you have to be a special sort of person to be a torturer? I simply can't understand why someone would want to inflict deliberate pain upon a powerless stranger.'

He sipped from his glass before replying. 'It probably helps to be a sadist or some sort of psychopath, Fay. But, whether torturers are born or made, I don't know. However, you shouldn't overlook the perks of the job.'

'What do you mean?'

Slipping under the covers beside her, a cold smile drifted over his lips. 'Well, one of the AVH men talked to me after he'd finished his work.'

'He chatted with you after bashing you up?'

'That's right. He'd been up all night, while I'd hardly slept for days. He gave me cigarettes and coffee and talked to me.'

'What was he like?'

'He was a young man from western Hungary, and he spoke some German. He wasn't very bright, but he was a major in the AVH, and he earned far more than a professional person, let alone a worker or a peasant. He had access to special rations and a car, and to his mind, he was performing a necessary and worthwhile job.'

'Oh really?' she sneered.

'Well, let's face it, Fay, if the state sanctions torture, why shouldn't a young man take his chance to get on in life and prosper?'

'God, you sound almost sympathetic. Just a lad trying to get ahead, was he, Jack? Just happened to have chosen a rather deviant route, had he?'

'Fay, he was totally corrupted by his job. Torture has an entirely corrosive effect. Once you climb over the first moral hurdle that most of us cavil at, this act sets you apart from society. Hence the need for an *esprit de corps* with other torturers; men who understand your self-justification, and who not only won't condemn you, but will encourage you to go further in what you're doing.'

Her eyes slit with curiosity. 'Were there any women torturers?'

'Possibly, but I didn't encounter any. I suppose they're a rarity, like female murderers. We tend to think of men as the takers of life, and women as the makers of life.' His face screwed up reflectively. 'So, because she'd shatter such a stereotype, a woman torturer might be very effective, and certainly more chilling.'

The car pulled up by the isolated Sussex building. Eve leapt from it, slammed the door to, and marched up the cobbled path. She shoved open the main entrance, and passed through the dark hallway. Fists clenched, she transformed her irate expression into a mask of fury. Holding this guise, she burst into the beamed lounge to confront its occupants.

Rupert Eaton had draped a toga over his pinstriped suit, and a droopy laurel wreath sat askew upon his balding head. But his attempt at a stoic look buckled before Eve's wrathful gaze. Gwen Chambers too looked away.

'Greed I understand, initiative I applaud, but disobedience I will not tolerate,' pronounced Eve in a vitriolic voice. Hauling from her bag some of the photos she'd inherited from Barber, she held them up one by one for the edification of her cowering audience.

'Jumping the gun, were we? Trying to make a little on the side, were we? You knew these pics were intended for later release into identified niche markets. But, ignoring my express instructions, you decided to flood the general market with them now, didn't you?'

Setting the snaps aside, she paced up to the cringing banker, and brutally tweaked his nose until his eyes ran with tears. Then she turned towards Gwen. Grabbing her hair, she jerked her head to one side.

'It's bloody lucky that I have a distrustful nature, Gwen, and that Zoë and I were masked in those pictures. Otherwise, you'd have screwed up everything.' Glowering into the other's fearful eyes, she yanked the dark hair viciously. 'Have I got through to you, Gwen?'

'Yes, Eve,' she whimpered.

She turned back to Eaton. 'You've been identified and pressurised by my boss, Rupert. So I presume you told him all he wanted to know about Horner's accounts.'

'I thought it best to do so, Eve.'

'Well, since your information has made him happy, it's likely you'll be left in peace.' The green eyes glared anew. 'During these proceedings, Rupert, did you mention my name?'

'Of course not, Eve.'

Her thumb and forefinger clamped the tip of his still red nose. She waggled it from side-to-side as she spoke. 'Rupert, under no circumstances whatsoever will you dare mention your relationship with me.' Staring into his streaming but mesmerised eyes, she squeezed her message home. 'Is that completely understood?'

When he assented devotedly, she released him. A telling nod for the benefit of both offenders concluded her rebuke. Then, rubbing her hands together in mercantile fashion, Eve announced that it was time they got on with their planned project.

Still massaging his glowing nose, Eaton screwed up his face in confusion. 'What on earth is going on, Eve? You promised we'd do number eight on my list.'

'That's right,' she replied brightly. 'So where's the money?'

'I've brought the money, Eve, but you don't appear to have brought Zoë with you.'

'Zoë's otherwise engaged. Anyway, we don't need her.'

The banker lifted his anxious eyes to meet her direct stare. 'With respect, Eve, we do need Zoë. Magnificently formed though you are, you aren't sufficiently endowed to perform Zoë's role in number eight.'

'I know that,' she conceded good-naturedly, 'but Gwen is.'

The older woman gulped. 'Eve, I've never acted in my life. And who's going to take the photos, if I'm on the other side of the camera?'

'Gwen, you're a woman. This means you can act.' Focusing an icy gaze upon the photographer, Eve picked up her camera. 'Think of it as your first starring role, Gwen. Think of it as a chance to win back my trust. Think of it as a reminder never to cross me again.'

'And you'll be…?'

'Yes, I'll be snapping away, Gwen, and afterwards I'll get the films developed by a more secure source.'

37

MONDAY 12 SEPTEMBER 1949

Catching the sound of Arthur's shrill whistle, Moon shuffled into Horner's room, but failed to suppress a yawn. Repeated shifts of watching Jack's house were beginning to take their toll. Slouched behind the desk, the 'Dossboss' peered sternly at his lackey

'Eric, how much sleep have you had lately?'

'I'm okay, guv.'

'Well, mind you get your rest, lad. I need you in tip-top condition, and I'm sure Maisie does too.'

'Leave it out, guv.' Even his jug-handle ears were tinged scarlet. 'Please!'

'Eric, I'm only trying to....'

'You put it on the floor, guv,' said Moon, when Barber looked around bemusedly for the ringing phone.

With a fierce grunt, he leant precariously from his chair and clutched the receiver. Panting while he listened, he then found sufficient breath to gasp out some instructions before ringing off.

Moon waited for the heaving belly to still. 'Mrs G., guv?'

Nodding, Arthur rubbed his scaly palms together. 'She's invited herself around this afternoon, Eric. I reckon our Fay's beginning to crack.'

'She's in on it and all then?'

'Right up to her neck, lad. Still, it can't hurt to hear what she's got to say for herself.'

Fay mounted the stairs to the attic, and found him staring out of a dormer window. He turned when she spoke.

'Barber wants to see you again on Wednesday, Jack, just after my own interview.'

'Why did you ring him?'

She paced further into the room, and glanced at the photo of her cousin Caroline with her son. 'I rang him to arrange an informal chat. I decided that this would be in my own best interests. So I'm seeing him this afternoon. Then I'll be going home, Jack. I want to get a decent night's sleep before I pick up Oliver at the airport tomorrow.'

Her altered domestic arrangements left him unconcerned. He stared at her darkly for another reason. 'So what are you going to do, Fay, if you find out that Barber's got something on you?'

Her face hardened. 'In that eventuality, I'll take such measures as I deem appropriate. But there's no need for you to worry, Jack. Just concern yourself with your own problems.'

Eric opened the door for the lady. When Fay flashed him a cute smile of thanks, his nose shifted several shades to scarlet. Stepping past him into Horner's office, she found Arthur enthroned behind the huge desk, puffing regally on his pipe. Adjusting her thoughts, Fay gazed about the room, like a little girl transferred to the wonders of a Christmas grotto.

'Well, lass, what have you got to say to Uncle Arthur?'

Having fashioned her lips into a slightly anxious pout, her eyes latched onto his serpentine gaze. 'Can I come and sit next to you, uncle?'

'Of course you can, lass. Make yourself at home.'

Fay sauntered languidly towards the desk, the sway of her hips set near optimum. Holding Barber's gaze, she swung her bottom through an extravagant arc and eased it onto the desk. Planting one hand upon its surface, Fay thrust her bust towards the podgy figure behind it.

Barber converted his grave demeanour into one of indulgence. 'No point in sticking them in my face, lass. Wed nigh on thirty years and never strayed. Some marriages are like that, Fay.' He paused, lardy lips playing with a smile. 'Then again, some aren't. So save your big tits for young Jack. Mind you, I'm not sure how much time he's got left to savour such delights.'

Fay sat back and sighed. 'Well, Arthur, if you've no interest in me, why haul me up before you next Wednesday?'

'Lass, my only interest lies in solving this case, and my only rewards go to them as helps me. Do I make myself clear? You help me, Fay, and I'll reward you.'

'Arthur, what exactly are you after?'

'My quarry, lass.'

'But Jack hasn't done anything. He's been locked up in Hungary.'

'Fay, how do you know what he was up to while he was away for three months? Were you in contact with him?'

Crossing her legs elaborately, Fay addressed her upraised knee. 'What does DOSS do, Arthur?'

'My organisation does all sorts of things, lass. Now, what were you doing for Horner while you were in Paris?'

'All sorts of things, Arthur.'

'You still a Party girl, Fay?'

She threw him a saucy glance. 'Well, I like a good time. I'm off to one next week.'

'Why did you join the Party, lass? Bit of a rebel were you, a bit of a romantic? Fancy all that free love, did you, Fay?'

'Free love, Arthur?' she retorted contemptuously. 'Where've you been? Love always comes with a price tag, lad, even for them as wed nigh on thirty years.'

Pricked by both her barb and her mimicry, his florid face deepened in hue. It required a two match rekindling for him to recover his composure.

'Why did you borrow the file on Noel Field, lass?'

'I thought my interview was on Wednesday.'

'We're just chatting, Fay. You did borrow it, didn't you?'

'Arthur, I see loads of files.'

Barber blew her a whorl. 'Well, it doesn't matter, lass. It's totally irrelevant to my investigation. You can tell Jack that Noel Field doesn't figure in this case at all.'

'So what does figure, Arthur?'

'Was Horner's safe open, when you ran in to help a dying man?'

'I've no idea. I just did my nursie bit.'

'What's "overloaded" mean, Fay?'

Eyes coquettish, she jacked up her brows, and thrust her shoulders back. 'Arthur, you said you weren't interested in that sort of thing.'

'What do you know about the Karakum Desert, lass?'

'I bet it's sandy.'

'What's a WB-29?'

'Sports car?'

'Have it your own way, lass.' His paw tapped against her bottom. 'So lift your lovely bum off my desk, Fay, and off you go. We'll talk again Wednesday. Say the right things, and it could even mean a new job for you. There'll be plenty of vacancies. That, I can promise.'

'Well, I do like a man who promises me a good time.'

The hoods drooped over his eyes. 'Oh, we'll have a right good time on Wednesday, lass. Mark my words. I've got a ton of questions for you to answer, Fay, and by the time I've finished, you'll wonder what hit you.'

She responded with a stagy pout. 'You're no fun, Arthur.'

'Oh, it's fun you're after. In that case, I'll see what I can do for you.'

'I can hardly wait,' murmured Fay, as she slid from the desk.

'Well, don't wait, lass. I'm done with you for now.'

She paced slowly towards the door, sensing the cowled eyes following her. When he called out her name, she halted, and peered over her shoulder.

'As you vamp out of the door, lass, tell Eric I want him. But not too husky with the voice, Fay, because he frightens easily.'

Absorbed in thought, seeking the sanctuary of her office, Fay descended the stairs from the fifth floor. Twenty minutes later, Sandra mounted them. Looking tired and harassed, she entered the room next to Horner's office from the corridor. Although a door at its far end connected the two rooms, on Barber's orders, it was now locked.

Sandra's temporary domain was long and narrow, and made yet more attenuated by filing cabinets lining one wall. These held Horner's personal files. Atop each cabinet were papers which Sandra had extracted from them. Resuming her solitary task, she broke off investigations to answer the phone, when Eve rang from DOSS headquarters.

'Found anything?'

'Well, Eve, there are a few interesting items. But I've seen nothing that remotely resembles this vaunted "Treasure Trove" of Horner's.'

'Have you found a red leather case?'

'No, there's nothing like that here.'

'That means the "Treasure Trove" isn't there.'

'Now you tell me!' she retorted peevishly.

'Sandra, I only found out about the red case yesterday.' Eve switched to a conciliatory tone. 'By the way, I've got some money for you. We've been financed by a splendid old girl, and there's more loot coming later from some pussies.'

'Whatever you say,' managed Sandra in a punch-drunk voice.

'Another thing, the Treasury's returning DORA's accounts. So, from tomorrow, you can start putting them into some sort of order.'

'Thanks a million, Eve!'

'Well, get one of the twins to help you. I imagine they can read and count, and only one of them is needed to keep watch on Jack's place.'

Sandra acquiesced with a long-suffering sigh. 'Where can I find you, if I need you?'

'I'll be busy, Sandra.' Her voice thickened with malice. '"Uncle Arthur" just rang me. He wants someone to be "unsettled a bit", to quote his woolly words. So I'll just have to see what I can come up with at such short notice.'

Knowing now what she had to do, Fay stepped out of the lift and into the security foyer. Ahead of her, she saw Sid Yates, and the jolly sergeant who checked the men. She favoured the policeman with a broad smile, which she narrowed down to nothing when handing Yates her ID. In his logbook, he recorded her name, number, and time of departure.

'Well, Sid, it's nice to see that someone's not been affected by recent upheavals. So how's Donald McCloy?'

'He's up in court soon,' Yates replied in a surly tone.

'I expect he'll get life for what he did.' Turning towards WPC Vi Thorpe, Fay flashed a convivial smile. 'Vi, I'm just popping out for some fags. I'm back on them, unfortunately. So do I still need to have my body patted?'

'Afraid so,' said Vi, her round face blushing slightly.

They entered a small side room. It was furnished solely with table and chair, plus a potted plant so withered as to be unidentifiable. An ashtray on the table was crammed with butts.

When Fay passed over her handbag, Vi poked around its interior and then returned it. 'Well, I can't see any state secrets in there.'

'Took those out last week, Vi.'

Grinning, she asked Fay to raise her arms. Her hands landed with the weight of a fly. 'I really hate doing this, Fay.'

'That's understandable. So when do the strip searches begin?'

'Bloody never, I hope.'

'Must we do this again when I return? I'll only be gone for a bit.'

'It's the rules, Fay. That little Sid sod makes sure we obey them. He reported one officer to that fat old git in charge, because he let some bloke back in without another search.'

Once outside, Fay walked quickly to a tobacconist and made her purchase. Then she hastened to a telephone box in a side street.

Extracting nail-scissors from her handbag, she made an incision into its lining. Through the tear, she withdrew a rolled strip of paper. It had lain concealed ever since they had presented her with the bag. It gave a London number. She dialled it, pressing Button A when a cautious foreign voice answered.

'This is "Natasha",' said Fay, first in English and then in Russian. 'I need to travel immediately.'

The man told her to wait. As she did so, Fay drummed a pencil against the coin box. Soon he returned with coded instructions, which she jotted down on a scrap of paper she'd brought with her. After replacing the receiver, Fay folded the paper into a tight wad.

She peered out of the kiosk's glass partitions to check that the street was deserted. Then she undid the top of her russet blouse, thrust the wad deep into her cleavage, and refastened the blouse. On the way back to DORA, she dropped the shredded phone number down a drain hole.

Fay passed through DORA's front entrance, and chatted briefly with the receptionist. Following the usual ritual of entry, Vi conducted a brief and uneventful session in the search room. Then Fay returned to the fourth floor, and made her way to Lucy Temple's office.

'I've never seen you doing a crossword before, Lucy.'

Hunched behind her dormant typewriter, Lucy glared at the wall clock. 'Well, I've never been this bored before.'

'Why not just take off? I'll lock up.'

'Lock up what?' retorted Lucy sourly.

'The CPV, once I've had a drink.'

Laying her puzzle aside, Lucy frowned anxiously. 'Fay, who's on duty downstairs, one of the heavy-handed lot?'

'No, Vi's there.'

Leaping to her feet, the secretary grabbed her things.

'Lucy, I've got to pick up Oliver tomorrow, so I'll take the day off. But tell Jack that I've left him something in your royalty file.'

'Will do! See you when I see you, Fay.'

Once Lucy had scooted from the room, Fay poured a scotch and sipped it twice. Then she went into her own office, locked it, and reached for a book. It was one of three copies of the same tome, which she'd dotted around her bookcases when she first joined DORA.

Fay undid her blouse, and retrieved the paper containing their instructions. Following the sequence of numbers she'd jotted down, she referred to the relevant pages, lines and words in the book. Each word she wrote upon the same scrap of paper. At length they formed a viable set of 'travel plans'.

Treating the town of Poole as a surname, Fay selected a fictional first name, and penned both into her address book. The time of her rendezvous she entered as digits of a telephone number, prefixed by the letters of a randomly selected London code. The street and house number of her destination became 'Sylvia Poole's' new 'address'. Then she took a photo from her bag and wrote a brief message upon its reverse.

She unlocked her door and went into the Ladies. Rolling the decoded instruction into a ball, Fay flushed this down the toilet. After checking that it had not resurfaced, she returned to her room, replaced the book on a shelf, and picked up her coat. She locked her office, returned to Lucy's room, and inserted the photo into an envelope. On this she wrote simply 'Jack'. A tight smile to her face, Fay stared at the name for a few seconds, before placing the envelope in Lucy's royalty file and locking the cabinet.

She downed the remains of her scotch, and resisted the temptation to pour another. When she found herself gazing sentimentally around the room, she stamped down hard on her thoughts. It was better just to go. She locked Lucy's office, dragged her eyes from the door that led into Randall's room, and then hurried down the stairs to the third floor.

Stepping out of the lift, Fay discovered that the personnel in the foyer had changed radically. Vi and the jolly policeman were gone. The latter's replacement was another DOSS heavy. A squat, bullet-headed man in a loud suit, Ken Flack was built like the proverbial tank. He peered coldly at Fay's profile, as she waited for Yates to log her details.

Taking back her ID, Fay spun around when she sensed a presence behind her. Clad in navy, the elegant redhead seemed to be fighting a smile.

'Follow me, Mrs Galbraith.'

'Why?' demanded Fay, brow creased with concern. 'Who are you?'

'An official of DOSS,' Eve answered coldly. 'Now, follow me.'

Once both were in the search room, Eve closed the door, and gazed in disgust at the laden ashtray. Having binned the dog-ends, she looked around the room. Tutting like a proud housewife, she hauled the bamboo cane from the pot plant, and tossed its shrivelled remains into the waste-bin. She was about to snap the cane and add it to the rubbish, when she noted that Fay was palpably trembling. Ever ready to extemporise, Eve laid the bamboo on the table.

'What's that for?' asked Fay in an edgy voice.

'What do you think,' Eve replied with deliberate ambiguity.

Seeking to restore her composure, Fay squared her shoulders, and studied Eve's face. 'Haven't I seen you before somewhere?'

Her question elicited solely an icy smile, followed by the order to hand over her bag. Eve emptied its contents onto the table, inspected Fay's purse and cosmetics, and leafed attentively through the address book. After returning the contents to the handbag, she told Fay to remove her coat. Slipping off her mac, Fay held it before her. Eve palpated its lining, foraged in the pockets, and dumped it on the table.

Fay's inquisitive stare had developed into a look of awareness. 'I recognise you now, although I can't get over how much you've changed. You're Mary Wilcox.'

'Wrong, Mrs Galbraith. That timid and distraught soul is no more. The woman you're dealing with goes by the name of Eve Loxton.' She picked up the bamboo, and tapped it against her palm.

Fay's eyes watched transfixed. 'What are you up to?'

'I'm deciding what to do about you, Mrs Galbraith.'

'What do you mean?'

'Well, if I didn't thoroughly check what might be secreted about the person of a Soviet spy and communist courier, I wouldn't be doing my job properly. But, I suppose we'll find enough stolen documents in your house.'

Fay swallowed hard. 'What on earth are you talking about?'

'When you get home, Mrs Galbraith, you'll discover that the men who've been watching your house have now obtained search warrants.'

Fay wound both arms around her body. 'I'd like to go now.'

'You'll leave when I say,' Eve retorted harshly. 'So have you ever illegally removed documents from this building?'

Glancing uneasily at Eve's assured face, Fay protested her innocence in a loud voice that hardly masked her discomposure. Frigid gaze unyielding, Eve flexed the cane again.

'Of course, you could have some documents about your person right now. Well, a strip search would establish the truth of the matter.'

Fay's eyes glistened. 'You cow!'

'Don't expect me to moo, Mrs Galbraith.'

'Please, don't make me undress,' begged Fay, her lips quivering.

Eve paced behind her, and tapped the cane against Fay's bottom several times. 'I really ought to thrash you for what you did to poor Mary Wilcox. But, since I'm pressed for time, I'll let you off for now.'

Whimpering in relief, Fay brushed at her eyes.

'But don't think that I'm finished with you, Mrs Galbraith. In fact, I've hardly begun.'

Returning the stick to the table, Eve strode from the room.

There were few occasions when Janice Marlow dressed soberly. But when she sat astride her powerful *Triumph,* garbed in black leathers and boots, a pink bandana was her sole concession to flamboyance.

When Fay emerged from DORA, and hurried towards her husband's car, Janice adjusted the kerchief over the lower part of her face. Reaching up to her helmet, she yanked goggles over green eyes. As Fay got behind the wheel, Janice lifted her gauntlets from the tank, and tugged them over milky hands. Then she kick started her machine.

PART FIVE

THE FINGER OF SUSPICION

SEPTEMBER 1949

38

WEDNESDAY 14 SEPTEMBER 1949

The choreography of Randall's second 'interview' was similar to the first. Opposite him, Barber's cumbrous body sprawled behind Horner's desk. To his right, Pratt perched stiffly behind a narrow table, eyes shining ascetically in his gaunt face.

To his left, Eve sat behind another table, set at right-angles to the desk. Attired in cream blouse and sienna outfit, her bare legs were crossed at the knee. Slides raised her red hair above remarkably small ears. Chin propped on palm, she stared intently at him.

Pratt began the questioning. 'Randall, have you seen Mrs Galbraith today?'

'No.'

'She was supposed to meet with us here this morning.'

'Then that's a matter between you and her.'

Fiddling with his bow-tie, Pratt read from his file. 'Randall, are you now, or have you ever been a member of the Communist Party of Great Britain?'

'I was a member of the Party from January 1936 to September 1938.'

'Why did you leave?'

'I didn't leave.'

Pratt's brows rose. 'What does that mean?'

'It means that I was expelled from the Party.'

'Why?'

'The sin specified was "Trotskyism".'

Barber's voice pursued the smoke streaming from his mouth. 'Why did you join the Party, lad?'

'For the same reasons as others did. It was the Popular Front period, when the CPGB had "no enemies on the left". People joined to fight fascism. The Party harnessed their idealism, and then led them to the knacker's yard of the Nazi-Soviet Pact in August 1939. At this point, those members, who still retained any shred of decency, left of their own accord.'

'So you're no longer a believer?'

'Correct. I'm no longer a believer.'

'Is Mrs Galbraith a believer?' inquired Pratt.

'Ask her.'

'I'm asking you, Randall.'

'And I'm not answering.'

'We shall note your refusal.'

'Well, make an additional note that I refuse to answer for someone else's beliefs.'

'We know she was in the Party.'

'You used the past tense.'

Lifting her chin from her left palm, Eve ostentatiously flashed her rings. 'Does Fay's husband know about your affair, Jack?'

'I've no idea.'

'Approve of that, do you?'

'What?'

'Adultery, Jack. Do you approve of adultery?'

'Not particularly,' he replied, lighting a cigarette.

'But, in your case, it's alright, is it?'

'In our case, it just happened.'

'What if we should inform her husband?'

'I couldn't stop you.'

'When did you first meet Fay?'

He ran a rapid search of his memory before answering her query. 'I met Fay through friends in June 1936.'

'Were these friends in the Communist Party?'

'Why should that matter?'

Eve fingered her rings. 'Was Fay already married then, Jack?'

'Yes, she was.'

Barber interrupted his pipe-lighting ritual to intervene. 'Why did you appoint Fay to her job in DORA in June 1944?'

'I didn't appoint her. Horner did.'

'But you were already there, lad, weren't you?'

'Yes, I joined DORA in May 1940.'

'Did Horner consult you about appointing her?'

'To the best of my knowledge, Horner never consulted anybody about the appointments he made.'

Disapproval written on his lips, Barber raised his pen. 'So you met Fay in June 1936, and she was appointed to a post in DORA in June 1944. So were you bedding Mrs Galbraith throughout the intervening years?'

Randall half-smiled on hearing this quaint word. 'No, I wasn't.'

Arthur wrote quickly, puffed vainly, and hunted for matches. 'So when did you two first cuddle up in your adulterous liaison?'

Staring back grimly at Barber's hostile look, he composed a devious reply in his head, and then opted to lie when he spoke.

'We had our first fling in spring 1946. The following August we agreed to end the affair, although we remained friends as well as colleagues. However, we started seeing each other again in March 1947, and since then, it's been an intermittent relationship.'

'So, since this first fling in spring 1946, you and Fay have deceived her husband,' asserted Arthur, his voice lingering over almost every word. 'That means that both you and Fay are capable of deceit to satisfy your own ends, doesn't it?'

Jack shrugged his response.

'When were you promoted to head your section, lad?'

'May 1945.'

'Bit young, weren't you? You were only thirty.'

'Well, Horner wasn't hidebound by things like that. He gave jobs to those who could do them, irrespective of age or sex.'

'Or political persuasion,' suggested the 'Dossboss' coldly.

Randall ground out his cigarette, but said nothing.

'So who promoted Fay to the post of your deputy, and when?'

'Horner promoted her, and it was in June 1946.'

'So you had nothing to do with it? You were simply flinging with Fay at the time?'

'That's right,' Randall replied brusquely. 'Both facts are correct.'

'Quite a picture, isn't it?' suggested Barber, staring balefully at Jack's expressionless face. 'Two former communists occupy the main posts in DORA's European Communism Section. Both see loads of secret stuff, and then they bunk off to bed together.'

'What's the question?'

'Did you and Fay discuss these matters?'

'Which matters?'

'Secret matters,' Arthur elaborated, in an irked voice.

'Well, it was our job to see secrets, and often to discuss them, but we rarely did so in bed. When I get under the sheets with a woman, it's not in order to natter about politics.'

Quashing any further digression, Barber asked if he and Horner had ever discussed the Soviet atomic bomb.

Jack nodded cautiously. 'Horner showed me a memo he'd written in October 1948.'

'And what was in it, lad?'

'Horner contended that there had been an accidental explosion in the Karakum Desert, because the Russians had "overloaded" their nuclear device. In view of this, he speculated that Moscow was probably in the market for "short cuts". I think that was his phrase.'

Barber scooped up his pen. 'What does "overloaded" mean?'

'I asked Horner that same question, and he sent me off to read a booklet.'

'Well, go on, lad. What did this booklet say?'

Rummaging in his memory, Randall lit another cigarette. 'If I recall things correctly, it discussed how to initiate the fast nuclear chain reaction needed to detonate an atomic bomb. Evidently, a minimum quantity of uranium, which scientists call the "critical mass", is required for that purpose.'

'And how much is this minimum quantity?'

'I've no idea. It certainly wasn't mentioned in the booklet. But, if through ignorance too high a minimum is set, then presumably a device is "overloaded", and this would result in an uncontrolled nuclear explosion.'

'So obtaining the correct figure for the critical mass from the West would constitute a shortcut for the Russians, in their quest to stage a successful atomic test?'

'That seems a fair conclusion.'

'Was there any other discussion between you and Horner about the Russian bomb?'

'No.'

The pale eyes stared fixedly at Randall. 'Did you know that Horner kept a diary?'

Shoulders taut, Jack shook his head.

'Now, under the date 12th October 1948, Horner wrote, "Randall is a fervent admirer of Beria." So why should he write that?'

'I imagine he was being facetious. Horner showed me some photos of Beria and asked me my opinion of him. I made some derogatory remarks.'

The sleek, smirking figure of Pratt stood. His tread gingerly feline, he loped over to Randall, as though walking on springs, and placed a photograph before him.

'Is that one of the photos you're referring to?' asked Arthur.

Jack stared at it, and shuddered involuntarily. 'Yes, this is one of the photos Horner showed me.'

An inscrutable smile surrounded the pipe. 'Tell me, lad, have you ever met the MGB colonel shown with Beria in yon photo?'

Randall inhaled tensely before muttering his response. 'I've been in a room with him.'

'You've been in a room with him,' parroted Arthur, his tone suggesting an illegal homosexual act had occurred. 'And where exactly was this room?'

'In Hungary.'

'My, he gets around! So what's his name?'

'I don't know.'

'You don't know?' Bafflement invaded Barber's face. 'So what was this nameless MGB officer doing in this Hungarian room?'

Jack crushed out his cigarette and forced himself to decline another. 'This colonel was present at some of my early interrogations. He was also there at the end, when I was drugged in Pécs prior to being shipped back to France.'

'And what did you and Colonel X talk about?'

'He only spoke once, right at the end.'

'Strong silent type, was he, lad? So what did he say?'

Jack grimaced before dredging out a response. 'The colonel said, "Mr Randall, do you think anyone in England will believe your story?"'

Dousing a cynical smile, Barber reached for his matchbox. 'Was Horner aware you'd been a member of the Communist Party?'

'I've no idea. He never mentioned the matter.'

'Have you served as head of section continuously since May 1945?'

'I only held that rank when I was in Britain. Whenever I was sent abroad, I handed over responsibility to whoever was then my deputy.'

'Was that the case when Horner ordered you to Paris last May?'

'Yes, it was, I handed over my duties by letter to Fay. She was resuming her post in DORA on 1st June.'

The cherrywood took, and Arthur snuffed out his match. 'In August 1944, Horner put up a report to "higher authorities". In it, he advocated the dismissal of five of his employees who'd been Communist Party members. Did you know about Horner's recommendation?'

'No, I didn't.'

'Did you know that your name headed this list of five?'

'How could I?'

'Fay Galbraith was the second name on the list.'

Jack shrugged.

'So Horner *did* know you'd both been in the Party.'

'What are you asking me?'

'You said he didn't know.'

'No, I said he never mentioned it. Check your notes.'

'Do you know the other three names on the list?'

'You've got the list.'

'Did you know Vic Welles had been in the Party?'

'Why are you asking?'

'And Leo Ikin?'

'Same answer.'

'And Donald McCloy?'

'Ditto.'

'More deceit,' contended Arthur, smoke seeping from his mouth.

'I've answered all your questions about myself, and too damned many about Fay.' Checking himself, Jack reduced his voice-heat to simmer. 'If you want to know if the others were in the Party, ask them. And, if you're unhappy with their answers from a security point of view, then I'm sure you can find the means to resolve such matters.'

'I already have, lad. Those employees of this now defunct department, who have a satisfactory security status, will be offered positions elsewhere. But certain folk will receive no such offer.' He waggled a sheet of paper. 'As per contract, Jack, I'm giving you six weeks' notice, effective from today, with your pay remaining at the same munificent rate as now. Naturally, you'll have no further access to sensitive material. From tomorrow, lad, you'll only be allowed to see newspapers. Understood?'

Randall nodded.

Barber sat back, basking in his chair like a benign toad. 'Anyway, lad, I won't detain you just now. But I'll need to talk to you again. So, unless instructed otherwise, you're to pop in daily, by noon at the very latest, and read the newspapers until six. Grand way to earn your keep, isn't it?'

Lucy stared back anxiously when he slouched into her office. 'What happened, Jack?'

'Well, Lucy, I've now had two intense sessions with that bunch from DOSS, and I've told them nothing but the truth. However, I've an awful feeling that, not only do they think

I'm lying, but they also suspect me of being involved in something else altogether.'

'Come and have a drink.' Grasping his hand, she led him over to the CPV.

'I've been sacked too, Lucy.'

She squeezed his hand, only releasing it in order to pour drinks. 'You'll get another job, Jack.'

'Not with the government, I won't.' He downed the Cognac. 'And have you seen Fay? Evidently, she missed her so-called "interview".'

'Well, Fay said she was taking yesterday off to pick up Oliver, but she said nothing about today. She mentioned too that she'd left you something in the royalty file.'

Crouching, Randall opened the cabinet drawer. He found the envelope addressed to him, tore it open, and withdrew a dog-eared photograph. Taken in Budapest in May 1947, it showed Caroline King, or Karola Király as she'd become, together with a young boy. Just as Fay had said, Zoltán was the spitting image of Imre.

He flipped the photo over and found Fay's brief message: 'I've decided to put some real space between us. I've loved you a little – now and then – as I think you have me. Take care of yourself.' He reread her words, and then tore the photo into shreds. Having stuffed these into the envelope, he shoved this into a pocket, and poured another brandy.

Lucy frowned. 'What's happened to Fay?'

His only response was to sink the contents of his glass.

'By the way, Jack, I'm transferring to my new job tomorrow.'

'I'll miss you, Lucy.'

'Same here.' Watching him wield the bottle again, her mouth puckered. 'Jack, don't go completely off the rails.'

'Lucy, right now, I've got nothing to keep me on them.' He drained his glass, pressed a fond kiss to her lips, and waggled a farewell wave.

On exiting from the lift, Randall wished he'd put more fire into his belly. Apprehensively, he gazed at the counter in the centre of the foyer. Standing by it were Phil Dove and Ken Flack. When he handed over his ID for Yates to record his departure, Sid held onto it.

Dove twiddled his moustache. 'We want your fings, Jack.'

Flack's icy smile revealed a gold-capped tooth. 'Get your kit off, pal, so we can inspect it.'

When Randall squared his shoulders, Dove hooted with laughter. 'Fancy takin' us on then? What are you, Jack, eleven stone top whack? Ken's fuckin' 'ead weighs more'n that.'

Grim-faced, he turned towards the search room, flanked by the two 'Dossers'. There he stripped off his clothes. As usual, when standing naked in the presence of men, he felt deeply uncomfortable. Mercifully, they left almost at once.

Forty minutes later, a sadistic smile playing over his handsome face, Dove returned the garments. 'We couldn't find nuffin' special there today, Jack. Maybe next time, eh? And Mr Barber wants to talk wiv you again. Nine-firty, Friday morning. Don't be late now.'

Randall dressed hurriedly. When he emerged from the search room, the only person in the foyer was Eve. Standing behind the counter, she stared at him fixedly.

'Was that your doing?' he snarled.

Ignoring his question, her long fingers dangled a crumpled envelope. 'I believe this is yours, Jack.'

He paced up to her, and snatched the offering from her hand.

'It was like doing a jigsaw, Jack. So who's the woman in the photo?'

His eyes narrowed. 'First, you can tell me who you are.'

'My name's Eve Loxton. Now, who's the woman in the photo?'

'Someone I once knew.'

'What about the boy?'

'He's her son.'

'So who wrote the stuff on the back, someone else you once knew?'

Gazing at her derisive expression, he balled up the envelope and thrust it into a pocket. 'Can I go home now?'

'Oh, I should think so.' She returned his ID. 'After all, tomorrow's another day.'

Slipping off her heels, Sandra clambered athletically up the ladder to the dovecot, and addressed two bored Delaneys. 'So what's Jack up to?'

'He's been wandering around his attic, just drinking.' Yawning, Delilah lowered her binoculars. 'It's not very interesting.'

Delphine rested the camera in her lap. 'Do you think Fay will be coming round, to provide us with a bit of action?'

'I doubt it,' said Sandra solemnly. 'Fay's disappeared. She was meant to meet her husband at the airport yesterday, but she never turned up.'

39

FRIDAY 16 SEPTEMBER 1949

That morning in Budapest, the trial of László Rajk and his so-called 'accomplices' began before the People's Court. Yet it was hardly the preeminent matter circling around Randall's mind, as he breakfasted on cigarettes and coffee.

Having come to a decision, he mounted the stairs to his attic, and unhooked the picture of baby Zoltán and Caroline from its place. Opening the frame, he extracted the photo and ripped it into tiny pieces. Then he returned to the lounge, lit a sheet of newspaper in the grate, and sprinkled the shredded snap like confetti upon the flames. For good measure, he added the remains of the photo Fay had left him.

Relieved of even the vestiges of paternity, he set out to attend his latest 'interview' at DORA.

When he entered the foyer, a young policewoman gazed at him brazenly. Her curly hair fringed a pale face dappled with freckles. Doll-like lashes crested flirtatious fawn eyes. Lips arcing in a saucy smile, she lounged across the counter, bottom tight-rounding her skirt. Dragging his eyes from these appealing contours, Randall shoved his ID in front of Eve.

Smiling cynically, she recorded his details and returned the pass. 'Fancy women in uniforms and black stockings, do you, Jack? Now, there's a surprise. But you won't be seeing that outfit much longer. Madge is transferring to DOSS, because of the better pay and prospects, and the more varied work. So I'm just putting her through her paces.'

'I'll bear that in mind,' he retorted coolly.

'It's not hard to distract you, is it, Jack? Of course, your inability to resist any sexual challenge might be your downfall.'

He hammed a bored expression. 'Can I go now?'

'No,' said Eve coldly. 'You haven't answered my questions.'

'You haven't bloody well asked me any.'

'Temper!' said Eve in a peremptory tone. 'Tell me, Jack, which of you headed the spy-ring, you or Fay?'

'What the hell are you talking about?'

'Did you get some of the money too, or did it all go to Horner?'

He screwed up his face in exasperation. 'What money?'

'Where's Fay, Jack?'

'How should I know?'

'Why didn't you go with her?'

'Where to?'

She glared at him icily. 'Note how he answers my questions with questions of his own, Madge; a typically evasive technique.'

'Have you finished?'

'For now,' said Eve abrasively.

The person in Horner's room was not Barber, but Christopher Pratt. Seated behind the grandiose desk, he motioned Randall to sit at the table in front of it. After some five minutes, during which Jack twiddled his thumbs but eschewed smoking, Pratt looked up from his file.

'Randall, where is Mrs Galbraith?'

'I don't know.'

'In that case, you can go to your office and read some newspapers until six. Try and earn your salary while it is still being paid.'

'You brought me in here early, just to ask me one question?'

Pratt stroked his bony chin. 'Randall, we will bring you in whenever we like and ask you whatever we choose. Is that understood?'

Not trusting himself to speak, he nodded.

A smug smile stretched Pratt's thin lips. 'However, should you have any information to volunteer, we can continue.'

'I've nothing to say.'

'Well, we think that you have plenty to say, Randall, and that one day you will say it.' He teased a drooping lock of greased hair into his quiff. 'Return to this room promptly at three p.m. Mr Barber wishes to talk to you.'

Unclenching his fists, Jack stalked from the room, and descended the stairs to the fourth floor. When he wandered into Lucy's office, a slim blonde in a blue dress looked up from a file. Coming to her feet in one graceful movement, Sandra smiled and introduced herself. Impressed by her imposing height and classic legs, he smiled back.

'We're going through the records of your section,' she disclosed.

'Then I'll leave you to it,' he replied, hauling a pile of newspapers from his in-tray.

He sat at the low table facing Horner's desk. Barber slouched behind it, toying with a pipe cleaner.

'Where's Fay, lad?'

'I've no idea. In fact, I'm sure you know far more than me about her whereabouts.'

Arthur's pouchy cheeks swelled merrily, when he unclogged the blockage in his pipe. 'Well, we do know that Fay should have picked up her husband from the airport on Tuesday. And, suffice it to say, lad, she didn't arrive and she hasn't been home since.'

Randall frowned in concern, but said nothing.

Barber blew through the pipe's stem. A blob of brown liquid formed, which he wiped on the sleeve of his blazer. Then he reassembled the pipe.

'Supposing I said her husband's car was found in Poole in Dorset.'

'What if you did?'

'Boat to France, Jack, and where to then? Do you think Fay's booked herself into a Hungarian room?'

Again he made no reply.

'Why didn't you go with her, lad?'

'Where to?'

'Didn't she want to take you with her? Has our Fay got another lad to fling with way out east?'

Jack shrugged bemusedly.

'Why did you stay, lad? You know we're going to nab you soon.'

'What for?'

'You know what for.'

'I really don't know what you're talking about.'

''Well, you'll soon find out,' Arthur asserted antagonistically. 'Any road, I'm off. But you stay put. My lasses have more questions for you.'

Madge Nichols lounged across the low table, causing her bottom to poke up even higher than did the foyer counter. He had legs to contend with too, once Sandra perched upon the table, a notepad balanced upon crossed knees. Eve planted herself between the other women, and shoved a photograph before him.

'Look at it, Jack.'

Randall complied, and started involuntarily.

'Have you seen the man in this photograph before?'

He nodded.

'So who is it, Jack?'

'That's Csillag.'

'Chill-log,' parroted Eve. 'Hungarian for "star", you said. But I'm going to call him, Max Stern; "Stern" being German for star. So how many times did you meet Max Stern?'

'Just once.'

'How many times did Fay meet with Stern?'

He stared into her probing eyes. 'Why should Fay have met him?'

'Just answer the question.'

'I can't. The only people who can answer that question are Fay and Stern. I suggest you ask them.'

'All right, I'll ask Fay.'

'But you can't ask Fay.'

'Why not?'

'Because she's not here.'

'So where is she?'

'I don't know.'

'Then how the hell do you know she's not here?' Gaze unflagging, Eve switched subjects. 'Where did you go after meeting Stern in Paris on 28th May?'

'I've already told you. I was kidnapped and imprisoned in Hungary.'

'Prove it.'

'How?'

'That's your problem, Jack.' she retorted belligerently. 'Anyway, now go and read your papers again until six.'

Once he'd left, Eve grinned at Sandra.

'You can ring our builders now. Tell them to start work tonight.'

On exiting from the lift, he was hardly surprised to see the heavies barring his way.

Dove squared his massive shoulders. 'Word is you're carryin' somefink out, Jack.'

He took a deep breath. 'I'm carrying a wallet, a packet of fags, and my house keys.'

'Not for you to say, pal.' Flack's gold tooth glinted in his wolfish smile. 'Same drill as before.'

Once more he stripped in the search room, and again they left at once with his clothes. Five minutes later, they returned them. Randall dressed rapidly, and stormed out of the search room. Eve awaited him in the foyer, arms folded, a supercilious smile dominating her face.

He glared at her. 'What is this ritual humiliation designed to achieve?'

'I think you know, Jack.'

'For God's sake, what do you want?'

'That should be obvious,' she replied. 'I want a confession.'

'What the hell do you want me to confess?'

'You know what, Jack.'

He shook his head in frustration. 'I've no idea what you're after, and you won't extort anything from me like this.'

'Jack, I don't need you naked in order to get a confession out of you. That was merely a little demonstration of my power over you, and your increasing loss of control. And that's only the start.' She underscored her assertions with a telling nod, 'Anyway, come in on Tuesday at eleven a.m.'

At home that evening, he took a phone call from Wendy. She informed him that she'd been offered a new post, and that she wanted to stay with him on Saturday. Isolated, with his life spinning out of control, he bowed to her wishes without demur.

40

SATURDAY–SUNDAY 17–18 SEPTEMBER 1949

Initially, they remained somewhat reserved with each other, as they sought to rekindle their relationship. When their conversation turned to financial matters, Wendy admitted that her scam with him had fed the worm of greed. During his three months' absence, she'd used Horner's signed blank forms to divert some handy sums into new accounts of her own.

However, she neglected to mention that she'd funnelled further funds her way, during that brief period between Horner's death and Leo Ikin's arrest. Not only had these sums come from a fresh source, but they had also greatly exceeded the amounts involved in her earlier embezzlements.

Now bored with money matters, Randall poured fresh drinks and handed Wendy a glass of wine. His eyes widened, when she emptied it in rapid gulps.

'Oh, what the hell!' she exclaimed. Leaping to her feet, she turned up the heat in her eyes and flung her arms around him. 'If you're going to be picked up soon, Jack, we might as well enjoy a last session together.'

Madge peered through the absent Delilah's binoculars at the scene in the attic. 'You get a really good view of things up here, don't you?'

Eve stifled a yawn. 'Well, we're a bit blasé, Madge. We've seen Jack in action several times before.'

'Wendy's got a really lovely bum, hasn't she?'

'It's even fatter than yours is,' sneered Eve.

'That's what I meant, Eve, really lovely.' Her impudent smile gave way to a reflective pout. 'Some blokes really like coming at the job from the back, don't they?'

Ever keen to advance her education, Delphine stopped shooting to ask why.

'It's all down to genes,' contended Eve, 'and more in certain blokes than others. It all comes from the time, Delphine, when our hairy ancestors operated on all fours or semi-erect.'

'I reckon Jack's a bit more than semi, Eve.'

'Yes, Madge, we can all see that. The point I was trying to put over is whether you've ever seen a monkey use the missionary position.'

'I've never seen a monkey at it at all, Eve. We're a bit short of monkeys in Balham. Not many missionaries either.'

Squinting into her telescope, Eve grinned, and then shook her head. 'Just look at him! Jack knows he's done for, but he can't help himself, can he? He's just like some condemned bloke scoffing his favourite breakfast before his execution.'

Delphine made a face. 'Do you think Jack actually knows what his favourite breakfast is?'

When he came through the door, bearing a laden tray, Wendy sat up, smiling in delight. 'Jack, it's ages since I had breakfast in bed.'

'I thought I'd give you a treat.'

'Another one?'

He set down the tray. 'I still find it hard to believe that DOSS is running interviews for new posts on a Sunday.'

'They told me they have to, Jack, because of the number of former DORA employees they need to process.'

He frowned. 'When will you be back?'

'Sometime this afternoon, I imagine.'

'So I'll show you where I keep a spare key, in case they arrest me while you're out.'

The midday sun streamed into the lounge of Eve's flat. Sprawled on her stomach on the sofa, Madge watched her boss emerge from the kitchen with a mound of sandwiches. Dumping the plate on the coffee table, Eve set to work with a corkscrew.

'So how did your appointment with Claudio go?'

Madge pushed up onto her elbows. 'I'm seeing him again tomorrow.'

Eve filled two glasses with wine and eased one across the table. Sitting up fully, Madge rapidly demolished a sandwich.

'Eve, did you recruit me just to wiggle my bum in Jack's direction?'

'Don't be such a silly cow.' Slipping off her shoes, Eve sank back into the comforts of an armchair. 'I took you on because you're bright, ambitious, and willing to learn. But, if you feel undervalued in your temporary role as sex-object, I can get someone else to fill in.'

'No, don't do that, Eve. I'm rather enjoying myself.' Following a speculative sip, she peered at her glass. 'Nice wine this.'

'It belonged to Horner. There's a load more back at DORA. "Uncle Arthur" let me have Horner's entire cellar, after he and the blokes had nicked all the spirits.'

'Typical,' muttered Madge. Setting down her drink, she stared at the rings adorning Eve's left hand. 'Are you still married?'

'No, Madge. But I always wear my rings. I find it comes in handy on occasion.'

'What about your husband?'

'What about him?'

'Did he go off with someone?'

The green eyes frosted. 'That's exactly what the bastard did.'

'Did he marry her?'

'Jimmy never got the chance, Madge. We were never divorced, and he snuffed it in the summer of 1947.'

'Was he a lot older than you?'

'No, he was only four years older,' said Eve, attacking a sandwich.

'So what happened to him?'

'He lost his footing on a cliff. He always was clumsy.'

'And her?'

'She drowned, Madge.' The tip of Eve's tongue snaked along her upper lip. 'Out of her depth, wasn't she?'

'How old was she when she died?'

'The bitch was only twenty-six, same age as you.'

Madge frowned uneasily, downed the remains of her drink, and changed the subject. 'Any news of Fay?'

'There certainly is.' Smiling maliciously, she refilled Madge's glass. 'I ensured that all of Fay's moves were known to me. Janice followed her car to Poole, and after she phoned me this news, I sent some reinforcements there. They kept Fay under observation, until she surrendered to Barber of her own volition last Wednesday.'

'She just gave herself up?'

'That's hardly a surprise, Madge. It's quite in character for Fay to surrender on her own terms to men. But she got a real shock when Barber transferred her into my custody. So last Wednesday evening, Fay was deposited in our safe house.'

Madge puckered her lips. 'Eve, who's in charge of this business, you or Barber?'

'I am, of course. Barber will try to interfere though, because, like most men, he can't properly delegate. But most conveniently, the Home Office and MI5 have just launched another attack upon the independent status of DOSS. So his attention will be diverted, and ultimately he'll have to cede total control of this investigation to me.'

Swallowing the last of her sandwich, Eve downed her wine, and stood. 'Anyway, his methods would never work on Jack. To get a woman's man like him to confess will require a woman's touch. Luckily, I've managed to convince Eric of this.' She tugged at her sleeves. 'So, drink up. We've got to go over to DORA soon.'

Impeccably dressed and wearing full war-paint, Wendy reciprocated Sandra's smile when they met in DORA's foyer. Exchanging small talk, they proceeded by lift and stairs to Horner's room. After Sandra had introduced her to Eve and Madge, Wendy sat behind Randall's 'usual' table.

'That's a lovely dress,' lauded Eve, who'd commandeered Horner's desk for the occasion. 'Classy material and superb cut, it must have cost a pretty penny.'

'I've a generous boyfriend.'

Eve smiled benignly. 'We rather thought you'd paid for it by dipping into DORA's shambolic finances.'

'I'm sorry,' said Wendy calmly, 'but I understood that this was an interview for....'

'Wendy, you've been embezzling money from DORA, haven't you?'

'What on earth are you talking about?'

'So far, Wendy, we've traced seven bank accounts in your name, each with a generous balance that bears no relationship to your salary. Yet you haven't withdrawn from any of these of late. So I can only assume that you've managed to clean out a big bundle of cash from one of Horner's many unregistered accounts.'

'Oh, for goodness sake, Eve, I was just a clerk. Mr Ikin was in charge of the Finance Section and its operations. Mr Ikin sought to keep some of DORA's money out of Horner's reckless hands, so that salaries and expenses could still be paid. For this purpose, he got me to open multiple accounts in different banks, and then he transferred funds to them.'

Smiling cynically at this smart response, Eve ordered Wendy to hand over her handbag. Tipping the contents onto the desk, she opened Wendy's purse. The jumble of coins induced a sceptical lift of her brows. At the sight of the ornate brass key, her eyes narrowed.

'Wendy, you've only got six shillings and eight pence in your purse. So where's the rest of your haul?'

'Eve, there isn't any haul.'

'We've been following you, Wendy. Over these last few days, you've bought lots of clothes and jewellery, and always paid cash. Want to see our photos?'

Wendy shook her head dully.

'Now, your only chance of staying out of jail is to collaborate with me. If you don't, I'll hand you over to the boys in blue. They'll charge you with fraud and embezzlement, and you'll be looking at years in jail. So, are you going to afford me your full cooperation?'

'What damned choice do I have?' Shoulders slumped in defeat, Wendy looked up fearfully. 'What happens to me now?'

'Now you get time and space to think. Nice quiet place in the country. You'll love it. We'll pay off your rent and move your stuff, and say you've been transferred abroad.' Standing, Eve drew a set of handcuffs from her pocket, and approached the seated woman. 'On your feet, Wendy, and then stick your pandies behind your back.'

'Why must you cuff me?' The crestfallen voice quavered, as she rose leadenly to her feet. 'I said I'd cooperate.'

'Well, these will remind you vividly of the criminal status you'll enjoy if you don't.'

She closed the cuffs around her prisoner's wrists, patted Wendy's behind, and urged the stunned woman towards her escorts. Switching off her smile, Eve waited for the trio to leave. When she rang Randall's number, he answered promptly.

'Jack, you'll be spending tonight and tomorrow without being troubled by a woman's cold feet. See you Tuesday.'

41

TUESDAY 20 SEPTEMBER 1949

Eve awaited him at the lift. Throughout their ascent, he felt her eyes peering intently at his profile. With Eve dogging his footsteps, he trudged up the stairs to the fourth floor. Turning to the left, he stopped abruptly, halted in his tracks by a newly-installed door. Set in a solid frame and surrounded by a partition wall, it blocked the corridor. Spinning around, he glared at the woman hovering behind him.

'What the hell's that?'

'Looks to me like a door, Jack.'

'Why's it there?'

'Privacy, Jack. There are still some former employees of this defunct organisation in the building, finalising their transfers. And we don't want them trespassing into areas where they've no business to be.'

'I don't like prisons,' he retorted savagely.

'It's hardly a prison, Jack.' Intensifying her look of derision, Eve fished in a pocket of her black jacket and pressed a key into his hand. 'This one's for you.'

His distrustful expression lessened, when he unlocked the door and pushed it open. 'Do I get to keep this?'

'For as long as is necessary.' She eased past him. 'Come on, Mr Barber's waiting.'

Grimacing, Randall pocketed his key and stepped through the open doorway. Eve locked the door behind them. Then she urged him before her, and together they ascended to the fifth floor, where Eric stood sentinel outside Horner's room. Jack glanced over his shoulder, but Eve was already heading down the stairs.

Ensconced behind Horner's desk, Arthur had only to pat two pockets before finding his pipe. Randall reciprocated by pulling out cigarettes, but he refrained from lighting one.

'Jack, where did you go after meeting Stern in Paris on 28th May?'

'I've already told you. I was imprisoned in Budapest and Pécs until early September.'

Barber played hide-and-seek; the matches hid and Arthur sought. Tapping each pocket in turn, he hunted them down while he spoke.

'Eve and I have been following the Rajk trial in the press, lad. We've even read translations of the broadcast trial, monitored by BBC external services. So we know that Noel Field's name has been mentioned in the proceedings. But I don't care a bloody toss about Rajk or Noel Field, lad. What I do care about are British traitors, who hand over the secrets of the atomic bomb to the Soviet Union.'

Jack shook his head in stupefaction. 'So that's what you're trying to frame me for.'

'Lad, I don't need to frame you. The evidence is there.'

'What evidence?'

'Eve will enlighten you tomorrow.' Radiating accomplishment, Barber guided the matchbox through a pocket's torn lining. He placed his catch upon the desk and eyed Randall coldly. 'You knew the Russians had tested a bomb successfully, didn't you?'

'What?'

'Oh, come on, lad! Fay had a good nose round Horner's open safe on the day of his heart attack. She saw the initial report, and she'd have told you all about its contents.'

'Let me get this absolutely straight. Are you saying the Russians have exploded a nuclear device?'

Barber's paw patted against the desk in mock applause.

Randall stared back coolly. 'That's the first I've heard about it.'

'Well, lad, soon everyone will know the Russians have the atomic bomb, because President Truman will be making an announcement to that effect.'

'I see.'

'Do you, Jack? Do you also see that this will come as a shock to the great unwashed? America's nuclear monopoly wasn't meant to end so soon, if at all. So this means there'll be a surge of righteous anger across the USA, with demands that someone be blamed?' He stoked the cherrywood and expelled a cloud of acrid smoke. 'There'll be a hunt for traitors, lad, and the finger will point at Britain because of our record. The Yank press will wheel out the case of Allan Nunn May in 1946. And, to propitiate American wrath, we'll just have to find another traitor, another "atom spy".'

Eyes cold with fury, Randall clenched his fists beneath the table. 'So I'm to be the human sacrifice, am I?'

'Stop playing the persecuted innocent,' snarled Barber, the flab of his chins now blotched in angry shades of red and plum. 'This will simply be a case of a traitor being brought to justice.'

'That's exactly what the producers of the rigged Rajk trial are claiming too.'

'But, our evidence hangs together a damn sight more convincingly than that load of tosh they're regurgitating in Budapest.'

'You really believe you're going to get a conviction?'

'Yes, I do. If I were a juryman hearing the evidence to be presented against you, lad, then I'd vote to convict.'

'Well, I think that when they hear your so-called evidence, you'll be laughed out of court. That is if your fatuous charges ever reach that far.'

'Lad, you're forgetting something. There'll be your confession too.'

'Now you're forgetting something, lad. I haven't made a confession.'

'But you will, Jack.'

Arthur lifted the phone and dialled. After three rings, he slammed down the receiver. Heaving his bulk from the chair, he doddered across the room to collect his hat and coat.

Randall pocketed his cigarettes. 'Can I go now?'

'Nay, lad, wait for Eve to fetch you.' Struggling into the sleeves of his mac, he spoke between grunts of effort. 'Talking of Eve, lad, has she been treating you all right?'

'That rather depends on how's she's meant to treat me,' he replied caustically.

'Meaning?'

'Nothing.'

The jowls shook appreciatively at this response. 'But if you've got any complaints, lad, just put them into me in writing, in triplicate, and they'll be thoroughly investigated.'

'When?'

'When you're in jail, Jack.' The grin rolled his cheeks into wads of blubber. 'Any road, just be grateful that we haven't "minimised" you.'

'Minimised?' he echoed inquiringly, despite suspecting that he knew precisely what Barber meant.

The lids drooped to cloak the expression in Arthur's eyes. 'It comes from the acronym "M.I.N.I.", lad, which stands for "Murder in the national interest". Mind you, it's not necessarily ruled out. So don't get too complacent.'

'I won't,' Randall replied sombrely.

'Any road, for now you won't be "minimised". The government needs a trial, you see, to show that it's alert, concerned, and decisive. All the things governments must pretend to be. It'll be in camera, of course.'

'Have you decided upon my sentence as well?'

'Judge does that, lad.' Arthur relit the pipe. 'But we'll find one uncharitable enough to hand you the maximum of fourteen years.'

Puffing jauntily, he stomped from the room. Shortly after his departure, Eve entered.

'Nice little chat?' she inquired brightly.

'Can we go?'

'Of course, Jack. You lead the way.'

He took the steps down to the next floor at a canter, and was relieved to discover that his key still worked in the new door. The next staircase too he descended at the double, before walking smartly up to the lift and opening its gate.

Eve was slightly breathless when she joined him. 'Such energy, Jack! But now you can rest in a car. You'll be driven home.'

He grimaced. 'What about tomorrow?'

'A car will collect you, and bring you to our meeting at five o'clock.'

'And after that?'

The viridian eyes glinted. 'That rather depends upon how much you please me, Jack.'

42

WEDNESDAY 21 SEPTEMBER 1949

When the car halted near DORA's entrance, he stared morosely at the bovine necks of Dove and Flack. Wedged like granite blocks in their seats, neither man had spoken during the trip from Ealing. Nor had Sandra Jansen, seated beside him in the rear, found overmuch to say.

She alighted from the vehicle in one languid movement, beckoned him to follow, and linked her arm in his. Struck by a foreboding that he might not enjoy free air for some time, Randall gazed at cloudless skies framing the street's sun-drenched rooves. But, when Sandra's arm tautened, he let her steer him into the building.

As her star guest entered the foyer, Eve switched on a smile that was worthy of any society hostess in radiance and integrity. Then she pranced up to him and grasped his free arm. 'Jack, it's so nice of you to come. We've such a lot to talk about.' Her hands tightened around his bicep. 'So shall we go up?'

'I can still walk unaided.'

'I know, Jack. But I'm in the mood to hold onto you, and I'm sure Sandra is too. Anyway, we mustn't keep Madge waiting.'

'Why, is she in charge today?' he needled.

Eve smiled afresh and icily. 'No, Jack, she's not. As you should know by now, I'm always completely in command.'

'Completely in command,' he echoed, grey eyes hardening. 'Well, since you're taking full responsibility for this performance, Eve, I'll remember that when I seek redress.'

'Somehow I don't think you'll be doing that, Jack. Now, let's go up.'

The women only released his arms in the lift. After exiting from its confines, he walked ahead until confronted by the newly-installed door on the fourth floor. Eve fished out her key, but Randall produced his own and inserted it unbidden. The door sprang open and they passed through.

'Did you really think we'd changed the locks, Jack?' Her shammed look of hurt quickly dissipated. 'Anyway, you can leave it open. There's no one else in the building now, besides us and the blokes.'

He absorbed this disquieting news without response. Plodding on, Randall approached the stairs to the fifth floor as if ascending the scaffold. But any thoughts of axe or rope were dispelled by Madge Nichols. She'd replaced her uniform with a 'cowgirl' outfit of jeans, check shirt, and tan boots.

'Like the togs, Jack? My uncle's a sailor and he brought them back from the States.' She spun around to show off his favourite feature, and then twirled again to face him. 'I'm going to a fancy-dress party later.'

'Now, I'm sure Jack's just dying to get started,' said Eve. 'So show our guest to his seat, Madge.'

Clamping his arm in her hands, Madge led him to the table in front of Horner's mammoth desk; the later now adorned by urns and vases crammed with chrysanthemums.

'We thought the flowers might help you relax, Jack. There's a new chair too. It swivels, so you can spin round and look at each of us lovelies in turn.'

'I suppose it's the thought that counts,' he muttered. Taking his seat for the performance, he stared dejectedly ahead.

Two high-backed chairs were already in place to each side of him. Sandra settled on the one to his left, pad resting upon upraised knee. Facing him, Madge lounged across the table. He stiffened when he felt Eve's hand on his shoulder.

'Why not write your confession, Jack?'

'Eve, I've got absolutely nothing to confess.'

'Absolutely nothing, you say.' She came into view and stood beside Madge. 'Now, we'll deal with your spying and treachery in a bit, Jack, but what about the rest of it?'

'The rest of what?'

She sat upon the table's edge. 'Jack, look at it this way. In the unlikely event that I can't nail you as an "atom spy", I'll get you for something else. There's no way you're going to wander off scot free. So, if you own up to the spying and write your confession, I'll have a quiet word in the right places and get a bit knocked off your sentence.'

'Eve, I won't confess to something I haven't done.'

'So how about confessing to something you have done?'

'Like what?'

'Well, Jack, I can't imagine that a person with such an unblemished character as yours could possibly be involved in Wendy's embezzlements. However, if something does turn up, then I shall be forced to add it to the other charges. So I hope you're getting the picture.'

He smiled sourly. 'Yes, Eve, I'm getting the picture.'

'Well, here are some others.'

Eve picked up a folder already lying upon the table. She located some photographs, and set them before him like a meticulous waitress. 'These come from your cousin Jessica's collection. Enlarged versions of some of them featured in a pre-war calendar, which has recently been reissued. Now, that is you frolicking in the altogether with Pam, Louise, and another woman, isn't it, Jack?'

He focused upon the stoned expression blighting his youthful face; an all too regular feature of his life at eighteen.

'I've also got some receipts signed by you, Jack. These acknowledge that Jessica paid you in cash for the right to reproduce some of these pics.' She fashioned a superior smile. 'Profiting from lewd and indecent images; not innocent of that, are you, Jack? Now, you must admit that it would be very easy for me to nail you for that escapade.'

Retrieving the photos, Eve replaced them in her folder. 'In case it hasn't occurred to you, Jack, I can hold the same threat over Pam and Louise, when encouraging them to talk.'

She paced over to the desk, and exchanged the folder for a thick file, which she set before him, open at the first page. Then, like a teacher about to help a pupil with learning difficulties, she moved the free chair alongside him. Once seated, Eve tugged the arm of his chair, encouraging him to spin to the right. Adjusting her own seat so that it faced him, she perched upon its outer edge.

'So let's examine what you've been up to, Jack. Let's have a really good look at some of the things which might interest a jury.' Her fingers rapped his knee, as if his attention had already wandered. 'Now, right at the start of that file, Jack, is a copy of Horner's diary entry for 10th September 1948. I can show you the original, if you're sceptical. Sandra, please read it out for our guest?'

Leaning across, Sandra recited the extract: '"Discussed with Randall the situation in the USSR, and the vital necessity for that state to obtain the atomic bomb in the near future".'

Eve winched up her brows. 'Any comment, Jack?'

Faced with the prospect of being constantly assailed by a dead man's ambiguous diary entries, he smiled grimly. 'Horner viewed Soviet acquisition of nuclear weapons favourably, as an essential element of his conception of stable spheres of influence in Europe.'

'Did you share his view?'

'I just listened to his lecture.'

Eve treated him to a pitying look. Then she pointed at the file, and directed him to reread Horner's memorandum conjecturing an abortive atomic test in the Karakum Desert. Swivelling to his left, he turned the page and complied.

'Turn to the next page, Jack. Now, you've seen those photos of Beria and MGB Colonel Yuri Volkov before, haven't you?'

He glanced towards her. 'Volkov, is that his name?'

Eyes filled with reproach, she signalled that he should spin back. 'Jack, you *know* his name is Volkov.'

'On the contrary, Eve, I've only just learned it.'

'Well, let's try a different angle. Do you admit that you've met both Colonel Volkov and Max Stern?'

'I hardly had much choice in the matter,' he responded mordantly.

'That's not what I asked, Jack. Do you admit that you've met them both, yes or no?'

He grimaced. 'The answer has to be yes.'

'Turn the page, Jack. What do you see?'

He swivelled back to his task. 'I see a photograph of Volkov and Stern with a chunk cut out of the middle.'

'Have you seen that photo before?'

'I've seen the uncut version before. It was taken in Paris in May 1946.'

'May 1946? Are you sure about that, Jack?'

He nodded confidently.

'Turn it over. What's written there?'

'"Paris, May nineteen forty-something",' he read aloud. 'The last digit's been cut out. But you can check with Vic Welles about the 1946 date. He issued this photo to Horner last October.'

She ordered him to spin back to face her. 'Vic's gone into hiding. It seems that Leo Ikin's death rather unnerved him.'

Randall frowned impotently.

'So who's been cut out of that photo, Jack?'

'There was a third man in it.'

'So who was the third man? Was it you, Jack? You were in Paris in May 1949, the most likely date when that photo was taken. And, by your own admission, you've met both Volkov and Stern, haven't you?'

His head shook in frustration. 'I don't believe this!'

Crossing her legs, Eve tugged the hem of a navy skirt primly over her upraised knee. 'It *was* you in the photo, wasn't it, Jack?'

Glowering, he leant back. 'Let's get something straight, Eve. The third man, the one who's been cut out of that photograph, was someone I've never seen before or since. Moreover, that photo was taken in May 1946, not in May 1949.'

Her eyes had never left his face. 'Well, let's try May 1946. Were you in Paris then?'

His brow furrowed in recall. 'Yes, I was, twice.'

'So what were you doing there?'

'I was making deliveries for Horner to his men in the field, during the so-called Paris Peace Conference. Because of this meeting, people from all over Europe could come to Paris without evoking overmuch suspicion.'

'What were you delivering?'

'I've no idea. The contents were sealed. I was just the courier.'

'Then give me the names of those you met.'

'No names were used. I made contact through recognition procedures.'

'So your contacts could have included Volkov and Stern, couldn't they, Jack?'

He gazed at her coldly. 'I did not make contact with either Stern or Volkov in May 1946. Furthermore, I repeat that I am not the missing man in that photo.'

'But you can't prove any of that, can you, Jack?'

'And can you prove that I *was* in that photo?'

'I don't think we need to prove it,' she replied coolly. 'Merely to conjecture such a possibility at your trial should suffice.'

'Eve, this is madness. It's just inference, not evidence.'

'Well, this isn't inference, this is fact. Horner met with Stern at Lord's on 3rd May 1949. Read out the extract from his diary for that day.'

She pointed at the file, and he spun his chair back.

'"Discussion with Stern at Lord's",' recited Randall in a muted voice. '"He interested in the background of my five former Party members".'

'Turn to the next page, Jack, and you'll see a scorecard dated 3rd May. On the back of it, are written Stern's instructions as to where and when Horner was to meet him in Paris.'

He studied both sides of the scorecard, and then complied with her command to turn to the page following.

'And, lo and behold, we have a Paris menu dated 11th May, as well as Horner's diary entry for the same day. Read out Horner's entry, Jack.'

He breathed out heavily before acceding. '"Further discussion with Stern in noted Paris restaurant. Randall is the preferred candidate for the task that Stern has in mind".'

'Now, Jack, look at the back of the menu. There you'll find that Horner has detailed the procedure whereby you were to make contact with Stern in Paris. Then read on.'

He stared at the instructions. These chimed precisely with those given him verbally by Horner for making his fateful contact. Next he studied Horner's diary entry for Friday 13th May 1949: 'Conveyed to Randall Stern's instructions regarding their forthcoming meeting in Paris on 28.5.49.'

Eve again ordered him to face her. 'Well, Jack?'

'Eve, I know nothing about any meetings between Horner and Stern.'

Her eyes gazed piercingly into his. 'Jack, you followed Horner's instructions to the letter, and ended up by contacting Stern in Paris on 28th May. You're not going to deny that, are you?'

He grimaced. 'No, I can't deny that.'

'So where did you go after meeting Stern?'

'I keep telling you that I was taken to Hungary.'

'Taken? Well, perhaps I can concede that you travelled to Hungary. Sandra, kindly read out Horner's entry for 9th July 1949.'

Sandra eased her head over the dossier and recited: '"Met with Stern in Richmond. Randall is apparently in Hungary, dutifully fulfilling his function".'

'"Dutifully fulfilling his function",' echoed Eve accusingly.

'My function as a fall-guy,' he snarled.

'That's not what it says there, Jack.' Her eyes narrowed. 'What were you carrying for Horner?'

'I wasn't carrying anything. When he sent me to Paris, I was under the impression that I was to collect something there.'

'So what were you meant to collect?'

'I don't know.'

'But you and Fay occasionally acted as couriers for Horner, didn't you? So, during the three months when you seemingly disappeared, Jack, did you carry microfilm from Horner to Paris or Budapest?'

'No, Eve, I didn't, because, as I've constantly explained, during those three months I was imprisoned in Hungary.'

'But, Jack, Horner was offering photos and other information for sale to Stern. It says so upon the back of the scorecard, and it even gives the astronomic prices he anticipated receiving.'

She gazed unwaveringly into his face. 'It's all so clear, Jack. Having lost a fortune at cards, Horner saw an opportunity to get hold of some real money. He offered to sell atomic secrets to Beria, by putting his proposition to Max Stern. He knew that Stern had links with Colonel Volkov, one of Beria's top men.'

Randall stared, almost mesmerised, into the dark green eyes.

'Beria agreed to pay up, Jack, on condition that Horner used you and Fay as couriers for conveying this crucial information. You and Fay; two dedicated communists, who weren't in it just for the money, like Horner. So Fay sets up the network in Paris, and when she's due to come back to London, Horner sends you out there.'

He gazed mutely at her intense expression, before shaking his head clear. 'Then why the hell did they take me to Budapest?'

'Well, when you went to Budapest to dutifully fulfil your function, perhaps you made a direct delivery from Horner to the Russians. Perhaps they also gave you further instructions there about which atomic secrets they wanted Horner to supply.'

'So where did Horner get all this atomic information?'

'Jack, we both know that Horner had sources everywhere,' she responded smoothly.

Eyes narrowing, he sat forward combatively. 'Eve, this spy ring is a figment of your imagination. And where's the evidence that Horner took money from Moscow?'

'His personal accounts, plus depositions from his banker and Ursula Conrad, all strongly suggest that he received money from Volkov through Stern.'

Randall slumped back in his seat.

'What about Fay, Jack? Are you going to tell me that Fay wasn't a Soviet agent, or that you never knew about her treacherous little ways?'

He took a deep, calming breath before he spoke. 'Eve, you know that all of your so-called evidence against me is entirely circumstantial.'

'Well, I'd say that it was deeply incriminating.' She lounged back in her chair. 'So why not write your confession, Jack?'

'Go to hell!' he snapped, thrusting to his feet.

'Going somewhere, Jack?'

'I'm going away from this bloody madhouse.'

She clasped his hand. 'I'd like you to stay, Jack.'

Whipping his hand from her grasp, he charged out of the room.

Eve smiled coldly. 'You'd better ring down, Madge.'

43

WEDNESDAY 21 SEPTEMBER 1949 [continued]

Randall stumbled from the lift into the foyer. Panting, he stared at the obstacle course before him, and shuddered.

'Where you scarperin' off to, Jack?' Planted like a Colossus between search room and counter, Dove glanced towards his mate. 'Looks real dodgy tonight, don't 'e, Ken?'

On the other side of the counter, Flack's arms folded across his massive chest. 'Well, the commie bastard's trying to move stuff out, Phil. Stands to reason.'

'Yeah, tonight's the night.' Dove nodded at the door to his left. 'In you go, Jack. Usual drill.'

Trembling from both fear and desperation, Randall inched forward, his eyes fixed upon the gap between Dove and the search room door. Beyond the huge man barring his escape, he could see the foyer's exit door wedged ajar.

'You 'ear me, Jack?' boomed Dove, who hadn't moved save to twiddle his tash. 'Do as you're told now.'

Crouching, both to lose height and to gain a sprinter's start, Randall stared at the gap. Mouth dry, he breathed in deeply twice, and then pelted like a rugby winger weaving along the touchline.

Dove's fist lifted Randall off his feet, when it smashed into his stomach. Hurled by the blow against the wall, he lay crumpled upon the cold stone floor, stunned and gasping. Whistling tunelessly, Dove dragged his victim by the heels into the search room.

Squatting in a corner of the search room, with his back to the door, Randall noted goose pimples on his forearm when he consulted his watch. It was nearly four hours since the heavies had left with his clothes. His stomach was sore, and there was an appreciable bump on his head.

When he heard the door open, he threw a glance over his shoulder. As Eve and Madge entered, he turned back to the wall.

'The blokes aren't far away, Jack, so don't give me any grief.' Eve prodded him between the shoulder-blades with the tip of her shoe. 'So up you get. We're going walkies.'

He thrust off the floor into a standing posture, and turned his head towards her. 'Now you've had your fun, Eve, I'd like to go.'

'Go, Jack?' Her lips twitched in amusement. 'Ideally dressed for the Tube, isn't he, Madge?'

Madge spluttered. 'Where are you going to put your ticket, Jack?'

'I want my bloody clothes.'

'Say please, Jack.'

He took a deep breath. 'Please, may I have my clothes, Eve?'

'They're upstairs. So let's go and get them.' She dangled a pair of handcuffs before his eyes. 'Pandies behind your back, Jack. I'm not taking any more chances with you.'

'Go to hell!'

'Do it, Jack, or else I'll fetch Ken, and the blokes say he packs the hardest punch of all.'

Such prospect cowed Randall's short-lived mutiny. Clenching his teeth, he placed his hands behind him. Once Madge had removed his watch, Eve shackled his wrists.

'Thought you'd like a bit of bondage,' she contended airily, before patting him on the buttock. 'Now, let's go.'

When he stayed put, she clouted his behind. He turned hesitantly, still with his back to her. Eve shoved him, and he shuffled into the middle of the room.

Lashes lifting lewdly, Madge grinned. 'Jack certainly looks pleased to see us, Eve.'

'That's hardly a surprise, Madge. He's showing us what a big boy he thinks he is.' She inspected him in profile. 'Looks arrogant, doesn't it? Jack's still playing games, Madge. He thinks he's still in charge. He doesn't want to confess.'

'I suppose that's one way of looking at it,' murmured Madge, her stare unabashed.

'Right, Jack, we'll take you up to your new quarters. Don't worry, the blokes won't see you. They're on reception. See how considerate I can be.'

'My new quarters,' he protested bitterly. 'You've no damned right to imprison me like this.'

'No right?' Eve stepped behind him and tugged the links of his cuffs. 'Possession is nine-tenths of the law, Jack, and you are now fully in my possession. Now, let's go.'

When he didn't budge, she walloped him on the backside. He winced, but refused to move. She whacked him again, but still he stood his ground.

'Are you enjoying yourself, Eve?'

The redhead smiled brazenly. 'I admit that it's something I've always wanted to do, Madge. But since he's being difficult, I'll get Ken.'

'Why bother? The usual method for a stubborn mule is carrot and stick.'

'Very astute of you, Madge, and I suppose you want the carrot.'

Her lips bunched lubriciously. 'Okay with you?'

'Perk of the job, Madge.' Glancing at the table, Eve grinned. 'Fancy that, my stick from the flowerpot is still here.' Clutching the cane, she tapped it against Randall's rump. 'So, Jack, where Madge leads, you will surely follow.'

Shorn of options, he trailed Madge into the deserted foyer.

'Delivered by hand,' announced Madge, on entering Horner's room.

Sandra smothered her laughter. 'Did you tow him all the way?'

Gwen grabbed her camera, and proceeded to take several shots, before Eve intervened.

'Sandra, fetch another set of cuffs, please. And, Madge, park Jack in that nice new room our workmen have prepared these last few days. New door too, Jack. While you were squatting in the search room, they replaced the one connecting Horner's office to Ursula's old room with a sturdier number. It's got a spyhole too, so we can keep an eye on you.'

Taking his arm, Madge escorted her prisoner into the confines of his new quarters. Dejectedly, Randall glanced around his cell.

The partition wall upon the far side had been removed, leaving the ablutions, once used exclusively by Horner and Ursula, as an integral feature of the now larger room. The uncurtained shower and washbasin were fully exposed. But, a cubicle had been built around the WC, with a truncated door affording a modicum of privacy.

Plywood sheets, screwed to the frames, blocked off all but the top few inches of the windows. A single bright bulb hung unshaded from the ceiling. In the middle of the room, its legs bolted to the floor, stood an iron bedstead with railed ends. Its double mattress was covered by a sheet, and a feather-filled duvet lay folded upon it.

When Sandra and Gwen entered, he glanced towards the door leading into Horner's room. It was then that he noticed the large mirror inlaid into the wall next to that door. The reflected scene, showing his naked body surrounded by four women, had an inevitable effect.

Eve directed him to stand by the end of the bed. She took the fresh set of handcuffs from Sandra, and closed one cuff around his left wrist, just above the existing fetter. The other she clipped around a headboard railing. Having unlocked the original cuffs, she handed these and the keys to Sandra. Then she pulled from her pocket a large ring holding a single key.

'Once I've locked you in, Jack, you can use this key to free your wrist. So I'd better put it somewhere you can reach easily.' Smirking, she stared at his revitalised erection, and then knelt before him. 'Now, don't think your luck's in, Jack.'

He heard the other women laugh, as a grinning Eve slid the key ring over his penis, and then took her time adjusting it to her satisfaction. He was aware too that Gwen was snapping his latest humiliation. But, all amusement was effaced when Eve came to her feet, peering ice-eyed at her captive.

'Jack, I don't think you appreciate what's hit you yet, so we'll leave you to brood over your unenviable situation. But I advise you to sleep in your clothes. They're hanging on the wall over there, and we'll collect some more from your flat later.'

Turning, she clicked her fingers, and held out her hand, demanding Gwen's camera. The photographer scowled, but complied. Then Eve ushered the other three women into Horner's room, and locked the cell door.

Next to it, hung Horner's immense map of the USSR, which Madge and Sandra unhooked from the wall. All four women then stared at their stunned prisoner through the two-way mirror, which the map had concealed.

'That map's too fiddly,' contended Eve. 'We'll get something else to cover the glass later. But for now, ladies, we've got some time off. So let's go and let our hair down.'

44

THURSDAY 22 SEPTEMBER 1949

Randall slept but fitfully after the women left. The permanent light disturbed him, as did the constant raising of the spyhole's cover. He was dozing when they came for him.

'On your feet,' bellowed Dove, his huge hand jolting the slumbering man's shoulder. When he whipped the duvet from the bed, Jack felt relieved that he'd heeded Eve's advice, and slept in shirt and trousers.

Throwing him a towel, Flack nodded at the ablutions. 'Quick wash and brush-up, pal. Mr Barber's ready and waiting.'

Emitting a zoic noise that many British MPs would have envied, Arthur stretched across Horner's desk for his pipe. Then he slumped back in his seat, panting, pale eyes gazing balefully at Randall.

Sitting at his usual table, Jack sensed Dove's presence towering behind him. Flack and Moon huddled in chairs to his left, both wearing the vacuous expressions of patients in a doctor's waiting room.

'"Nature has given women so much power, that the law has wisely given her little".'

Jack glanced at the obese oracle, whose pronouncement had broken the silence. He was assiduously unclogging his pipe with a spent matchstick.

'Who said that, lad?'

'You did.'

Barber glared tolerantly. 'Doctor Samuel Johnson, lad. It's summat I always keep at the back of my mind.'

Randall remained silent. Unwilling to volunteer conversation, he was saving himself for the inevitable questioning. Moreover, he fancied that Barber was planning to expound, once he'd plundered his pouch for tobacco and tamped it down in the pipe's bowl.

'Do you know which governmental department has the highest proportion of female employees, lad?'

Jack shook his head.

'It's mine, lad, the Department of Special Security.' A match flared, and Barber, sucking greedily on the stem, almost disappeared behind a cinereous cloud. 'Do you know which department is the only one offering men and women the same rates of pay and promotion prospects?'

The answer was obvious, but he let it fall from the oracle's lips.

'Mine again.' Arthur puffed proudly. 'You see, Jack, women have so much to offer, which our laws and conventions do so much to restrict. At first, it was hard for me to really appreciate the full range of their talents. But, once I did, I've always tried to move not just with the times, but ahead of them.'

He exhaled several large rings, as if smoke-signalling his message to a distant tribe.

'It was the last war that really opened my eyes. Women were doing so many things. There they were, lad, in the armed forces, in special operations, driving buses, keeping farms running, producing munitions, and all the rest.'

Content to remain mute, Jack rubbed his stubbled chin.

'But, when peace came, the men returned from the forces and wanted their civilian jobs again; so society chased women back to the kitchens and nurseries. It was always meant to be like that, of course. The wartime slogan, "Do the job he left behind", was hardly an offer of permanent employment, was it?'

When Barber's pipe expired, he laid it to rest in an ashtray. 'I've tried in my small way to uphold the banner of progress, Jack, and gone out of my way to recruit talented lasses into DOSS. You see, lad, I don't think women have realised their full potential yet. I like to think there's much more to come from them, and that I'm helping their advance, by opening up new avenues.'

A wax-seeking fingernail drilled into his ear. 'For example, as you know by now, lad, I use women interrogators. I reckoned I might as well put their love of talking to good use.'

Pondering the purpose of these maunderings, Randall was jerked back into the real world when Barber spoke again.

'Jack, do you still maintain that you spent the weeks between late May and early September locked up in Hungary?'

'Yes, I do.'

'Why keep on playing that worn-out record, lad?'

'Because it's the truth, that's why.'

'Trouble is, lad, we don't have one jot of independent testimony to support your version of events. But, what we *do* have is a mass of evidence proving you're an "atom spy".'

'I'm not an "atom spy", and you don't have a shred of evidence to prove that I am.'

'So why were you released from your so-called prison in Hungary? Am I supposed to believe that Marshal Beria himself decided to let you go?'

'Well, he may have done,' Jack ventured weakly.

'Have you met Beria?'

'Of course I bloody haven't!'

'But you've met one of his men, Colonel Volkov, haven't you?'

'Yes.'

'In a Hungarian room?'

Randall nodded peevishly.

Arthur fabricated an incredulous smile. 'It's not exactly a cast-iron alibi, is it, lad?'

'No, it's not.' Frustration added mettle to his tone. 'But it's still the truth.'

The interrogator reached out for his pipe. 'Where's Fay, lad?'

'I don't know.'

'How many times did you meet with Max Stern?'

'Just once.'

'Where were you during the three months you were absent from DORA?'

'I was locked up in Hungary.'

Barber's grin flaunted the stained yellow teeth. 'You never learn, do you, lad?'

When the 'Dossboss' jerked his pipe in signal, Dove pinioned Randall's arms. Flack and Moon swung into action too. Hauling Jack from his chair, they twisted his wrists behind him, allowing Dove to cuff them.

Lids cowling most of his eyes, Arthur beamed coldly. 'Jack, despite my advanced views upon the status of women, there are certain tasks I reserve exclusively for the lads.'

Clamping Jack's arms in vice-like grips, Dove and Flack dragged him into the centre of Horner's room. Fearfully, he gazed at Eric Moon.

Doffing his jacket, Eric arranged it over the back of a chair. He slid the tie from his collar, coiled it neatly, and placed both it and his wedding ring upon the desk. Having unbuttoned his spotless white shirt at the neck, he rolled up his sleeves, revealing chunky forearms tattooed with mermaids.

Stooping markedly from the waist, Eric repeatedly flexed his fingers. Then, having gauged distance and jostled his feet into position, he crouched in front of Randall. Fit for purpose, Moon looked up, sniffed twice, and unleashed a flurry of fists.

Dry-mouthed, unable to quell the terror he felt, Jack had tried to steel his stomach in anticipation of the blows. The first two overwhelmed his feeble defences, and the next four seemed to knock all the air out of his body. He slumped, gasping, saved from total collapse by the strong hands grasping his arms. When the pain bit fully, he groaned. His eyes filmed, and he swallowed on the nausea.

Barber trudged forward to stand by Eric. 'Where's Fay, lad?'

'I don't know,' stammered Randall in a quavering voice.

'How many times did you meet Stern?'

'Once.'

'Where were you from end of May to the beginning of September?'

Yet again the right answer was wrong, the truthful reply false. He emitted it almost in a whimper. 'I was locked up in Hungary.'

When Eric thrashed him in each set of ribs he screamed, and blinked maniacally in a vain endeavour to stanch the sweat stinging his eyes. Barber lit his pipe, snuffed the match, and repeated his questions like a mantra. Tone pleading, Randall bleated his answers.

Dove and Flack about-turned him, and Eric clouted him several times in the kidneys. Jack yelled in agony, and his captors released him. Crumpling onto the floor, he sobbed into the carpet, the smell of dust in his nostrils.

Barber squatted cloddishly next to the writhing body. 'Why do it this way, lad?'

Randall vomited in response.

Planting a half-hearted kiss upon his sulking lips, she bundled him through her front door, and immediately closed it. Then she gathered her strewn clothes, poured herself another brandy, and shivered in the late evening chill. Switching on the gas fire, Eve sat on the floor before it.

So, that was that! One more young man seduced and dismissed, and now as relevant to her life as his stain upon her sheets.

'What the hell are you up to, Eve?' she muttered to herself.

Financial circumstances and ambition had forced her to indulge 'Red Freddie'. Otherwise, the men in her life were getting younger and prettier. Was she only interested in girlish-looking, smooth-skinned boys? Was there something of the man in her, epitomised by her facile conquests and guiltless disposal of them afterwards? Eve sank half of her glass, and wondered whether she should just stick to women. Then she shrugged away such passing concerns, for there were far more pressing issues on her agenda.

Eve had a pretty good idea about what Barber would be up to with Jack, and intuition told her that he'd fail. Once that happened, she'd finally be left in complete command of proceedings; free to follow her own ideas in her name-making case against Randall and Fay.

First, she would delve into the backgrounds of her three prisoners. Then she'd apply pressure against every vulnerable point she detected in their personalities. And, in order to glean data about potential pressure-points, she needed all the witnesses she could muster.

Randall seemed to present the least difficulty in this respect. Not only did she have Fay and Wendy to hand, but his cousins Jessica and Amanda were available too. Then there was Pam Armitage, predatory and bisexual like herself. Eve allowed herself an anticipatory smile at the prospect of interrogating Jack's wayward stepmother. However, access to others might not be so simple, she reflected. Could she find

Eleanor Vere, who featured briefly, but relevantly, in the diaries of Walter Finch?

Despite her vendetta, she was convinced that Fay was an even more complex character. Would Jack reveal any insights? He knew Fay far better than her husband. Indeed, when told that Fay had been arrested on grounds of national security, Oliver Galbraith had appeared more relieved than bothered. His primary concern was whether this placed any restrictions upon his travel plans as a salesman.

However, there was someone else who might flesh out her picture of Fay, and it was high time she took a drive to Willesden. Draining her glass, Eve switched off the fire, and headed back to bed.

Randall crawled across the floor of his cell to puke into the toilet. Although in considerable pain, he fancied that Moon had pulled some of his punches. No bones were broken yet, and his face remained untouched.

45

FRIDAY-SUNDAY 23-25 SEPTEMBER 1949

The pale mask of Christopher Pratt figured amongst the male circle on Friday, when Arthur and Eric reprised their roles; jabbing questions and punches at their victim, like close-working boxers. Randall cringed and whined, flinched and groaned, effused sweat and tears. But he never deviated in his answers, as the blows fell upon his bruises.

The only modification to events came as he again lay gasping into the dusty carpet, when he heard Pratt's voice lifted in dissent.

'Sir, no matter how much I deplore Randall's treachery, I cannot condone this brutality against a defenceless man.'

'What do you want, lad, a fair fight? Marquis of sodding somewhere rules? Do you think Joe Stalin abides by rulebooks? You fight fire with fire, lad. That's the only way to stamp it out.'

'Sir, I really must protest….'

'Just piss off, lad! You're no bloody use to me.'

When she revealed her identity and the purpose of her visit, Dave Holt admitted her reluctantly, but without questioning her authority. Eve followed behind him, observing the slow ascent to his bedsit.

Grunting, he hauled on the banister to his right, and dragged a lame left leg up the stairs. The stump of his left arm was cocooned by a folded and pinned shirt-sleeve. She could only wonder why he didn't rent a downstairs room.

Once they entered his austere bedsit, he turned his terrible face towards her. Divided between normality and hideousness, it might have served as an ideal subject for a Bosch painting. His single eye scrutinised her from head to foot.

'They all redheads in your mob?' he asked in a gravelly voice.

Eve felt this reference back to his earlier visitor unfair, since Janice's mop was merely marmalade.

'Don't you like redheads?'

'I was married to one when I went to war. But she didn't hang around long after they carried me back.'

He related this in a matter-of-fact tone, but Eve noticed his shoulders tighten. Then she looked around the room, and caught sight of a photo depicting a handsome, laughing, young man in uniform.

'Is that you?'

The intact side of his face frowned. 'Yeah, twenty-one I was then. A month later, I caught a packet on the Somme.'

Eve did her sums. So now he'd be about fifty-four. Strangely, the good side of his face looked much younger than that, although the blonde hair was now mostly white. The mess on the left had no age; it was simply a testament. The skin was burned and scarred, a few tufts sprouted above it from his scalp, and the missing eye was represented by the black patch which concealed it.

She surveyed the room again. A kitchenette, piled with unwashed dishes, led off from a wall that hosted a battered table. Two chairs were pushed beneath it. A wireless and an ugly vase topped a scuffed sideboard. A camp bed took up most of another wall, with the bedclothes tucked and turned down in military fashion. She bet it took him ages to produce that result.

There were two tatty armchairs; one occupied by a black Persian cat, the other by a tiny tabby. Near the bed was a litter-tray lined with newspaper. Although it hadn't been used recently, the acrid smell of cat's piss still hung about the room.

'Do you have a job, Dave?' she asked lightly, feeling her way into his existence.

He explained that he ran a newsstand for the evening papers, and suddenly bawled out, '*News! Star! Standard!*'

Eve started at the sound. The Persian yawned cavernously. Pacing over to the bedsit's sole window, she stared out of it at the matching window of the house next door, which stood but a few yards away. She could see directly into the room, towards which she jabbed a finger.

'Was that Fay's room?'

She heard an assenting grunt behind her. Dave was now sitting in an armchair, the tabby in his lap. Turning, Eve folded her arms across her bust.

'Did you know Fay well, back in the late nineteen-twenties?'

He ruffled the cat's fur a little. 'I talked to her sometimes in the street.'

'So she knew who you were and where you lived?'

'Well, she could hardly miss seeing where I lived, could she? Not from there.'

'What about you, could you miss seeing her?'

He made a snorting noise. The tabby turned over and he tickled its tummy.

'Pretty girl, was she?'

Nodding cautiously, his eye fixed her with an inquisitive stare. 'Why all these questions about Fay? Is she in trouble?'

'Would you expect her to be in trouble?'

A brief pause prefaced his response. 'Yeah, I would. Specially if she's still carrying on like she did then.'

'What did she do, Dave? Give you the odd flash of her frillies?'

The living side of his mouth seemed to be sneering. 'I saw a sight more than that, lady. Fay never closed her curtains, and always undressed by candlelight. Stood in the middle of the room there, peeling off her clothes real slow, like some stripper. I used to sit in the dark and watch her.'

'Did she know you were watching?'

'What do you think?'

'You didn't have to look, Dave.'

'Of course, I bloody did!' he shouted. 'I'm a man, or I was. The little tart knew I had to look. And it wasn't some act of charity for a mangled war hero, if that's what you're thinking. No, she got a real turn-on from doing it, like she was practising her moves on me.'

Eve refrained from observing that some men were never satisfied.

His fist clenched tightly, and an anger born of impotence seethed through his words, as his mind replayed scenes from twenty years before.

'And it didn't stop with her striptease. Afterwards, she touched herself all over, standing in the window there. For an hour every night she never moved out of my sight. So I just watched till she put out the candles. And that was a tease too. She used to bend over them, blowing them out one by one, all the time sticking out her smashing arse for me to see.'

'When did you last see her, Dave?'

Composing himself, he tickled the tabby's ear. 'It was just after her old man died – funny that, I almost felt sorry for the little trollop that night.'

On the third day they rose again to their assigned tasks; Saturday's session seemed shorter, the pain more intense. As he squirmed on the floor, his bloated interrogator wheezed into a perilous knees-bend posture.

'Sorry, you fell over again, lad.'

With that Randall exited stage-right, toted like a sack of spuds by Dove and Flack. Now he was prostrate on the floor by the iron bed, trying not to stir rib cage or stomach as he breathed. Whenever he failed in this endeavour, the excruciating pain pumped fresh tears to his eyes from a deep well of anguish.

Next door, Arthur clawed at an itchy armpit. 'So what do you reckon, Eric? How's Jack reacting to this drubbing I decided to give him.'

Moon shuffled uneasily. 'It ain't workin', guv.'

'What the hell do you mean?'

'Jack don't like blokes, guv. 'E don't like talkin' neither. 'E likes 'is little secrets. So 'e's gone and dug 'is 'eels in.'

'But, Eric, he's scared shitless when he's in your hands.'

'Don't mean 'e'll cave in easy, though. Course we can break 'im in the end. But, it'll take time, guv, and 'e'll be really messed up. Ain't no bleedin' use like that, is 'e? Not if you wants 'im on trial.'

'So you think I was wrong to intervene in the matter and try the direct approach?'

'Never said that, guv,' he parried prudently. 'You're the boss, and you done what you reckoned you oughta.'

'But you think it's a job for Eve and her lasses, don't you?'

'Yes, guv, this needs a woman's touch.'

Following a grudging nod of assent, Barber phoned to the floor below. A few minutes later, he stomped across the room to confront Eve, hovering in the doorway. When he gruffly announced his decision, her eyes glinted. Restraining any other sign of triumph, she manufactured a gracious smile.

'Thank you, sir. You won't regret your decision.'

'Make bloody sure I don't, lass, because I'll hold you fully responsible if owt goes awry.'

'I appreciate that. But don't worry, sir. I'll provide you with a watertight confession.'

Barber sanctioned her new role with a curt nod, and then lumbered into the corridor. Shutting the door behind him, she sprang over to Moon and playfully tweaked his nose.

'Oh thanks, Eric, I owe you one.'

'Well, 'e's all yours now, Eve, like I reckoned. So I didn't mess 'im up as much as I could've.'

A jagged smile flickered beneath Moon's glowing nose, when Eve crushed his nozzle affectionately between her fingers. Then she bounded into the cell, and grinned at the pain-filled face at her feet.

'Well, Jack, you're finally in my clutches.'

That night the quartet gathered around a table in Horner's room.

'So what's your plan regarding Jack?' queried Sandra. 'I presume we're not going to torture him like the blokes did.'

Placing her emptied wineglass on the polished surface, Eve frowned in thought for a few seconds. 'No, we'll torture him in a different way.'

'What do you mean, Eve?'

'Well, Sandra, to my mind, torture is about making people lose things they cherish. It's about taking away things like dignity, conviction, love, honour, trust, status. Things like that.'

'Taking away sex too?'

'That too, Madge. And in Jack's case, once we finally get rid of his sexual appetite, we'll have got rid of his lies as well.'

'Well, whatever you say, Eve.'

'In any case, once you've made people really aware of what they've lost, they've got all the tools they need to torture themselves.'

'And that's the real torture, eh?'

The question elicited an assured smile. 'Yes, Madge, that's what I reckon.'

Sandra frowned. 'That's all very well in theory, Eve. But, what are we going to do with Jack in practical terms?'

'Well, I want to pierce his layers of lies and see what makes him tick. I want to expose his vulnerabilities, like open wounds. I want him to feel emasculated, guilty, loathed and traduced. I want to leave his mind in such a state that he just won't care if he confesses himself into clink.'

'Is that all?' chorused her listeners.

'Well, something like that,' muttered Eve, with a slight lessening of confidence. 'And, another thing regarding Jack, it's hands-off all round. Do as much teasing and tempting as you like, but nothing else unless I expressly order it.' She pinched a cigarette from Madge's packet and lit it. 'Anyway, our overall objective regarding Jack can be summed up in my maxim, "No libido, no lies".'

Gwen topped up her glass. 'Eve, how exactly are you planning to use Wendy Page in this business?'

Free hand cupping her chin, Eve smiled. 'In Wendy I see a young woman who enjoys acquiring and spending lots of money. So, manipulated properly, her admirably avaricious nature can be exploited to unearth loads of loot from Horner's Byzantine accounts.'

'Eve, have we actually got anything on Fay?'

'Yes, Madge, we do. When they searched her house, the blokes found a stash of FO documents. They also stumbled upon Fay's diaries, which I've been reading with great interest. But, until I'm ready to visit them in the safe house, I've told Janice to ensure that Fay and Wendy keep penning their "autobiographies".'

'Perhaps you could tell Janice to write one of her own,' suggested Sandra drily.

Eve grinned. It wasn't a bad idea. Trying to fit together a coherent picture of Janice Marlow's life, from the snippets she let fall, was like trying to complete a jigsaw with several pieces missing. Where did this bit go, or this? She didn't even know Janice's age.

'Anyway, I'll deal with Fay and Wendy later, once we've got Jack up and running.' The green eyes flashed with irritation. 'Why the hell "Uncle Arthur" had to intervene with his crude, traditional methods, I'll never know. He's put everything back by days, if not weeks.'

The next morning, all four women entered their captive's cell. Sandra and Madge eased a wincing Randall into a sitting position in his bed. Once they'd piled plump pillows behind his back, Gwen placed a tray on his lap.

'What's this?' he asked warily.

'Porridge, Jack. It'll slide down easily, if you're still sore.'

'Sunday papers too,' announced Madge perkily, littering his bed with the press. 'Just like the Ritz, isn't it?'

'No,' he snarled, 'it's just like a prison, where you get beaten up. It's just like bloody Hungary.'

'In bloody Hungary,' remarked Eve unsmilingly, 'you'd have been strung up for what you've done. That's what they do to traitors there, Jack. Yesterday, the People's Court in Budapest sentenced László Rajk and two of his fellow-accused to death. You can read all about it.'

Expression lightening, she placed his fountain pen and a pad of writing paper atop the pile of journals. 'However, I want you to use your pampered lifestyle for more than just a bit of reading. Over the next few days, Jack, you will write.'

'Write what?'

'Your confession.'

'I've nothing to confess to.'

'Then write your "autobiography", like you claim you did in Hungary. Who knows? It might amount to the same thing.'

PART SIX

ACT OF CONFESSION

OCTOBER TO NOVEMBER 1949

46

SUNDAY 2 OCTOBER 1949

Taking her time, Eve shackled his wrists to the barred headboard behind him. Then she paced to the side of the bed, pulled the duvet over his chest, and followed up with an accusatory glare.

'Still malingering, Jack?'

'No, Eve,' he retorted acidly, 'I'm still recovering.'

She sat on the edge of the mattress. Crossing her legs, she slicked the hem of a green skirt over her knee. 'So have you settled in all right?'

'Settled in?' he fumed. Glowering at her smug expression, he jangled his fetters against the iron headboard. 'Eve, I'm a bloody prisoner!'

'Well, people adapt,' she replied in her silkiest voice.

'Do they really? So would you like to be me, chained and cooped up like this?'

Her lips drifted into a sardonic smile. 'Jack, you get three meals a day, all your washing done, free electricity and hot water. You have women at your beck and call. Some men are just never satisfied.'

He screwed up his face to terminate the conversation, and then cannily rearranged his features into an expression of supplication. 'Could you let me have some more cigarettes, please? I've run out.'

Her brows soared above rounded eyes. 'I forgot to mention the free fags.'

Sandra glided into the cell, bearing a cardboard box. 'This has just arrived, Eve, I think it's Jack's new lead.'

Her expression like a child's at Christmas, Eve tore open the carton and pulled out a set of leg-irons connected by a lengthy chain.

'Just the job! Now, this will make things much easier.' She beamed at Randall, whose expression was markedly less joyous. 'American, Jack, a gift from the land of the free. Well, the irons are. But we've had a nice light chain knocked up in one of our workshops.'

Stretching towards the foot of his immovable bed, she clamped one of the irons to a leg. Then she lifted the duvet, and locked the other around his ankle.

The principle was obvious to the scowling man. They could now free his wrists permanently. And, if he was minded to go 'walkies', he could gather up the long chain, and shuffle off to the ablutions or some other fascinating corner of his whitewashed cell.

He glared at his jailer. 'How the hell do I get my trousers on?'

'You don't, Jack, except when we take you to interrogation.'

'Otherwise, I just crawl around naked, do I?'

'Well, you have done so far,' said Sandra. 'Not that we mind. But we'll get you some fetching nightshirts, so you can veil your newfound modesty.'

'Can these come off now?' demanded Randall, rattling his cuffs. 'If you must chain me up like a dog, Eve, can't you just limit yourself to this manacle around my ankle?'

'Perhaps, Jack.'

'For God's sake, I'm not likely to be running off anywhere, am I? Barber's thugs have seen to that.'

'Well, that particular episode was certainly a flagrant error. Not that the blokes ever had a chance with you.' Her eyes seemed to lighten in shade as she subjected him to a gelid stare. 'We both know that it will be a woman who gets you to confess, don't we, Jack?'

'Do we?' he sneered.

She unlocked the cuffs. 'Better now?'

With a slight groan, he eased his arms from their outstretched position, swung them forward, and planted both hands on his stomach.

'Jack, I want you to write another "autobiography". The last version, like your previous efforts, is totally unacceptable.'

'I've run out of paper.'

'Then I'll supply you with some more.'

His response was a mulish look.

'Anyway, you've had enough bed rest. So we'll start your interrogation tomorrow.'

'Eve, I can barely slither over to the toilet.'

'Jack, I'm not negotiating. I'm telling you we start tomorrow.' She eyed him coolly. 'Now, Madge will bring you some cigarettes. Sandra will supply you with some nightshirts, once they arrive. While I'll be back later, bearing fresh writing paper. See what I mean about women being at your beck and call?'

Accompanied by Sandra, she left the cell, leaving the door unlocked behind them. In Horner's room, the two women joined Madge, who'd been left on observation duties.

In place of the huge map of the USSR, which had once covered the business side of the two-way mirror, there stood a large wardrobe with no back or fittings. Its doors were wide open, and Madge was availing herself of an unimpeded view into the makeshift cell.

'I still say he's malingering,' muttered Eve.

'If he is, he's been putting on a really good act,' observed Sandra. 'Crawling across to the loo on all-fours, convincing groans at strategic moments, plus the odd howl of agony.'

Eve met such mitigation with a sneer. 'What do you reckon, Madge?'

'The proof of the pudding is in the eating,' she replied sagely.

'Well, I want that pudding on his feet. We've wasted too much time already, because Barber was in such a damned hurry.' Her features knitted into a thoughtful frown. 'Has Claudio finished your costume, Madge?'

'Yes, I collected it this morning.'

'Well, here's what I want you to do.'

Wearing her 'cowgirl' outfit, Madge entered the cell, and hung her new costume on a hook next to his suit. Then she wiggled over to the bed and sat on its edge.

Emitting a grunt of pain, Randall twisted his torso to face her. 'Madge,' he whispered urgently, 'help me get out of this madhouse.'

'Jack, are you implying I'm a loony?'

'No. But you'd be mad to let Eve corrupt you.'

'Perhaps I'm already corrupt, Jack, and enjoy working for people who reward such talents.'

'You haven't fallen into that abyss yet,' he insisted.

'Are you sure?' Her audacious expression slowly mellowed. 'Anyway, I've brought you some fags.'

Fishing in a shirt pocket, she produced the packet, and placed it on the nearby chair. Withdrawing a cigarette, she lit it, took a puff herself, and then poked it between his lips. He inhaled greedily, while Madge sauntered over to her bottle-green outfit.

'Like it, Jack? Eve sent me to her tailor. I've picked up loads of tips about dressing from her.'

'So you're really going to hitch your fate to hers?'

'Well, Eve's a winner, Jack, and I like winners.'

'I could think of other words to describe her.'

'I'm sure you could, given your parlous situation.' Her lips curved into a teasing smile. 'Anyway, I'm going on a date this evening, wearing my new suit. So I want to be clean and spruce. And, since our shower downstairs isn't working, I thought I'd use yours. You don't mind, do you, Jack?'

As he stared at her disbelievingly, Madge unbuttoned her shirt. Unsurprisingly, the exposure of well-formed breasts secured his undivided attention; he even stubbed his cigarette. Dropping the shirt to the floor, she sat on the bed and thrust out a booted foot.

'Jeans can't come off without the boots coming off first, Jack.'

The flippant smile seemed etched upon her face, as she watched him frenziedly haul off both boots. Rising to her feet, Madge wriggled out of her denims, and paraded around the bed, enjoying his desperate gaze.

Switching on the shower, she made a womanly retreat from the water until it warmed. Then she slipped out of her Claudio-created thong, and cast a wanton look over her shoulder at his tortured face. Stepping into the shower, Madge lathered herself serenely, before poking her head out of the cubicle with a look of entreaty upon her face.

'Can you wash my back for me, Jack?'

His visceral reaction was worthy of one of the dead, creaking upright on the Day of Judgement. Thrusting the shrouding duvet from his naked body, Randall came to his feet and groaned. Cursing his ribs, and hampered by the chain he was forced to gather up and feed out, he stumbled towards paradise nonetheless.

'Oops! I dropped the soap,' announced Madge helpfully.

He watched her bend, relishing the curvaceous bottom which she exposed to maximum advantage. The pace of his advance quickened to that of an express snail, with the paid-out chain snaking behind him like a spoor. At length, panting and grunting, he leaned against the cubicle.

Madge rewarded him for his services to genetic predisdisposition with a soggy kiss, and invited him to hop in. Having surmounted the slippery slope, he received the slippery soap, when she slid it into his hand.

'Jack, go gently with my back. It's a bit of a whatsit zone for me.'

Twirling around, Madge beamed at the mirror. On the other side of it, Eve took her latest photo. Standing beside her in the wardrobe, Sandra disembowelled a red jelly baby.

'Well, one part of Jack's pain-racked body can never be accused of malingering.'

'As they say, Sandra, you can't keep a good man down.'

'And Madge is certainly enjoying things to the full.'

'Well, Jack's supposed to make a clean breast of things while he's here.'

'Why the photos, Eve? Surely, we've got more than enough.'

'Sandra, these are to demonstrate that Jack's philandering never ceases, whatever his circumstances. I might need to show them to Fay and Wendy, should they still be feeling a bit loyal to him.' She handed the camera to Sandra. 'Anyway, I'd better go and break things up.'

Striding into the cell, Eve handed a towel to a giggling Madge, who draped it around her body. Collecting her clothes and suit, she slipped next door.

Now confronting Randall, Eve bolstered her words with a steely stare. 'I'm glad you can now manage an erect standing position as well, Jack. But soon you won't need any sexual treats. Because by the time I've finished, you could have every woman you've ever laid dancing around you naked, and you simply won't care. All you'll want to do is confess. And I'm not joking, Jack. I don't joke about things like that.'

She tossed him a towel. 'I'll let you malinger for the rest of the day, Jack, during which you can rewrite your "autobiography". But tomorrow we'll talk again, next door this time.'

47

MONDAY 3 OCTOBER 1949

'Out you come,' ordered a smirking Madge, standing by the door connecting his cell to Horner's office. Dressed in flannels, white shirt and striped pullover, an unfettered Randall emerged gratefully from the monotonous confines of four walls into the brightly lit room.

It had been transformed since he was last there in September. Now pushed against a wall, the vast desk was draped with an ochre cloth, upon which stood candles and flower-filled vases. Urns and jugs, crammed with dried flowers, were dispersed around the large room. Pre-Raphaelite prints dotted the white walls. Rugs woven in bright colours obscured most of the charcoal carpet. Cushions in a variety of hues littered the floor. A suite covered in cerise velvet surrounded a low *art déco* table.

Sandra lounged in an armchair, watching him. 'Amazing what you can get from the Ministry of Works, Jack, when someone owes you a favour.'

'So how are the bruises?' asked Madge chattily, patting a spot on the sofa to indicate where he should sit.

'Yellowing,' he replied brusquely.

Taking a seat next to him, her eyes widened over a roguish smile. 'I'll bring you a fresh bar of soap later.'

Ignoring Eve, who sat facing him, Randall gazed at the room's far corner. A cubicle now concealed the entrance to the narrow room where Horner had once stored his files. Most of its two walls were formed of mirror-glass. And, given that one could also enter that room from the corridor, he surmised that somebody might be sitting in the cubicle, observing him from behind two-way mirrors. Turning his head, he smiled grimly on seeing the closed 'wardrobe'. He had no illusions either about the mirror fixed into the wall inside his cell.

'Right, Jack, today we're going to talk about your family.'

When Eve spoke, he finally faced her, his expression refractory. 'Why the hell do you need to pry into my family?'

'Well, firstly, I'm a secret policewoman, so I'm bound to be a bit nosy. Secondly, you tell lies, Jack, so we need to study certain matters in more detail. And, last but not least, I need to know what makes you tick.' She tugged a sleeve of her navy jacket. 'Furthermore, your latest scribbled "autobiography" is totally inadequate. There's even less information in it than in the personal dossier Horner kept on you.'

'I've lived a very sheltered life, Eve.'

'Then let's drag it into the open. And do remember that we'll be talking to our witnesses about you. So don't try a load of flimflam.'

'Which witnesses?'

Ignoring his question, her gaze dropped to the file resting upon her lap. 'Now, I'll bowl you an easy one to begin with, Jack. You were born on 20th October 1914 in Shropshire and christened John Gareth, weren't you?'

He responded with a surly nod.

'Be your birthday soon,' said Madge brightly. 'Perhaps we'll knock you up a cake.'

'And, surprise, surprise, Jack, it's my birthday too,' announced Eve. 'Amazing, isn't it? Same day and month, but I'm five years younger.'

He remained silent.

'Now, both your father Luke Randall and your mother Miranda Haynes were born in 1888, and they married in 1913,' Eve recounted from her notes. Raising her head, she speared him with a piercing stare. 'Is your mother still alive, Jack?'

He lit a cigarette before answering. 'My mother died when I was a baby.'

'Did she really? But when exactly?'

Squeezing shut his misty eyes, his voice was low and hoarse when he finally replied. 'My mother died giving birth to me.'

'So you killed your mother on coming into the world,' expounded Eve with studied callousness. 'What an auspicious start to your life.'

He glared at her impotently.

'Did you ever feel that you'd murdered the most important woman in your life, simply by being born?'

'What do you think?' he retorted bitterly.

'I don't know, Jack. I was hoping you'd tell me.'

'Go to hell!'

Her stare was of sufficient duration to induce in him a bout of self-torturing reflection. Then she ran a finger slowly down her file, as if selecting from a range of questions.

'The First World War had just started when you were born, Jack. Tell me about your father's involvement in it.'

'Luke served throughout the war, and after it too. He didn't return home until 1921. He was wounded three times, and received all manner of decorations. People told me later that he exhibited a total recklessness in battle.'

'You were never in the armed forces, were you, Jack?'

'I was in a "reserved occupation" during the Second World War.'

Eve's eyes hardened markedly, as did her voice. 'What did that involve, Jack? Spying for the Russians, and screwing the wives of men at the front?'

He drew smoke deep into his lungs. 'I sought to have my exemption cancelled several times, but without success. I have never spied for the Russians. While the only women I slept with during the last war were single.'

'What amazing restraint,' Eve remarked scathingly. 'Now, regarding your father's reckless bravery, I suppose it stemmed from losing much of his reason to live, when his beloved wife died bearing you. Would you agree?'

'I've always thought that probable,' he replied despondently.

'So when did you and your valiant father first meet?'

'In November 1921, shortly after my seventh birthday.'

'Who'd been looking after you prior to your father's return?'

'Luke's older sister Daisy. Her husband was killed on the Western Front. But she continued to care for me, as well as her three daughters, even after she was widowed.'

'So what happened when Luke returned to Britain in 1921?'

'He ordered that I be sent back to Shropshire.'

'To the house where you were born, and your mother died?'

Pinching his lips, he nodded.

'How big was this house?'

'Fourteen rooms, as I recall, and set in several acres of land. My grandfather was a successful entrepreneur. Luke inherited the house from him, as well as a London flat and a sizeable chunk of capital. Daisy too received a generous bequest, plus a London flat.'

'Tell me about that first meeting with Luke.'

'Well, there's not much to tell. Daisy took me to Shropshire, and introduced me to this tall, tanned man with a clipped moustache. He stared at me strangely and said, "I am your father, Jack". Then he pointed at the woman standing next to him and said, "This is Miss Grace Slade, your governess." Then, without another word, Luke picked up his hat and left for London.'

Having jotted some notes, Eve looked up. 'Luke certainly seemed pleased to see his little boy for the first time, didn't he?'

Randall responded with silence.

'There's something else, Jack. When we searched your flat, we couldn't find any photos of your mother.'

'There aren't any,' he explained grimly. 'After my mother died, Luke destroyed every picture of her. He even forced Aunt Daisy to hand over any photographs she had of Miranda.'

'Does that mean you've no idea what your mother looked like?'

'That's right.' He blinked back tears welling in his eyes. 'I just imagine her.'

'Fancy having to imagine your mother,' remarked Eve in a soft, emphatic voice.

She stared at him for a good minute, before dropping her eyes to mark her notes with ticks. Then she laid some typewritten sheets on the table.

'Care to sign this, Jack? You can read it first if you like.'

'What is it?'

'Your confession, Jack, drafted along the lines of our long talk on 21st September.'

'I'm not signing a pack of lies.'

'But you will, Jack, later.' Grinning assuredly, she picked up the 'confession' and tucked it into the file resting on her lap. 'So let's talk about Grace Slade, your governess. Was she good at the old "three Rs"?'

'Miss Slade certainly taught the basics well, and she also instilled into me the rudiments of French, history and Latin.'

'Did Grace run the house for your father?'

'She was in charge. However, there were several staff who dealt with the household and the grounds. Miss Slade's life was hardly onerous.'

'Was your father ever there during her reign?'

'He visited once or twice a year. Even then, he was usually cloistered in his study, perusing the accounts, and he never once stayed overnight.'

Eve eyed him shrewdly. 'Did he talk to you during his visits?'

'He managed the odd exhortation about obedience and character,' Jack responded in a jaundiced tone, 'but we never had a conversation. He housed, fed, and clothed me, and paid for my education. But there was always distance between us, like some unbridgeable chasm.'

Eve flipped a page of her file, studied her notes, and inquired how he'd reacted to boarding school, when he was sent there in 1925. He reflected briefly before replying.

'I disliked the absence of women, the vile food, and the mindless traditions. On the other hand, I had fine teachers for art, history and languages.'

'Were you bullied there?'

'No, I wasn't. Although brighter than most, I wasn't rated a swot because I was also good at sports.'

'So when did you leave boarding school for university, and what did you study?'

'I left school in summer 1932. That autumn I went to university in London to study languages. I graduated in summer 1936 with a degree in Russian and German.' He smiled cynically. 'That seemed to cover Europe's options in the 1930s.'

'We'll discuss the options you chose in the thirties later, Jack.' She closed her file. 'Now, to show how considerate I can be, we've collected paints and canvases from your flat. We'll put everything in your cell later, once you've written another "autobiography".'

He responded with a curt nod.

'Now you can toddle off to your room.'

When he stood, Madge took his arm, as though they were going for a stroll, and escorted him into his cell. Sitting on the bed, the impish smile spread across her face.

'Let me have your clothes, Jack, and then I'll chain you up.'

48

TUESDAY 4 OCTOBER 1949

Rural Surrey was the location of a secluded safe house maintained by DOSS. Following a stroll around its grounds, Eve returned to the house and found her way into its large kitchen. There she spent some time drinking tea, and nattering with Janice Marlow and the other women. Then she picked up her briefcase and mounted the stairs.

She unlocked a door, half-opened it, and caught sight of the toilet and wash-basin partly concealed by a screen. Stepping fully into the room, she locked the door, and stared about her.

The view from the barred window offered a vista of fields and trees decked in autumnal hues. Beneath the window was a desk, its surface strewn with magazines. Hanging from another wall was an unchallenging painting, below which was a bed. Wendy Page covered much of its surface, a hazy smile playing about her lips.

The heat from a wood-burning stove made the room stuffy. Eve lowered her briefcase to the floor, and unbuttoned her sienna jacket. Prodding a white blouse into the waistband of her skirt, she stared sternly at her prisoner.

'On your feet, Wendy, I've come to have a serious talk.'

The recumbent figure didn't budge. 'First, fetch me some proper clothes. I'm sick to death of these damned nightdresses.'

'You only get your clothes when you cooperate.'

'Just how am I supposed to do that?'

'In my briefcase, there are selected records from DORA's Finance Section, which you can utilise to track down Horner's hidden accounts.'

'Oh, can I?' Wendy retorted abrasively. 'So what's in it for me?'

'Ten per cent of whatever you find for me.'

'Twenty.'

'Fifteen, plus some slacks and a sweater.'

'I want those before I start.'

'You're hardly in a position to make demands, Wendy.'

'Well, you're not in a position to refuse them. Not if you want Horner's money.'

Reluctantly, Eve conceded the point. 'I'll get you some clothes later. But I also want you to write a new "autobiography".'

'For God's sake, I've already written a dozen of them.'

'And in none of them do you mention Jack Randall.'

'Why should I?'

'Don't be obtuse, girl. You know what I want. You're going to have to shaft him.' She paced over to the bed. 'There's something else, Wendy. Where did you get that ornate brass key, which I found in your purse when we took you into custody?'

'I don't know what you mean,' she retorted limply.

Without a word, Eve grabbed Wendy's hand in both of hers and bent it into a wrist-lock. Eyes filming, the victim screeched with pain.

'Now listen, you insolent hussy. If you sod around with me anymore, I'll hand you over to the judicial system. And for all that thieving from public funds, Wendy, you'll spend your best years behind bars.'

Prompted by both threat and pain, tears seeped from the dark eyes.

'Now, I'll give you one last chance. Where did you get that key?'

'I got it from Horner's desk,' she shrieked.

Eve released her hold. First dabbing her eyes, Wendy flexed her wrist.

'You're learning, Wendy.' A frigid smile attended Eve's words. 'Now, I'll get you some clothes. Then you can write another "autobiography", describing in microscopic detail your relationship with Jack Randall. After that, you'll start work on the accounts. And when I return tomorrow, you can tell me everything you know about that key.'

'Is that all?' queried Wendy facetiously.

'No, there's something else. You lied to me just now, Wendy, and your overall attitude is most unsatisfactory. You need to wake your ideas up.' Grasping a towel draped over the screen, Eve threw it onto the bed. 'You'll need that after your cold shower.'

'I've got a nightshirt for you, Jack.'

Scowling, he reached out and fingered Sandra's offering. 'I suppose it could double as an artist's smock. But if you unchained my ankle, I could get dressed in my own clothes.'

'Sorry, Jack, but Eve's orders are that you only get unchained and dressed, when she calls you through for interrogation.'

Shrugging, he pulled the garment over his head, climbed out of bed, and paid out the chain attached to his fettered ankle. 'When's my next session with the titian Torquemada?'

'I'm not sure. Eve's away, talking to witnesses. But, she wants me to ensure that we've got a correct chronological record of your movements in the twenties and thirties.'

Seated on his bed, she shuffled papers around her file. Then she recited a litany of the foreign trips he'd made as a boy, in the company of Aunt Daisy and his cousins. Next came a list of the 'improving' trips around Europe, funded by his father, which ensured that his teenaged son was absent whenever Luke holidayed at his country house.

Perched behind his easel, Randall squeezed paint onto his palette, and then turned towards her. 'Not a fact out of place, Sandra.'

She jotted some details and then looked up. 'Where were you in summer 1931?'

He returned his eyes to the canvas, seemingly in order to apply some crucial dabs to the landscape he was painting. 'I was in Shropshire with my stepmother.'

'What about 1932, Jack?'

'I was in Shropshire once more, again with Pam. That summer the house was sold, and in the autumn I went to university in London.'

Sandra added more notes and ticks. 'Where were you after that?'

'During my first long vacation in summer 1933 I was in Nazi Germany.'

He then listed the European countries he'd visited and sometimes stayed in during subsequent years. Once Sandra had completed her record, he reached out for another tube of paint.

Silently, counting off a minute, Eve studied her haggard prisoner before speaking. 'Not enjoying your stay with us, Fay?'

Hunched upon the bed, the other woman's white-knuckled hands gripped the hem of her nightdress, yanking it tight over her knees. 'Why am I here?'

'Why?' responded Eve incredulously. 'You're here because we found a stash of secret documents in your study, when we searched your house. Bedtime reading, were they, Fay, or were they waiting to be microfilmed and sent to

Moscow?' She smiled spitefully. 'We also found your diaries.'

Fay hunched her shoulders higher. 'I suppose you've read them.'

'I've read every word, Fay, and noted every bloke.' Easing her bottom onto the desk by the barred window, Eve opened her file. 'So why did you just drive off into the night after our last meeting?'

'That's not hard to fathom.' Her lips pinched with loathing. 'I felt so soiled by you that I had to get far away from the scene, both physically and emotionally.'

'Life's full of little ironies, isn't it, Fay? So, because I made you a bit flustered, you buggered up your escape plan, didn't you?'

'If you want to put it that way,' snapped Fay, directing most of her irritation at herself.

'What were you intending to do if you hadn't been so flustered?'

She glared at Eve's mocking expression, but her reply was addressed to her upraised knees. 'My original intention was to leave the following morning, the Tuesday, after I'd spent Monday night putting my affairs in order. I suspected you were watching me, so I planned to leave in the direction of the airport, and then change my route and head for Poole.'

'When were you expected in Poole?'

'On the evening of Tuesday 13th September.'

'But, instead, you arrived there the previous night. In short, you panicked, didn't you?'

'I wasn't thinking very clearly,' Fay conceded in a sour tone.

'What was to happen in Poole?'

'I was to sail from there to France.'

'Where were you to go after that?'

'Somewhere in the Soviet sphere of influence, I imagine.'

'Did you actually visit the address in Poole?'

'No, I didn't.' Pausing, she yanked at her hem once more. 'By then, I'd realised that I couldn't go through with their plan. And, since I was deadbeat, I booked into a hotel.'

'With just your handbag?'

'That's right,' said Fay shortly. 'Of course I had very little money with me and no fresh clothes.'

'Why abandon the car?'

'I thought you'd be looking for it.'

Eve grinned. 'Actually, we weren't at first. Even though Barber's watchers reported that you hadn't arrived home by eight that Monday, this still didn't ring any alarm bells.'

'By eight?' Fay's mouth curled in a disbelieving sneer. 'Is that when they knocked off for the night?'

'Well, there wasn't any money for overtime in your case, Fay. It was all being spent on watching Jack. In fact, the blokes had no idea that you'd disappeared until the police passed on Oliver's concerns, after you failed to meet him at the airport. So it wasn't until late on Tuesday that they first learned the make and registration of Oliver's car.'

'God, you're as inept as I am.'

'I wouldn't bank on that,' Eve retorted sharply. 'I knew exactly where you were, even if Barber didn't. So don't ignore the fact that you're now dealing with women.' She glanced at her notes. 'Anyway, penniless and agitated, you rang Barber from Poole, and surrendered to him on the Wednesday evening. Then he handed you over to my jurisdiction.'

Slipping from the desk, Eve paced over to the bed. Towering above Fay, she stared remorselessly at her downturned head. 'Since then, Fay, you've been living here in the lap of luxury. But, you've failed to provide me with any relevant information in these pathetic "autobiographies" you've written.'

'I've told you all I know,' the other insisted in a tense tone.

'Don't talk such rubbish. Look, Fay, even if we ignore the escape plan, that pile of documents in your possession marks you down as a Russian spy.' Eve mimed her much practised look of stupefaction. 'I suppose you're deluding yourself that you'll get off with a judicial slap on the wrist. Well, you can forget that, Fay,' she asserted harshly. 'If you don't cooperate, then you're heading for a very long stretch in prison.'

Hugging her knees, Fay clamped her eyes shut to veil her troubled thoughts. Then she half-opened them to direct a shifty look at her nemesis. 'What does this cooperation entail?'

'Firstly, a full confession of your espionage activities since 1938, which is when I believe you were recruited by the MGB, or whatever it was called then. NKVD, wasn't it?'

Fay nodded.

'Then I want you to write about Jack.'

'Write what?'

'I think you know, Fay.'

Lifting her head, she gazed into Eve's face. 'Where is Jack?'

'He's in my clutches too.'

'So what are you going to do with him?'

'Send him to prison for a very long time as an "atom spy".'

'I see,' Fay mumbled, almost inaudibly.

'I hope you do see,' said Eve menacingly, 'or else you'll be joining him in the dock and then in clink.'

A heavy frown wrinkled Fay's brow. 'You want me to provide evidence to send him to prison?'

'Yes, you'll be the primary prosecution witness to substantiate Jack's confession.'

Her eyebrows shot up in surprise. 'He's confessed?'

'He will confess,' said Eve assuredly. Pursing her lips, she assessed her prisoner's reticent expression. 'Fay, I can't believe that you're actually in love with Jack.'

'That's not the issue. But there is such a thing as loyalty.'

'Oh, is there?' Eve parried cynically. 'Well, Jack didn't seem overly bothered by your disappearance.' Extracting a wad of photos from her file, she passed them to Fay. 'These show him enthusiastically screwing your rival Wendy, shortly after you vanished.'

Fay glanced through the snaps, laid them aside, and glowered at Eve. Unfazed, the redhead detached a brown envelope from her file and tossed it onto the bed.

'Those show him in a bit of a lather with my colleague Madge the other day. Anyway, I'll leave them with you to help spur your pen.'

'You're utterly vile,' said Fay, her look of sheer loathing wasted, since she directed it towards her knees.

'I prefer to say I'm effective,' Eve countered clinically. 'Let's be clear, Fay. I detest you as much as you detest me. But I do have a sneaking admiration for your intelligence and abilities, and the totally selfish way in which you conduct your life. I see no real point in incarcerating a woman with such redeeming qualities.'

Fay glanced up cautiously. 'But you will if you have to.'

'Good, Fay. I do believe you're getting the message.'

'I do believe I am.'

'So it's time to put pen to paper again. If I like what you've written, you'll get some clothes.'

'I understand.'

'Now more good news,' announced Eve in a treacly tone. 'From now on, one of my girls will supervise your showers. And she'll be looking, Fay, to remind you that you'll get a damned sight more than looks in prison.' She paused for effect. 'So if you want to avoid such a fate, you know what to do. Got enough writing paper?'

49

WEDNESDAY 5 OCTOBER 1949

Madge poked her head around the opened cell door. 'Jack, do you want a cup of tea? I've just made a pot.'

Randall looked up from his painting. 'Any chance of some Cognac instead?'

'You know I can't, Jack. Eve says you've got to keep a clear head for concocting your lies.'

'Black coffee?' he ventured optimistically.

'Keeps you awake at night, Jack.' Her feline smile broadened. 'So how do you want your tea, two sugars and extra bromide?'

He heard the door locking and shook his head. Even without the chain, he was hardly in a position to escape. His clothes had disappeared from the cell. So all he had to wear between interrogations was a penitential white nightshirt, which was again doubling as a smock.

Keys rattled, the door reopened, and Madge wiggled in, bearing two steaming Utility mugs. She placed them upon the floor, and then eased herself onto the bed.

He stuck his brushes into a jar of turps. 'So is Eve still away, interviewing so-called witnesses?'

'Yes, she is, Jack.' Madge lolled back on her elbows. 'Sandra's away too, until later today, while Gwen's on another job until tomorrow.'

He gazed inquiringly into her flirtatious eyes. 'Does that mean I'm under your sole command just now?'

'I suppose it does, Jack.' Extravagantly fluttered lashes topped off her wanton smile. 'So let me think of some orders I can give you.'

Eve padded into the room and locked the door.

Dressed in sweater and slacks, Wendy huddled by the stove, staring at feet encased in woollen socks and fluffy slippers. Her face was pale, her eyes bagged from sleeplessness and tears. She greeted Eve's entry with an audible sniffle. Then she pulled a soggy hanky from her sleeve and sneezed into it dramatically.

'I hope you haven't got laryngitis as well,' remarked Eve, unmoved, 'since I'm expecting you to do quite a bit of talking.'

Wendy glanced at her jailer. Recalling her ordeal of the previous evening, her lips tightened vengefully.

An icy jet of water had buffeted her body for what seemed like an eternity. Her initial screams of rage had become moans of misery, and then despairing whimpers. After being dragged back to her cell, she'd shuddered uncontrollably until finding the strength of purpose to dry herself. Then she'd crawled into bed and cried herself to sleep.

Eve stared intently at her prisoner before speaking. 'Let's talk about that key. You took it from Horner's desk drawer on the day he died, didn't you?'

Again surveying her feet, Wendy nodded.

'What were you going to do with the key?'

Wendy managed a bleak smile. 'I was hoping to find Mr Horner's "Treasure Trove".'

'I see.' Eve's vapid voice masked the surge of excitement which had coursed through her. 'What convinced you that such a thing existed?'

'Mr Ikin's behaviour, I suppose.'

'So tell me about Leo Ikin.'

Wendy hunched forward, hands clasped around upraised knees. 'Mr Ikin's greatest passion seemed to be booze. But he knew his stuff, and because he realised I knew mine too, he gave me quite a lot of leeway. So, although he was always threatening to transfer me, when I was cheeky to him or when I arrived late, it was just bluster. He depended upon me and he knew it.' Unclasping her hands, she inspected a crease in her slacks. 'Anyway, on this particular day I wanted some money from the main safe.'

'You had access to the main safe?'

'No, only Mr Horner and Mr Ikin did. I always had to stand well back while Mr Ikin ran through the combination. But, on this occasion, I could see a red leather case inside the safe.' She raised her head, and stared at the glowing logs in the bowels of the stove. 'So I asked what was inside the red case. "Oh, I expect its Horner's 'Treasure Trove'", Mr Ikin replied. I think he was quite drunk that day. Mind you, he was always a little drunk.'

'Exactly when did you see this red case in the safe?'

Wendy puffed her lips in recall. 'I first saw it there last August. I saw it there on subsequent occasions too, when the safe was opened. But, on the Thursday before Mr Horner died, I noticed it had gone.'

Eve calculated backwards from the date of Horner's death. 'So that would be the first of September.'

'If you say so. Well, I innocently mentioned its absence and wondered where it might be. And Mr Ikin answered in that nasal voice of his, which always seemed to worsen with drink, "Skull in Palestine". At least, it sounded like that.' She managed a mirthless smile. 'It was a riddle. He liked answering in riddles sometimes.'

'"Skull in Palestine",' echoed Eve incredulously. 'Are you certain he said that?'

'That's what it sounded like.'

Eve frowned. 'How did you know about the key?'

'I didn't. But when I was telephoning in Mr Horner's room on the day he died, I saw this open drawer with pills, a gun, and a key in it. The key had a faded label attached to it, which I later threw away. The letters "TT" were written on the label. So I grabbed the key from the drawer.'

Eve phased out her frown. 'You probably picked up the right key. The trouble is that we've no idea where to find this case containing the "Treasure Trove". So give this "Skull in Palestine" mystery some more thought.'

The younger woman nodded, but didn't speak.

'Now, have you written a new "autobiography"?'

'I started it,' Wendy responded sullenly.

'Why didn't you finish it?'

The dark eyes narrowed in a hostile glare. 'It was because I spent most of the night shivering, not sleeping.'

Eve's shoulders lifted in a shrug of unconcern. 'What about tracking down Horner's accounts?'

'I glanced at what you left me, but I'll need more documents to make any progress.'

'Have you made a list?' inquired Eve sharply.

'Not yet.'

'Well, I suggest you do so as a matter of urgency.'

Jaw set stubbornly, she took on Eve's baleful expression. 'I'll get round to it later.'

The green eyes became slits in the stern pale face. 'Wendy, you really do need to wake your ideas up. So you'll be taken for another cold shower to aid that process. Two minutes for neglecting to write the fresh "autobiography" that I specifically asked for, and another two minutes for making no serious attempt to find me any money.'

The knuckles whitened in Wendy's clenched fists. 'You utter cow!'

Eve responded to her look of hatred with a glacial stare. 'I'm not at all pleased with your attitude. I intend to make you fully aware of how seriously I view these matters.'

Tears seeped from the bruised eyes. 'You hideous, callous bitch!'

'Call me one more disrespectful name, girl, and I'll add a minute for each word.'

On returning from her latest interview, Sandra poured a drink, and then slumped on the sofa.

Lounging over Horner's desk, Madge sipped some wine. 'So, did you see Jack's cousin Amanda?'

'I had that great pleasure,' said Sandra fractiously. She reclaimed her gin from the floor. 'And I've got Pam's cousin Louise tomorrow.'

'Well, if you're really good, perhaps Eve will let you talk to Pam as well.'

Sandra failed to suppress the shudder evoked by such a prospect.

'Anyway, what was Amanda like?'

'Prissy, bitter, intense,' Sandra recited. 'But, she gave me some useful information about Jack's time in the Communist Party.'

50

THURSDAY 6 OCTOBER 1949

Dressed in her own clothes, Fay sat at the kitchen table in the safe house, and poured scotch from the bottle provided by her jailer. Opposite her, Eve studied the fragmentary life story she'd distilled from Fay's 'autobiographies'. Intent upon filling in the many remaining gaps, she glanced at her prisoner, and then consulted her file again.

'Let's check a few things, Fay. You were born in Hendon in May 1913, at which time your mother was thirty and your father thirty-seven. She was Swiss, and he was a British engineer, who'd spent the first decade of this century working in Tsarist Russia. Having made his fortune, your father left Russia and went on a sort of "Grand Tour" of Europe. He met your mother in Switzerland, married her in 1912, and took her to London. He bought a house in Hendon, and set up a factory in Wembley. When the First World War broke out, he played a vital role in British war production. Am I right so far?'

Fay nodded curtly.

Looking up, Eve locked eyes with her. 'So how were things at home?'

'Disastrous.' Fay took a pull at her drink. 'Mother was schizoid. As her condition worsened, she spent lengthy periods in mental hospitals. Whenever she returned home, she seemed to exist on a diet of alcohol and pills.'

'And how did you get on with your father?'

Full lips puffed into a ruminative pout. 'When I was little he was the perfect father. He would always spend time with me after work, no matter how long his day had been.'

'Why did he teach you Russian?'

'He was convinced that it would be a major language of the future. It also allowed us to enjoy a secret world, into which my mother, my nanny, and the servants couldn't intrude.'

'What happened to your mother?'

'Father took her back to Switzerland, as though he was returning a faulty piece of machinery. In her Swiss sanatorium she continued to deteriorate, and in autumn 1927 she killed herself.'

'You don't seem to have had much time for her, Fay.'

'True enough. I saw only a weak woman with no dignity, who was unable to fight for her rights.'

'Did you visit her while she was vegetating in Switzerland?'

'Up until her death, I stayed with my Swiss grandparents every summer following the 1914−18 war. That was how I learned German.'

'What was your father like, once he was single again?'

'Well, both he and his circumstances had changed drastically by then. His business had suffered in the post-war slump, and the struggle to keep it afloat brought on a stroke, shortly after mother's death.' Fay paused to swig more whisky. 'Unable to run his business, he was forced to sell up at a loss. And, to help pay his debts, our lovely home was sold and most of its contents auctioned. Then he and I decamped to a small, rented flat in Willesden.'

'So what happened to you?'

'As there was no money for fees, I was removed from my private school. I was just fifteen then. My father told me that I must now support myself, so I went out to work.'

'Was your father really flat broke?'

'I doubt it. Somehow he'd held onto a stash, which he used for one purpose only. Since the stroke obliged him to spend much of his time in bed, he seemed determined to get as much pleasure from this exigency as he could. So I had no option, but to watch him share his bed with a string of youthful tarts, as he conducted a costly exercise in self-delusion.'

Feigning puzzlement, Eve screwed up her face. 'Now, certain entries in your diary for 1928−29 are written in German, and they all mention a girl called Natasha. So who was she?'

Fay dropped her eyes. 'There was a Russian fairytale I'd read when young. Olga, the little girl featuring in it, did lots of naughty things. But whenever she was challenged about them, she blamed her behaviour on her *alter ego* Natasha.'

'So Natasha is Fay when she's being naughty,' clarified Eve's mocking voice. 'So it's no surprise that you chose Natasha as your party name, when you became a naughty little commie and spy.' She glanced again at her file. 'Now, who was this Herr Heinrich, who had so much fun with naughty Natasha?'

'Heinrich was Henry, a partner in a firm of solicitors. I'd started work there as a general dogsbody in June 1928.'

'That August, there's an entry in your diary which reads: *"Herr Heinrich musste Natasha sechs Pfund bezahlen! Mensch, das war billiges Geld!"* So why did Henry stump up six pounds, and why was it such easy money for Natasha?'

Pouring more scotch, Fay granted herself an abrupt smile of recall. Then she peered at her interrogator through lidded eyes. 'He was paying for sexual services, rendered in his office one evening. And, that weekend, I went shopping for a dress I'd long admired.'

'So you were a youthful tart too, Fay.'

She held Eve's probing gaze. 'I prefer to say that, unlike mother, I was a survivor.'

'You knew what to charge, did you?'

'More or less,' she responded casually. 'One night, I waylaid one of my father's tarts, and invited her to have a drink in our lounge. I got her to talk about what she did with her clients and how she charged them. After a few gins she was very forthcoming, and I was impressed by how matter-of-fact she was about the whole business.'

'Nice to know what you're worth, isn't it?' Eve remarked drolly. 'Now, from October 1928 to March 1929 there are several more references to Natasha and Herr Heinrich, while a Herr Gerhard puts in appearances too. So shed a little light, Fay.'

'Herr Gerhard was Gerald, a friend of Henry's. He was a dapper, silver-haired and silver-tongued man, about my father's age. A partner in another firm, he had a flat in Harrow which he'd let close friends use. I went there first with Henry. Later, I indulged Gerald as well. Both got an added thrill from the fact that I was still underage. So I adjusted my rates to accommodate this factor.'

Eve masked her admiration for Fay's articulate and unapologetic display. 'So how did you feel about selling your body?'

'I didn't feel anything. I let Natasha handle that problem. She was the tart, and it was her who was paid. I was completely detached from the whole process. I just took my body to the sessions, and let Natasha earn the money.'

'Fay, are you sure you didn't inherit your mother's split personality, as well as your father's sex drive?'

'Spare me your amateur psychoanalysis.'

'Did you have any other clients?'

'There were some others I picked up locally, but they were so casual that I didn't bother to record them.'

'Now, your father died in April 1929, just before you turned sixteen. How did you feel about that?'

Fay lowered her eyes. 'Naturally, I was upset.'

'But you weren't devastated, were you?'

'Well, we'd grown apart.'

'The last entry in your diary for 1929 is undated, Fay, and there are no further entries until you start an entirely new diary in June 1931. So let's examine those few words you wrote.' Erasing a cold smile, Eve read from her file. '"*Vor einige Wochen, eine Höllenfahrt"*. To translate: "Some weeks ago, a descent into hell". So what does that refer to?'

'Father's death, of course.'

'Fay, you've just told me you weren't much bothered by it.' Eyes piercing, Eve looked up from the detailed notes she'd made of Dave Holt's evidence. 'This refers back to your last night in Willesden, doesn't it?'

Shaking her head in denial, Fay reached for her drink and sank the remains of the scotch.

'Let's have the truth, Fay.'

'That *is* the truth.'

'Really? Now, when you lived in Willesden you put on candlelit performances, didn't you?' Eve tutted theatrically. 'Don't you remember teasing that helpless bloke sitting in the dark next door, Fay? Well, he saw what happened just before you left Willesden for good. Quite unusually, someone switched on the electric light in your room that night. So give me your version about this so-called descent into hell.'

Fay poked a cigarette between her lips and lit it. Then she reached for the bottle in the centre of the table and poured a generous measure. First downing a slug of scotch, she stared at the tabletop, and then took a deep breath. 'I tried writing about it later, but "a descent into hell" was all I managed to put down. Even Natasha couldn't handle what had happened.'

Eve switched to her most unctuous voice. 'Then let's hear about it now. Best to get these things out in the open, don't you think?'

Smoke seeping from pinched nostrils, Fay parked the cigarette, gulped more scotch, and then levelled her eyes at Eve's. 'Two local tarts visited me that night. Jenny was a skinny redhead. The other was Mollie, bottle-blonde and masculine-looking. They didn't like my independent operation, or the fact that I'd entertained some of their clientele. They warned me to get off their patch. When I told them to get lost, they grabbed hold of me and hauled me up to my room.'

Reclaiming her cigarette, she dragged on it tensely. Her eyes moistened, but she kept them locked upon Eve's face. 'Mollie was incredibly strong. She held me down easily, while Jenny tore off my clothes. Then they gagged me with one of my stockings, and bound my wrists behind me with the other.'

Fay closed her eyes briefly, as if to dam welling tears. When she reopened them, she focused intently upon the task of refilling her glass, while her face contorted with disgust.

'Keep going,' commanded Eve unsparingly.

Purging her expression of all emotion, Fay took a long pull on her drink. The gaze she now directed at Eve was as dispassionate as her words. 'While Mollie pinioned me, Jenny collected some of my candles, and used them to rape and sodomise me. Then Mollie took her turn. After that, they joined forces. Is that enough damned detail for you?'

Eve's face remained impassive. 'Life's a real bitch, isn't it, Fay? You can play with blokes like they're toys, and you despise weak women. But, you keep coming a cropper at the hands of nasty, skinny redheads.' Smirking, she consulted her file, before eyeing Fay again. 'So let's fill in a few more gaps in your life story. After you fled Willesden, were you still on the game?'

'Hardly,' she replied flatly. 'Not after that hellish experience.'

'Where did you go after you left the flat in Willesden?'

'For a year I lived in bedsits. I left the law firm too, and went to work in a shop. The wages were pathetic, but I was cushioned by the savings I'd made earlier. Then, shortly after my seventeenth birthday, I arranged to share a flat with my cousin Caroline. She was three years older than me, and working as a translator. She got me a job with the same firm.'

'Were there no men in your life?'

Fay stubbed her cigarette. 'For some two years I was celibate. I was eighteen when I next indulged.'

Studying her notes, Eve made a show of totting up some numbers. Then, with brows elevated in a spurious show of prudery, she looked up. 'So how would you rate the forty-odd blokes recorded in your diaries in the two-year period before you married Oliver.'

'Well, they varied, of course,' she retorted glibly, 'and was it really as few as that?'

'Bit of a nympho, aren't you, Fay?'

She eyed Eve coolly. 'Strange, isn't it, that not only are words like "nymphomaniac" and "promiscuous" applied solely *to* women, but very often *by* them as well.'

A tinge of pink scurried across Eve's pale complexion. Then she shook off her momentary embarrassment, and settled for scowl and goading voice. 'Now, you married Oliver in June 1933, shortly after your twentieth birthday. Love at first sight, was it?'

'He was well-off, he could be controlled, he proposed.' Fay reeled off the words like an epitaph. 'I told him the conditions under which I'd accept his proposal, and so it came to pass.'

'So there's dull old Oliver, some twenty years older than you. He's a straightforward and successful breadwinner, who's frequently away on sales trips. Behind him, he leaves a young wife with her own agenda. But he copes, by being one of those men who doesn't want to know or see, as long as the shit isn't actually visible on his doorstep. Is that a fair summation, Fay?'

'I've always ensured that he is never publicly embarrassed.'

'So Oliver keeps you in comfort, and ignores the politics and infidelities. In return, you do the wifey bit when he's home, and dole him out the odd bout of high-class sex. And, being a former whore, as well as a consummate actress, I'm sure you've performed your role to perfection.'

'I got what I wanted from the marriage, and so did he,' retorted Fay in a businesslike tone. 'I've never seen any virtue in poverty. Moreover, I firmly believe that a woman should use all those powers she has, in order to organise her life to her advantage.'

'At least we agree about something,' said Eve seriously, cupping her chin in a palm. 'But, all in all, Fay, it seems that life has taught you to despise the weak and to exploit the old. Presumably, that same outlook underpinned your political views in the thirties too. Did you see yourself as working for the radiant new Soviet star in the east against the feeble, old, appeasing democracies in the west?'

When Fay made no answer, Eve switched subjects.

'Now, you were just twenty-three when you first met Jack in June 1936. Were you already in the Party then?'

'I'd joined his branch in West London that April.'

A needling smile appeared on Eve's lips, as she fiddled with the rings on her fingers. 'According to your diary, Fay, it was on your third wedding anniversary, while poor old Oliver was flogging tractors in Latvia, that you first climbed into bed with Jack.'

'So what was wrong with that? I fancied him.'

Eve jotted some details and then capped her pen. Closing her file, she passed over a sheet of paper, and switched on an icy stare. 'I want you to recite those extracts from my latest version of your trial testimony, just as though you were in court.'

Fay shrugged, and immediately complied. On conclusion, she reached out for her glass, and glanced at her jailer to assess her reaction.

Eve converted her pout into a scowl, and then abandoned this too in favour of a glare. 'Fay, that was utterly woeful. Your performance lacked all conviction. There was as much dramatic edge to it as when my mother reads out knitting-patterns. You'll have to do far better than that.'

'Well, it's not easy to convey credibility, when one's lines contain so many blatant lies.'

'Fay, stop behaving like the leading lady in a morality play. Of course there are some lies in your script. There have to be, to make the case against Jack hang together.'

Leaning back, Eve bunched her hair with both hands, and then shook the red mane back into shape. 'Now, the jury mustn't suspect that you can run rings around Jack. Rather, they need to believe that you were utterly dominated by him, and he could make you do whatever he wanted. They must believe that Jack kept you in line as his agent, not only by sex and blackmail, but by violence. They have to think, what else could the poor woman do?'

'God, why is it all so important?'

'For this reason,' said Eve sternly. 'In the very near future, I want you to show Jack what he'll be up against when you go into the witness box. I want Jack to appreciate what a jury will hear and see. This means your performance must demoralise him. And, to do that, Fay, you must embrace those lies you're going to tell. Embrace them like a lover, and smother them with conviction.'

'I can't make that load of tripe sound convincing.'

'I don't like the word "can't",' countered Eve coldly. 'So, under my direction, we're going to rehearse your testimony until it's absolutely compelling. And if I don't get a real performance from you, Fay, I'll make sure you stand in the dock with Jack.'

Thrusting to her feet, Eve paced around the table, and brought her face close to that of the seated woman. Green eyes constricting into slits, her voice thickened with menace.

'Now, since this is absolutely your last chance to avoid prison, Fay, imagine what would happen to you behind those walls. Because there'll be plenty of women like Jennie and

Mollie around, and they'll be queuing up to pounce on a toffee-nosed tart like you. So think candles, Fay, and worse.'

Fay shuddered convulsively, and then gazed intently at the tabletop. Eventually, her eyes locked onto Eve's penetrating stare.

'All right, you win.'

'I usually do, Fay. So let's hear that testimony again.'

51

FRIDAY 7 OCTOBER 1949

Slowly pacing around the cell, Eve read through Wendy's latest 'autobiography'. On conclusion, she halted by the desk where Wendy sat with a mound of documents before her. Other papers, late of DORA's Finance Section, were spread in a logical pattern over the bed.

Eve leant over the seated woman's shoulder. 'Now, what have you found for me in the way of funds?'

Compliantly, Wendy plucked a single sheet of paper from a folder. She showed off her findings to Eve, who stared at the sums unearthed and was unable to suppress a pleased grin.

Wendy handed her another sheet. 'I'll need more records to get at other accounts. That's a list of the documents I need.'

'I'll see to it directly I get back to base.'

Eve slipped the list into her file. Then she placed Wendy's 'autobiography' on the desk. 'Now, this is certainly an improvement. But there's still not enough detail on Jack. So don't be reticent. Really let rip about your relationship with him in the next version.'

'Why do you want me to go so much harder on Jack?'

'Well, in the unlikely event that I can't nail him for espionage, I'm going to have to put him away for other crimes, including fraud.'

'But Jack's frauds were pretty insignificant. I stole much more than him.'

'I know that, Wendy. But do you want to squander your loveliest years behind bars?'

'Of course not,' she murmured.

'Then you'll load your crimes onto Jack. You're the one who can really fix the evidence against him from all that documentation.'

Wendy grimaced. 'I'll do what you want, if only to avoid another cold shower. Just don't expect me to feel good about it.'

After locking the cell door, Madge turned, still adjusting her new navy outfit. Sandra stared at her sternly, and then wielded the gin bottle in liberal fashion.

'You're cutting things really fine, Madge. You know Eve will be here soon.' Curling up in an armchair, Sandra sampled her drink, and nodded approvingly. 'That's a really smart costume Claudio has made for you.'

'It's an absolutely smashing fit too, Sandra. It took him hours to measure me up for it, and he knocked something off.'

Curbing her smile, Sandra glanced up when Eve slipped into the room. Having fixed herself a gin and downed half of it, Eve beckoned her deputy, and handed her a slim file.

'Sandra, I want you to investigate this talk Jack had with a bloke called Peter Repnin in summer 1939. It was at that party of Jessica's that Beatrice mentioned. Jessica brought it up when I spoke to her.'

'Is Jessica back then?'

'Yes, she and Rita snuck back into Blighty a week ago. So we made a deal. She accepts the loss of her archive, and I forget about her criminal misdeeds. Anyway, you'd better question those who were at Jessica's party.'

Sandra screwed up her face. 'Does that mean I have to see Pam?'

'Why?' asked Eve, restraining her amusement. 'Is there a problem?'

'Eve, can't you see her? I'll do the others.'

'All right,' she replied affably, 'I'll talk to Pam.'

'Thanks,' muttered Sandra in relief.

'So have you managed to track down Eleanor Vere yet?'

'Well, I think we've finally found her right address. And she's married. Her name's Eleanor Todd now.'

Eve nodded in satisfaction. 'There's something else, Sandra. I've discovered from Fay why her name was in Herbert Pilling's address book.'

'Well, surely it was because she was passing him stuff to be microfilmed.'

'No, Sandra, they weren't linked in that business in any way. They met quite by chance at a party given by some of Fay's leftie friends. And, although he was with someone else that night, Pilling fancied Fay, and took her details for a later assignation.'

'Did they meet up?'

'No, and that was the really ironic bit. Two days after the party, Pilling had his fatal car crash. In any case, Fay didn't know his real name. He'd introduced himself by an alias.'

'So when did she realise who Pilling was?'

'Well, I had to show Fay a photo of him before the penny finally dropped.' Grinning, Eve topped up her glass. 'You should have seen her face, when I explained how she'd come to our attention. So I gave her a little lecture about the pitfalls of promiscuity.'

Wendy goggled at the sum deposited in the account. It had taken her several hours to finally unearth it from Horner's secret holdings. Shaking her head dazedly, she looked up from the desk, and gazed through the barred window at the horizon of tree-studded hills.

Returning her attention to the records on her desk, she drew a pristine sheet of paper before her, and assiduously checked all the figures. Yes, it really *was* that much! Her smile of delight lasted until other thoughts intruded, when it gave way to a circumspect frown. The question now was what to tell Eve?

'Nothing,' she answered herself aloud.

Seated upon the sofa in Horner's room, he glanced at Madge. Kneeling on the floor, she lolled across the coffee table on folded arms, bottom poked high for his delectation. When she gazed at him over her shoulder, her smile rivalled that of the Cheshire Cat.

'I'm doing the notes this time, Jack, because Sandra's busy investigating more of your dark deeds.'

Staring at the mirrored cubicle, he frowned. 'Who's in the hidey-hole today, Madge?'

'The what, Jack?'

'Madge, that cubicle's simply a mass of see-through mirrors, just like the one in my cell. So who's in there?'

'I honestly don't know, Jack,' she whispered. 'Eve keeps these things to herself, but there's probably nobody in there.'

Eve strode into the room and settled into her armchair. Peering coolly at the man opposite, she opened her file. 'Jack, let's talk about your stepmother Pamela.' Uncapping her pen, she cocked her brows. 'Soon after your father married her in March 1930, she became pregnant. But what happened then?'

'Pam had a miscarriage that autumn. The prognosis was that she couldn't have another child. Luke left her early in 1931.'

'Bastard!' hissed the two women in unison.

Sensibly making no comment, he awaited Eve's next question.

'Later, Pam got the Shropshire house as part of her pending divorce settlement. But what provision was made for you, Jack?'

'Well, there was a condition in the settlement that I should have a home there until my eighteenth birthday in October 1932. So effectively, though not legally, I was made Pam's ward until then. Luke also set up a trust to pay for my school and university education.'

Eve ticked her script. 'When did you first meet Pam?'

'It was summer 1931 in Shropshire.'

'So how did you rate Pam as a woman all those years ago?'

'I found her icily stunning,' he replied candidly. 'Even when young and vulnerable, there was a glacial quality to her beauty.'

'Were you and Pam alone in the Shropshire house in summer 1931?'

'No, Jessica was there on occasion, as was Pam's cousin Louise.'

Eve made another tick. 'Now, I've got a photograph taken by Jessica that summer, Jack. It shows you with a great big bandage over your arm. So come over here and roll up your left sleeve.'

Hesitating briefly, he stood up and walked to her side. Unbuttoning his cuff, he furled his shirtsleeve to the elbow. Eve grasped his forearm, traced a finger along the serpentine scar, and then released him.

'That looks nasty, Jack. How on earth did you do that?'

'I was running through a copse of trees on our land. I tripped, caught my arm on some sharp bit of wood, and slit it open.'

Fingers drumming against her file, she frowned sceptically. 'Is that all? I was expecting a somewhat meatier narrative.'

He offered her an insipid smile in recompense. 'Sorry, Eve, it was a simple teenage accident that gave me this scar.'

Mouth pursed in dissatisfaction, she dismissed him. Waiting until he and Madge had disappeared inside his cell, Eve stood and gesticulated towards the cubicle. Then she walked over to the room's main door and into the corridor. When the other woman emerged from the narrow room leading to the cubicle, Eve stifled a yawn.

'We'll discuss everything tomorrow. I've had a long day. So I'll just show you out.'

52

SATURDAY 8 OCTOBER 1949

Eve motioned Pamela Armitage towards the settee. After providing them both with drinks, she settled into her armchair.

'I thought we'd have a proper chat today, Pam.'

A blasé smile preceded the drawled retort. 'Does that ruling mean I can't mention anything *im*proper, Eve?'

'The point I'm making is that you revealed nothing of substance when I phoned you.'

Delaying her response, Pam drew cigarettes from her bag. She inserted one into an ivory holder and lit it in elaborate fashion. 'So what more is there to tell?'

'That's what I intend to find out. Anyway, could you see and hear all right in the cubicle yesterday? It was the first time I'd used it.'

'There were no problems at all, Eve.'

'And what did you think of Jack's performance?'

'Well, I was most intrigued to hear his views about me when I was young.'

Eve lounged back in her seat. 'So let's hear your version of life with young Jack.'

Pam sipped scotch pensively and then set down her glass. 'Well, Eve, early 1931 was a truly bleak period in my life. I was feeling exceptionally confused and vulnerable. I was barely twenty-two, I'd recently miscarried, and I'd just been deserted by my so-called husband. And, while I may have thought that I knew a lot about life, in fact, I knew next to nothing.'

'So how did you deal with your situation?'

'I had no master plan, Eve. I simply operated from day-to-day. But, of one thing I was quite certain; I would never again allow a man to treat me as Jack's father had done.'

'You're preaching to the converted, Pam.'

'I don't doubt it.' She darted Eve a shrewd glance. 'Anyway, in the summer of 1931 Jack was due in Shropshire and, the way I was feeling, I hardly needed the added burden of a sixteen-year-old adolescent. But he had nowhere else to go. Previously, he was sent abroad in the summer, while in the shorter vacations he stayed with friends. However, I soon began to appreciate his company in that hateful house since, apart from brief sojourns by Jessica Deacon and my cousin Louise, there were no visitors.'

'So where did things go wrong between you and Jack?'

'Well, I wouldn't say that things went entirely wrong between us, but back then our relationship certainly went awry. Moreover, while I hate to admit it, I wasn't entirely blameless in the matter.'

'Was there some catalyst in your dealings with Jack?'

Smoke seeping from her nostrils, Pam nodded. Then an almost dreamy expression illuminated her face. 'It began when I went to a party, my first venture into society for many a moon. I wore this gorgeous cream creation and little beneath it. Unsurprisingly, men surrounded me like moths around a flame, and I flirted outrageously the entire evening.' Her lips tautened reluctantly in recall. 'Possibly, I drank a little too much as well. In those days I rarely touched alcohol.'

As if to underline the transition, she reached for her glass. 'Since I was still formally married to a local nob, I was deemed off-limits. So I drove home erratically and alone. Then I went to my room to change, only to discover that the damned zipper on my gown had caught. And, short of tearing it apart, there was no way I could get out of that dress without assistance.'

'And there was nobody in the house except Jack.'

Muting her smile, Pam nodded. 'He was reading in the library, as he often did. So I summoned him, instructed him on how to proceed, and the zipper parted perfectly.'

'Then you thanked him profusely, and sent him back to his books,' suggested Eve in a wry tone.

'No, I didn't,' Pam admitted, dabbing quite unnecessarily at her hair. 'Naturally, it wasn't hard to divine his thoughts, as he stood there ogling a woman half out of her dress.'

'But he was nearly six years younger than you, Pam.'

'True. But, various adventures abroad ensured that he was already more accomplished in sexual matters than was I. My sole experience had been at his father's hands, and he made most inexpert use of those.'

Pam extinguished and ejected her cigarette. 'So I asked Jack what he expected to happen next, and what he intimated came as a shock to my then innocent self. However, it was not this which determined matters. Rather, it was the controlling expression that I saw on Jack's face. It was as if this look had been handed down like an heirloom from father to son. Moreover, it made me realise that I was in danger of handing on myself as well.'

Her features softened; a concession reflected in her words. 'In retrospect, it's possible that I read too much into that look at the time. Perhaps my hatred for Jack's father simply coursed through me once more. But, I felt what I felt, Eve, and I was determined not to have another Randall ride roughshod over me.'

Pam stared at her clasped hands, and then looked up. 'So I decided to settle matters there and then. I invited Jack to kiss me, and he did so, most delightfully. At this juncture, he obviously expected to proceed to the next stage. Instead, in an icy tone, I ordered him out of my room. I saw this look of utter bewilderment upon his face, but he left. And that was that.'

'You saw Jack next in summer 1932, Pam, when you were arranging the sale of the house in Shropshire. So how were things between you when you two met up again?'

'Initially, Jack stayed well out of my way. He was always polite and obedient when our paths did cross, and his personality was noticeably more urbane. But mostly he avoided me, and retreated to "Stone Pool", a small lake on our land. There he would just swim, read, and sunbathe.'

'Until?' prompted Eve, showing off her knowing look.

Eyes half-lidded, Pam smiled brazenly. 'Until my afternoon walk somehow took me towards "Stone Pool". And there he was; tall and handsome, nearly eighteen, and lying naked in the sun.' Veneering a lip with her tongue, she let her shoulders shrug ingenuously. 'Well, I thought, "Damn it, why not?" He had it, and I felt like taking it. So I did, there and then.'

'That all seems eminently reasonable.' Eve flicked up her brows inquiringly. 'Presumably, you came back for more at your convenience.'

'Whenever it suited me, I summoned Jack to what I call a "command performance", and I never had cause for regret.' She paused to drain her glass. 'Unlike his father, who was sexually violent and selfish, Jack accommodates women's moods and desires. I fancy that this accounts for much of his success with them.'

'So for certain women he's quite ideal.'

'He is indeed,' said Pam, toying with her treasured jade bracelet. 'He's intelligent and interesting. He does what is required of him, and does it very well. He makes no demands, and he causes no scenes. I'm sure Louise and Fay could provide you with equally glowing testimonials regarding his overall performance.'

'Of course, there'll be no more performances for several years, once I put Jack away.'

'Well, such is fate.'

Grinning, Eve stood to refill their glasses. 'How did he get that scar on his arm? You heard him say yesterday that he got it when running through a copse.'

'I'm afraid that was the truth, mundane though it be.'

'Oh, well,' said Eve, enacting a thwarted shrug over what had proved to be a dead end. Passing a scotch to Pam, she reseated herself, and took a generous pull at her own drink. Then she welded her gaze to the other woman's face. 'You go both ways, don't you, Pam?'

The fair brows rose above slightly widened eyes. 'I go any way that suits my interests, Eve. In any case, I abhor sex discrimination, except when it works to my advantage.'

This retort triggered matching smiles from both women.

'So when did you and Jessica Deacon become lovers?'

Reaching for her scotch, Pam sipped it reflectively. 'Our relationship began late in 1931 in London, Eve. I'd moved there, after Jack returned to boarding school, because I had no intention of remaining isolated in that odious Shropshire mausoleum. But, to say that we were lovers, save in a sexual sense, is to oversimplify things; for I was quite wrong for Jessica's needs. Jessica is tediously possessive, and has no interest in men whatsoever. And, while I had no problem crisscrossing the boundaries of gender, I had no intention of being owned by either woman or man.'

'How long did your affair with Jessica last?'

'Well, it wasn't until summer 1932 that we finally called it a day. But there had been countless rows and rifts before then; mostly prompted by the fact that I took my pleasure wherever it was to be found. Strangely, we got on better after we split up than before.'

Vacating the armchair, Eve took a seat on the sofa next to Pam. Withdrawing several photographs from a folder, she spaced them over the table. 'Four snaps from this rather graphic collection feature in a recent calendar of Jessica's.'

'Yes, I know. Jessica informed me of the fact, and assured me that the same financial arrangements would pertain as of old. She told Louise as well. But I doubt that Jack knows anything about it.'

'Jessica took the original pics in early 1933, didn't she?'

'That's correct,' said Pam, leafing casually through the photos. 'We'd all decamped to London. The Deacon sisters were cohabiting in the Belgravia apartment they'd inherited from Daisy. Jack was sharing a flat in Earls Court with fellow-students. Louise and I were renting a small place in Chelsea, and it was there that these photos were taken.'

'And what set off this orgy?'

'Well none of us were angels, Eve, and we'd all drunk plenty that night. Then Jack produced some hash of which we all partook. Thereafter, for want of a better phrase, things just happened between us, and Jessica photographed these spontaneous events. However, unbeknown to the participants, Jessica showed a selection of these racy photos to some of her clientele, and very soon she could hardly meet demand.'

'So Jessica realised that this was where the money was.'

'Exactly, Eve, and until the war put a stop to such activities, she made an excellent living producing risqué calendars. These featured mainly Louise and myself, together with a sprinkling of her other models.'

'Wasn't it chancy for you to pose for such pics, Pam? After all, you were well-known in society and frequently photographed for magazines.'

'As you say, there was a risk.' Plucking a *Du Maurier* from her pack, she loaded it into her holder. 'So, to ensure that Louise and I could not be identified in our unclad state, we utilised arty lighting, streaming hair, hats, masks, and suchlike. As a result, we were never detected, Eve, not even in Jessica's best-seller.' Smirking, Pam brandished the photo. 'An unidentifiable me performing a handstand, and Jack....' She let her words tail off.

'Who's the third woman in these pics?'

'That slender beauty was my then girlfriend. She was a model, although hardly of probity.'

'Was Jack often at your place, Pam?'

'Well, on occasion I'd command his presence there, and sometimes Louise would.'

'Didn't he paint you both there as well?'

'Yes, he did.' An almost sugary expression coated her face. 'In fact, he painted me twice, and let me choose one portrait to keep for myself. So I selected that which I thought portrayed me best. It was an utterly gorgeous painting, Eve. Unfortunately, it was later stolen by one of my besotted admirers. I was dreadfully upset.'

'Jessica told us that you sold it.'

Pam diluted her sour look into a lemony smile. 'Well, I was offered a very fine price, Eve. One can't be overly sentimental.'

'So when did you last pose before Jessica's camera?'

Pam polished off her scotch before responding. 'With the onset of the war everything juddered to a halt, and when peace came I was in my mid-thirties. So I turned my attention to alternative sources of finance.'

When Eve pointed at her empty glass, Pam nodded. Having replenished their needs, she returned to her armchair, and filched a fag from Pam's pack.

'Now, how involved was Jack in all this?'

'Well, when Jack learned that he was on sale through Jessica's orgy photos, he was most annoyed. But, since he always needed money as a student, he was pacified when offered royalties. However, Jessica diddled him. She only paid him a trifling sum for each photo sold, whereas Louise and I were most generously rewarded.'

Eve's face screwed up in frustration. 'Are you saying that Jack was only involved in porn once, when Jessica shot those photos at your place?'

'Yes, Eve. But I can always say that there were other occasions.'

A broad grin effaced Eve's frown. 'You're my kind of woman, Pam.'

The blue eyes widened above an audacious smile. 'I realised that from the moment we first met, Eve.'

Ignoring the challenge, Eve simply posed another question. 'Did you ever stay with Jack when he was abroad?'

'During his university year abroad, Jack chose Vienna as his base. I visited him there in 1935.' Pam paused, both to kill her cigarette and to imbibe. 'Do you know about the soap?'

'Soap,' echoed Eve. 'What about it?'

'In Vienna Jack gave me a bar of soap to take to London.'

Eve leant forward with interest. 'Did it contain anything?'

'I think that goes without saying, but I've no idea what.'

'So what happened to it?'

'It was collected from me by a polite, intense man. He was obviously foreign, and decidedly Jewish. He didn't say his name. He merely uttered a password which Jack had given to me in Vienna.'

Crushing out her butt, Eve reached for her file and jotted a few notes in it. Her eyes skated over what she'd written. Then she closed the file, and peered at the older woman.

'Well, I think that's all I need from you just now.'

'What a pity,' said Pam, gaze as candid as her tone. 'Could I not interest you in a meal, Eve, or anything else for that matter?'

'Pam, for me it's always business before pleasure, and right now I'm extremely busy. Anyway, you've got a whole herd of male admirers.'

The full lips pinched in disdain. 'A herd of balding bellied bores.'

'Well, you can't have everything.'

'I really don't see why not,' said Pam, miming an extravagant pout. 'But how did you know about my herd?'

Eve deflected the question with a bland smile. 'I'm told that you're getting engaged to "Smarmy", once this unhappy business with Jack is over. He is queer, isn't he?'

'Irrevocably so. However, his projected career demands the fiction of a wife, while mine demands his factual fortune.' She lowered her voice in entreaty. 'Would you care to attend the wedding, Eve? I could do with some good company while I endure that charade.'

'I'd love to, Pam. In return, can I offer you an invitation to Jack's confession?'

'Now, that I'd love to witness.'

'Well, it shouldn't be long now,' said Eve confidently. 'First, I'll need to accompany Jack on some more mendacious wanderings down memory lane. But, I'll let you know when to pop in.'

After Pam had left, Eve phoned Sandra's flat. Once she'd established which twin was on the line, she instructed her to collect a set of prints which Gwen had produced from old photographic plates.

'I'd like some classy enlargements made, Delilah, and I want them by next weekend.'

53

TUESDAY 11 OCTOBER 1949

Sandra escorted him into Horner's room. Once Randall had assumed his usual place on the settee, she left. Ignoring his presence, Eve continued to peruse her file. With no option but to await her favour, like some disgraced courtier, he studied the woman seated opposite.

She wore a sienna costume teamed with a black silk blouse. The red mane spilt over her shoulders. Appreciating the bold colour combination, his eyes ran over her slender figure and downturned face. Reluctantly, he conceded that he found her exceptionally attractive, and from certain angles quite beautiful.

As though she'd read his thoughts, a smile flitted across Eve's lips. Eventually, she looked up. 'Jack, before I confront you with Fay, I want to tidy up a few loose ends. We've had very interesting talks with your cousin Amanda, as well as with Pam, and her cousin Louise Grainger. Now, I warned you that I'd be able to check the validity of your answers.'

He stared back into her probing eyes.

'Jack, you've lied to me constantly,' she asserted, summoning from experience the tones and demeanour of a wronged wife. 'Now, most have been little lies. But they create this aura of mendacity about you. All of which suggests that you're likely to withhold or distort the truth about the bigger issues too. You must see that.'

Pausing for effect, Eve let the didactic mingle with the dogmatic in a complex facial expression. Then she consulted her file once more. 'Now, you told us on 3rd October that you only slept with single women during the war. But Louise was still married, when you were sleeping together at the war's end. Just a little white lie in this case, was it?'

He reached for his cigarettes and lit one. Lugging deeply on this prop, he took on her accusing stare. 'Louise stayed with me, because her first husband had decamped with his secretary, and she didn't want to be alone. She was going to divorce him and later she did. As far as I was concerned, Louise was a single woman, and she viewed herself likewise.'

Eve nodded indifferently. 'What was Louise's job at that time?'

'She was a government scientist.'

'What did her first husband do?'

Her change of tack induced his frown. 'He was an official in the Ministry of Supply.'

'What was his role in the ministry?'

'It was something to do with procurement.'

'Procuring what?'

'Raw materials that were in short supply.'

'And what topped his list?'

'I'm not sure.'

'You're not sure!' she stormed, jabbing a finger at his face. 'Jack, you knew from Louise that her husband was involved in procuring uranium for the Anglo-American atomic weapons programme, didn't you?'

'It must have slipped my mind.'

'I don't like slippery minds,' she retorted frostily. 'You used your affair with Louise to pump her for information, didn't you?'

'What do you mean?'

Leaning forward, Eve stared at him balefully. 'Before he deserted her, Louise's husband leaked things about his work, which she, being a very able scientist, comprehended perfectly. Later, she was able to explain certain things to you: like the various isotopes of uranium; the function of heavy water; the meaning of nuclear fission and chain reactions. Are you going to deny that you had such conversations with Louise?'

'Why should I deny it? I was interested in the potential of atomic energy. It's hardly irrelevant to mankind's future, as the bombs on Hiroshima and Nagasaki have demonstrated.'

'Did you pass these morsels to your Russian masters?'

He snorted in exasperation. 'I don't have any Russian masters. In any case, this is simply more circumstantial evidence, isn't it?'

She sat back, relentless eyes fixed upon his face. 'It all goes into the pot, Jack, and I've got some more ingredients to add.'

'Like what?'

'Like this,' she retorted. 'When you went to university in London, your cousin Amanda was already a student there. Now, Amanda was a member of the CPGB for several years, wasn't she?'

He stubbed his cigarette. 'I suggest you ask her that.'

'We have, Jack. Amanda says she joined the Party in 1932, and left it in September 1939, in disgust over the Nazi-Soviet Pact.' Eve tented her fingers, and then interlocked them into a rickety tepee. 'Remind me, Jack, when did you join the Party?'

'January 1936.'

'During the all-pals-together Popular Front period, you told us.' Her eyes focused accusingly upon his. 'But, Amanda says you attended some Party meetings with her in late 1933, when the international communist line was uncompromisingly hostile towards others on the left. Is that correct?'

'Yes, I went to several Party meetings then.'

Disengaging her hands, she sat forward aggressively. 'Another lie, Jack?'

'Not at all. I'd just come back from Hitler's Germany. I was nineteen, and I was looking for some answers. I went to CPGB meetings for that reason. But, as you said, Eve, the then Party line was utterly sectarian. So I had no incentive to join it. I'll repeat what I told you earlier, I joined the Party in January 1936.'

She glanced at her file. 'You left university in June 1936. What did you do then?'

'I worked as a journalist.'

Her eyes rounded quizzically. 'But, in summer 1936 the Spanish Civil War began. Why didn't you volunteer to fight there in the International Brigades?'

'I didn't want to get killed.'

'Was that the reason? Both Amanda and Fay say the Party forbade you to go, because you were being groomed for greater things.'

He held her stare, but didn't speak.

'Here's another discrepancy, Jack. You told us on 14th September that your first fling with Fay began in spring 1946, didn't you?'

He pursed his lips, but remained silent.

'In fact, you two were having an affair long before the war, and it continued until Fay and Oliver left for the USA in 1942.' Her eyes bored into his. 'So do you want to change that bit of your story?'

'All right,' he muttered, 'I admit that I did sleep with Fay back then.'

She regaled him with a look of triumph. 'So you lied about when your affair with Fay began. Now, why not say it out loud, Jack? Confess to one lie at least.'

Randall stared at the floor, and in a subdued voice admitted his lie.

'At last we're getting somewhere.' She gave him a full terror-of-the-deep smile as reward, and then lolled back in her seat. 'Let's talk about your meeting with Peter Repnin.'

Disconcerted, he looked away.

'It was June 1939. Jessica gave a do. You were there, and so were Pam, Fay, and Amanda. Remember it, Jack?'

Toying with his matchbox, he nodded charily.

'Another guest was Repnin, who worked for Soviet intelligence. Fay says that it was he who recruited her, following her phoney expulsion from the Party in September 1938. Repnin instructed her to hold herself in readiness, until she was in a position to be of use to the Russians. That time came in 1942, when she and Oliver went to Washington. There Fay had several affairs with American officials. But this was just pillow-talk stuff. It was only when Fay joined DORA in June 1944 that her spying career really took off. Now she could get her hands on documents.'

'So Fay says all that about herself.'

'Fay says your expulsion was also rigged, Jack. Thereby allowing you, like her, to distance yourself from the Party, and be available for later recruitment as a Soviet spy.'

'Well, that's news to me, Eve. I didn't agree with the grounds for Fay's expulsion, whether rigged or not, and I said so. Partly for that reason, partly because I'd expressed my own doubts about the Party line, and partly because I was involved with Fay, they expelled me too. There was nothing more to it than that.'

She eyed him stonily. 'Fay, Amanda, and Pam, all say you had a long conversation with Repnin at Jessica's party. Fay says you were talking in Russian. Do you deny that?'

'Some of it. I did talk to a man calling himself Repnin, but our conversation was conducted in a mixture of Russian, German, and English.'

Her response to such quibbling was a dismissive flick of the fingers. 'Jack, you're impossible!'

'No, Eve, I'm just stubborn about facts and the truth'. He exchanged the matchbox for a cigarette and lit it. 'Repnin was no more Russian than I am. He spoke lousy Russian, dire

German, and abysmal English. For what it's worth, I reckon he was Czech.'

'Are you going to deny that he worked for Soviet intelligence?'

'Not at all. He tried to recruit me too, but I declined his offer.'

'So you say, Jack.' Again she consulted her file. 'When Fay was in the USA, did she contact you?'

'I never heard a word from her. The next time I saw her was when she turned up in DORA in June 1944.'

'You told us that you played no role in her appointment.' Eve fashioned a cocksure smile. 'Yet Fay says that Horner contacted her because she knew Russian, and that it was you who'd supplied this information to him. Care to comment, Jack?'

'By all means,' he replied assuredly. 'In early 1944, Horner asked me to provide him with the names of any British citizens I knew, who were fluent in Russian. Naturally, I gave him Fay's name amongst others?'

'Naturally?'

'Well, how many native-born Russian-speakers do you know, Eve? Anyway, what Horner did with my list was his business. As I said, it was he who appointed Fay. I had nothing to do with it, except to alert him to her existence.'

'How did you and Fay get along between June 1944 and the resumption of your affair in spring 1946?'

'We rarely saw each other. During the war, DORA was quite a large organisation and spread over several buildings. I worked in the one we're in now and Fay in another. When our paths did cross, she showed absolutely no interest in me. Presumably, she was involved with some other man.'

'Several, according to her diaries,' Eve supplemented brightly.

He shrugged his indifference. 'Anyway, I had Louise in my flat around this time, while for most of the latter half of

1945 I was abroad. Fay moved into this building when both I and my then deputy were absent, in order to take charge of the section. It was only when I returned to Britain in early 1946 that things started up again between us.'

Nails tapping against her file, Eve glanced at her list of questions. 'In summer 1935, you got Pam to carry a bar of soap from Vienna to London. This was later collected from her by some foreign bloke. So what was so valuable about it, Jack? Did it contain microfilmed instructions for Soviet agents in London?'

'No, Eve, it contained diamonds.'

Her brows arched with incredulity. 'And who were they for?'

'The relatives of a Jew I knew in Vienna. He anticipated the Nazi take-over of Austria, and wanted his kinsmen to fix up an escape route for him and his family.'

'That's a really murky tale, Jack.'

'It was a really murky world, Eve.'

She held his assured gaze for several seconds before posing her next question. 'Jack, how often did you see Caroline King in Paris?'

Extinguishing his cigarette, his brows knitted in a frown. 'What do you mean?'

'When she was in Paris, Fay met her communist cousin Caroline, who now rejoices in the name Karola Király. She was working for the Hungarian legation there, until she was recalled to Budapest last May.'

'Well, since Fay neglected to mention such details to me, I'll have to take your word for it.'

'Most gracious of you, Jack,' she retorted acidly. 'Now, you were Fay's superior in a spy-ring. Moreover, you contacted her each time you passed through Paris, when you were carrying microfilm from Horner for Soviet intelligence. So did you hand over information to Caroline for onward transmission as well?'

His smile forbearing, he slowly shook his head. 'Even by your abysmal standards of evidence, Eve, those accusations are utterly ludicrous. I was Fay's superior in DORA, not in this nonexistent spy-ring. I never once saw Fay between her departure for Paris and my kidnap there last May. While any microfilm I carried for Horner went to his men in the field, not to Soviet intelligence.'

'I also asked if you met with Caroline,' she reminded him coldly.

Grey eyes narrowing, Randall leant forward belligerently. 'Yes, I *did* meet her, Eve, but not in Paris. I met Caroline in a cell in Budapest, sometime in June, when our jailers brought us together for a confrontation. She was white-haired, skeletal, and could barely stand. In a whispered monotone, she denounced me and herself as "imperialist spies and Titoite provocateurs". After that, I never saw her again, and I'd be very surprised if she was still alive.'

Eve's lips parted in a parody of astonishment to exaggerate her gasp of disbelief. 'Oh Jack, the things you come out with!'

54

THURSDAY 13 OCTOBER 1949

The handover took place at the recently erected door in the fourth floor corridor.

'All yours,' boomed Brenda Higgins, ushering Fay into Madge's charge.

'Do I have to sign for her?' she inquired brightly.

'Just don't bloody well lose her,' advised Brenda, flashing a brutal smile. 'Eve would be rather upset if her key witness disappeared. And the person what lost her would be even less happy.'

Frowning apprehensively, Madge watched her waddle off. Then she double-checked that the door was securely locked. Pointing ahead, she then followed as the shackled woman trudged into her former office.

'Must be nice to be back in your old place again, Fay.'

The prisoner reviewed her surroundings. 'I could see out of that window before.'

'Still, it's only for a few days, if everything goes to plan.' She slid the mac off Fay's shoulders and unlocked the cuffs. 'Anyway, there's a nightie for you to change into.'

Fay glanced at the younger woman. 'I suppose you too will be standing and staring while I undress.'

'Well, those are Eve's orders. But it's really not my cup of tea. So I'll give you five minutes to change. Just don't mention it to Eve.'

Spinning on her heel, Madge left the room.

In the safe house, Eve locked the cell door behind her, and peered at the woman lying in bed. 'What's this, Wendy? Why aren't you working on the accounts?'

'I've finished them,' she retorted smugly. 'I cracked the final set last night. The details are on the desk.'

Crossing the room, Eve opened the folder. Once she'd tallied the figures, her eyes widened in delight. 'That's the lot, you say?'

'That's your lot,' confirmed Wendy; neglecting to mention that she'd be bagging the big one for herself. Holding the covers over her bust, she propped herself on one elbow. 'You've really made a mint out of me, haven't you?'

'How can you possibly say that?' goaded Eve.

'Well, besides laying you golden eggs from Horner's stashes, just think of what you got when you shut down my own accounts.'

'But that was stolen money, Wendy.'

'And you've handed it all back to the government, I suppose.'

'No, I've re-stolen it to finance the government's business. However, since the money in your very first account seems to have been honestly acquired, I've left that intact.'

'Thanks a million!' Wendy retorted acidly.

'Anyway, you clever little accountant, I really ought to reward you.'

Still clutching the covers, Wendy drew herself into a sitting position. 'So set me free.'

'I could do that. After all, I've now squeezed every penny out of you, Wendy. Nor do I need you for Jack's trial, now that Fay is being so cooperative.'

The dark eyes ignited with delight. 'You mean I'm free?'

'Well, that depends.'

'On what?'

Folding her arms, Eve produced a disconcerting smile. 'What would you do to gain your freedom?'

Thinking of the life-changing sum of money, which she could only access if she was at liberty, she answered at once. 'I'd do anything.'

'Given an open-ended offer like that, Wendy, just be grateful that you're not my type.' Smirking, Eve sat on the edge of the desk. 'So I'll be satisfied with some grovelling.'

'What do you mean?' asked Wendy nervously.

'Come over here, throw yourself at my feet, and beg for your freedom.'

'But I'm not wearing anything.'

Eve's smile seemed almost apologetic, 'I know,' she said, reaching down to slip off her shoes. 'But that will simply add to your sense of degradation.'

'I don't understand. Why must you humiliate me?'

'For two reasons, Wendy: firstly, because I want to; and secondly, because I can.'

Evening meal delayed, bloated belly rumbling, Barber trudged towards the office of the PUS. Munching on his moustache helped a little, since it still tasted of lunchtime's pea soup. He was about to be called to account by yet another vulture circling the carcass of DOSS. The usual suspects, MI5, SIS, and the Home Office, had all tentatively dipped their beaks into his exposed hide. Now it would be the turn of 'Puss'.

Plodding through the open door of the office, Arthur slumped onto a chair unbidden, and wrenched the cherrywood from a pocket. Ready with attack as the best form of defence, the pipe thumped viciously against his open palm, which understudied for the role of Puss's shiny cranium.

Brollied, but not yet bowlered, the PUS toyed with his umbrella, as if seeking to engage first gear. Then he swivelled it into neutral. 'Barber, you and your bungling thugs have made an utter hash of things. An innocent man is dead.'

'Innocent?' countered Arthur, gruff voice straining for derision. 'There were whispers that Ifor Evans was planning to talk to the press.'

Puss moved one foot forward dinkily, and rammed his brollie into second. 'Barber, the one thing saving you and your blundering outfit from the chop, is the fact that you have somehow got your ham-fisted hands upon an "atom spy". So where do things stand regarding Randall's confession?'

Almost choking with relief that the 'minimising' of Evans no longer seemed to be an issue, Arthur's voice emerged as a hoarse whisper. 'I'm reliably informed that it's imminently forthcoming.'

There was little else he could come up with other than this load of flannel, because this was all Eve had told him. Nor was he in any position to gainsay her, since the latest round of attacks upon DOSS had left him with no time to check her contention. In any case, he was sure she'd come up trumps. He could feel it in his water.

'I am asking, Barber, because our cousins across the Atlantic are quite unable to understand why we are so intent upon trying the stubborn Mr Randall. They remind us that we have to hand the self-confessed spy, Mrs Galbraith; a lady who has betrayed not only our own secrets to the Russians, but theirs too.'

'I doubt our Fay got hold of much from a wartime fling with some State Department lad.'

'It was quite a fling, Barber.' Strangling his stringy smile at birth, Puss pursed his lips like a bugler. 'The FBI memorandum we have received runs to over fifty pages. Its lurid contents reveal Mrs Galbraith to be a serial seductress, who had liaisons with numerous officials in wartime Washington, from all of whom she extracted classified information.'

'So it's the footling FBI that's stirring things up, is it? So just inform them that, if they insist on interfering in our investigation, we might have to publicise the fact that....'

'Barber!' It was the same authoritative voice which had once bawled out his fag's name, but was now invested with a warning note. 'As you well know, there is a tacit understanding about such matters between our two nations. As long as we make no mention of such peccadilloes, then our American cousins will continue to overlook the small matter of....'

'Aye, I know about that,' growled Arthur.

Puss fiddled with his umbrella. Seemingly unable to engage third gear, he settled for neutral. 'Although it pains me to say so, Barber, our masters agree with you that it can only be Randall who stands in the dock. We would be the world's laughing stock, if we revealed that this country's secrets were betrayed upon such a grand scale by a female master-spy?' His beaky nose twitched rabbit-fashion. 'Perhaps mistress-spy is more apt in this instance.'

The brollie jiggled again. This time he got into third and even managed a smooth change into fourth. 'Thus, there can be no question of indicting Mrs Galbraith, nor, indeed, of portraying her as other than a pathetic accessory to the man's crimes. So get Randall's confession, Barber, and get it soon.'

Pocketing his pipe, Arthur slumped back in his chair, confidently compressing his paunch with both paws. 'Are we done, lad?'

Puss planted the bowler on his head, caught up his rolled umbrella as if to cleave Barber's skull, and then dropped it to regulation position. 'I'll be in touch about that other matter.'

Fangs bared in a lupine grin, Barber dredged himself from the chair and lumbered triumphantly from the room.

55

SUNDAY 16 OCTOBER 1949

When Eve entered his cell, Randall lay sprawled on top of the bed in a nightshirt. The chain securing his ankle to the bed lay in coils on the floor. Beneath the bed was a tray containing his last, barely-touched meal. He made no resistance, when she grasped his wrists and fettered them to the iron frame above his head. Then she emptied his congested ashtray into the waste-bin, and laid it upon a nearby chair.

Unbuttoning her beige jacket, she clambered onto the bed. Mouth set in an irksome smirk, she propped herself on one elbow beside him. 'You know, Jack, it's simply ages since I shared a bed with a bloke. I don't think you appreciate just how much time I'm devoting to you.'

'Well, I'd be delighted to leave here this very moment, if that would help matters.'

'No chance,' she said, playfully tweaking his nose. 'So does time go slowly in here?'

He rattled his shackles. 'What do you think?'

'Still, you get plenty of time to think, don't you? Time to work on your next round of fabrications. Now, don't get me wrong, Jack. I know a lot of what you say is true. But it's all interwoven with loads of lies and evasions. So it's my job to unpick the tapestry of your life, and get at the real truth.'

'I think we've had this fruitless conversation before.'

'It's hardly fruitless. I'm utterly fascinated by this case. It's like peeling an onion layer by layer to get at the hard core of truth. And, that's you, Jack; a hard-core philanderer and traitor, shielded by a skin of charm and deceit. But we're getting there now.'

'Are we?' he sneered.

'So what do you think about when you're alone?'

'I'm hardly going to tell you.'

'Do you think about your past conquests, all long gone? Do you think about going to prison, Jack?'

He nibbled his lip, but remained silent.

'No women in prison, Jack. But you'll cope, because when you get there, you won't care a damn. Take my word for it. In any case, perhaps a bit of erectile dysfunction will be a blessing in disguise for you.'

'Bit of what?'

'Just a phrase I made up. Reckon it'll catch on?'

'Probably, Eve, if the world fills up with women like you.'

'And just what do you mean by that?' she demanded, theatrically steepling her brows.

'Eve, you know damn well what sort of woman you are.'

'Yes, that's true, Jack. I'm extremely ambitious, highly professional, absolutely amoral, and utterly ruthless. Of course, not all women can boast such a range of virtues, while others have yet to cultivate these traits to the same level as have I. But, when all is said and done, Jack, we are the stronger sex.'

Randall showed no inclination to dispute this.

'You've got nice hair, Jack. Like my Jimmy's – dark and wavy.'

'So where's this Jimmy? Chained up in a kennel for the night?'

'No, Jack,' she responded, tugging his hair. 'Jimmy was my husband. He ran off with some fat, round bitch. But he's dead now.'

'I don't see you as a grieving widow, Eve.'

'Oh, I did grieve, Jack, when he ran off. But not when he went over the cliff, screaming away, as Eric tossed him into the void.'

Randall gulped. 'What about the woman he ran off with?'

'She drowned,' said Eve distantly. 'I really enjoyed watching the bubbles come to the surface, as I held her under the waves. Nice little spot to die, down in Devon.' She jabbed his nose and grinned. 'Would you have done that?'

'I'm not an utterly ruthless woman, Eve.'

She twisted his nose until he winced. 'I sense you disapprove of what I did, Jack. But I reckon she got her just desserts.'

Eyes watering, he made no comment.

'Jack, did you know that Ifor Evans was involved in a hit-and-run accident?'

His eyes flickered, but he remained silent.

'Poor old Ifor, there he was, toddling along a country lane, thinking about his knighthood, when suddenly this car came round a bend.'

'Eric again?'

'No, Jack, it wasn't, but I believe Ken Flack was in the area. And, another thing, did you know that Ursula Conrad is dead?'

His lips curled in disgust. 'You're certainly making sure the truth won't come out.'

'Fair dos, Jack! Ursula died of a brain tumour. We took her to a hospital we use, but it was inoperable. Poor old girl just went into a coma. Doctor helped her on, but she'd had it anyway. In any case, Ursula wouldn't have been "minimised". Despite his quite advanced views upon female emancipation, Barber remains wedded to inequality when it comes to "minimising" women. Rather sexist, isn't it?'

'How does that fit in with the death of Jimmy's woman?'

A glacial smile prefaced her reply. 'Oh, that was private stuff, Jack; private and personal, a bit of freelancing.'

He breathed out slowly. 'Do you think you're sane, Eve?'

'Yes, Jack, I'm perfectly sane.' She stared at him unblinkingly. 'Tell me, is this like talking to your torturer in Hungary?'

He smiled wanly. 'I only told one person about that.'

'And she told me. Trouble is, Jack, you don't know what else Fay is going to say. But you'll soon find out.'

His eyes closed briefly upon his troubled thoughts.

'You've really ballsed-up your life, haven't you, Jack? Especially when you consider how privileged it's been.'

'Privileged,' he echoed bitterly. 'Do you mean I was privileged to cause my mother's death, without ever knowing her or her love? Or that I was privileged to have a father, who deigned to exchange about one hundred words with me in my entire life?'

'Damaged from an early age, were you, Jack? Well, so are loads of kids without your advantages, but they don't all turn into traitors. Actually, I was referring to such privileges as intelligence, good looks, charm, and a fine education. But none of that seems to have got you anywhere, except this cell.'

He eyed her uncertainly. 'All my own fault, is it?'

'Well, no one else is to blame, Jack.' She held her cold smile. 'And soon, you'll have to face up to further facts about your life. But I'll save those for a birthday treat.'

'I'll look forward to it.'

Pushing to her feet, Eve subjected him to an icy stare. 'Don't get too cocky, Jack, because in the very near future a woman will cause your downfall. That, I can promise you.'

Sandra glanced at Fay, who sat on a mattress, hugging her knees. Seating herself on a desk jammed into one corner of the cell, she opened her file.

'Is this stuff about your cousin Caroline King actually true?'

'Amazingly enough, it is,' Fay replied, in a tone more jaded than sarcastic.

'So how did you get in touch with her?'

'Well, after she was posted to Paris, Caroline contacted her mother in London. Her mother informed me of Caroline's address, and I got in touch with her. But we were very careful. We went out of our way to find some obscure bistro for our get-together.'

'You only met her that one time?'

Eyes uneasy, Fay nodded. 'We arranged to meet again, but Caroline didn't turn up. I rang her, but her phone was dead. Later, I went to her address. The concierge said she'd returned to Hungary to see her sons.'

'Have you no idea what happened to her?'

'None at all. Jack told me that she'd been caught up in the purges in Hungary, but he didn't elaborate.'

Easing herself further onto the desk, Sandra pinioned one thigh with the other. 'Did Jack know you'd contacted Caroline in Paris?'

'I doubt it. I certainly didn't tell him.'

'Did Jack meet with Caroline in Paris?'

'I can't see how he could have done.'

'Can't you?' responded Sandra sternly. 'Well, here Eve wants you to strengthen your evidence, because she'll be alleging that Jack met Caroline in Paris several times, and that he handed her material to be conveyed to Soviet intelligence. So she wants you to work that into your testimony. Eve also wants you to provide far more detail about your own meetings with Jack, while you were in Paris.'

A momentary expression of distaste marred the haggard prisoner's face. 'I'll devote my full powers of invention to all of that.'

Sandra frowned before posing her next question. 'Do you believe Jack really *was* kidnapped and handed over to the Russians?'

'Yes, I do, but I'm not sure why. All I can tell you is that, months before it happened, my MGB handler asked me to provide him with a detailed biography of both Jack and myself. He also wanted information about other former Party members working in DORA, namely Vic Welles, Leo Ikin, and Donald McCloy.'

Waggling a foot, Sandra pondered this reply. 'Doesn't that suggest that the Russians had *not* recruited Jack as a spy?'

'Not at all,' Fay countered shrewdly. 'It only suggests that he hadn't been recruited by the MGB.'

Ignoring this point, Sandra stared at Fay, budded lips the centrepiece of her incredulous expression. 'Fay, given what's happening now in Eastern Europe, not to mention the likely fate of your cousin, are you really still a believer in that monstrous system?'

'One expects the current imperfect system to change or reform.'

'Oh, does one?' Sandra retorted icily. 'Perhaps it would be better for oneself to change or reform, wouldn't one say?'

Fay gazed back obdurately. 'If you want the desirable end, you have to accept some of the repugnant means. As Stalin once said, "You can't make an omelette without cracking eggs".'

The tall blonde wrinkled her nose in contempt. 'Except the eggshells cracked by bullets are human skulls, Fay. And does anyone really know how big this bloody omelette is going to be?'

56

WEDNESDAY 19 OCTOBER 1949

Accompanying Sandra into Horner's room, Randall noted the rearranged furniture. A row of three armchairs now confronted the swivel chair in which he sat. Then, to his surprise, Sandra produced a set of handcuffs. Having shackled his left wrist, she clipped the other cuff to the chair's wooden frame. Smiling, she eased herself into an armchair, dipped into a pocket, and castrated a green jelly baby.

'Why manacle me, Sandra?'

'It's because we can't risk you attacking Fay.'

He jacked up his brows. 'Why would I attack her?'

It was Eve, standing behind the middle armchair, who responded. 'You might want to, Jack, once you've read a transcript of her confession. I'll let you have a copy later, so you can appreciate the full beauty of Fay's deeds. You see, it's all about authenticity, and Fay's confession is loaded with detail about real codes, real microfilmed documents, and real meetings with real Russian controllers. She's a genuine expert witness.'

His eyes latched onto hers. 'Just how long has she been in your hands?'

Eve granted him a condescending smile. 'Fay's been our guest since shortly after her abortive attempt to defect.'

'You mean she never even left Britain?'

'Well, why would Fay really want to slip behind the Iron Curtain, Jack? Like you, she'd seen the queues and shortages there, which make our own seem like paradise. She'd felt the overt political terror as well. Of course, like any theoretical believer, she could ignore such facts, but only until she had to face up to one practical question. Did she really want to spend the rest of her life under such conditions?' Skirting the armchair, Eve paced over to his side. 'Anyway, after faffing about for a bit in Poole, Fay turned herself in two days after you last saw her.'

Eyes narrowing, he stared up at her. 'So she was already in your hands when Barber's thugs were beating me up, because I couldn't tell him where she was.'

'That's right,' she confirmed blithely, ruffling his hair.

'Well, if Fay's confessed to being a Russian spy, then that's her problem.'

'Wrong, Jack, it's yours. It's your fault for being a man.'

'Again?' he queried in a contemptuous tone.

'Don't you see, Jack? You made her do it. We'll have to do the usual stereotypes, like weak, infatuated woman under the thumb of an evil male seducer, and all that crap. But it's you who'll have to carry the can.'

'Eve, what are you wittering on about?'

'In the popular mind, Jack, *real* spies are men, while the typical female agent is a Mata Hari, gathering up whispers from pillows. So a woman working in a secret job, who hands over tons of classified information to Moscow, like Fay has done, would shatter this comforting misconception.' She gave his nose a tweak, gentle by her standards. 'I really liked the idea of a "Spy Queen", Jack. But with so much prejudice around, I knew I'd never get away with reversing your roles. So this means it has to be you in the dock.'

'Then you admit that you'll be framing me?'

'Jack, we both know you've been up to something with the Russians. So, if we magnify your role a bit, it doesn't alter the fundamentals.'

He glared at her grinning face. 'As I said, you'll be framing me.'

'We'll just be adding some verisimilitude to your treacherous deeds. Anyway, look on the bright side, Jack. You'll be a master-spy, and that has a certain cachet.'

'Stuff the cachet! You'll imprison me for something I haven't done.'

'But only for fourteen years, Jack. So when you get out, you might still have enough going for you to make it as some pensioner's toy boy.'

'A what, Eve?'

'Toy boy, Sandra. It might catch on. Fay and Pam must have had loads of them.' She switched off her smile. 'Anyway, she'd better come in.'

Gliding over to the door leading to the corridor, Sandra opened it to admit Madge and Fay. Face drawn, her bearing lethargic, Fay averted her eyes from Randall's hostile glare. When she slumped onto the seat facing him, Eve sat side-saddle on its arm, while Madge and Sandra curled up in the remaining armchairs.

'Not even a Judas kiss for you, Jack,' Eve observed.

'Fay, why are you doing this?'

Her lips twitched, but she refused to look up. 'I'm sorry, Jack, but it has to be done this way.'

'You're sorry?' he snarled. 'Well, that excuses everything.'

Her eyes glistened. 'For God's sake, Jack, don't you realise that my whole life's been dragged through the mud during these past weeks?'

'Fay, I didn't lead your life, you did.'

'You can't run away from your past,' purred Eve. 'It's like your shadow, Fay. You can try ignoring it, but it's always there, right behind you.'

'It's there in your diaries too,' said Sandra pugnaciously.

'All those blokes!' added Madge, her tone hinting more at envy than censure.

Eve slipped both hands around Fay's neck and prised up her chin. 'So how does he look, Fay? A bit betrayed, do you reckon? He doesn't look like he loves you.'

'He never did,' snapped Fay.

'I suppose you're wondering why she's turned against you, Jack. Well, beyond her patriotic duty in shopping a treacherous sod like you, there's the simple fact that Fay really can't face jail.'

'Just a parlour red, aren't you, Fay?' goaded Sandra scornfully. 'Can't possibly go to prison for your beliefs, can you?'

'Prison,' echoed Eve melodramatically. 'Heavens above, Fay might meet some real members of the working class there. Not the heroic, class-conscious militants of her drawing-room fantasies, but nefarious elements of the Lumpenproletariat, like her old friends Jenny and Mollie.'

'Jack, I just can't face the prospect of prison,' insisted Fay in a subdued voice.

'It's not something I'd planned for myself either,' he retorted acidly.

'But you're a man.'

'What the hell's that got to do with it? I haven't done anything.'

Her eyes took on his angry glare. 'Yes, you have, Jack.'

Eve smiled supportively. 'Jack, do you remember the message on the back of that photo which Fay left for you? The one you tore up, and which I found that first time I had you properly searched?'

'What about it?'

'Well, Jack, we asked you many times if you knew where Fay was.'

'And I told you just as many times that I didn't know.'

'But, you knew from her message that she was planning to defect to the East, didn't you?'

'I may have suspected it, but I didn't know it.'

'So you suspected that Fay was involved with the Russians?'

Scowling at her crafty expression, he nodded reluctantly.

'So, if you're as honest and loyal as you claim to be, why didn't you turn her in to the authorities?'

He held Eve's gaze. 'I wasn't feeling overly patriotic at the time.'

'But that's hardly the judgement a loyal citizen should make. So we'll work that sentiment into your trial. The jury will lap it up.'

He managed only a defeated grimace as response.

'Now, Jack, the central motif of your trial will be your word against Fay's.'

'I think I've realised that by now,' he retorted grimly.

'So who do you think the jury's going to believe? I reckon they'll prefer the Svengali version.'

'Perhaps they'll prefer to assess the facts.'

'No, Jack, they'll assess the performances. A trial is theatre.'

Eve stood and paced behind Randall, who observed Fay's eyes follow her like a dog. Her shoulders straightened, as if jerked into position by a puppeteer. From behind him, Eve ordered her prisoner to perform some of the testimony she'd be giving in court.

He watched Fay compose herself. But, once she adopted her role, the incriminations poured out in persuasive fashion. Terror-stricken looks buttressed her accusations against him, and there were lots of seemingly real tears. The finale featured an extremely plausible show of contrition, together with Fay's expressed determination to lead a new life. If he'd had two free hands he might have applauded.

'You know, that was really good,' lauded Madge.

'She almost convinced me,' conceded Sandra in a vinegary voice.

Parading a triumphant smile, Eve returned to Fay's side. 'A fabulous performance, darling,' she gushed 'Just like a Pavlovian doggie. Reckon you can beat that, Jack?'

Whether or not she was still performing, Fay's jutting jaw and determined tone portrayed utter conviction when she spoke again. 'Jack, under *no* circumstances am I going to prison. I just want to go home to Oliver.'

'After the suspended sentence,' explained Eve, 'it will be back to Oliver, that paragon of understanding husbands. The Galbraiths will fashion a new life together. Fay's going to be a housewife; it's her current *raison d'être*, she tells me. So, back to your cell, Fay, and give it a good dusting before your departure.'

Once Fay and Madge had left, he glanced at Eve, whose confident demeanour spoke for them both. She paced up to Randall, and planted her hands upon the arms of his chair. Her eyes gazed intently into his, and then dropped to his crotch.

'Still feeling cocky, Jack?'

Randall was in his cell, and Fay was under escort to Surrey. Patiently, Eve awaited the arrival of her favourite DOSS carpenter. Punctual as ever, Harry was a jovial man with a barrel chest and beefy biceps. Skilled in his craft, he immediately powered into action.

Once Eve had sufficiently enjoyed the ripple of some serious muscle, she left to shower and change. Then, following Harry's departure, she spent her time adorning a wall in Horner's room.

57

THURSDAY 20 OCTOBER 1949

He awoke with a start. Eve's inverted face grinned down at his from above the iron bed head. He shot her a half-hearted glare.

'What's the time?'

'It's just after midnight, Jack.' Pacing around the bed, she sat on its edge. Her face jelled into a spurious show of concern 'So how are you feeling since confronting Fay? A bit betrayed, I suppose.'

Ignoring her question, he posed his own. 'Do I get to know why you're here tonight?'

'I'm going to take you next door.'

'I wondered when you'd get round to nocturnal interrogations. They were the norm in Hungary.'

'Jack, I'm far too unorthodox to have norms,' she retorted in an imperious tone. 'We're going next door for other purposes.'

Standing, she strode across the cell to where his clothes now hung again. Having selected the roomiest shirt, she returned to the bed, whisked the duvet from it, and ordered him to stand up. As Randall manoeuvred his chained leg onto the floor, she flashed him an equivocal smile.

'I have to agree with Madge. Keeping a naked man chained up in a nearby cell could prove to be quite a time-saving device for some women.'

'I thought I was a sexual pariah and untouchable traitor.'

'Well, you are most of the time, Jack. But today's our birthday, so I thought we should celebrate.' She tossed him the shirt. 'Slip that on. It's more versatile than a nightgown. After that, turn around and stick your pandies behind you.'

His eyes darted suspiciously towards the open door. 'Who's in Horner's room?'

'Nobody, Jack. The only people there are frozen in time in pictures of the past, and it's these I want you to confront.'

'You've already shown them to me,' he said dismissively.

Lidded eyes added menace to her sinister smile. 'But I've got some new ones, Jack, which you simply *couldn't* have seen before.'

Having buttoned the thigh-length white shirt, he inched his hands behind him. Eve pulled cuffs from her pocket, closed them around his wrists, and then unfettered his ankle.

'Now, that wasn't so hard, was it?' Her palm landed a light slap upon his buttock, which she converted into a playful grope. 'You lead the way, birthday boy.'

He trudged towards the doorway and peered warily into Horner's empty room. On entering it, he took stock of the latest changes. A wide pelmet had been fixed to one wall, and from it hung two sets of closed black curtains. He was soon confronting this funereal display, when Eve planted him on the settee.

She slipped out of her black jacket and draped it over a chair. Long fingers cajoling a white blouse into her waistband, she posed before him. The Stygian backdrop accentuated the hues of both blouse and hair. Then she drew back one set of curtains to reveal a wall studded with photos, all featuring a teenage Randall. Arms meshed across her bust, Eve stared fixedly at the manacled man slouched on the settee.

'As you are aware, Jack, those pornographic pics of you with three women were taken at a drug-fuelled orgy at Pam's place. Moreover, you profited financially from some of them, didn't you?'

He chose to stare at his knees.

'Won't look good at your trial, will it, Jack? If you were prepared to sell your body to support your degenerate lifestyle, then you'd sell the nation's secrets too. That's how the jury will reason.' Her eyes widened in appeal. 'Jack, it would be far less humiliating if you confessed, and later pled guilty at your trial.'

'Forget it, Eve.'

'You're certain you won't confess, aren't you?'

Lips tightening obdurately, he denied her a reply.

'Well, I'm certain of something too, Jack. I'm convinced that by the end of this session, I'll have turned your head inside out.'

Randall gazed at the intense expression upon her face. 'Any chance of a smoke before you attempt to mess with my mind?'

'Of course, Jack. My programme allows for a whole range of birthday treats, prior to attaining my objectives.' Her indulgent smile morphed into an approving pout. '"Mess with your mind". I like it. It could catch on.'

She headed towards the desk and vanished from his view. Her chatty voice sounded behind him. 'Fancy a drop of classy Claret? That's what I'm having. If you prefer something stronger, there's VSOP brandy. We found a bottle in some filing cabinet.'

He vacillated. It was a month since he'd touched spirits. In his current plight, keeping a clear head seemed sensible. Yet the alternative was attractive too. He asked for a Cognac.

With cigarettes and matchbox tucked into her waistband, Eve carried over glasses and bottles, and deposited them by his feet. Seating herself beside him, she bent forward to pour their drinks. Then she straightened up, lit a cigarette, and anchored it between his lips. As he smoked, Eve sampled her wine. Then she deposited her glass on the carpet, plucked the butt from his mouth and stubbed it. Smirking, she scooped up the brandy, fed him sips, and again set down an empty glass.

Turning towards him, she trailed fingers down his neck until thwarted by the buttoned shirt. Eve darted him an ambiguous glance, and then leisurely unfastened the garment down to his navel. 'Well, I did say it was more versatile than a nightgown, Jack.'

Rounding her eyes, she undid the remaining buttons. Her gaze homed in on his groin. 'Looks somewhat limp, Jack. Are you putting up a rare show of resistance, or are you just feeling less cocky? Or is it that you don't fancy me anymore?'

'Who says I ever did?' he retorted in a surly but strained tone.

Her lips curled haughtily 'I bet you wish that was true, Jack.' She topped up her wine, and sipped it as she stared. 'Now, that's much more like it. It's really perked up. But soon we'll look at the new photos, and let's see how rampant you are then.'

She drained her glass and placed it on the floor. 'To my mind, Jack, this continuing activism of your libido indicates that there are still lies lurking within you. And that's what it boils down to. You want to fuck your interrogator both metaphorically and literally, don't you? You want to screw up my investigation by your deceit, and screw me into the bargain. Well, you won't succeed on either score.'

When he glared at her challenging expression, she pushed the open shirt to each side of his erection. 'Now, supposing I took advantage of this display, like the women in those pics on the wall. Would you tell me to stop? Would you try to escape from my attentions? Of course, you wouldn't.' Her taunting smile augmented. 'But, despite the temptation, I can't do that, Jack, since from the outset I designated you as sexually off-limits. So I'll just put it back under wraps.'

After refastening the buttons of his shirt, Eve pushed to her feet. She collected a sheet of paper from her jacket, tucked it into her waistband, and replenished her glass. Pacing over to the 'orgy' photos, she scrutinised them closely, as though viewing a gallery of old masters. Then, with drink in hand, she positioned herself before the closed set of drapes, and eyed him inquiringly.

'Would you like to see your mother, Jack?'

Smiling icily, Eve hauled back the curtains to reveal four sepia-tinted prints. 'Now, it can't have been much fun having to imagine your mother all this time. But this array should give you some pointers.'

Randall barely heard her, as he gazed at a photograph of a young woman fronting a sun-splashed garden. She posed in Edwardian dress, with broad-brimmed, feathered hat and parasol. Her attractive face featured the deep-set eyes and hawkish nose which he'd inherited from her.

There were two other photos of Miranda Randall. One was of her wedding. Both she and Luke stared back with fashionable solemnity. A young Aunt Daisy hovered to one side, while Jessica and Nancy Deacon, then beribboned tots, proffered posies and shy smiles. In the other picture, his mother was seated indoors, her hair coiled weightily upon her head. Her body seemed bulkier, but her face was gaunt and the eyes leaden.

He screwed up his face. 'Who took these photographs?'

'Walter Finch, Daisy's passive paramour. He never overcame the pitfall of admiration from afar, even after she was widowed. You should read his diary, Jack, if you want a study in repressed desire.' Eve paused to quaff some Claret. 'He left everything to Jessica, his talented *protégée*. So, along with his equipment, she inherited his photographic plates. That's how these shots of Miranda were preserved, despite Luke's best efforts to erase her memory. We've enlarged them, of course.'

Eve pointed at the picture of Miranda seated. 'She's pregnant there, Jack. That's you inside, devil-swelling in her belly.' Her gaze drilled into his disturbed psyche. 'But she looks somewhat anxious, doesn't she? Perhaps she knows you're going to kill her.'

She paused again to savour both her wine and his overt distress. 'Or perhaps she's just wondering about the point of it all. You see, Luke was having an affair. It was in Walter's diaries. He met the lady in question as well, when he travelled up to Shropshire with Daisy and her husband in July 1914. He photographed her too.'

Eve gestured towards the fourth photo, which portrayed a curvaceous and vivacious young woman. 'Her name's Eleanor Vere, or Eleanor Todd as she now is. She was twenty then, and I reckon she looks a lot like Fay. Take after Luke quite a bit, don't you, Jack?'

He forced himself to take on her supercilious stare.

'God, but he loathed you, Jack. We talked to Eleanor recently. When Luke was on leave in 1915, she tried to reignite their affair. She told us he'd spat out a passing reference to you. "That vile brat", said Luke, "has robbed me of the only woman I ever loved". Nice thing to say to the woman he'd been screwing while the wife was out of action. Men can be so inconsiderate and hurtful, can't they?'

Eve drained her glass and placed it on the floor. 'Now, what was it you wrote in early 1931, Jack, after Luke left Pam? In her letter to you, Pam related that she'd discovered your father was conducting an affair while she was pregnant. And I found your reply to her, which you apparently never sent. It was in that big trunk in your attic.'

She tugged the letter from her waistband, unfolded it, and recited the relevant extract: '"Pam, what you write forces me to reflect upon my own relationship with Luke. I have often wondered whether my father has made me pay for his own guilt all these years. Has he made out that my birth robbed him of the only woman he ever loved, while at that time he was involved with another? If that really was the case, I honestly don't think I could cope with it."'

She eyed him coldly. 'That's what you wrote, Jack. So how are you coping?'

As the tears rolled down his cheeks, Eve wafted her hand in the direction of the 'orgy' photos. Her lips curled disparagingly. 'What would Miranda have said about that charming display, Jack? Pornographer, philanderer, drug addict, communist, spy, traitor, and God knows what else. How would your poor mother have reacted to such a litany of shame? You might well have killed her, if you hadn't done so already.'

She paced across the room, sat by his side, and hauled up his downcast face by the chin. 'Jack, you don't really care that your mother has to confront such a spectacle, do you? What's wrong with a life devoted to sex and lies, all overlaid with betrayal? None of that bothers you, does it? You're protected by your lies. So you don't need to confess anything, do you?'

Shoulders heaving, he wept uncontrollably; crying the tears deferred over the years by 'manliness'.

Bringing her face close to his, Eve treated him to an assured smile. 'But deep in your being, Jack, you know full well that you *do* need to make a confession. So why not admit it, if only to yourself? And to aid that process, I'll let you have a long, self-torturing think about things. Shall we say for about three weeks, Jack? What's milling around your anguished head should have festered enough by then.'

Eve collected her glass and poured more wine. Grinning, she toasted the pictures of Miranda Randall.

'Jack, I always said it would take a woman to make you confess.'

58

FRIDAY 11 NOVEMBER 1949

Attired in a midnight-blue evening dress and long matching gloves, Pam Armitage sauntered towards him. Eve joined her. Like visitors at a zoo, they studied the passive figure before them. Wrists cuffed behind his back, ankle chained to Horner's desk, Randall's panda-like eyes peered back dully.

Pam laid a leather-gloved hand upon the forearm of her hostess. 'Has he given you much trouble, Eve?'

'No, Pam. Ever since Jack's confrontation with some home truths, he's hardly spoken. For days, he's just been staring at pictures of his mother.'

'So what has he been thinking about?'

'He's been thinking about confessing, Pam. I've let the strains and stresses bubble away inside him, and now I fancy his head should be properly cooked.'

'What on earth is he wearing, Eve? It looks like a cross between a toga and a nappy.'

'Oh, that's just a sheet I wrapped around him. It's for the unveiling.'

Pam winched up her silky brows. 'So what exactly will you be revealing?'

'A new man,' said Eve laconically. 'My objective has been to beget a new man from the husk of the old.'

Eve straightened the sienna jacket she wore over a peachy blouse. Then she led her guest to the suite positioned around the laden coffee table. Settling upon the settee, Pam watched Eve uncork two bottles of Horner's *Chablis Grand Cru.*

'Eve, it was so thoughtful of you to invite me to this ceremony.'

'Think nothing of it.' She passed over a glass, and then eased herself into an armchair. 'So why are you all dolled up, Pam?'

'Well, I was planning to go to the theatre later.' She sipped her wine, and then stared blatantly at the redhead. 'That is, unless I should be unavoidably detained.'

The main door opened and Eve's colleagues entered. Gwen swamped an armchair with her large frame, while Sandra's lithe body settled in another. Madge supplied them with drinks, and then perched on an arm of Sandra's chair. Following some desultory conversation between the women, Eve set down her glass and stood. Pacing over to the figure swaddled in the grotesque 'toga', she stood in profile to indict him; coaxing indignation into both her visage and her words.

'Let's summarise your life, Jack. You killed your mother, and were justly repudiated by your father. Thereafter, you took sexual advantage of a host of gullible women, and were unfaithful to every one of them. Then, as the high point of your career, you betrayed your country. And to think a woman died, so that scum like you could be born.' Turning, Eve summoned a sisterly smile for her audience. 'But, thanks to your help, ladies, we can now reveal a truthful and emasculated Jack Randall; a veritable new man.'

Slowly, she untwined the sheet from his torpid body. When it fell to the floor, Eve stepped back to admire the detumescent perfection of her exhibit. Soon the other women crowded around for a closer look.

Pam stared disbelievingly at her stepson's unresponsive manhood.

'Bloody hell,' groused Madge indignantly, 'not a peep!'

'Jack, that's not very flattering,' lamented Sandra.

Sniggering behind her camera, Gwen took several shots.

Madge frowned in frustration. 'Well, you've got what you wanted, Eve. No libido and therefore no more lies. So are you happy with this blob of a bloke you've produced, this so-called new man?'

'Madge, I've simply made Jack confront his life,' Eve asserted piously, 'and this is the inevitable result.'

'So can Madge and I go now?' asked Sandra in a disenchanted voice.

'If you want,' said Eve offhandedly.

Once they had left, she turned towards the photographer. 'Hand over your camera, Gwen, and then take the rest of the evening off.'

'But, Eve,' she begged, 'please, let me print these. They're brilliant shots, and I promise I won't....'

'Damn right, you won't!' Beaming a remorseless glare along the line of her outstretched arm, Eve snapped her fingers. 'Camera, Gwen, and don't make me tell you again.'

Her face like thunder, Gwen complied. Wordlessly, Eve escorted her to the exit leading into the corridor. Then she closed the door behind her and locked it.

'Am I a prisoner too?' drawled Pam.

'Just say the word and I'll unlock it.'

'I've forgotten what the word is.'

Reseating herself on the sofa, Pam poured more wine, and then stared at Randall. Her face a portrait of revulsion, she shuddered. 'Eve, please remove your hideous new man from my sight.'

'I will, once he's signed something.' Eve pointed at the document on the desk behind him. 'There's the confession I've written out for you, Jack. Are you now prepared to sign it?'

Apathetic eyes confronting her steely glare, he nodded. Immediately unshackling his wrists, she handed him a pen, and he signed each sheet.

'*Bunosséget elismeri?*' questioned Eve in Hungarian. 'Do you plead guilty? Oh, come on, Jack! I learned it especially for this occasion from the transcript of the Rajk trial. And you say what?'

'*Elismerem,*' he whispered. 'I plead guilty.'

'*Az egész vonalon?* On all counts, Jack?'

'*Az egész vonalon,*' he murmured in confirmation.

'Good boy, Jack!' Smiling like a beatific shark, she patted his head. 'Pleading guilty to your life, that's what I like to hear.'

Freeing his leg from the desk, she shoved him gently towards his cell.

Still panting from her run downstairs to fetch another camera, Gwen Chambers entered the room next to Horner's from the corridor, and passed from there into the cubicle. Easing her sizeable bottom onto a chair, she surveyed the panoramic view provided by the two-way mirrors, and focused her camera in anticipation.

Eve locked the cell door and walked towards the desk, where she poured herself a large brandy. After holing most of it in one, she set down her glass, and watched Pam posing narcissistically before the mirrored cubicle. Eve pouted admiringly at the sight; hoping that at forty she too might have such flawless skin and unspoilt figure.

Pam's eyes latched onto Eve's mirrored gaze. 'Anything wrong?'

'Are you still planning to go to the theatre, Pam?'

She glanced teasingly over her shoulder. 'That rather depends upon you, Eve.'

Eve padded towards the other woman. 'Fancy your luck's in, do you?'

'Well, isn't it?' The striking blue eyes stared avidly at the reflection of both her own beauty, and that of the redhead poised behind her. 'Now, wouldn't this make a stunning photograph?'

Eve slipped her arms around the firm, svelte waist. 'The gloves certainly add a novel dimension. Will you be keeping them on throughout?'

Pam reached behind to grip Eve high on the thighs. 'I thought you might enjoy the feel of leather against your skin at a later juncture.'

'Pam, this was always going to be a test of wills.'

'True, but I'm sure you won't regret it.'

'But *you* might, Pam.'

'Why on earth should I?'

'Because I rather fancy a "command performance".'

Pam smiled invitingly. 'That hardly presents me with a problem, Eve.'

'That's good. Because I'll be in command, Pam, and I'm a *very* bossy person.'

PART SEVEN

FEELINGS OF RELEASE

DECEMBER 1949 TO JULY 1950

59

THURSDAY 15 DECEMBER 1949

Nose buried in the *Manchester Guardian*, Barber read how Traicho Kostov had been sentenced to death for treason. He noted how in their final pleas to the court, Kostov was the only one of the eleven accused to maintain his innocence regarding the main charges.

A knock sounded on his door. Closing the newspaper, Arthur bellowed permission to enter. Resplendent in navy outfit and blue blouse, Eve strode punctually into his office and seated herself on the chair by his desk.

'I've just been reading about Kostov, lass. He's the latest one for the high jump. So that's a nice little present for Stalin's seventieth birthday next Wednesday.'

'Was Noel Field mentioned in Kostov's trial, sir?'

'Nay, lass, but Field didn't know any Bulgarian reds.'

'Do we know anything more about Field's wife and brother?'

Shaking his head, Arthur tracked down his pipe. 'Nowt's been heard of either one, since they vanished behind the Iron Curtain in August. Any road, who cares? This whole business is just about red bigwigs settling scores and bumping each other off.'

'It's probably the only pleasure on offer to the downtrodden sods in Eastern Europe.'

'I agree, lass. Yet, whatever I think of Kostov and his ilk, I can't help respecting the man's courage in denying most of the charges against him. Especially, if you consider how brutally they must have worked him over beforehand.'

'Your point being, sir?'

The bushy brows crept upwards slowly and slyly. 'No chance of young Jack doing a Kostov and denying everything in court, is there?'

'None at all,' she declared confidently. 'Jack will confess to any crime, and put his name to any lie.'

The jowls wobbled with his satisfied nod. 'I'm asking, Eve, because I was shown an SIS report from Vienna some days back.' Barber stoked the cherrywood as he spoke. 'This concerned a defector from the Hungarian People's Paradise, some AVH lieutenant.'

She cocked her brows in query.

'Well, this lad was on duty in AVH headquarters in Budapest last June. He told our friends in MI6 that an Englishman was being held there at the time, but nowt else, no name or description.'

'Pretty vague stuff, sir, and even if true, it doesn't mean this Englishman was Randall.'

'But it's a sign of the times, lass. The competition's really envious of the kudos we've earned by unearthing an "atom spy" for HMG. They'll do anything to undermine us.'

'I realise that, sir,' she responded soberly. 'Anyway, what's the situation with our own little defector?'

Like shields the lids sagged over his eyes. 'Well, not only has young Pratt's resignation gone through, but I'm hearing that MI5 have taken him onto their books.'

'So we've got the SIS and Five trying to queer our pitch. Nothing new there, sir. But we've got Randall, of course, while they've got sweet FA to offer our masters.'

He performed his pipe-smile. 'Aye, lass, we're right out of sight of the other riders in the "atom spy" stakes.'

'So how are the preparations for Jack's trial coming along?'

'Typically, the papers got lost in committee for a time. But it'll be going ahead, Eve. We'll have to get Christmas out of the way first, and then there's likely to be a General Election.'

'The powers-that-be will hardly want a spy trial going on during that bun fight, will they?'

'Nay, lass. But, once it's done with, they'll whisk Randall quickly through the lower courts and set a trial date. So he'll just have to vegetate a little longer.'

'Well, that won't present any problem, sir. It's like he's already adjusted to doing time. Just get the authorities to give Jack some books and paints when he's finally popped into clink, and I foresee him being a model prisoner.'

Lolling on the sofa in Horner's room, listening to the Light Programme, Sandra glanced up when Eve arrived at DORA for the first time in a fortnight. She eased herself into a sitting position.

'Eve, how much longer will I be babysitting Jack?'

'It could be a while yet.' Eve lowered herself into the chair behind the huge desk. 'So I'll get Brenda and Norma to relieve you and Madge for a bit. Mind you, Jack won't like it if I send away his two favourite ladies.'

'I doubt he'd even notice.'

'How is he then?'

'He's just a shadow of his former self, Eve. He hardly smokes, he sleeps a lot, and his skin's gone quite pale. He's also developed a passion for chocolate cupcakes, so he's getting a bit podgy.'

'Does he still read?'

'A bit, when he's awake. I left him a Rupert Bear annual as a joke, and he devoured it at one sitting. Later, Madge brought in some of her younger brother's comics. Jack really enjoyed those.'

'Gone back to his childhood, it seems. And has he been signing a copy of his confession regularly?'

'He's never missed a day, or created any problem when told to sign.'

Eve narrowed her eyes. 'I trust there's been no renaissance of his libido.'

'Hardly,' retorted Sandra drily. 'Yesterday, Madge complied with your standing orders. There she was, prancing around starkers in front of Jack, and he just fell asleep.'

Eve grinned. 'Well, he won't be the first bloke to do that.'

60

THURSDAY 5 JANUARY 1950

Barber struggled from his mac, and hung it and a battered trilby on the coat stand. Glancing around the room, he noted that both armchairs were occupied. His old foe, DCI Unwin, glowered at him from one. The other was commandeered by the representative of MI6. Pale of countenance, with grizzled hair and trim moustache, Basil Villiers nursed a scotch and soda.

Taking the only free place, Barber flopped gauchely onto the settee. 'So who are we waiting for?'

Villiers' hazel eyes homed in on the 'Dossboss'. 'Some fellow called Smythe. Chap's standing in for the PUS.'

Arthur shone a blubbery beam upon Unwin. 'Lad, would you like to get me a scotch?'

'No, Barber,' snarled the Special Branch officer. 'I would most definitely *not* like to get you a scotch.'

'Over there, old chap,' said Villiers, thumb waving vaguely in the manner of a novice hitchhiker.

Arthur dredged himself from the spongy recesses of the sofa. He wheezed over to the drinks cabinet, poured himself a whisky, and then sank again into the depths.

A balding man with a bulbous nose slipped into the room. He coughed to demand attention. Portentously opening his file, he stared at its solitary entry, and then looked up.

'My name is Quentin Smythe. My function is to convey to this meeting, upon behalf of the PUS, a decision of HMG. The proceedings initiated by the Department of Special Security against Mr John Gareth Randall are to be discontinued forthwith, and Mr Randall is to be set at liberty today.'

'What?' demanded Arthur in a strangled voice, his ruddy complexion deepening in shade. 'What the hell do you mean, lad?'

'Precisely what I said,' retorted Smythe coldly.

Barber's face purpled. 'What is this, a stitch up?'

'Tell him, Villiers.'

'We've had another report from Vienna, Barber.'

Arthur's hue had dulled to a savage crimson. 'What are you talking about, lad?'

'I'm talking about another AVH defector, Barber, whom we shall refer to as Captain Horváth. He too served in AVH headquarters last summer, and he told SIS station in Vienna that an Englishman had been incarcerated there; a man by the name of Rondoll.'

'Who the blazes is Ron Doll?'

Villiers treated him to a clever smile. 'The joys of Hungarian pronunciation, old chap. The unaccented letter "a" is like the "o" in our word "hot". Only when Captain Horváth actually wrote down the name Randall, did we realise about whom he was speaking.'

'In other words,' declared Smythe in his reedy voice, 'Mr Randall was imprisoned in Budapest, just as he informed you.'

'Oh, was he?' bellowed Barber. 'Can't you bloody see? This is just a load of Soviet disinformation. The MGB must have learned by now that we're holding Fay Galbraith and Randall. So now they're planting cover stories upon alleged defectors to boost Randall's alibi. And you're bloody well falling for it.'

'What a convoluted and cynical mind you have,' countered Villiers suavely. 'Randall really *was* in Hungary. Unbidden, Captain Horváth provided a more than adequate description of him, right down to the conspicuous scar upon his left forearm. So why can't you accept this simple fact, Barber? Or don't you like facts in DOSS?'

'Facts are relative to one's objectives,' growled Arthur. 'They can be changed, suppressed, or ignored.'

'However, HMG's decision will certainly not be changed, suppressed, or ignored,' said Smythe sharply. 'Unwin, be so good as to fill in the remaining detail.'

Thrusting forward in his armchair, Terry Unwin gazed vindictively at Arthur's sanguine face. 'Barber, your so-called "atom spy", Jack Randall, just isn't in the same league as the one MI5 has now got its hands on.'

Arthur puffed his chubby cheeks. 'I'm not with you, lad.'

'We're questioning an atomic scientist, Barber. He's been passing gen to the Russians for years.'

'Fuck!'

Unwin smirked. 'No, Fuchs.'

'What?'

'This scientist's name is Fuchs, Dr. Klaus Fuchs.'

Smythe swept his file under an arm like a swagger-stick. 'Therefore, given that Dr. Fuchs has such superior credentials for the role of "atom spy", HMG no longer require the services of Mr Randall or Mrs Galbraith. Both are to be released today, Barber. So see to it at once.'

Once Smythe had scuttled away, Villiers levered his cadaverous body upright. He sneered at Barber's beetroot face. 'What terribly bad luck, old chap.'

Following Villiers from the room, Unwin paused long enough to flick cigarette ash into the seated man's whisky. 'You've had it coming to you, Barber, you fat fucking slug.'

Left alone in the room, Arthur was stuck. Despite almost manic grunts of effort, he floundered in the settee's deep cushions. He tried bouncing; treating the sofa as a trampoline, with his tonnage providing sufficient spring for liftoff. At the end of his tribulations he lay helplessly beached, sucking in gusts of air.

One last titanic effort brought him farting to his feet. He grabbed his mac and hat, and blundered breathlessly into the corridor outside. Staggering down the stairs, he heaved open the door of the building, and lurched into the street, like a drunk.

Glowering in his Waterloo office, it took Barber two tries to ignite the cherrywood. 'Nowt to say, lass?'

Eve had sat glumly throughout his tirade. 'Why can't they try Jack as well as this Fuchs bloke?'

'For God's sake, Eve, the bloody government hardly wants an epidemic of spy trials. And, given the choice of Jack or Fuchs in the dock, who's going to impress the Yanks most?'

'Fuchs, of course,' she muttered moodily. 'But all that bloody work for nothing. And it's not as if Jack is innocent. I know he's been up to something.'

Barber inspected his grimy nails. 'You've got your orders, lass. Go and release Jack and Fay into the community.'

Attired in a suit that was now tight around his waist, Randall stood before Horner's desk, staring at Eve through lacklustre eyes.

'Sorry about that,' she said busily. 'Case of mistaken identity, it seems. You look a bit dazed, Jack, so it'll do you good to walk to the station. Bit of fresh air.' She stepped around the desk and stuffed some paper into his hand. 'A few quid to get you started.'

Shaking her head despairingly, Eve retrieved the notes from his flaccid hold. She extracted the wallet from his inside pocket and shoved the money into it.

'Your bills have all been paid while you were my guest. We forged your signature on the cheques, Jack. Don't mind, do you? And the girls have taken your stuff out to your place, and tidied up a bit. They got some coal and food in too,'

Frowning at his bewildered expression, Eve made a shooing gesture. 'Off you go, Jack, you're free. You're rehabilitated, comrade. So try and look on the bright side.' She turned him in the direction of the door. 'Anyway, it was lovely having you.'

As he plodded towards the exit, she smiled remorselessly.

'And no hard feelings, Jack.'

The car lurched around the corner, swung into their drive, and braked by a trim privet hedge. Oliver Galbraith flung open the driver's door, and his wife alighted from the passenger's side.

'I hate this damned house,' snapped Fay.

'So do I,' snarled her husband,

'Now, I suppose, you'll tell me how intensely you hate me too, for all the slights and humiliations you've endured these many years.'

His baleful glare intensified. 'I really wanted them to jail you, and to throw away the key.'

She stared at him coolly. 'Well, they didn't. So bring my cases in, and then run me a bath. After that, you can take me out for a meal. I'm hardly in the mood to cook.'

Nodding robotically, once the commands came, Oliver trudged to the rear of the car and opened the boot.

Fay studied the browbeaten face beneath sparse, grey hair. 'When are you away next?'

'On Tuesday, for eight days.'

Lips pursed in satisfaction, Fay pondered her latest instruction, before tossing it to him like a bone. 'You may come to my room on Sunday for an hour, but no longer than that.'

Catching the gleam of gratitude in his eyes, Fay puffed her lips in satisfaction to acknowledge this rapid restoration of the old order.

'I barely recognised Jack when he returned,' said Delilah in a disdainful voice. 'There just wasn't any virility about him.'

'I only took a couple of shots for the record,' reported Delphine sniffily. 'Anyway, he closed the curtains in the lounge.'

'Well, I hope he keeps them closed, Delphine, if he intends to present himself to the world like that.'

61

FRIDAY 6 JANUARY–WEDNESDAY 1 MARCH 1950

On the day following his release, Randall awoke fully-dressed on the floor of his lounge, huddled beneath the duvet he'd stripped from his bed. Unable to jettison the ambience of the past three months, he'd left the light on throughout the night, and closed both the curtains and the room's door. He'd found some Cognac in the kitchen too, and reacquaintance with alcohol had left him with a slight hangover.

Further readjustment to his environment was determined by needs. With ablutions no longer integral to his surroundings and food no longer served up to him, he was forced to visit the bathroom and kitchen. But he remained reluctant to venture into the other rooms.

Once he'd rekindled the fire from its embers, he tentatively drew back the curtains to reveal a murky sky, which seemed to squat upon his head. However, there was sufficient natural light to point up the dismal wallpaper which rendered the room so dreary. The colours he had lavished upon the attic had never touched the lower floor. Crumpled and unshaven, he gazed at the uninspiring walls; viewing there all manner of images from the recent past, as though they were projected from his mind and screened before him.

His 'film' was interrupted by the sound of the front door opening. Wendy called out his name. He didn't answer, but he heard her ascending the stairs. She came into the lounge, frowned at his dishevelled appearance, and then glanced sternly at the half-empty Cognac bottle and crammed ashtray.

'Madge paid me a visit and said you'd been released,' she explained, 'although I've no idea if she was acting on her own or on Eve's behalf.' She paced further into the room. 'I used the spare key. You told me where to find it, when we were last here together.'

'It seems like a very long time ago,' he murmured.

'So how are you, Jack?

'How do I look?'

'Not as good as you did back then.'

He smiled wanly.

'I wasn't sure whether to come. But, now I'm here, I can at least apologise for those dreadful lies I wrote about you for Eve.' Her eyes moistened. 'I'm not proud of my behaviour, Jack. I just wanted to avoid prison, and later I was desperate to be released from their safe house.'

'I'm not going to judge you, Wendy. Eve has a way of making people do things they don't want to do.'

'That I know to my cost,' she murmured resentfully. 'Anyway, I'm going now. But I'll come back in a few days.'

'There's no need.'

'I reckon there's plenty of need, Jack.'

On the Sunday, Prime Minister Clement Attlee announced that a General Election would be held in February. Five days later, Wendy let herself into his flat again. Randall managed a tepid grin, when she congratulated him upon having shaved and bathed.

'Have you been out yet, Jack?'

'I did some shopping.'

She sat next to the fire. 'You must have brought some coal in too. Goodness me, all that exercise!'

'I did some press-ups too. Not many. I felt as weak as a kitten and pretty flabby.'

'Well, it's a start,' she said, tacking an encouraging smile onto her words. Then her lips pursed in query. 'Jack, have you still got a job?'

'I'm not sure. Yesterday, I received a letter from somebody in the Treasury. It seems I'm currently on sick leave, and they're reviewing my future status.'

She stared at the glowing coals. 'I think you should talk about what happened to you.'

'With you?'

'Have you got anybody else to listen?'

He shook his head.

'Tell me what happened, Jack. It will do you good.'

'Not yet.'

A week later, he was tackling a patch of bindweed in his garden. Glancing up when the street level door opened, he tensed as Eric Moon stoop-walked down the steps. Grasping his spade in both hands, he watched Moon approach and proffer him a thick brown envelope.

'My guvnor says you're to 'ave this.'

'Will it explode?'

When Moon gurgled merrily, Randall rammed his spade into the soil, and opened the envelope. It was stuffed with used fivers.

'My guvnor wants to know if that'll do you, Mr R.'

'Tell him it will do for a start,' he replied coldly. 'Is that understood?'

The red nose sniffed. 'I gotcha, Mr R.'

As the light dimmed, and he put away his gardening tools, Wendy trotted down the steps. With an approving smile, she squeezed his bicep.

'You're looking more like the old Jack. Colour's coming back to your face too.'

He pulled off his gardening boots. 'So are you staying or going, Wendy?'

'I'll stay for a while. And have you got any wine, Jack? I feel like talking.'

That evening, as the levels of two bottles fell with regularity, he told her something of his ordeal as Eve's prisoner.

She peered at him inquisitively. 'That's not everything though, is it?'

'No. I'm still dealing with certain matters in my head.'

Later, having phoned for a taxi, he helped her don her coat. She turned to face him, and then linked her hands behind his neck.

'I think you should kiss me goodnight, Jack. It'll do you good to hold a woman in your arms again.'

Following a formal confession to MI5 on 30th January, Dr. Klaus Fuchs was arrested by Special Branch three days later. On Friday 3rd February, he appeared before Bow Street Magistrates Court and was remanded to the care of Brixton Prison. A week later, he was again remanded by magistrates, and committed for trial at the Old Bailey.

The following day, Randall travelled to the East End in search of an Italian-owned store. It was there that he had bought the paints with which he'd decorated the attic. His concern that it might have disappeared in the Blitz was unfounded. The store had survived, and the paints were still available – at a price. Thanks to Barber's bundle, he was able to afford them and their delivery.

As a bonus, he was directed to another shop which could supply him with an essential component for his shower. Again he paid without demur the inflated price imposed by shortages.

On 24th February, the results of the General Election were announced. As in July 1945, the Labour Party was victorious, but now with a greatly reduced majority. Randall had opted not to vote. He'd ignored the press and the radio too, except when listening to music on the Light Programme while he painted.

He'd finished the main bedroom, colouring the walls terracotta and jade, and the ceiling azure. Now he was near to completion with the lounge, using the same colours, but in a different combination.

That evening, Wendy turned up again. Wandering into the lounge, she nodded approvingly, and then gazed at him seriously.

'Once you've finished decorating the rooms, Jack, perhaps you should try a proper painting. It'll do you good.'

On Wednesday 1st March, Fuchs pleaded guilty to four breaches of the Official Secrets Act. His trial at the Old Bailey lasted eighty minutes. At the end of it, the Lord Chief Justice sentenced Fuchs to fourteen years imprisonment.

62

SATURDAY–SUNDAY 4–5 MARCH 1950

Lolling on her sofa, nursing a gin, Eve pouted ruefully. 'It would be nice to go out for a decent meal, but we're both skint. So what's it like being broke and forty-one?'

Pam Armitage crowned a haughty stare with a lift of silky brows. 'You mean thirty-nine, Eve.'

'Going backwards, are we?'

'Not at all,' said Pam. 'I reached forty and didn't much care for it. So I decided to remain thirty-nine.'

'Pam, you can't be thirty-nine for the rest of your life.'

The older woman exhaled a stream of smoke towards the flaking ceiling. 'Well, when I've ceased being thirty-nine, Eve, which may be for a considerable time yet, then I shall simply become ageless.'

'Ageless?'

Pam angled her head into a pose that had so enthralled Cecil Beaton and other society snappers. Softening her eyes, she practised the gaze that had melted the hearts, stirred the loins, and emptied the wallets of a whole raft of household names.

'Yes, Eve, ageless,' she repeated in her refined alto. 'That is to say, without age, beyond age, not caring a fucking toss about age.'

Eve responded with a toothy grin. 'So that's ageing taken care of. Now, what can you do about my poverty, Pam? All

I've got in the world are some decent clothes, and this mortgaged dump of a flat.'

Stubbing her cigarette, she eyed Eve inquiringly. 'Don't you have any little moneymaking schemes up your sleeve?'

'I might have, if I could find Horner's "Treasure Trove".' She scowled in frustration. 'But all I've got is this riddle clue that Wendy gave me; "skull in Palestine", spoken in a nasally voice.'

'How bizarre!' exclaimed Pam, hands patting together in delight. 'So let me hear how it might sound.'

Nose pincered between her fingers, and trying not to laugh, Eve uttered the words 'skull in Palestine' several times. Head cocked, neck flexed in another practiced pose, Pam listened attentively. Then she made her pronouncement.

'Well, Eve, to me it sounds like "School Prince Palatine".'

'What the hell's "Prince Palatine"?'

'Who,' corrected Pam, a reproachful stare complementing her scathing tone. 'Don't you know any history, Eve?'

'Just what I've lived through,' she retorted sourly, 'and I didn't think much of that. I was far too young to flap in the "Roaring Twenties". So all I got was the nonstop fun of slump, war, and cold war.' She grabbed and drained her glass. 'But I still don't get it.'

'English Civil War, Charles the First's nephew, dashing cavalry leader,' prompted Pam.

'That's the Prince Palatine?'

'Exactly. And what was his name?'

'I've no idea,' confessed Eve, twitching her shoulders to mime a shrug of indifference.

'His name was Prince Rupert.'

Eve swore in self-directed fury. Then she squeezed her eyes shut, and counted silently to twenty to regain her composure.

'Rupert! School, Eton! Pam, I reckon Horner deposited his "Treasure Trove" of secrets in Rupert Eaton's bank for safe-keeping, when he lost heavily at poker, just before he died. He probably hoped to recoup his losses later, either by blackmailing people, or by selling his secrets as a job lot to the highest bidder.'

'Eve, I've no idea what Horner intended to do with his secrets, but at least we now know where they are. However, what I totally fail to understand is why you didn't think of Eaton.' She widened her eyes to underscore the criticism. 'After all, he was Horner's banker.'

'I certainly did think of him. But, Rupert expressly undertook to inform me, if the "Treasure Trove" ever turned up at his bank.'

'That's you all over, Eve, *far* too trusting.'

Grinning, Eve leapt to her feet. 'I'm going to phone Rupert.'

Wendy let herself into his flat. She found him in the lounge. 'So what have you been up to, Jack?'

'I've been painting a landscape.'

She smiled in surprise. 'Where is it?'

'Drying in the attic.'

She left the room, returning a few minutes later. 'The colours are simply gorgeous,' she lauded. 'Now, is your shower fixed?'

'Yes, the plumber came last Tuesday.'

'That's good, because my hair needs a wash.' She eyed him seriously. 'I've brought some things with me, since I'll be staying tonight.'

He tensed and frowned.

'In the spare bedroom,' she clarified.

'I wasn't expecting otherwise.' His brow furrowed further. 'What's this all about?'

'I'll let you know later.'

Eve topped up their drinks as she spoke. 'Rupert's prepared to reveal the combination that unlocks the door to the vaults, Pam. Then we can use our key to access Horner's strongbox. Unsurprisingly, he's set certain conditions to such generous cooperation.'

'So enlighten me.'

Eve spent some time doing precisely that.

'Now, that sounds like fun,' said Pam brightly. 'Sunday is usually such a dreary day. But how did Eaton know about me?'

'He didn't,' Eve admitted. 'He asked for Zoë, but I told him she was unavailable. However, he seemed perfectly satisfied, when I said I had another beautiful blonde to hand.'

The blue eyes softened. 'You said *that*?'

Eve grimaced. 'Well, I had to think quickly.'

'So tell me what this Eaton's like.'

'A bit like "Smarmy".'

'Oh, you mean repulsive. Now, that should add a certain edge to the proceedings.'

His eyes opened blearily when she called his name. Focusing upon the door of his darkened bedroom, he made out a head poking around it.

'Fancy breakfast in bed, Jack? It's all ready.'

'What's the time?' he grunted.

'About ten. I'll fetch the tray.'

As he dragged himself, yawning, into a sitting position, Wendy padded barefoot into the room. She rested the tray in his lap, switched on the electric fire, and then raised a corner of the duvet.

'Move over a bit, Jack.'

He stiffened. 'Wendy, I'm not sure....'

'Well, I am.' She reached for the hem of her nightdress and hauled it over her head. Wriggling into the space next to him, she grabbed a slice of toast, and grinned. 'Your face, Jack! If I didn't know better, I'd say you'd never seen a naked woman before.'

He switched his disconcerted gaze to the tray, and lifted up a mug of coffee. 'Wendy, what are you up to?'

'I'm just trying to help.' She laid a hand upon his arm. 'Tell me what happened, Jack. It will do you good.'

Once breakfast was disposed of, he stared straight down the bed. Haltingly, he recalled how he'd reacted to the pictures of his mother, and the confirmation of his father's infidelity.

She pressed a kiss against his shoulder. 'Jack, it's high time that we stopped feeling sorry for ourselves, and did something about Eve.' Her fingers trailed lightly over his chest. 'But, there's something else we should undertake first. It might do us both good.'

'I'll try,' he murmured.

Having escorted the women into his office, Rupert Eaton hooked both thumbs into waistcoat pockets, and stared at Pam in awe. 'I've seen your face many times over the years, Mrs Armitage, but I've never had the pleasure of....'

'No, you wouldn't have.' Pam's withering look underscored her disdainful tone.

'Well, that's the introductions over,' said Eve busily. She turned towards the banker, ready with the words from his 'script'. 'Mr Eaton, we want to know the combination that unlocks the door to your vaults.'

Porcine eyes bulging expectantly, he responded with equal ritual. 'Madam, any banker who agreed to tell you that would deserve to be severely punished.'

'Before or after?'

A frisson of delight surged through his portly frame. 'Madam, it can only be before.'

Eve grabbed a pinstriped arm. 'Now, Pam, while I cuff Rupert to his chair, you need to put on that outfit he's provided. And don't forget your stick.'

She escorted Rupert down to the vaults. Typically, he insisted upon retaining his socks. Soon Pam swayed regally down the steps.

'Pam, where's the mask and all the rest?'

'Eve, I refuse to wear such a ridiculous ensemble. It would simply make me look cheap. However, I have brought the cane.'

Eve watched her swish it through a couple of dry runs, a sweetly sadistic smile playing over her lips. Then she addressed Eaton. 'What's the first number of the combination, Rupert?'

'Just two,' he muttered sullenly.

'Two, Pam,' said Eve, penning the number into her notebook.

Pam brought the stick down tentatively for the first blow, and then swiped a little harder for the second.

'Next number, Rupert,'

Anticipation etched upon his face, he boomed it out.

'That's eight, Pam.'

Following the performance of this octave, she could hear Pam panting.

'Next number, Rupert.'

'Zero.'

Pam sighed with relief. 'Thank goodness, my arms ache already.'

Eve smirked. 'Sorry, Pam, but under the terms of our agreement, Rupert insists that a zero means ten.'

She squashed her bust against his chest. 'How do you feel, Jack?'

Tightening his arms around the voluptuous body, he smiled gratefully. 'I feel something like a man again.'

Having run the combination, Eve pushed open the door to the vault. Using the key Wendy had stolen, she unlocked Horner's strongbox, and withdrew the red leather case. Noting with satisfaction that another key was taped to its underside, she used this to unlock the case. Extracting certain of its contents, she glanced through the papers, and gave several impressed nods. Then she loaded the case into her rucksack and hoisted this over a shoulder.

In the antechamber, a scowling Pam sat astride a chair, massaging her aching arm. Lowering the rucksack to the floor, Eve approached the fettered banker. Pincering his nose, she twisted slowly.

'Rupert, you undertook to inform me immediately, if Horner's "Treasure Trove" was ever deposited in your bank. But you neglected to do so, didn't you?'

'Just a slight oversight, Eve,' he responded nasally.

'I'm afraid I can't overlook oversights,' she announced in an icy tone. Releasing his nose, she peeled off her jacket, and picked up the cane. 'So let's go through that combination again, Rupert. Pity about all those zeros.'

The coal fire blazed brightly. Glass held aloft, Wendy studied the wine's colour in the dancing flames. Then she glanced at him and fashioned a suggestive smile.

'Jack, I can stay with you tonight too, if you want. I'm not travelling to Switzerland until Tuesday.'

'A lovely thought, Wendy, but there's no need. I'm feeling something like my old self, thanks to you.'

'So what will you do?'

His face hardened. 'I'll call my solicitor tomorrow.'

63

MONDAY 20 MARCH 1950

Puce-faced, Arthur reeled out of Smythe's room, like a wounded bull elephant.

Moon shook his head as though it was still heaped with obloquy. 'That was a right bollockin', guv.'

'It will be a bloody sight more than that, Eric, unless we get this sorted.' A livid tug freed his pipe from the blazer pocket's torn lining. 'Do you know where I'd like to stick this?'

'No, guv.'

'Nor do I,' snarled Barber. 'There's quite a range of options.'

Plodding towards their car, he caught sight of a telephone box. 'Eric, ring Eve and tell her to be in my office at three o'clock sharp.'

'Eve, in this job, like all those involving the use of power, you have to know when to kick arse, and when to lick arse.' Barber's cumbrous body fidgeted in his chair. 'So when your position is stronger than t'other person or group, you can kick. But when it's weaker, you have to lick.'

Both impressed by this crude but flawless logic, and wary about where it was leading, Eve pecked agreement.

'There's also the third version, the standoff. That's when neither side is in a position to impose their will, and they have to compromise. But, let's get back to the first two, lass, because this is a quintessential kick-and-lick job.' He battered his clogged pipe on the desk, as though hammering in a nail. 'Now, I saw Smythe this morning, and I had my arse well and truly kicked. So now I'm going to kick yours, Eve, metaphorically speaking. And do you know what I want you to do then, lass?'

'I suppose you want me to do some metaphorical licking,' she answered sourly.

'Good lass, you always were very quick on the uptake. Now, I've extemporised upon this matter of power, Eve, because Jack Randall has brought up a matter which concerns us.'

'So what's his problem, sir?'

'Well, he appears to have several, Eve.' Foraging inside his blazer, he withdrew a sheet of paper and scanned its text again. 'Let's consider the main charges detailed by Jack's lawyer. Among them I note "wrongful arrest", "unlawful imprisonment", "physical and mental abuse", "false witness", and "perjury".'

Eve squirmed in her chair. 'So who's been named in the charges?'

'Me, Eric, Phil and Ken are cited, as well as you and three of your lasses. Lesser complaints have been lodged against Fay Galbraith, Pam Armitage, and Wendy Page.

'So what the hell does Jack want?'

'He wants "adequate redress" for his grievances. And, if he doesn't obtain such redress from each person named by 30th April, lass, he intends to "pursue restitution against any recalcitrants through other avenues".'

'What does he mean by "other avenues"?'

'He doesn't say. The press and the courts are obvious possibilities, of course. And, in such eventuality, Eve, suspension, dismissal, and even jail are all on the cards, which won't much help anyone's career.'

'Won't Randall just settle for money, sir?'

'Only up to a point.' Barber kindled the pipe and a cloud of smoke belched into the air. 'I sent Eric round with another brown envelope. I thought the amount it contained right fair, but Jack didn't. Any road, we've now agreed a final sum. But, he's made it crystal clear that the cash only absolves me and the lads from the bashing we gave him.'

'Meaning?' asked Eve, her voice riddled with suspicion.

'Meaning, I'll still be held responsible for the actions of my female subordinates, unless Jack receives "adequate redress" from you and your lasses by 30th April.'

'The slimy bastard! He's leaning on you to make you lean on me.'

'That's right, lass, and I'd do exactly the same in his shoes.'

Eyes that had just flashed in anger became gelid slits. 'So let's "minimise" him.'

'Don't be so bloody daft, Eve. We can't "minimise" him. He's taken out too much "insurance". Already there are lawyers involved, happen the press too. Jack could have planted accounts of his so-called ordeal all over the bloody place. And these would simply pop up into the public domain, if he was bumped off.'

'But we can't just give in to him,' she protested fiercely.

'Yes, we can, lass.' Barber fumbled frenziedly in his pockets until he found matches. 'Look, Eve, DOSS is in an extremely precarious position. Because of the Fuchs success, MI5 are currently the golden boys. They're dying to absorb us, and they've a fan club favouring such a move. I'm fighting on all fronts for the very existence of DOSS. The last thing I need right now is some public scandal.'

Masking her impotent fury, Eve pulled out her cigarettes and added her contribution to the smoke-filled room.

'So, lass, Smythe wants me to make the Randall problem go away. And, in the interest of DOSS, I'm going to do just that. This means that any bugger impeding such an outcome gets thrown to the wolves. Understood?'

Smoke hissed from her lips, but she said nothing.

'So, Eve, I want you and your lasses to provide Jack with "adequate redress".'

'I know what he's got in mind by that,' she countered bitterly. 'It'll be more like retribution.'

'Well, if you know what Randall's got in mind, Eve, you'll know how to satisfy him. Then that will satisfy me, and I can satisfy Smythe and Puss, and they can satisfy the minister. Then everyone's fucking happy.' The lids slid down Barber's eyes. 'So get on with it, lass, if you want to keep your job. Go and make Jack happy. Do just what he asks.'

64

WEDNESDAY 22 MARCH 1950

Laying aside an item from the 'Treasure Trove', Sandra stifled a yawn. 'Eve, does every French politician have a mistress?'

'It goes with territory, Sandra. According to my historical adviser, they all fancy themselves as the reincarnation of Louis the Fourteenth. But, since these Latins don't know what a guilt-complex is, there's nothing we can cash in on there.' She placed a gin and tonic next to the tall blonde. 'Anyway, what else have you found?'

Dangling a photo, Sandra smirked. 'There are some extremely fetching pictures of one of Pam's suitors wearing women's underwear.'

'Yes, I saw those. But I haven't mentioned it to Pam, just in case.'

'In case of what?'

'Well, he's loaded, Sandra. So if he should marry again, as I'm led to believe he might, we can put the squeeze on him with those pics.' Planting herself on the settee, Eve plucked a cigarette from her packet and lit it. 'So what else has caught your eye?'

Sandra's face screwed up unhappily. 'There's this rather sordid story about some married royal and his mistress. I wish they wouldn't do such things. It tarnishes their aura.'

'What aura, Sandra? They're human beings, just like us.'

'No, Eve, they're different.'

'Are they?' queried Eve, blasting smoke from her nostrils, like a goaded dragon. 'Monarchs may sit on thrones, but they shit on thrones too. They're not super-humans.' She reached out for another bundle of papers. 'Anyway, let's get on with this stuff from the "Trove". Right now, it promises to be the only way we can replenish our coffers.'

Randall answered the persistent ringing of his doorbell, and stared curiously at the two callers. Matching looks of contrition glowed upon each doll-like face.

'We must talk to you about something terribly important,' beseeched Delphine, 'for we come from on high.'

'If you're from some religious sect, ladies, I'm really not interested.'

'But we come from on high,' they chorused, synchronised fingers pointing above his conifer screen. 'And we took the photos.'

'Which photos?' he asked in bewilderment.

'Photos for Eve,' they divulged in unison.

'You work for Eve?'

His question set off a barrage of responses, with each twin speaking in turn: 'Eve removed the photographs we took of you... And put us on half-pay... But now she's sacked us... So after Friday we've nowhere to live... And we've got no money.'

He frowned. 'Let's start again, ladies. Who are you?'

'Delilah and Delphine Delaney,' they refrained.

'So you lived up there, and took photographs of me when….' His voice tailed off into an audible exhalation. 'Were there many?'

'Oh, hundreds.'

'Are they all in Eve's hands?'

The heads shook in tandem, wily smiles dancing on their lips. 'Eve took the negatives and prints we'd left in the darkroom. But we kept one set of prints in our private album.'

When Delphine thrust a hefty tome into his hands, a quick flip through its contents had him flushing to his ears. 'Is this the lot?'

'No,' chirped Delilah, proffering him a foolscap envelope. 'Perhaps you can use the contents. Eve doesn't know about them.'

He withdrew the photographs of Eve on his sun-soaked balcony, which they'd taken in August. As he perused them, he was already mulling over certain possibilities. 'Twins, what do you want for all of these?'

'Food, new digs, and some spending money.'

'Well, you'd better come in.' Letting them by, he followed them to the lounge. 'Now, twins, when exactly does your lease expire?'

'On May 1st, but Eve wants us out by this Friday.'

'That figures. Yesterday, I had a call from Eve to arrange the visits of her and the other penitents. The first arrives on Sunday.' He eased a wad of Barber's cash from his back pocket. 'Well, ladies, I've got a deal for you, if you're interested.'

'Eve, I've just read this paper from the "Trove", which alleges that a bunch of Cambridge students were recruited by Soviet intelligence in the thirties. It says that some of them were, and possibly still are, employed by the FO, the SIS, and MI5. Guy Burgess, Donald Maclean, Kim Philby, Anthony Blunt, John Cairncross,' detailed Sandra. 'Have you heard of any of these people?'

Shaking her head, Eve looked up. 'It's not our job to go chasing communists and spies just now, Sandra. But I might pass that gen to Barber later, providing he's a good boy. In any case, our priority is the Yanks, since they've got all the money. And now we've found Max Stern's address in the "Trove", I'm going to use him to get our message through to those who'll have to pay up.'

'So what exactly is this message?'

'Well, Sandra, after twenty years of rule by the Democrats in the USA, the swing of the pendulum is expected to propel the Republican candidate into the White House in the 1952 presidential election.'

'Go on.'

'Republican prospects will be enhanced, if they can put up General Eisenhower, the unbeatable "Ike", as their candidate.' Grinning, Eve took a long pull on her gin. 'Only there's a nasty big skeleton in Ike's cupboard, which could be ruinously rattled by his opponents.'

'And what's that, Eve?'

'Well, presidential candidates are expected to be blissfully married. But, during the war, Eisenhower had an affair with his female driver.'

65

SUNDAY–THURSDAY 26–30 MARCH 1950

On the Sunday, Gwen Chambers arrived at his flat, seemingly empty-handed. Having expected to receive negatives and prints of the photos she'd taken during his incarceration, he made no attempt to hide his displeasure. Blanching, she explained in a halting voice that Eve had confiscated them.

'Well, you'd better come up with something, Gwen, or else I'll make sure the whole damned book gets thrown at you.'

'I've got something, Jack, really graphic stuff.' Licking her lips nervously, she tugged a package from her handbag. 'I shot these from the cubicle in Horner's room. I can make you more prints too.'

He sifted through her photographs of Eve and Pam together. 'They're fantastic pics, Gwen. I'll take another three sets.'

She managed a feeble smile. 'Right, Jack. So can I go?'

'You can go when I've shot this film.' He lifted his own camera from the coffee table in his lounge. 'And you'll be developing it, Gwen. So don't botch the prints, or I'll simply take it all over again.'

'Jack, please, can't...?'

'Damn it, Gwen! You were only too happy to take humiliating shots of me.' He jabbed a finger at her scared face. 'So it's like for like, Gwen, and I'll just be taking photos, nothing else. However, I want you to learn what it's like being on the other side of the camera.'

Sandra Jansen turned up on Tuesday, armed with transcripts of the interrogations he'd undergone. She also handed him various drafts of Fay's confession, plus Pam's signed and perjured statements. Slipping out of her coat, she sat in an armchair and accepted a gin.

Having glanced through the papers, he laid them on the floor. 'Thank you, Sandra, that's more than "adequate redress".'

Sipping her drink, she hooked her classic legs over an arm of the chair. 'I thought you'd be more vengeful, Jack.'

'Men aren't as vindictive as women,' he asserted, trying not to heed the expanse of femoral flesh that she'd somehow caused to be revealed. 'It's a regrettable failing of ours.'

She straightened and raised her topmost leg. Her gaze was as direct as her question. 'So you're not going to demand sex from me?'

'No, I'm not.'

'Supposing I said that I wanted to go to bed with you, Jack?'

He grinned pliantly. 'Well, that's different.'

'How about painting me as well?'

'I'd love to paint you.'

Fidgeting her supple body, Sandra contrived to cause the hem to ride even higher. 'So when shall I come over?'

'What about next Monday to Wednesday, if you're free?'

She threw him a risqué glance. 'I'm sure I can fit you in, Jack, on each of those days.'

Clad in a beige mac, Madge Nichols was his visitor on Wednesday.

'So, Madge, what have you brought me?'

'Two pairs of handcuffs, Jack.

'Why handcuffs?'

'Well, you never know,' she averred sagely. Pulling a set from each pocket, she tossed them and their keys onto an armchair.

'Do you consider that to be "adequate redress", Madge?'

'Not really, Jack. But I was hoping to make it up to you later.' She flashed him an impish smile and widened her eyes. 'Sandra said you've done a painting of me from memory. Can I see it?'

He accompanied her up to the attic. As she stood staring at the painting, her smile became a pout, which she then recast as a scowl.

'From your face, Madge, I can only assume you don't like it.'

'Jack, it's smashing, but my bum looks big in it.'

'Madge, I *can* paint a woman's figure, and I assure you that you're magnificently in proportion.' Faced with her continuing grimace, his eyes narrowed in frustration. 'Madge, it's called perspective.'

'Jack, I don't care what it's called. My bum looks big in it. Can't you take a bit off each side?'

'I'm not a barber, Madge.'

'Tell you what, Jack. I'll pose for you properly. Then you can paint another picture and get me in proper perspective.'

Shaking his head in defeat, he grinned affably. 'Can you come over Thursday week?'

'That's fine, Jack. I'll be over early, so we can do a whole day's painting and "adequate redress". I'm free on the Friday too, in case there are still some things that need putting right.'

Around noon on Thursday, he opened the front door to Pam Armitage. Beneath a fur coat, she wore a navy sweater and slacks. Glancing at him arrogantly, she led the way up to his lounge, settled into an armchair, and demanded a scotch. Compliantly, he fixed her a whisky.

She gazed at him icily as she took the glass. 'So you fancy it's my turn to succumb, do you, Jack?'

'Let's say it's your turn to offer "adequate redress", Pam.'

'And what makes you think I'll play your sordid little game?'

'Pam, spare me the high moral tone. You were prepared to commit perjury to help put me in jail. All you have to do is to write to my lawyer and withdraw your testimony, just like Fay and Wendy have done. Once you've performed that task, as far as I'm concerned, that's an end to the matter.'

'You want me to back down?' Both her tone and demeanour exuded incredulity. 'Jack, you know I can't do that.'

'Very well, Pam, you've made your choice. So, when you've finished your drink, you can leave.'

'Leave, Jack? I haven't travelled all this way simply to be dismissed.' She sank her whisky and held out the glass. 'Since I'm here, and despite your high-handed manner, I'm prepared to show my goodwill.'

Randall carried off her glass for a refill. When he turned from barman's duties, it was to discover that she'd doffed her coat, and was now examining the cuffs which Madge had tossed onto the armchair.

'You know, I've never used these.'

'You surprise me, Pam.'

She darted him a half-hearted glare, and then, with cuffs and keys dangling from her fingers, she beckoned him follow with her drink. In the bedroom Pam studied her reflection in a mirror. Apparently finding some cosmetic flaw, her finger smoothed her lip while she eyed him in the glass. Then she glanced around the room.

'I see you've moved the bed next to the balcony doors.'

'After months without natural light,' he responded coldly, 'I find I can't get enough of it now.'

She sat on the bed. 'Well, I very much hope that there's something else of which you still can't get enough.'

66

SATURDAY 1 APRIL 1950

He opened the front door. Eve Loxton squeezed past him, close enough to impress her perfume upon his senses, and headed up the stairs. Randall ushered her into the lounge and offered her a drink. Requesting a brandy, Eve sank into an armchair, tugged the hem of a black skirt over her knee, and stared about her at the newly painted walls.

Taking the Cognac from his hand, her brows rose inquiringly. 'Are you enjoying this bout of retribution, Jack?'

'I find it very therapeutic, Eve.'

She subjected him to a penetrating gaze. 'Jack, you're damaged.'

'I'm perfectly aware of that. But the world's full of damaged people, doing all sorts of things. Some of them even get to be secret policewomen.'

Smirking, she sipped her drink. 'Is the painting therapeutic too?'

'It helps.'

Unfastening a sable shoulder bag, she fished within its confines for cigarettes and transferred these to a jacket pocket. 'Can I see what you've done of late?'

'If you want, although there's little new.'

As she headed towards the attic, glass in hand, Randall informed her that he needed to call his solicitor. She peered at him suspiciously, and then bounded up the stairs. Having made his call, he carried brandy bottle and a glass up to the attic, where Eve was inspecting his painting of Madge. Switching her gaze, she stared through a dormer window towards the dovecot across the street. Then her restless eyes fixed upon his.

'Jack, what's the importance of the thirtieth of April deadline?'

'Well, Eve, I've informed our main security agencies that, if they want to talk with me, I'll be available on that day. So I want to see where I stand in this business of "adequate redress", before deciding what I might tell them.'

'So what, if anything, do you think you've got to offer them?'

His gaze locked onto her probing eyes. 'They might value my insights regarding the working methods of DOSS, not to mention certain foibles of its personnel. For instance, would you welcome a fresh investigation into the violent deaths of your husband and his mistress?'

Her lips tightened, prior to their renaissance as a wounded smile. 'Jack, I was just playing games when I told you all that. I'd have loved it to have happened that way. But, her death was entirely accidental, while poor old Jimmy simply threw himself from a cliff after the bitch drowned. It was suicide, Jack. Balance of the mind disturbed and all that.'

He reacted to her sheer gall with a cold smile. 'Eve, just in case you feel like playing more games, please note that I've taken out "insurance". Moreover, those two murders, which you now term accidental deaths, figure amongst its terms.'

As anticipated, next came the fully-rounded eyes and gawping mouth. Ignoring her antics, he reminded her that they had other business.

'I'll need more anaesthetic,' she retorted. Reaching for the bottle, Eve poured a generous measure of Cognac and sank half. 'Jack, I've got two hundred quid in my bag. Will you accept that as my "adequate redress"?'

He eyed her stonily and shook his head.

'I might be able to lay my hands on some more.'

'Forget it, Eve.'

'What if your interrogator doesn't want to be fucked?'

'In that case, just finish your drink and go.'

'And there'll be no consequences?'

'There will certainly be consequences,' he replied icily, 'because I'll adjudge you not to have made "adequate redress" for what you did to me.'

'Which means?'

'It means that my lawyer will hand over to the police the evidence I've given her. And, if everything comes out, Eve, you'll lose your job, and it's likely you'll go to jail as well.' His grave expression gave way to a cynical smile. 'It's even possible you might be "minimised" beforehand, to save DOSS such embarrassment.'

She added more brandy to her glass and knocked back most of it. Her nostrils flared in fury. 'You're determined to have me, aren't you?'

'Let's say I'm determined to exercise power over you, Eve. I'm going to make you act in a way that you don't want to. After all, you forced both Wendy and me to act in such fashion, simply because it served your purposes. So I'm going to repay like with like, Eve, because I believe in the therapeutic qualities of retribution.'

She drained her glass, set it down, and emitted a hollow laugh. 'Today is All Fools' Day, of course, and I'd love to think that this was all just one bloody great joke.' Tearlets of frustration welled in the eyes which she averted from his ruthless gaze. 'So it's into bed or into jail,' she murmured.

Eve stood silently for several seconds. Then she slipped out of her jacket and paced towards him. As he stared into the mesmerising eyes, her arms linked around his neck. When her tongue engaged his, he buried his hands in the thick red hair. She broke off their embrace to retrieve and refill her glass, whose contents rapidly dwindled.

Setting her drink aside, Eve unbuttoned her blouse and peeled it from her torso. Holding his gaze, she removed her few remaining clothes. Arms akimbo, she stared at him haughtily.

'After all this, Jack, I hope you won't disappoint me.'

'I told you so!' whooped Delilah in the dovecot. 'You owe me half a crown.'

Scowling, Delphine refocused her camera. 'I really expected Eve to refuse outright.'

Delilah chuckled into her gin. 'It was just as well Jack foresaw that Eve would make a copy of the key to our flat, and would inspect it before going to his. While we were in our digs nearby, waiting until Jack rang to give us the all clear.'

'I wonder how much he had to bung the estate agent, Delilah, to ensure this lease ran fully until May 1st, and that there were no new clients inspecting the place until then.'

'Best of all, he hinted that we might rent his place, should he go off to France to paint. So, Delphine, make sure your camerawork serves his purposes.'

Hands locking behind his neck, Eve drew his inscrutable face close to hers. 'Well, that wasn't bad at all, Jack.' Pressing her body against his, she peered into his wintry eyes. 'And, while I'm pleased you've got your libido back, I must also assume that you're still full of lies.'

'Looking for another confession, Eve?'

She flashed a synthetic smile, and then intensified her gaze. 'Have you any idea why the Hungarians freed you?'

'I've a very good idea why I was freed, but it had nothing to do with the Hungarians.'

'Go on,' she urged, her voice almost husky, her fingers caressing his back.

Breaking free of her attentions, he sat up and found their drinks. Eve jacked herself onto one elbow to take the glass he handed her.

'It was Colonel Volkov who set me free, Eve, which means that it was probably Beria who ordered my release.'

'But why should the MGB free you?'

'It was probably because they'd established that I was on the books of Red Army Intelligence, the GRU.'

The viridian eyes narrowed down to slits. '*What* did you say?'

'It was the MGB which arranged my kidnap in Paris and brought me to Budapest, Eve. But I was already a deep "sleeper" for the GRU, who'd recruited me in 1939. So when I was imprisoned in Hungary, I tried communicating my status in various ways. Presumably, one of these efforts finally registered. Thereby allowing Moscow to sort out its bureaucratic problems and set me free.'

She downed a slug of brandy. 'You lying, cheating bastard! You really *have* been spying for the Russians all this time.'

'On the contrary, Eve, as I've told you many, many times, I've never spied for the Russians.'

'How can you possibly say…?'

'I've never spied for them, for the simple reason that I've never been activated, Eve. I suppose Moscow was waiting until I was really well-placed.'

She gazed at him ruefully, and then stretched across him to deposit her glass. 'I'm going to report this conversation.'

'Eve, be realistic,' he advised, stroking the back of her bare thigh. 'Currently, your rating in the intelligence community is extremely low. And, if you report that you heard this story while half-drunk, in bed, and on April the first, it will probably hit rock bottom.'

He slapped her taut buttocks and burst into laughter. She glared at his grinning face, and then wriggled onto her knees. Shoving him onto his back, she squeezed his nose.

'You sod, Jack! Bloody April Fool's Day! And I've fallen for it.'

Ignoring her assertion, he eased himself into a sitting position and eyed her coolly. 'Anyway, we've finished our business, so you can go. But you can come back next Saturday, if you want to.'

'Passed fucking muster, did I?' she muttered bleakly. 'Do you mind if I have a bath first?'

'Go ahead.'

Swinging her long legs so that she sat beside him, she smiled coyly. 'And can I stay the night?'

'Why, haven't you got anyone to torture?'

'Well, I'm sort of suspended until I've made "adequate redress" to you. So is anybody booked in for tomorrow?'

'Eve, why are you being so docile and accommodating?'

'Because you're in command.' Her eyes gazed compliantly into his. 'Jack, this GRU bunch you spoke about, I don't know anything about them.'

'Nor do I, Eve.'

'You must know something, Jack, given the job you did.'

'So are you still doing the job you did, Eve?'

She shrugged stagily and grinned. 'I think I'll have that bath.'

67

THURSDAY 27 APRIL – MONDAY 1 MAY 1950

'Have you finished it?' asked Madge excitedly, the moment he let her into his flat. When he confirmed that he had, she tore up both sets of stairs to the attic, with the artist following at a more stately pace.

'Oh Jack, that's so much better,' contended the model, once she'd reviewed the completed 'Madge II' with its 'reduced' posterior.

Now seated on a chair, Randall smiled to himself. He'd simply painted her from a more oblique angle. Yet he was pleased with the end product.

She peered over her shoulder, frowning slightly. 'Jack, what about the shape? Are you sure it's not too round?'

'It's not too round, Madge. But you could always go to a Cubist, if the species isn't extinct, and get a second opinion painted.'

She produced a hybrid of grin and frown. 'No, Jack, it's fine.' Following a modest shimmy of her rear, she swung it into his lap and beamed anew at her portrait.

'Madge, is it true that Pam has joined your lot?'

The feline smirk almost split her face. 'Yes, she's what Eve calls a consultant.'

'Is Eve planning to recruit Fay as well?'

'Well, she would if she could, Jack, because Fay has qualities that Eve looks for in women. But Fay can't be persuaded.'

'So what are these hidden qualities Eve is looking for?'

'You know all the women involved, Jack. What have they got in common?'

He hammed a reflective frown. 'Is it the ability to make my life a misery?'

'Jack, that's not fair! You can hardly accuse us of making your life a misery this last month. Most blokes would give their right arm to be in your position.'

A degree of warmth escaped his expression. 'Would they all have donated a limb to undergo my previous experiences?'

She prefaced her wise words with a theatrical flutter of the doll-like lashes. 'You never know, Jack.'

'So is this ability to handle me the magic quality that determines all these jobs for the girls?'

'Well, if we can manage you, we can manage most blokes, can't we? And that's what it's all about. It's a man's world out there, Jack, or hadn't you noticed?'

'Given recent events, Madge, I think you're probably asking the wrong man.'

She smiled impishly, and then kissed him. 'Anyway, looking at that painting makes me feel overdressed. So do you fancy some more "adequate redress"?'

Eve paced over to the lounge window, and gazed up at the dovecot cresting the line of conifers.

'There's nobody up there, Eve.'

'I know, Jack.' She waggled a key ring. 'I checked.'

A bland smile acknowledged her assertion. 'So pour yourself a drink, Eve. I'm just going to ring my lawyer.'

'Why?'

He rubbed the tip of her nose, and then gave it a gentle tweak. Delphine answered when he dialled, and gravely recited the name of a law firm. Randall asked to speak to 'Mrs

White'. Informed that she was unavailable, he promised to call back.

Coddling a brandy, Eve eyed him suspiciously. 'You always ring your solicitor just after I arrive.'

'Well, she likes to know that I'm still happy.'

She conjured up her wronged face. 'Jack, I'm hardly going to upset you at this late stage in the proceedings.'

'Meaning what?'

'Well, today's Friday and you're off to France with your paintbrushes in three days' time. At which juncture, the girls and I can resume our careers at DOSS, albeit under a slight cloud. So I've a vested interest in having you contentedly board that boat on Monday.'

'How the hell do you know all this?'

With difficulty she held a mocking smile in check. 'Well, when you let Madge rest from posing, she somehow stumbled upon your ticket. While, during a similar break, Sandra just happened to find letters from MI5 and the SIS, in which they declined any interest in talking with you.'

'Bloody snooping women!'

'Well, it *is* their job, Jack.'

'Eve, don't get too complacent. I haven't yet told my solicitor to put the other matters into abeyance.'

Spinning on her heel, Eve sauntered back to the drinks. Only when she'd refilled her glass and drastically diminished its contents, did she look towards him.

'Jack, let's agree that I've won. But I won't rub it in. In fact, since I'm in the mood to behave outrageously, I'll give you something to remember me by.'

That Monday, after depositing their cases on the landing, the twins investigated the vacant flat.

Delphine waltzed from the kitchen. 'Jack's left us lots of food.'

'Plus a bottle of gin,' exulted Delilah, gambolling from the lounge.

'Well, he seemed very pleased with our photographs.'

'Yet he was most selective in what he retained.'

Together they wandered into the master bedroom and then onto the balcony.

'Funny to be on this side of things, isn't it?' whispered Delphine, staring nervously in the direction of the dovecot.

Delilah followed her sister's gaze and clutched her hand. 'Do you think anyone's up there?'

Eve had ordered her to 'see him off the premises', as Madge phrased it, and their journey to Dover was good-humoured and uneventful. She didn't even question him about the time he spent in the Post Office, despatching registered mail.

As Randall expected of Madge, their leave-taking was dry-eyed and pragmatic. Following a flurry of waving arms and blown kisses, both expediently turned their backs, as the sea parted their lives.

68

WEDNESDAY 3 MAY 1950

As both peace offering and token of her indispensability, Eve clutched a slim file. It contained a summary of the data which Horner had gleaned about the 'Cambridge spy-ring'.

Summoned to the office of the 'Dossboss' that morning, she'd assumed they were meeting to formally lift the suspension imposed on her in March. But she changed her mind, when she observed the apoplectic colouring of Barber's face. It started off strawberry, with a hint of plum blotching his jowls.

'Lass, I told you to make Jack Randall happy.'

'And I did, sir,' she insisted. 'I made him extremely happy.'

Cheeks a restrained cerise, Arthur loosened his frayed tie. 'Well, you obviously didn't make him happy enough, Eve.'

'I'm not with you, sir.'

Drooping lids half-hooded his eyes, and a subtle shade of maroon chequered the chins. 'Lass, I don't give a toss about what you do out of hours or who with, as long as they are of age and consenting. But, what I do care about is you getting snapped while you're at it.'

He flung a wad of photographs across the desk. As she inspected them, Eve's brows zoomed skywards.

'What am I supposed to make of that lot, lass? There you are, prancing around Randall's sunny balcony in the altogether. Then you stretch out on the railing and have a little fiddle with yourself. What exactly was going on there?'

'It's not what you think, sir.'

'Don't tell me what I'm thinking, lass.'

'But the photos aren't all that clear,' she protested feebly.

'Not all that clear,' he snarled, complexion now dashed with damson. 'Well, these bloody well are!'

He bunged the next set across his desk. Eve leafed through them, a flush warming her temples.

'The head of my women's section is writhing around Horner's room in her birthday suit. She's with Pamela Armitage, who is similarly unattired, save for some fetching leather gloves. You do know who she's engaged to, don't you? Yon pics'll do absolute bloody wonders for old "Smarmy" and his political career.' He bit hard on the stem of the unlit pipe. 'Hardly the way for DOSS to win friends and influence in that party, is it, Eve? They'll close me down quicker than a vicar's fart, if they win the next election.'

'But we've just had one.'

'Well, we could have another one right soon. Bloody Labour Party's searching the slag-heaps for its so-called soul again. Meaning the quicksilver boys are sniffing after dull old Attlee's job. So divided they'll fall.'

'Well, if you say so, sir,' she agreed hastily.

'And these!' Skin tones rivalling a soft fruit selection on a market stall, he slung more photos towards her; shots of her final 'outrageous' session. 'Clear enough for you, lass? You and Jack performing on his balcony, with you cuffed to the railing. Using two sets, no less!'

The colour of Eve's face was a good match for her hair. Words being superfluous, she made do with a sickly smile.

'Why not do it in a shop window?' he rasped hoarsely, as though even a loosened tie was a ligature. 'Tell me, how can I be sure the competition hasn't got hold of these or worse? Is there owt else that might come out, lass? Nowt with animals, is there?'

'What the hell do you take me for?'

'What do I take you for?' he ranted, the darkest shades of his skin now aubergine. 'A liability, a ticking bomb, that's what I take you for.'

He hurled another package towards her. 'Shots of your lasses with Jack. Does a classy handstand, does leggy Sandra. And young Madge, mother a contortionist, was she?'

Eyes clamped shut, Eve inhaled deeply, counted to twenty, and groped for a rare word. Her eyes opened with a beseeching cast, to top an expression sculpted into contrition.

'I can only say that I'm sorry, sir.'

'Sorry you got caught, you mean.' A paw swiped dismissively. 'Any road, you're no bloody good to me, lass, too much of a liability. So off you go, Eve, and take your lasses with you. Clear your desks and hand in your passes by this evening. You'll all get three months salary. So don't say I'm not generous.'

'You're sacking me?' she whined disbelievingly. 'That's not fair!'

'It's as fair as life is,' he growled, stubby finger stabbing at the photos. 'And take yon mucky pictures with you.'

Hands moving robotically, Eve gathered up the miscellany. Having piled the snaps onto her forgotten file, like breakages on a tray, she stormed towards the door. Wrenching it open, she spun on her heel, lips quivering in a chalk-white face.

'Well, fuck you, sir! And fuck DOSS too!'

Barber nodded ponderously as the fury flew from his room; slammed door still vibrating on its hinges, her words still ringing in his ears.

'Aye, lass, just like you say,' he muttered wearily, 'and I reckon someone'll manage just that, and right bloody soon.'

'She'll be along soon. She's composing herself,' announced Sandra to the gathering in Eve's office. Dosing herself with a jelly baby, she distributed some opened registered envelopes to the attendant women. 'You can treat these as your redundancy notices. As you now know, we've all been sacked.'

Flicking through the photos, Madge glanced at Pam. 'These are good of you and Eve,' she remarked snidely. 'Here, have a look.'

'I've already seen them,' responded Pam glacially, directing a murderous glare at Gwen. 'I met my fiancé for lunch. He had a set to hand, and it transpires that his constituency chairman has received another.'

'Well, they won't mind,' asserted Madge sagely. 'Most blokes are only too happy to look at pictures of two women at it.'

'That's as may be,' retorted Pam. 'However, his chairman *does* mind the photos of me with Jack, which he received by the same post. I think it was the fact that I was both shackled and smiling that decided the issue. So, since I've apparently become a political liability overnight, my fiancé has terminated our engagement forthwith.'

'Oh well, chin up!' Following these latest wise words, Madge perused photos of her own antics. 'So who took all these pics of Jack with us in his flat?'

'The terrible twins, I imagine,' said Sandra distantly, engrossed in admiring shots of her own athleticism.

The door opened sedately to admit Eve. Having resealed the entrance with a soft click, she approached her desk. Extracting certain snaps from the pile, she studied them, and then held up several graphic pictures of herself with Pam.

'Did you take these, Gwen?'

The photographer nodded nervously.

'They're fantastically good.'

'Thanks, Eve.'

'We must have a little talk about them in the coming days.'

'Yes, Eve,' she muttered in a cowed voice.

'Eve, why did Jack post all these photos?'

'Well, Madge, like most men, he doesn't like to see women getting ahead. Anyway, that's all in the past, it's the future which beckons.'

'With two upthrust fingers,' remarked Sandra tartly.

'That's very negative,' chided Eve.

'So what's positive, great leader?'

'The following,' announced Eve, commanding them with her gaze, as she displayed another selection of photographs. 'I've decided to set up a company to market not only these pics, but also the products in both our back catalogue and the Deacon archive. In addition, I expect new items to come on stream in the near future. Therefore, I've appointed myself as chairwoman of the board, managing director, executive director, and personnel director. In one or other of these capacities, I'm now offering you all jobs.'

'Can't we be directors too?' griped Sandra.

Eve churned out a citric smile. 'Of course you can, just as long as you don't interfere with my efficient running of my company.'

Madge frowned. 'Aren't you going to employ any blokes?'

'There will be a bloke-quota, Madge. We'll employ some young, attractive men as telephonists, filing clerks, and secretaries. Then we'll have something to grope whenever there are problems at home, or simply if we feel like it. I'll see to it that you're on the interview board, Madge. In fact, you can be director of blokes. Think you can manage that? And you can be finance director, Sandra.'

'Oh thanks! So what am I going to use for money, Eve? There's almost nothing in the kitty.'

'Then I shall fund-raise as usual,' Eve retorted busily. 'I'm about to open negotiations with our transatlantic cousins.

But, for now, we'll have to get our loot nearer home. Got your shorthand pad, Pam?'

'My what?' she responded blankly.

'Pam, you're my PA? That posh telephone voice of yours clinched it.'

'But I....'

'Pam, now you've been ditched at the altar, you'll have to work for your living.'

Pam's face screwed up in inquiry. 'What on earth do I do as a PA?'

'You write down my commands in your shorthand pad, and then you ensure that they're performed to perfection.'

'But I don't know the slightest thing about shorthand.'

Eve shrugged. 'Anyway, Pam, phone Jessica, and tell her I'm offering her the post of marketing director. Then phone Rupert, and tell him I've decided to do number sixty-nine.'

'Who with?'

'With you, Pam. But we'll wait until you get over your broken heart. Next week suit you?'

'But I thought I was a PA.'

'No demarcation disputes,' pronounced Eve firmly. 'You'll all have to multitask in my organisation.'

'Multi-what, Eve?'

'Just something I made up, Madge.'

'I wish you hadn't,' she moaned. 'It sounds like hard work.'

'Well, what's that to a woman?' inquired Eve sternly. 'Look, we'll all have to turn our hands to everything, until we can afford to employ some drones. Now, where are the twins?'

'They're renting Jack's flat,' said Madge. 'But you sacked them, Eve, remember?'

'So re-employ them. We'll need all the photographers we can get.'

'You want me to do that?'

'Yes, Madge, I've just made you personnel director. And Gwen's art and publicity director, Norma's catering manager, and Brenda's head of security. Got that, Pam?'

'What about Janice?'

Frowning, Eve made an indeterminate sound.

Sandra raised her hand. 'Eve, if I'm finance director, who's going to be research director?'

'We'll find someone. And, come to think of it, Sandra, it's better that you become executive director.' Eve paused briefly and munched her lip. 'As for your other job of finance director, I'll see if I can get someone else to take that post.'

'Eve,' protested Madge, 'isn't it my job employing staff, if I'm personnel director?'

The chairwoman treated her to a severe stare. 'Madge, I hope you're not going to interfere with my efficient running of my company. I'm looking for a genuine work-ethic, teamwork, bonding, employment generation….'

69

MONDAY 29 MAY 1950

Wendy reread Eve's letter, which had recently caught up with her, and smiled vindictively. At last the opportunity to use her newfound power had arrived. And it had been worth the wait; for revenge was, indeed, a dish best eaten cold.

The Italian saying seemed even more apt, when the taxi drew up outside Claudio Bonomi's premises. Impressed by Madge's praise of his skills, she had made appointments with him both before and after visiting Switzerland.

Wendy paid off her fare, tipped generously, and walked up to the tailor's shop. She inspected the display in the window. Then she pushed open the shop's door, setting off the bell which announced her presence. Seconds later, the tailor emerged from his workroom.

'*Ciao*, Claudio.'

'*Signorina* Wendy,' he responded, flashing a dazzling and expectant smile. Putting up the 'Closed' sign on the door, he ushered her through to the back rooms and helped her doff her jacket.

She stared in delight at the rolls of cloth piled upon his shelves. Pacing slowly around the room, she pointed at various materials. 'I want dresses in that, that, and that, a suit in that, and some slacks in that.' She paused, as if envisaging an end product, and then glanced at Claudio, who was scribbling furiously in his notebook. 'Can you make swimwear too?'

'I make anything.'

'Well, I want a couple of these bikinis that people are now wearing, but skimpier.'

He frowned uncomprehendingly.

'Skimpier? Less in the way of material, and more in the way of me,' she explained. 'Anyway, you'll need your tape measure, because I may have gained weight while abroad.'

'I do not see. You look magnificent.'

'Still, you'd best measure me again, if that's not too much trouble.'

'Is not trouble,' he responded hoarsely.

The company's headquarters was a Victorian building located in a suburban back-street. Outside a plaque advertised 'GEMS Ltd.', an acronym formed from the initials of Gwen, Eve, Madge, and Sandra. Of several cramped rooms dotted over three floors, the managing director's office was the largest. Its furnishings, like those of other rooms, had embellished Horner's office during Randall's stay. But, following their collective dismissal, these trappings had found their way to Eve's new premises.

Behind a now modest desk, Eve lolled in the swivel chair. 'I met Eric down the gym, Sandra, when I was on the weights. The end is nigh for DOSS, it seems. "Uncle Arthur" has been offered a gong and an enhanced pension, as long as he clears his desk by the end of June.'

'Do you think he'll agree?'

'I should think so. Just look at the mess he's in. MI5 got their hands on Fuchs, while he had to let Jack off the hook. Then, once he closed down DORA and removed a competitor to the FO, those ungrateful sods stopped supporting his efforts to keep DOSS as an independent outfit. Worst of all, he can't even offer a female section any more. The only women left in DOSS are the tea ladies. So why go on?'

Sandra frowned. 'One could pose the same question about us, Eve. We're teetering on a financial knife-edge. Ursula's bequest is almost exhausted, while Eaton never responded to your offer to perform number sixty-nine.'

'I find that absolutely astonishing, Sandra. Still, we've got the porn.'

Sandra's lips pursed sceptically. The high quality photographs awaited firm orders. Dealers from Belgium and Germany had made approving noises about the samples offered them, but as yet that was all.

'Then there's my dollar diplomacy with the Yanks.'

'Eve, be realistic. Your negotiations have stalled, because of the top dollar prices you're demanding for items from the "Treasure Trove".'

'Oh, we'll be all right,' said Eve confidently. 'I feel lucky.'

Sandra's readiness to counter such optimism was thwarted by Madge, who came bustling into the room.

'There's a telegram for you, Eve.'

'That's my PA's job,' she muttered, as she tore it open. 'But I expect Pam is skiving again.' Moments later, Eve spluttered with laughter. 'Mystery solved,' she said, handing the telegram back to Madge.

'Well, read it out,' urged a bewildered Sandra.

Madge skimmed the text and then relayed its message between giggles: 'MARRYING LAND CHELSEA TODAY STOP HONEYMOONING COTE D'AZUR STOP BACK JULYISH BUT AVAILABLE IN EMERGENCY STOP LOVE PAM.'

Sandra glanced towards Eve. 'Sounds like we might get some treasure from the "Trove", doesn't it?'

'It does indeed. So get the twins to knock up some fresh pics of Lord "Land" in bra and suspenders. And we'd better get to work quickly, Sandra, if we're going to lay our hands on his dosh before Lady Pam spends it all.'

After Sandra had drifted from the room, Eve turned to Madge. 'Do you want to be my PA for a while?'

'Well, just for a bit. But am I still personnel director?'

'Why?' demanded Eve suspiciously. 'Do you want to appoint someone?'

'Fat bloody chance!' retorted Madge, frankness offset by a saucy smile. 'Now, do you recall that finance director you appointed over my head?'

Eve's brows rose but marginally in an otherwise masklike face. 'You mean Wendy Page?'

'Well, Miss Page is in my office.'

Pushing to her feet, Eve grabbed her shoulder bag. 'Give me five minutes, Madge, and then send her in.

Eve watched Wendy close the door with a firm push of a red-taloned hand. She wore an impeccably tailored black costume over a cerise blouse. A string of jet pearls encircled her neck. The shoulder-length hair was expertly cut, the make-up subdued.

Running her eyes over the woman standing by the mantelpiece, Wendy offered a stringent smile. Then she advanced towards Eve's desk, lowered herself onto the chair before it, and crossed her legs.

'You took your time arriving, Wendy.'

'I've been exceptionally busy,' the visitor replied with equal brusqueness. Layering manicured hands over her upraised knee, she stared inquiringly at the redhead. 'Tell me, Eve, what on earth made you invite me to join your merry band as finance director, given the nature of our last encounter?'

Eve's tense expression lightened to match her candour. 'It's simple enough. Besides me, Wendy, you're the only woman I know, who's consistently driven by the desire to be a serious moneymaker.'

'I see. So can you give me any indication of the current assets of your so-called company?'

'Twenty cartons of high-grade porny pics.'

'Any liquid assets?'

'Crate of gin.'

She shook her head despairingly 'That's you all over, Eve, when it comes to finance; living from hand to mouth, just waiting for something to turn up.'

'I wasn't just waiting for something to turn up,' she protested. 'I was waiting for you to turn up, Wendy.'

'Well, I'm already beginning to wonder why I'm here.'

'No, you're not,' scoffed Eve. 'The idea of working with me intrigues you. Let's face it, life's never dull when I'm around.'

Having digested this assertion, Wendy stared back through narrowed eyes. 'I'll give you two days of my time, to see if I think your venture is viable.'

Eve worked hard at making her smile seem gracious.

'Of course, before I make any commitment, I'll want to see everything relating to this business.' Rising to her feet, Wendy unclipped her handbag and poked around its confines. 'So come over to my new place on Wednesday evening, and I'll let you know my decision. That's the address.'

Eve took the proffered card, read the address, and gawped. 'How the hell can you afford to live there?'

Wendy smiled coldly. 'I'll let you think about that, while you're showing me around.'

70

WEDNESDAY 31 MAY 1950

'Of course I don't have to work,' said Wendy airily. 'I've got tons of money.'

Fidgeting upon the plush settee that she shared with her hostess, Eve brought the glass to her lips. Again her eyes flitted over the quality furnishings adorning the lounge of the Mayfair flat. The inspection served only to underline her worst fears.

'One of Horner's hidden accounts was a really big one, wasn't it? And you got your thieving little mitts on it, didn't you, Wendy?'

Setting her wine upon the low table before them, Wendy plucked at a sleeve of her black dress and drew it higher up her forearm. Whether intended or not, the effect was to fully expose a gold and onyx bracelet to Eve's envious gaze.

'How I became wealthy is neither here nor there, Eve.'

The narrowed green eyes lacked any real menace. 'I could find out all about it and really bring you down this time.'

'Eve, you're a civilian these days.'

'I could still find out though.'

'No, you couldn't,' retorted Wendy in a patronising tone. 'On this occasion I had the time to do things properly, and I wasn't so cocksure. I doubt that anyone could track down this particular transfer of assets.' She patted Eve consolingly on the knee. 'And, just between you and me, I spent some time in Zurich last winter, when I wasn't on the ski slopes.'

'You little minx! A Swiss bank account, no less.' Eve converted her admiring look into one of curiosity. 'But, if you're so filthy rich, why the hell are you offering to help me out at all?'

'Well, the trouble is, that at twenty-four, I find it hard to envisage myself simply squatting on my backside. And you're right about something too, Eve. Despite your appalling record, working with you represents a challenge. So, as long as full latitude is given to my outside interests, I'm prepared to give of my time and expertise to be your financial adviser.'

'Financial adviser? I can't see that catching on.'

'Well, call it what you like, Eve. But, the fact remains that you need my help. There will have to be some radical restructuring if you're to be viable. I'll draw up some proposals, and you can use your dictatorial tendencies to ram them through. Moreover, I suspect you're trading not only inefficiently, but illegally too.'

'Of course I am,' Eve replied caustically. 'It's in the nature of the beast. I'm dealing in porn.'

'I do realise that, Eve. However, I was referring to how your company is set up. I wager that you're not even registered with Companies House.'

'What's it got to do with them?'

'Rather a lot,' said Wendy silkily, 'but I'll see to it.'

A bland stare, confirming Eve's ignorance, was followed by a brow-furrowing frown. 'Now, before we go any further, Wendy, just tell me what, when, and how I get paid under this regime of yours.'

Wendy doused her smile with a sip of wine. Lowering the glass, she responded to Eve's probing stare with a severe one of her own. 'You will draw a reasonable monthly salary. Later, you'll receive royalties and dividends on shares, paid at six-monthly intervals.'

'Six months!' Eve hammed up her gawping face. 'How am I supposed to live? What about expenses? Where's my working capital?'

'Eve, just understand this. I will not countenance you sticking your fingers into the company till, whenever you fancy a silk blouse, or feel like impressing some lover.'

'Impress!' echoed Eve derisively. 'I'm still living in sodding Shepherds Bush.'

'That only goes to show how inept you are from the financial angle. So there must be a complete overhaul. I want a free hand and I want your full backing, Eve. But if you want me to work *with* you, since I've no intention of working *for* you, then you'll stay out of financial affairs completely.' Wendy held her frosty stare. 'Is that fully understood?'

It took a little time, but a surly nod eventually ensued.

'Now, Eve, you've seen your women work. How are they all coping?'

Eve pondered briefly before replying. 'Well, Jessica's hopelessly hidebound. She thinks porn should only be entrusted to some self-selecting elite. She'll never move the stuff on a mass scale.'

Wendy nodded agreement. 'You certainly need to expand your client base, which suggests to me the need for a new marketing strategy. Now, what about Sandra?'

'She's invaluable, on account of her intelligence and efficiency.'

'And the others?'

'Well, Madge has her moments, but so long as she lets blokes distract her, she's going to be playing in the second eleven. Gwen I no longer trust at all, the twins exist in a world of their own, while Janice is unpredictable, to say the least.'

'That leaves Pam.'

Eve shook her head bemusedly. 'And Pam is Pam. She has the brains and ruthlessness to make a real go of things. But she's so selfish and wilful that she makes me seem like the patron saint of altruism. And, besides her hedonistic nature, there's now the added distraction of her spending time impersonating Lady "Land".'

'Well, until we can attract some more talent, Eve, you and I will drive everything and retain the controlling interest. We'll need to form a new holding company. "GEMS" will be solely a distribution outfit.'

'But the others enjoy being directors.'

'I imagine they'll enjoy getting paid even more,' retorted Wendy archly. 'In any case, we must clear out the dead wood. Jessica and Gwen will have to go. The twins will be responsible for all photographic work, and you can run the office. This will leave Sandra, Pam, Madge, and Janice to work as saleswomen under my aegis as marketing director.'

'What about Norma and Brenda?'

'We could keep them on, Eve, to perform menial work. But, our objective should be to recruit women with brains and initiative.'

'It's a pity I can't entice Fay away from her feckless husband.'

'See what you can do,' said Wendy busily. 'Now, let's consider certain relevant financial matters. Obviously, I've got the capital to fund shares in our new company. What about you?'

'I'm flat broke.'

Coddling her wine, Wendy stared coolly at the pauper. 'In that case, I'm prepared to offer you a loan for share purchase, with the security being the deeds of your flat. Take it or leave it.'

Eve nodded submissively. 'What about my day-to-day extravagances?'

'Well, until things take off, your pocket money will have to come from me too.'

'You're really going to enjoy this role reversal, aren't you?'

'I shall delight in it.' Vindictive smile augmenting, Wendy set down her glass. She extracted a cheque from her bag and passed it over. 'This is your allowance for next month.'

Glancing at the amount entered, Eve gaped in horror. 'How the hell am I supposed to live on this?'

'Frugally,' suggested Wendy.

'For God's sake, I've got to have more than this.'

Wendy pouted, as if seeking a satisfactory compromise. 'Well, Eve, I could improve the overall financial package by offering you an incentive scheme. One that would compensate me for the way you treated me.'

Eve grimaced. 'I wondered when that would come up.'

'So, follow me.'

Pushing to her feet, Wendy led the way into her spacious bedroom. Halting near the doorway, Eve stared about her. Floor-length magenta curtains were drawn to. The deep-piled carpet was plum-coloured, as was the ceiling. Three walls were painted aubergine. Fitted wardrobes with mirror doors masked the fourth wall. A desk faced the wall of mirrors, with a low table positioned to its side, its surface cluttered with papers, bottles and glasses.

Wendy plucked an opened bottle of champagne from an ice bucket, poured a glass, and seated herself behind the desk. Eve perched on its edge and stared at their reflections.

'You must spend a lot of time looking at yourself, Wendy.'

'Actually, it was like that when I moved in, although the wardrobe space was most welcome.' Reaching into a drawer, she withdrew from it a cheque and handed it to Eve. 'This is your incentive payment.'

Eve scrutinised the cheque, which was made out to her for a handsome sum. It was dated, but not signed. Her face creased in exasperation. 'Since you've planned this whole bloody episode, Wendy, perhaps you could tell me what I've got to do to earn this.'

'What would you do?'

Staring at the sum involved, Eve gritted her teeth, and then muttered the expected reply. 'I'll do anything.'

'That's good. Now, this is a play in several acts. Perform them all, Eve, and I'll sign the cheque. If you fail just one, I'll tear it up. Is that clear?'

Eve laid the cheque upon the desk and nodded grimly. 'So what do you get out of it all, some perverse revenge?'

Wendy prefaced her assent with a remorseless smile. Pushing to her feet, she opened another desk drawer and pulled out a set of cuffs. 'Hands behind your back, Eve.'

When she meekly complied, Wendy shackled her wrists. Then she tapped Eve on the backside, and ordered her to stand in a corner of the room, facing her.

'Eve, you will remain like that for an hour, which is far less time overall than you had me in irons. You will not speak, unless spoken to. If you do speak out of turn, I'll add five fettered minutes for each word. Nod if you understand.'

Smirking, Wendy moved the champagne onto her desk, sat behind it, and opened a magazine.

Having freed Eve's wrists, Wendy poured more champagne. Then she paced across the room and opened a mirrored door. When she saw the tiled shower, Eve shuddered.

'Set on cold.' Wendy sipped contentedly from her glass. 'So get undressed, Eve, and in you go. But merely for a merciful two minutes.'

'You bloody cow!'

'Make that four minutes.'

Swallowing her next expletive, Eve shook her head dazedly. 'How the hell did I land myself in this mess?' she groaned.

'Greed, megalomania, callousness,' suggested Wendy icily.

Glancing at her gold watch, Wendy indicated that Eve might switch off the shower.

'Bracing, isn't it?'

Mute and trembling, Eve staggered from the cubicle and clutched the proffered towel. Wendy passed her a glass of Cognac. Having sunk the brandy in two gulps, Eve dried her body and briskly towelled her hair.

'Can I get another drink?'

Wendy flicked a permissive finger towards the cluttered table. Dropping the towel, Eve raked back her damp hair. She refilled her glass and made short work of its contents. Wendy came up behind her.

'Now go back under the shower for five minutes.'

'Please, Wendy!'

'Shall I rip up the cheque?'

Shoulders slumped, Eve tottered towards the cubicle.

When she lurched out of the shower again, shuddering convulsively, Wendy pointed at the Cognac. Hand trembling, Eve filled a glass and swiftly drained it. Then she found a fresh towel.

'Eve, do you think you should go under again?'

Dabbing at her eyes, Eve shook her head despairingly. 'Please, Wendy, I beg of you.'

'Then beg nicely.' Reseating herself at the desk, she watched Eve drop to her knees before her. Wendy slipped off her shoes. 'Really abase yourself, Eve. Grovel for your money, just like I had to grovel for my freedom.'

'How long did you imprison me?' inquired Wendy in a glacial voice, as she pushed Eve over the desk.

'Just a few days.'

'It was twenty-six days, Eve. Obviously, I've got better things to do than to lock you up in one of my rooms for that length of time. So I'll repay you now, and in a manner which might finally exorcise memories of how you humiliated me.'

Raising her head, Eve watched in the mirrors as Wendy grabbed her copy of *Tatler* from the table, and rolled the magazine up tightly.

'God!' she moaned, 'you and Jack really love this eye-for-an-eye stuff, don't you?'

Staring into a mirrored door, Eve rubbed her backside, checked the hang of her jacket, and then prodded and patted her hair. She turned towards Wendy, who was again seated at the desk. Smirking, the younger woman signed the cheque with a flourish and beckoned Eve to collect it. Pacing uncomfortably across the room, Eve snatched it from her hand.

'If this bloody cheque bounces, Wendy, after what I've just been through, then rest assured I'll bounce your head off one of your pretty walls, and to fatal effect.'

'Why should it bounce, Eve? Today's experience was worth every penny of the trivial sum I've just paid you.' She topped up her champagne. 'By the way, Eve, in a fortnight I'm travelling down to Nice for some sun and some fun. I've also arranged to see Jack. His place is just along the coast.' She converted her smug smile into a mouthed kiss. 'I presume you can see yourself out.'

71

FRIDAY 30 JUNE 1950

When she'd arrived at the station, Randall had picked up Wendy in his battered *Citroën*. The following day, they had driven out to view Renoir's house, visited outlying villages perched upon the foothills of the Alps, and then returned to his own quite civilised cottage near Cagnes-sur-Mer. Since then, save for dips in the sea, and forays for food and wine, they hadn't left it; sunbathing, lovemaking, and painting in his garden instead.

Until then he'd managed without women. With one exception, he hadn't even painted them, as he concentrated upon landscapes. The exception was a painting of Eve and Pam together, which he'd composed from memory. He invited Wendy to help him bury it in the garden, and then drive stakes through it for good measure.

Instead, she'd offered to buy it. She had also insisted on paying him for the portraits he'd painted of her in Ealing, as well as those he'd completed during her stay. The unsigned cheques, each made out for generous sums, were parked behind a vase. The sole catch in the proceedings was that she would only sign the cheques in London. And this underlying demand that he return with her to Britain was never far from their thoughts.

Mediterranean sunlight streamed through the window, as he served up croissants and coffee in bed. He sat pensively on its edge, while Wendy munched her way through breakfast without speaking. Then she dusted flakes of pastry off her bronzed breasts, and stared at him gravely.

'I'll stay for one more week, Jack, but no more. And, I must warn you of something. If you *don't* return home with me, not only will I be bitterly disappointed, but you'll never see me again.' Smouldering black eyes gazed deep into his. 'I don't like being rejected, Jack.'

'Have I ever rejected your advances?' he responded lightly. Then, setting the tray on the floor, he screwed up his face in query. 'But why choose me, Wendy? With your looks, not to mention your newfound riches, you could get almost any man you wanted.'

'But I want *you*.' Pulling him onto the bed, she squashed her body against his, before lifting her head to peer into his eyes. 'Jack, what do you really want from a woman?'

'Contentment would be nice.'

'Well, I can give you that,' she murmured. 'So, throughout these next seven days, I'll be doing my damnedest to get a favourable result.'

'You might not need that long,' he said, writhing beneath her touch. 'On the other hand, I might have a vested interest in making a last minute decision.'

Opening the front door, Eve's expression altered rapidly from surprise to suspicion. Standing before her, sporting a summery frock, was a tanned Pam Armitage, accompanied by a perspiring taxi driver.

'Eve, I'm ruined,' she announced dramatically.

'Oh, you don't look that bad, Pam. But where's "Land"?'

'I'll get to that,' she said in a hushed voice, wafting a cotton-gloved hand towards the luggage piled behind her. 'But, before I relate the whole sorry tale, could we bring in my few things and pour ourselves a drink?'

Once the driver had hauled in Pam's baggage and left, Eve fixed their tipples, and sat. The expectant expression upon her face prompted the uninvited guest to bat her lashes, and then drop her eyes.

'Well, Eve, all went swimmingly until we arrived in Monte Carlo. Rashly, I had allowed my suspicions to remain unaroused. Indeed, when I watched "Land" wager this enormous sum at the casino, I was terribly impressed.'

Pausing, Pam raised her eyes, injecting them with a hint of naivety that she could just about recall from her teens. 'What I didn't realise, Eve, was that this was the final instalment of his fabled fortune. Now all that's left is some paltry income from grazing rights on scrubby Welsh hillsides.'

Eve's scowl reflected her own financial concerns. 'Just how paltry is this residual income of his?'

'Well, it's not something I would have married him for. In fact, it's not even enough to pay some farcical blackmail demand that "Land" received recently.' Her tanned shoulders twitched with mirth. 'Can you believe it? These ridiculous people were seeking to extort money from him, merely because he likes wearing women's clothes?'

'And he doesn't?'

'Of course he does. In fact, when he sneaked out of our hotel after his final disastrous loss, he was wearing a nun's habit.'

'So where is he now?'

'In a priory, incommunicado.' Pam paused to make major inroads into her drink. 'Sister Hortense indeed! I've never been so embarrassed in all my life.' Her lips squirmed in response to jogs of memory. 'Actually, I have been. The trick, of course, is not to show it.'

Reflecting upon another failed venture, Eve produced her thwarted pout, and then poked a cigarette between her bunched lips. 'So what are you going to do now?'

'I'm not sure,' said Pam, eyeing the spare bedroom. 'I'm homeless too. I rented out my flat.'

Grabbing her gin, Eve lowered its level drastically. 'You can only stay here for a while, Pam. We can't risk murder charges by living together on any long-term basis.'

Pam nodded both thanks and understanding. 'Now, is there any chance of getting an advance on my royalties?'

'Not a hope in hell, Pam. Under the current finance system everything gets paid at regular intervals, and only when there's actually some money in the bank. It's ridiculous, I know, but you'll just have to wait six months, like the rest of us.'

'Six months,' she echoed dully. 'Oh, what is to become of me? Here I am, ruined and homeless, with nothing but the rags on my back.'

'Pam, you've never seen a rag, let alone worn one,' retorted Eve, eyes focusing on the cluttered hallway.

'A few shoes, the odd dress,' Pam acknowledged plaintively.

Anchoring raised brows above a sceptical stare, Eve prompted further confession.

'Well, there was this Texan oilman in Monte Carlo, who was kind enough to help a damsel in distress.'

'So where's this knight in greasy armour now?'

'He heard that I was married to a nun, and became terribly prim in the way that only frontiersmen can. Of course Americans have no sense of irony either.'

'What happened?' persisted Eve sternly.

Pam swigged scotch and sighed. 'I had to promise to disappear, simply to get my fare home. Anyway, he wasn't really my type, Eve, and his sexual technique, modelled upon his profession, was akin to sinking boreholes.' Pam fashioned a *'c'est la vie'* smile, which she soon remodelled into a 'life goes on' pout. 'Now, where can I get some lolly, Eve?'

'I don't know,' said Eve, as she refilled their glasses. 'My own financial arrangements have varied drastically. One was painfully short-term, at the hands of Wendy. The other is a long-term business model, centred on negotiations with the Yanks.'

The blue eyes glittered with interest. 'For the moment, Eve, I shall restrain my curiosity about the first event, in order to inquire about the humdrum alternative.'

'Well, recently I sent my actress friend Zoë as my envoy to the Yanks.'

Pam sat forward attentively. 'So what happened?'

Eve stubbed her cigarette. 'Initially, the crew-cutted creeps just stalled, and acted as though they ruled the world.'

'I think you'll find they do, Eve.'

'Then something happened, and I met this Yank Tom Quaid some days ago.'

'I see.' Pam lounged back on the sofa. 'Now, tell me about Wendy. Did she come into money?'

'In a way. She stole a load of it from the government.'

'And quite right too! After all, they'd only squander it on the indigent and feckless.'

'Pam, she stole it from the likes of you and me. Don't forget we're taxpayers.'

'Are you really?' Pam marvelled. 'What strange habits you have, Eve.'

'Do you know what I had to do to get some money from Wendy?'

'I'm sure you're going to tell me.'

'I'm not sure I want to.'

'Of course you do, Eve. Confession is good for the soul. You of all people should know that.'

When Eve had finished her tale, Pam shrugged. 'I can't see that anything untoward occurred.'

'Nothing untoward!' fumed Eve. 'You didn't have to endure twenty-six of the best, Pam. I expected the *Tatler* to be in tatters by the end.'

'But it wasn't, of course. So there I can only applaud Wendy's good taste. With her newfound wealth and status, naturally she had *Tatler* to hand. It's a most reliable instrument for such purposes, I always think.'

'What about the cold showers I had to endure?'

'Oh, Eve, you're such a baby. When I was at convent school, the nuns were always shoving us under cold showers; except, that is, when Sister Veronica was on duty. Then they were always lovely and hot when she came charging in to join us.'

The green eyes compressed with curiosity. 'Pam, you aren't really a Catholic, are you?'

'Parts of me are, Eve. I've never much cared for the restrictive aspects of the faith. Moreover, I'm sure it would be a far more tolerable and relevant religion, if women alone were allowed to become Popes.'

'I've missed your peerless wisdom, Pam.'

'Oh, you are in a grumpy mood.'

'That's because I'm broke, frustrated, and vulnerable. Of late, I've had no option but to let Jack and Wendy have their wicked ways with me.'

Taking Eve's hand, Pam patted it consolingly, and then hauled the redhead to her feet. 'Well, after a curtailed honeymoon with "Sister Hortense", followed by a rash affair with a derrick, it's about time I indulged in some wicked ways of my own. And don't worry about being broke, Eve. I won't charge you.'

In the spacious Paris apartment Quaid set down his drink. He stared approvingly at the Degas, and uncertainly at the Picasso. Then he redirected his look of envy from Stern's latest acquisitions to the other's bronzed face.

'So how was it on the Côte d'Azur, Max?'

'Sunny,' mumbled Stern, seemingly absorbed in swilling bourbon around his glass.

'And that's where Miss Loxton's representative offered the deal you put to me?'

'Like you say, Tom.'

'Do I know her?'

'Search me.' Stern jiggled his glass again. 'But she sure was a cute-looking bundle; young, tall, blonde, well-stacked, great legs.'

Glancing around the pastel walls once more, Quaid caught sight of the Millet. 'How come you got that off Horner?'

'Stevie and me made a deal.'

'Now, we heard something about that deal, Max. That guy Randall who was involved, he's in France too. Is that news to you?'

'No, Tom, it ain't. The cute dame said how Jackie's down on the Med, painting.'

'Max, I heard too, how Randall worked for the MGB and the whole show was an MGB blind. They got Horner to set Randall up, and then they took him east to debrief him and give him fresh orders. After that, they sent Randall home with this tall tale about being kidnapped and banged up in Hungary.'

'Could be what happened, Tom.'

'Then again, Max, I heard tell how Randall's a GRU sleeper, and the MGB brought him in without knowing, and that's why they had to cut him loose.'

Stern's head bobbed in a busy nod. 'Yeah, I heard that story.'

'So what do you reckon, Max? Why did Moscow send Randall back?'

'Hell, who knows?' Depositing his glass, Stern loudly cracked his knuckles. 'Maybe they just cut loose some guy who's been used, Tom. Some guy who's mad as hell at the world. Just to see what gives when he gets back home. I know for sure Stevie Horner didn't want Jackie back.'

Quaid screwed up his face. 'If that was their play, it looks like Moscow didn't make out so bad. DORA's closed down all the way and, from what I hear, DOSS is set to go under too.'

Stern shrugged his beefy shoulders. 'So Moscow got a result.'

'You reckon Randall's worth talking to?'

'What about, Tom? What he spilled to Moscow, if he sang there, is now in their files. But, if his story pans out, then he's just gonna play you that record all over again.'

Leaning forward conspiratorially, Quaid dropped his voice. 'Maybe we should take him out?'

His listener revamped tight-lipped disapproval into a cold smile. 'Hell, why risk it? Jackie ain't nobody's asset no more, Tom. He's just a painter. Why not leave him be?'

Quaid narrowed his eyes. 'I'll give it some mind.'

Stern's thick brows lifted inquiringly. 'So you gonna talk with this Loxton dame?'

'I already have, Max. I saw her in London. I was curious about what she'd got her hands on. And, what I liked about Miss Loxton's offer is she ain't greedy.'

Stern churned out a cynical smile. 'Yet, say yet, Tom.'

72

FRIDAY 7 JULY 1950

Pam laid aside her book and sipped some whisky. Setting down her glass, she dipped once more into a biography of Madame Pompadour. Three chapters later, she looked up when Eve opened the lounge door. Decked out atypically in a dark green dress, she hugged a briefcase under one arm.

Pam's brows lifted inquiringly. 'So did you get your down payment of hush money concerning Ike's wartime affair?'

Eve stifled a yawn, grinned, and patted her case. 'It's all in here.'

'Presumably, you were forced to spend the night with Mr Quaid, in order to clinch the deal.'

Shaking her head, Eve plonked the briefcase on the settee. 'Quaid wasn't there. But, he sent this very good-looking man as his representative, and our negotiations somehow took place in his hotel bedroom. It was no easy matter reaching a mutually acceptable agreement, but my powers of persuasion ultimately prevailed.'

Pam nodded approvingly. 'Now, let us turn to other money matters, Eve. I trust you've got some lolly for me.'

Eve delved into the case, and then stared at the blonde austerely. 'It's called a loan, Pam, to be set against your future royalties. It's all part of the harsh new economic climate that breezed in with Wendy.' She plucked pen and paper from her briefcase. 'So sign this.'

Having scribbled her signature, Pam grimaced, as if a turd rather than a wad of banknotes had been placed on the sofa. 'I can hardly stay at the Dorchester on that pittance.'

'You don't need to. There's a place nearby that's up for rent.'

'I suppose that must suffice in the short term.' She swilled her glass reflectively, and then looked up. 'Eve, if blackmailing the Americans over Ike's guilty secret proved such a financial success, why stop there? Why not assess who might be the presidential hopefuls in 1960, since you can be certain that American politicians and fixers are already thinking in those terms.'

'Why 1960?'

Pam composed a clever smile. 'That's because Ike will serve two terms, Eve. After all, you can't get your golf handicap down in just one.'

'1960,' muttered Eve, aghast. 'I'll be forty-one then.'

'And I'll be ageless,' purred Pam.

'But it's a brilliant idea, Pam; trying to work out who'll be up for president then, and who can be screwed. Thinking long-term, that's good. This could be our pension fund.' Eve nodded sagely, and then reached into the briefcase to extract a bundle of notes. 'But that's years away. Right now, it's time we went out for a decent meal.'

The week had passed, and Randall was driving back to Britain. At least he'd managed to run things down to the wire, and it had been well worth the delay. He exchanged smiles with his glamorous passenger, when she placed his hand on her thigh, and announced that she'd like some lunch. Giving her femur a parting squeeze, he removed his hand in order to change gear, and pulled off the *route nationale*.

The restaurant proved to be as expensive as it looked from outside. When the bill arrived, he stared at it bemusedly. But, just before popping off to the Ladies, Wendy surreptitiously passed him a wad of francs. In his newfound role as kept man, Randall paid the bill and tipped generously.

Wendy emerged from her titivations, looking confident, content, and beautiful. On leaving the restaurant, she linked her arm in his, and related a joke she'd heard. But their smiles quickly disappeared, when they saw two gendarmes loitering by the *Citroën*.

The burlier of the two addressed Jack. *'Suivez-moi, Monsieur Randall.'*

'Pourquoi?'

Once the officer had explained why he should follow him, Randall frowned, and then nodded reluctantly.

Wendy glanced at him anxiously. 'Jack, what's going on?'

He tried to keep the concern from his voice. 'I've got to talk to some men, Wendy, and you've got to stay here with one of the cops.'

'Why have you got to talk to some men? Who are they?'

He wasn't sure, although their identification by name suggested that the recent past had caught up with him again. Yet how was it known that they were returning on that particular day?

'Wendy, I'll fill you in later.' He kissed her firmly, and then unlocked the car's door. 'Why not sit inside?'

The gendarme led him across the car park, and pointed at the trio standing in the shade of a giant poplar. He identified Max Stern at once. By the cut of his clothes, the second man was British, and Jack had a good idea who employed him. The third man had his back to him. When he turned, Randall recognised him too. He was the man who'd been cut out of that fateful photograph taken in Paris in May 1946. As he approached the three men, Tom Quaid's hostile glare focused on him unabated.

'Mr Randall, we won't detain you for long,' said Basil Villiers, without identifying himself. 'We understand that you and the delectable Miss Page are travelling to England. Is that correct?'

'Why, is it now a crime?'

'Listen to the man,' advised Quaid in a threatening tone.

'Mr Randall, you must return to Cagnes and remain in the department of Alpes Maritimes. From now on, you must report weekly to the prefecture there. Later, you may be permitted to visit other parts of France. However, you must not leave France, and you will certainly not set foot in England.'

'And what happens if I do?'

Villiers' hazel eyes seemed to yellow, like a wolf about to dine. 'I'm afraid you will be liquidated, as our Soviet friends so elegantly phrase the process.'

'What?' gasped Randall. 'And why?'

'I think you know why, old chap.'

'Don't start that bloody nonsense again,' he retorted testily.

'Nonsense, Mr Randall? Tell me, were you privy to all of Horner's secrets?'

Jack smiled sourly. 'Of course not. Who was?'

'Precisely. Well, it now appears that a number of Horner's soap bars, and the secret material they contained, ended up not with his men in the field, but in Moscow. You were the courier on each occasion.'

'"It now appears",' echoed Randall derisively. 'Have you nothing more concrete than that? In any case, I never knew what I was carrying.'

'So you say,' remarked Villiers unperturbed. 'The trouble is that elements of our press have got a sniff of the matter in which you featured. Of course, we've slapped a D Notice on the story. However, should you return to our shores, it would be rather hard to keep matters under wraps. People would wonder why you weren't being interrogated.'

'I have been,' Jack responded acidly.

'I mean properly interrogated, old chap. Then people would wonder why you weren't arrested and put on trial. Naturally, a fresh trial, so soon after the Fuchs fiasco, would be too embarrassing. In short, we could not allow it. Hence the need for your liquidation before matters got entirely out of hand.'

'And if they miss you, Randall, we won't,' snarled Quaid.

'Jackie, go back to Cagnes,' counselled Stern. 'Leastways, there you get to stay alive.'

The rage and fear, which had so recently topped his emotions, surrendered their preeminence to self-preservation, and produced in him a strange feeling of relief. Their edict that he remain in exile cancelled out his own hasty decision to return. They insisted that he follow the path he'd originally chosen. So who was he to argue?

'What do I tell Miss Page?' he asked Villiers.

'You tell her that you are returning to Cagnes. Naturally, you do not tell her why.'

'Could you take her to Paris?'

'But of course.'

With that, Randall turned towards his car, from which Wendy had already emerged. The few needed words came to him almost too easily.

'I'm not going back to England with you, Wendy. I don't think it would work.'

Anger, not tears, showed in her eyes. 'You never were serious about returning, were you? Did you arrange this little show? God, but I'm sick to death of your secrets and your games, Jack. And, as you once reminded me, there are plenty more fish in the sea.'

The car carrying Villiers and Quaid braked alongside them. He pulled her cases from the *Citroën*. 'They'll take you to Paris, Wendy.'

He saw it coming, the well-deserved price of rejection. He did not evade it, but he certainly felt it. Cheek still stinging from her vicious slap, Randall loaded her luggage into the other car. When Villiers drove off, Wendy didn't look back.

Stern's car drew up. He switched off his engine and got out. Then he pointed at the canvases stacked in the *Citroën*'s back seat. 'Mind if I take a gander?'

'Go ahead,' said Randall, lighting a cigarette. He watched Villiers pull out into the RN7, caught a last glimpse of Wendy's profile, and gazed at the car until it disappeared.

'Jackie, I'll buy this, if it ain't sold.'

Heeling out his butt, he turned when Stern spoke. He was holding the painting of Eve together with Pam.

'The sale fell through,' Jack muttered ruefully.

Max reached into his back pocket. 'Dollars or francs?'

'Dollars, the franc's too volatile.' He watched Stern peel notes from a wad, and was impressed by the amount.

'I guess I owe you. That okay?'

He nodded. 'But you still owe me, Stern.'

'Keep painting, Jackie. I'll call by sometime to see what you've got. Keep them pictures of Wendy. If she don't come back, I'll buy the lot.'

Randall stuffed the first instalment of Stern's indemnity into his wallet; again a kept man, and still with women trouble.

It was almost dark when they returned to Eve's flat from a very long and costly meal. Pam headed off for a bath, while Eve sat in contemplation in the lounge, occasionally consulting her watch.

Wearing just the towel turbaned over her damp hair, Pam entered the lounge and fixed herself a drink. 'Are you coming to bed, Eve?'

'Not just yet. I'm waiting for a phone call from Quaid in Paris. I want to hear how things went today.'

'What things?'

Eve smiled vindictively when the phone rang in the hall. 'I'll tell you later.'

'I'll make sure you do', said Pam, heading for the bedroom.

Following her lengthy telephone conversation, Eve carried two glasses into the bedroom. Plonking a replacement scotch on the bedside table, she sipped her gin contentedly.

Lounging on the bed, swathed in a blue silk dressing gown, Pam reached out for her drink. 'Eve, you look so smug that you'd best tell me what you've been up to.'

Eve sat on the side of the bed. 'Well, as you know, Jack caused me to lose my job, Pam, a job I really loved. Later, Wendy took advantage of my poverty to humiliate me. So, naturally, I had to have my revenge on both of them.'

'Of course you did, Eve. So what did you do?'

'Initially, I began dropping hints all over the place about what I reckoned Jack had been up to. Then I got some well-connected women I know, as well as Gloria and her co-workers, to do the same. In this way, Pam, bits of the story reached the ears of journalists, MPs, and the security services.'

Eve took a long pull at her drink. 'I also ensured that Zoë mentioned a few things to Stern, when she was down on the Mediterranean. Later, when I saw Quaid, I fed him further titbits. Of course, nothing was ever made public, but once the press started to show an interest in the rumours, both our security services and the Yanks became nervous.'

Eve drained her glass. 'Then a couple of days ago, I received a telegram from Wendy, crowing about how and when she was bringing Jack home. So, just in case it hadn't been intercepted, I let Quaid and Stern know about it. Anyway, the upshot of it all is that Jack is exiled in France, and a devastated Wendy is returning home alone.'

Pam smiled callously. 'Oh, Eve, how clever you are. That really is a heartwarming tale.'

Slipping off her shoes, Eve went into the lounge for another gin. On her return, she stepped out of her dress, draped it meticulously over a hanger, and stowed it in the wardrobe. Then she picked up her hairbrush and drew it through her thick hair

'We're going to Claudio's tomorrow,' she announced. 'He's going to make something for your birthday.'

Pam stared in surprise. 'Eve, that's really sweet of you, but my birthday's not until February.'

'I know.' Eve smiled sardonically. 'But when she returns, a heartbroken Wendy will want Claudio to make her loads more stuff, to take her mind off her misery. And you can imagine how long he'll take to measure her. So it's best for us to get in early.'

'Well, that's tomorrow taken care of. So what are we doing tonight?'

'You know damn well what we'll be doing tonight.'

'I was just checking that you didn't have a headache, Eve.'

Laying the brush aside, Eve whipped the thong down her bare legs. A nimble flick of her left foot propelled it into her right hand. Balling it up, she utilised dormant netball skills to direct it onto the top of the laundry basket.

Pam eased herself into a sitting position and slipped out of her dressing gown. Lying back expectantly, she pumped her lips into an extravagant pout. 'Mmm! Sex tonight and shopping tomorrow, I definitely like the sound of that.'

'Sex and shopping,' echoed Eve thoughtfully, as she coddled her gin. 'Pam, that's brilliant! That could really catch on.'